big
NATE
THE CROWD GOES
WILD!

More

big NATE

adventures from

LINCOLN PEIRCE

Novels:

Big Nate: In a Class by Himself

Big Nate Strikes Again

Big Nate On a Roll

Big Nate Goes for Broke

Big Nate Flips Out

Big Nate in the Zone

Activity Books:

Big Nate Boredom Buster

Big Nate Fun Blaster

Big Nate Doodlepalooza

Comic Compilations:

Big Nate From the Top

Big Nate Out Loud

Big Nate and Friends

Big Nate: What Could Possibly Go Wrong?

Big Nate: Here Goes Nothing

Big Nate Makes the Grade

Big Nate All Work and No Play

Big Nate: Game On!

Big Nate: Genius Mode

Big Nate: I Can't Take It!

Big Nate: Great Minds Think Alike

Big Nate: Mr. Popularity

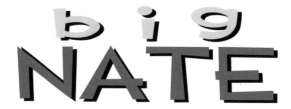

big NATE

THE CROWD GOES WILD!

by LINCOLN PEIRCE

Andrews McMeel
Publishing

Kansas City • Sydney • London

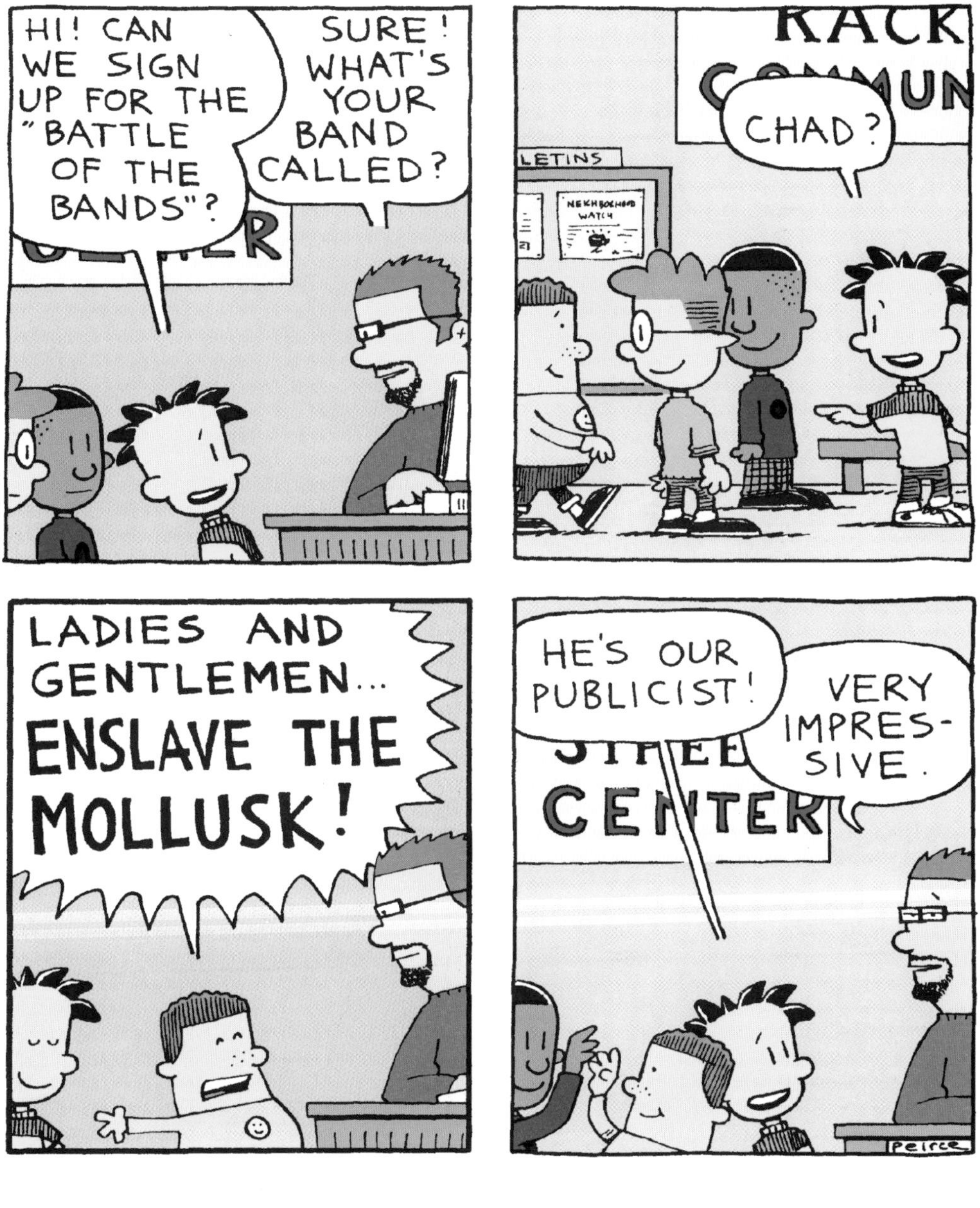
HI! CAN WE SIGN UP FOR THE "BATTLE OF THE BANDS"?
SURE! WHAT'S YOUR BAND CALLED?
LETINS
CHAD?
LADIES AND GENTLEMEN... ENSLAVE THE MOLLUSK!
HE'S OUR PUBLICIST!
VERY IMPRES-SIVE.
CENTER
peirce

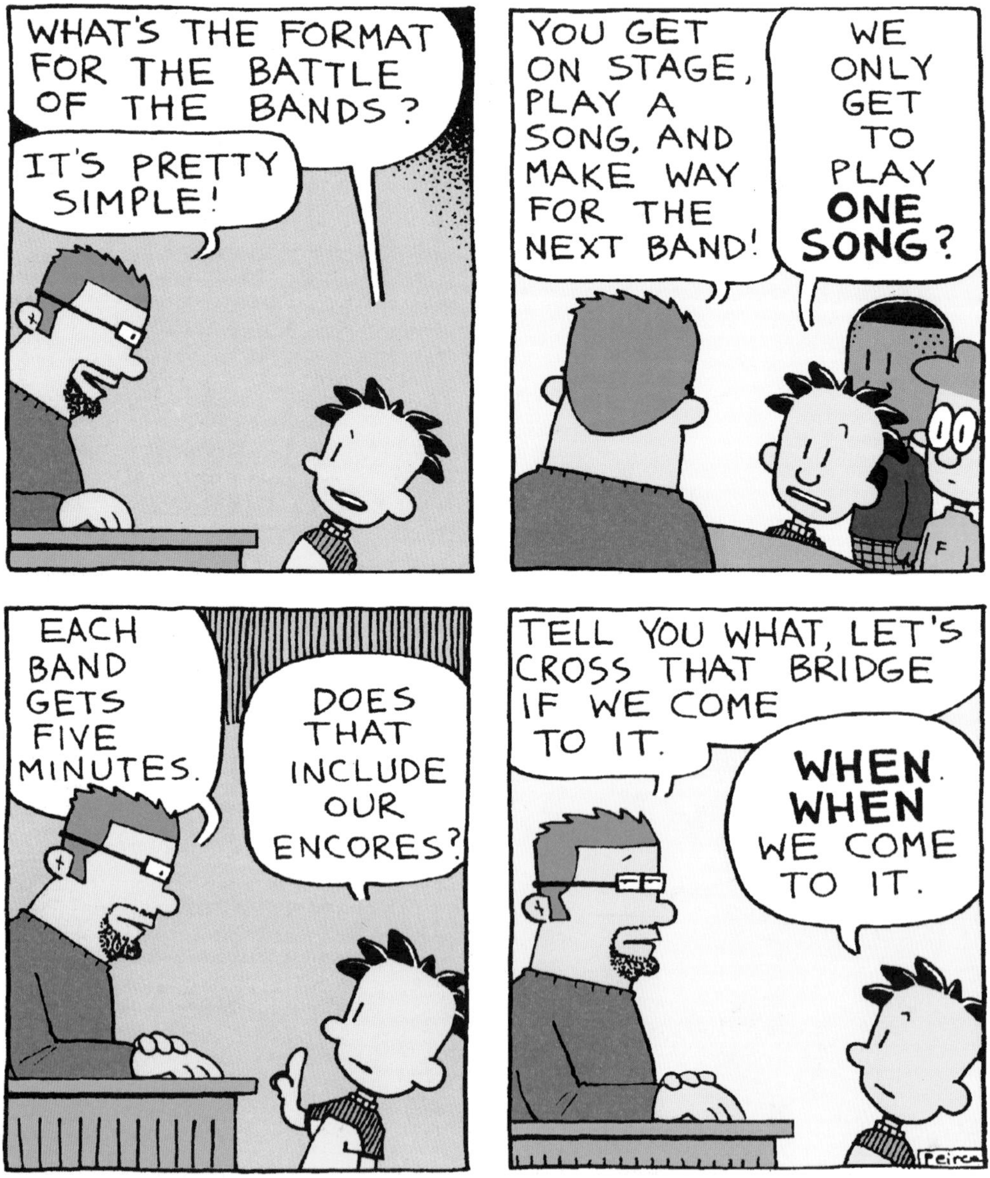
WHAT'S THE FORMAT FOR THE BATTLE OF THE BANDS?
IT'S PRETTY SIMPLE!
YOU GET ON STAGE, PLAY A SONG, AND MAKE WAY FOR THE NEXT BAND!
WE ONLY GET TO PLAY **ONE SONG**?
EACH BAND GETS FIVE MINUTES.
DOES THAT INCLUDE OUR ENCORES?
TELL YOU WHAT, LET'S CROSS THAT BRIDGE IF WE COME TO IT.
WHEN. **WHEN** WE COME TO IT.
Peirce

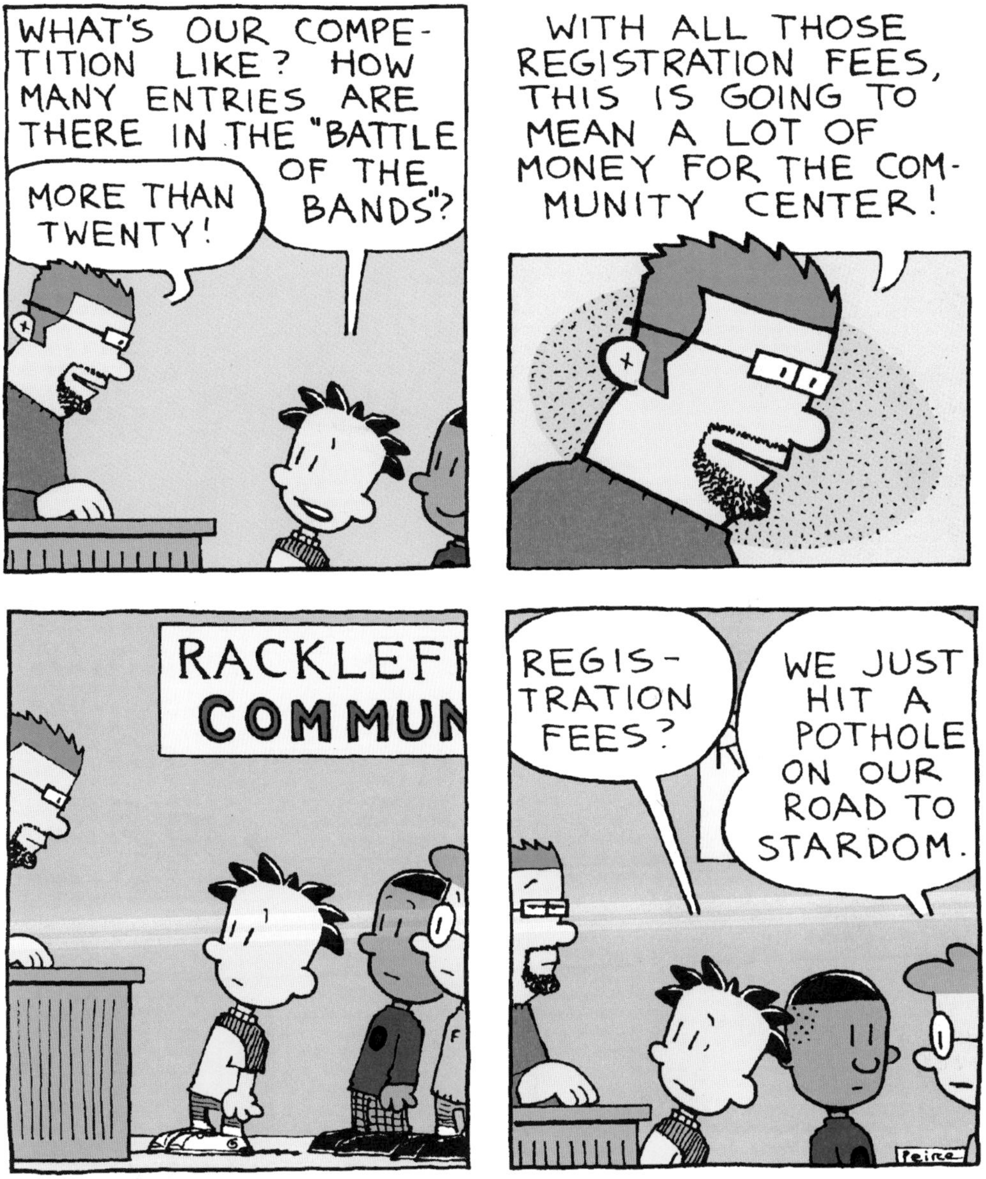
WHAT'S OUR COMPETITION LIKE? HOW MANY ENTRIES ARE THERE IN THE "BATTLE OF THE BANDS"?
MORE THAN TWENTY!
WITH ALL THOSE REGISTRATION FEES, THIS IS GOING TO MEAN A LOT OF MONEY FOR THE COMMUNITY CENTER!
RACKLEF
COMMUN
REGISTRATION FEES?
WE JUST HIT A POTHOLE ON OUR ROAD TO STARDOM.
Peirce

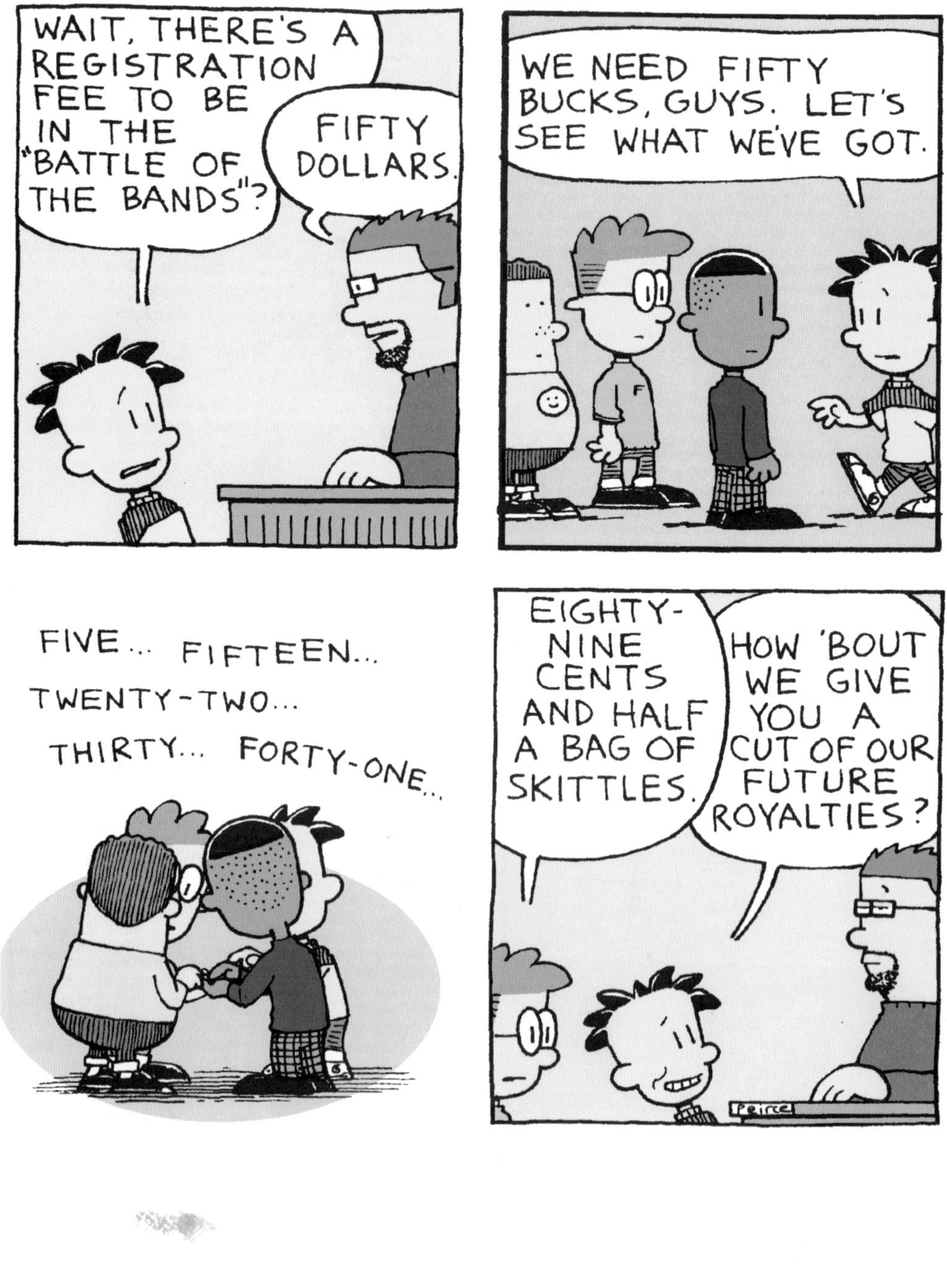

WAIT, THERE'S A REGISTRATION FEE TO BE IN THE "BATTLE OF THE BANDS"?
FIFTY DOLLARS.
WE NEED FIFTY BUCKS, GUYS. LET'S SEE WHAT WE'VE GOT.
FIVE... FIFTEEN...
TWENTY-TWO...
THIRTY... FORTY-ONE...
EIGHTY-NINE CENTS AND HALF A BAG OF SKITTLES.
HOW 'BOUT WE GIVE YOU A CUT OF OUR FUTURE ROYALTIES?
Peirce

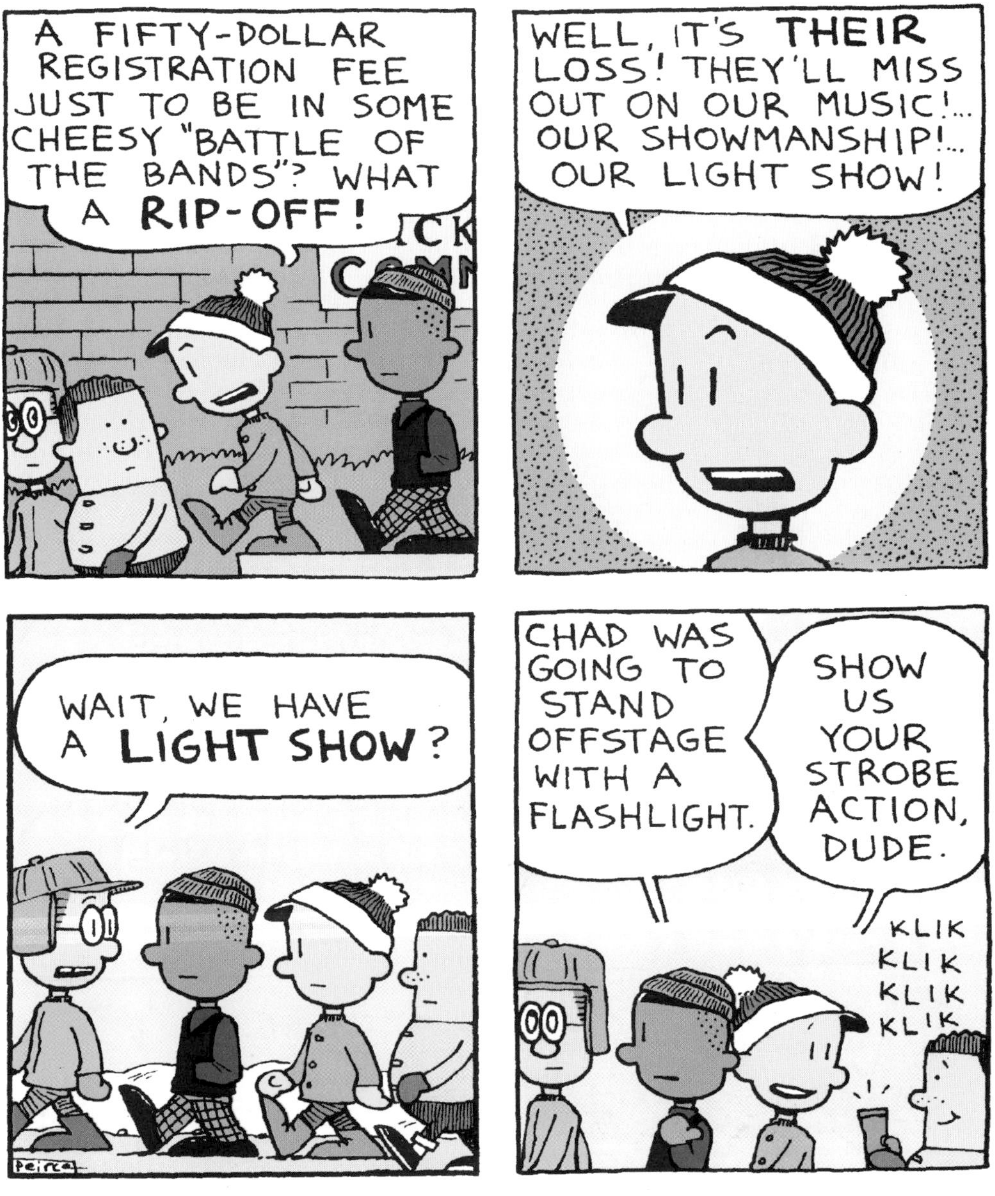
A FIFTY-DOLLAR REGISTRATION FEE JUST TO BE IN SOME CHEESY "BATTLE OF THE BANDS"? WHAT A RIP-OFF!
WELL, IT'S THEIR LOSS! THEY'LL MISS OUT ON OUR MUSIC!... OUR SHOWMANSHIP!... OUR LIGHT SHOW!
WAIT, WE HAVE A LIGHT SHOW?
CHAD WAS GOING TO STAND OFFSTAGE WITH A FLASHLIGHT.
SHOW US YOUR STROBE ACTION, DUDE.
KLIK KLIK KLIK KLIK
peirce

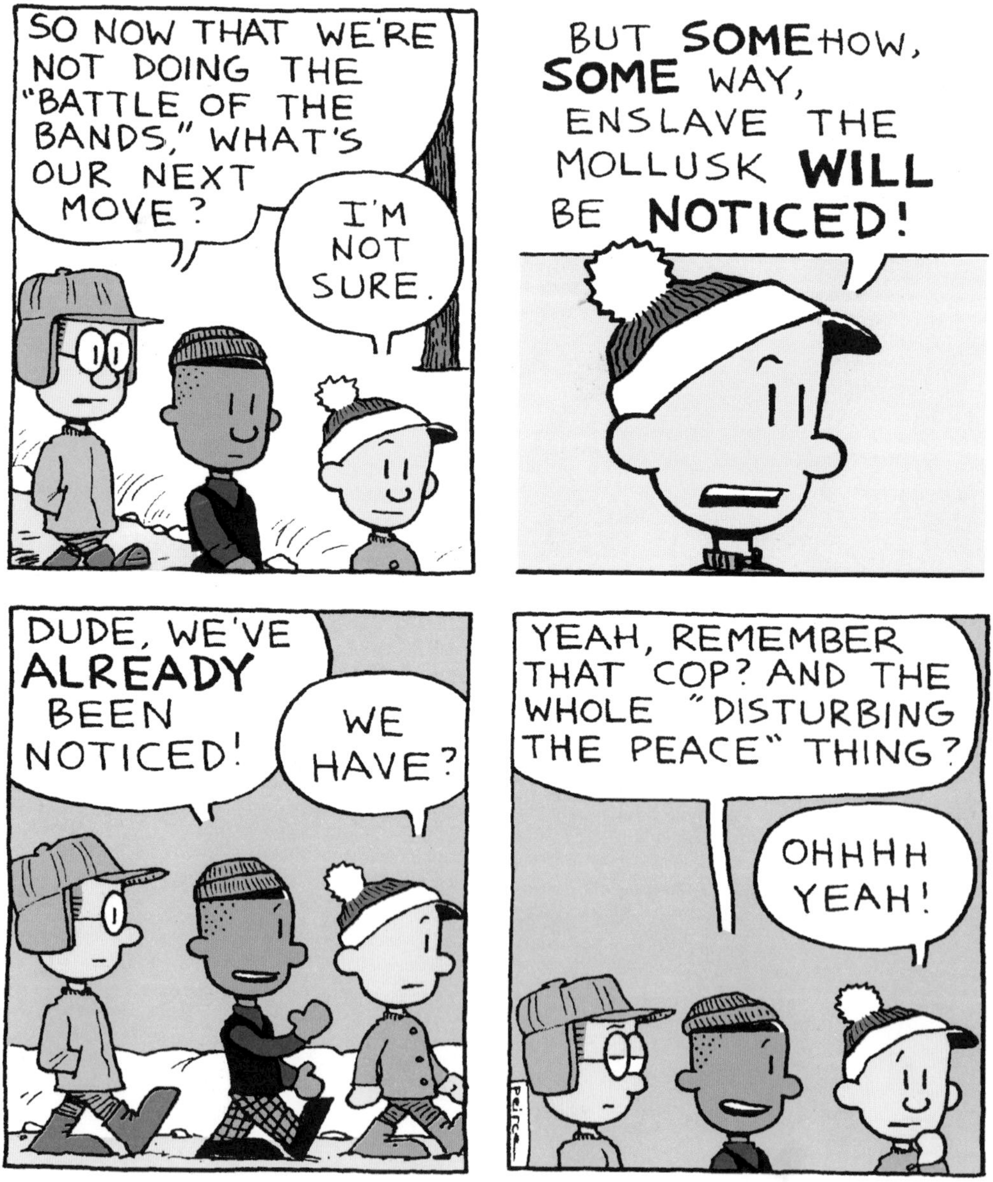
SO NOW THAT WE'RE NOT DOING THE "BATTLE OF THE BANDS," WHAT'S OUR NEXT MOVE?
I'M NOT SURE.
BUT SOMEHOW, SOME WAY, ENSLAVE THE MOLLUSK WILL BE NOTICED!
DUDE, WE'VE ALREADY BEEN NOTICED!
WE HAVE?
YEAH, REMEMBER THAT COP? AND THE WHOLE "DISTURBING THE PEACE" THING?
OHHHH YEAH!
Peirce

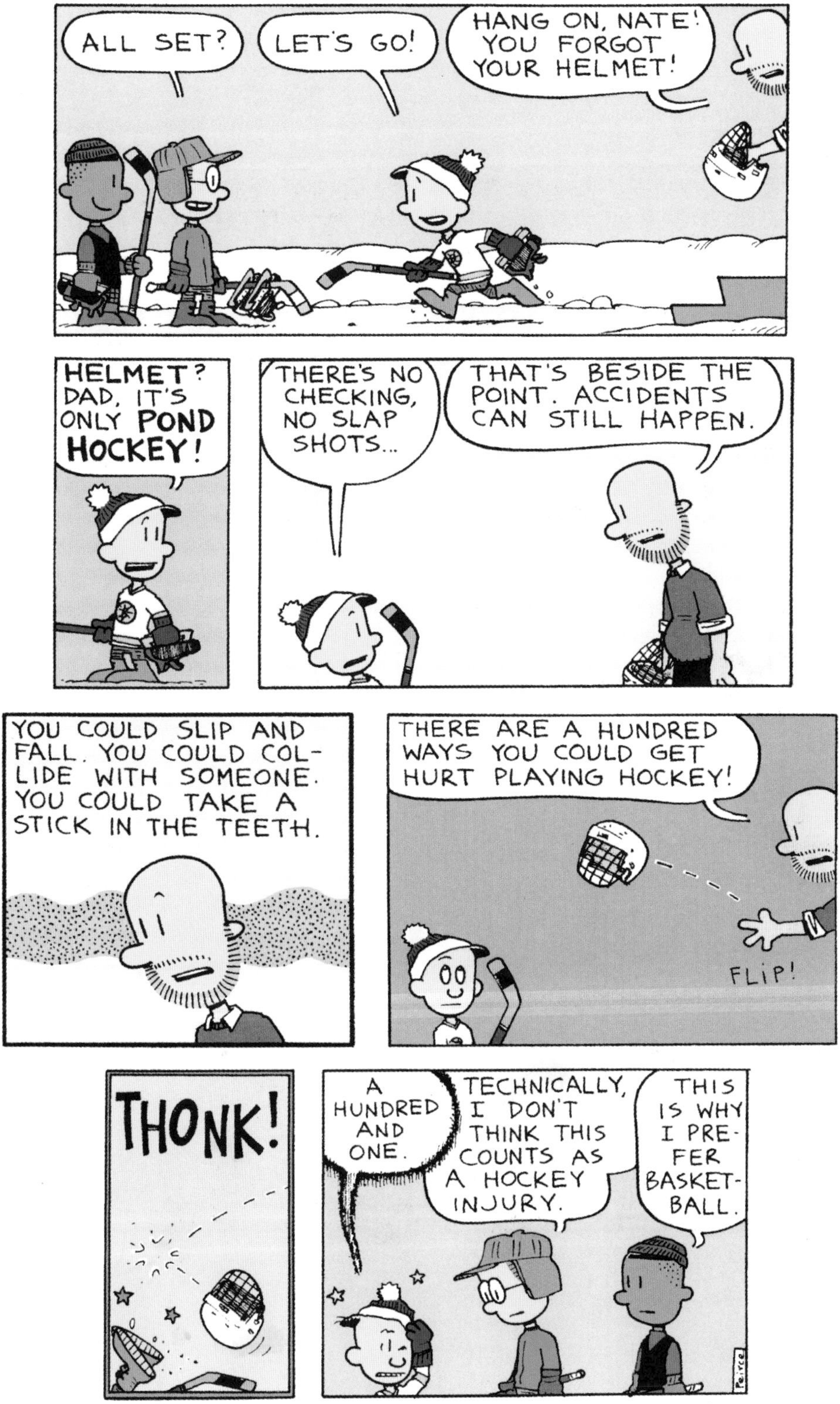
ALL SET?
LET'S GO!
HANG ON, NATE! YOU FORGOT YOUR HELMET!
HELMET? DAD, IT'S ONLY POND HOCKEY!
THERE'S NO CHECKING, NO SLAP SHOTS...
THAT'S BESIDE THE POINT. ACCIDENTS CAN STILL HAPPEN.
YOU COULD SLIP AND FALL. YOU COULD COL-LIDE WITH SOMEONE. YOU COULD TAKE A STICK IN THE TEETH.
THERE ARE A HUNDRED WAYS YOU COULD GET HURT PLAYING HOCKEY!
FLIP!
THONK!
A HUNDRED AND ONE.
TECHNICALLY, I DON'T THINK THIS COUNTS AS A HOCKEY INJURY.
THIS IS WHY I PRE-FER BASKET-BALL.
Peirce

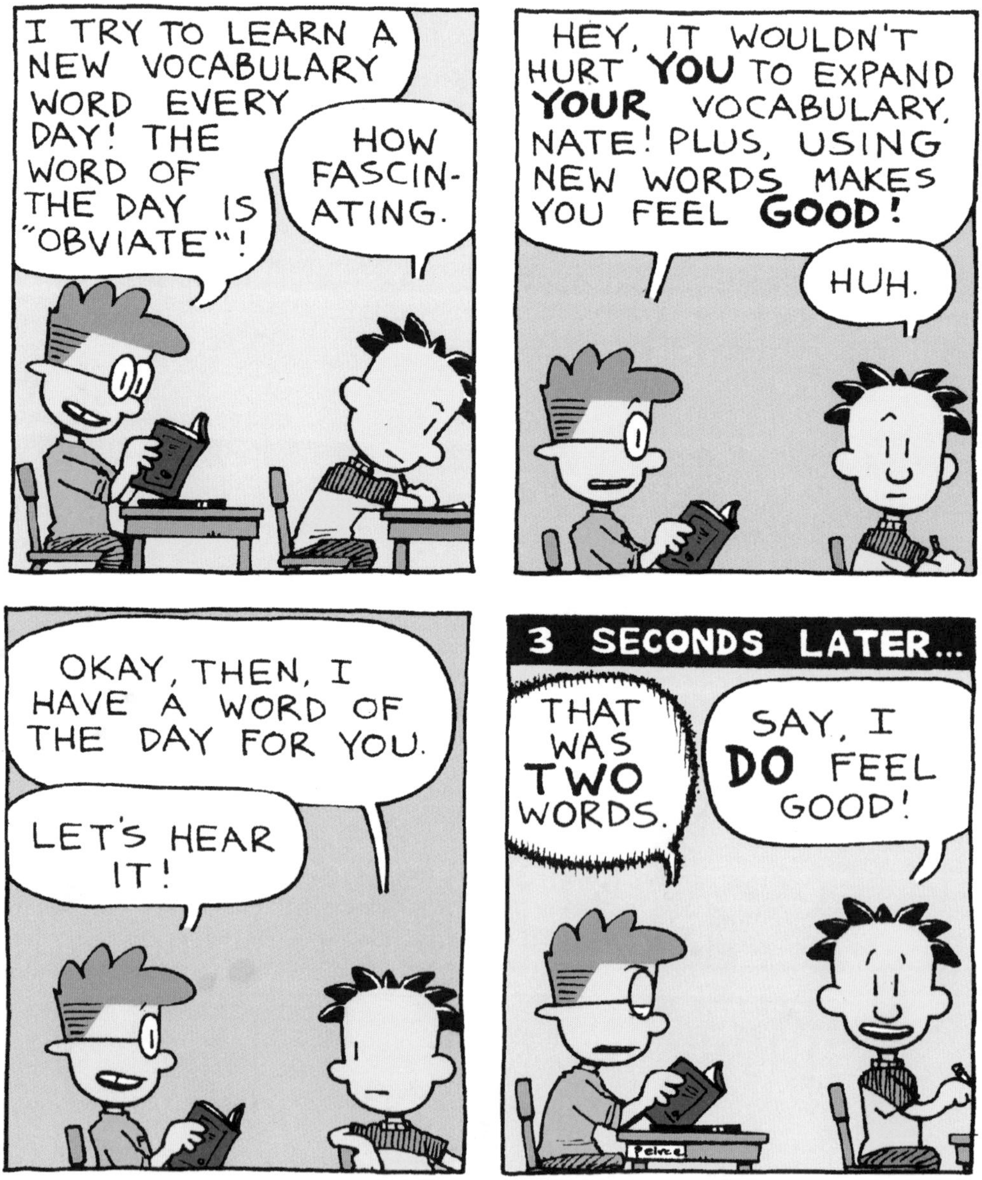
I TRY TO LEARN A NEW VOCABULARY WORD EVERY DAY! THE WORD OF THE DAY IS "OBVIATE"!
HOW FASCINATING.
HEY, IT WOULDN'T HURT **YOU** TO EXPAND **YOUR** VOCABULARY, NATE! PLUS, USING NEW WORDS MAKES YOU FEEL **GOOD**!
HUH.
OKAY, THEN, I HAVE A WORD OF THE DAY FOR YOU.
LET'S HEAR IT!
3 SECONDS LATER...
SAY, I **DO** FEEL GOOD!
THAT WAS **TWO** WORDS.

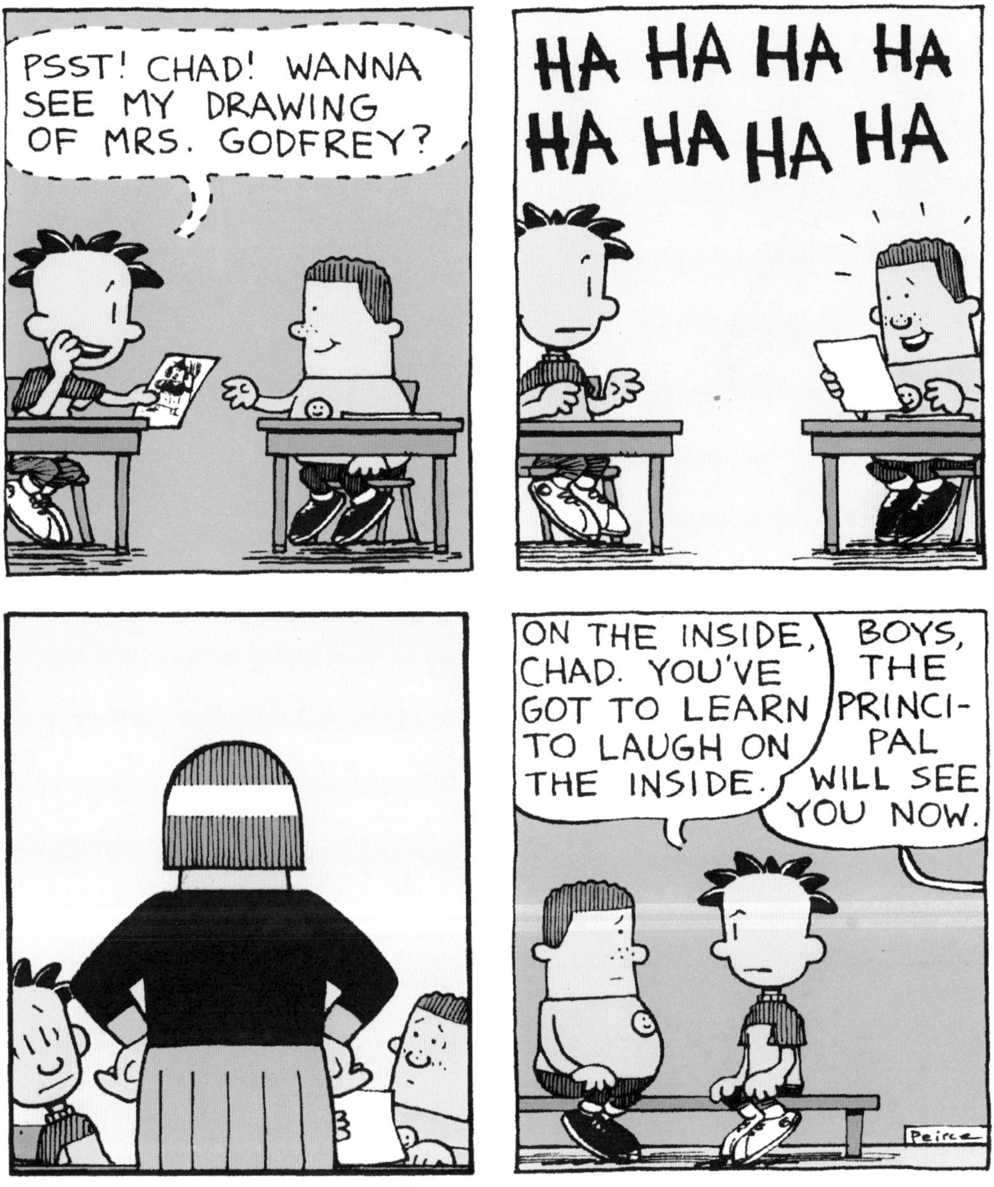
PSST! CHAD! WANNA SEE MY DRAWING OF MRS. GODFREY?
HA HA HA HA HA HA HA HA
ON THE INSIDE, CHAD. YOU'VE GOT TO LEARN TO LAUGH ON THE INSIDE.
BOYS, THE PRINCIPAL WILL SEE YOU NOW.
Peirce

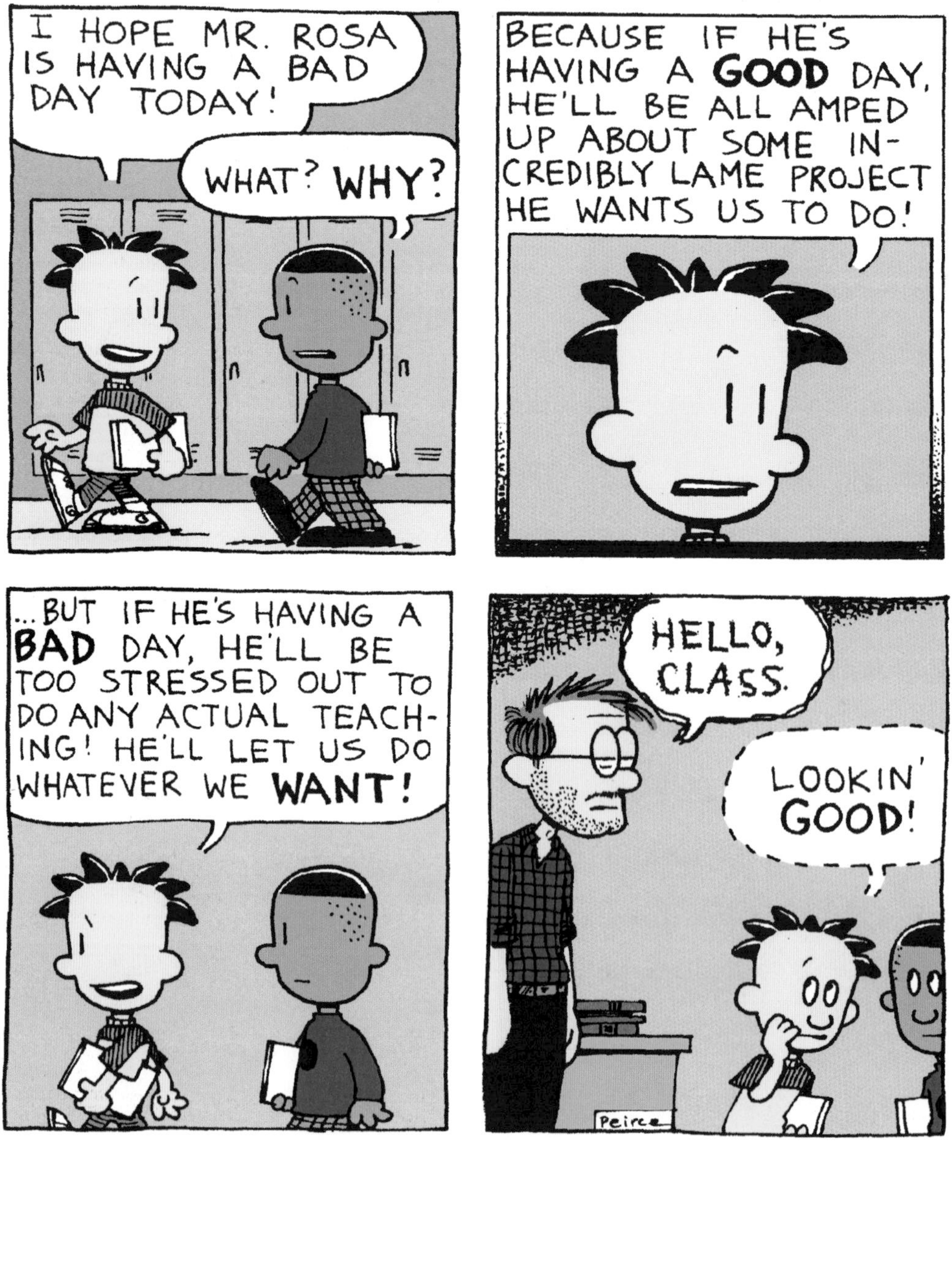
I HOPE MR. ROSA IS HAVING A BAD DAY TODAY!
WHAT? WHY?
BECAUSE IF HE'S HAVING A GOOD DAY, HE'LL BE ALL AMPED UP ABOUT SOME INCREDIBLY LAME PROJECT HE WANTS US TO DO!
...BUT IF HE'S HAVING A BAD DAY, HE'LL BE TOO STRESSED OUT TO DO ANY ACTUAL TEACHING! HE'LL LET US DO WHATEVER WE WANT!
HELLO, CLASS.
LOOKIN' GOOD!
Peirce

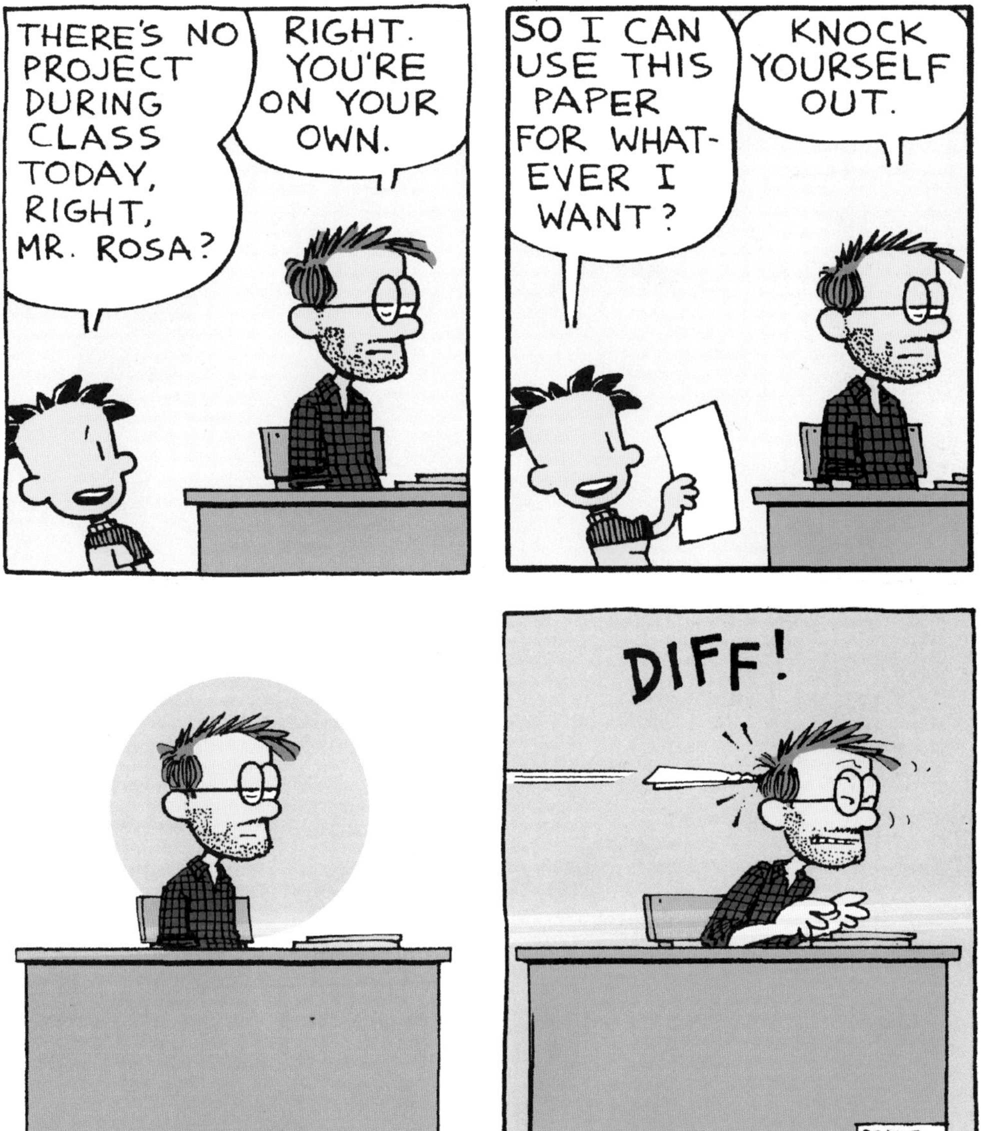
THERE'S NO PROJECT DURING CLASS TODAY, RIGHT, MR. ROSA?
RIGHT. YOU'RE ON YOUR OWN.
SO I CAN USE THIS PAPER FOR WHAT-EVER I WANT?
KNOCK YOURSELF OUT.
DIFF!
PEIRCE

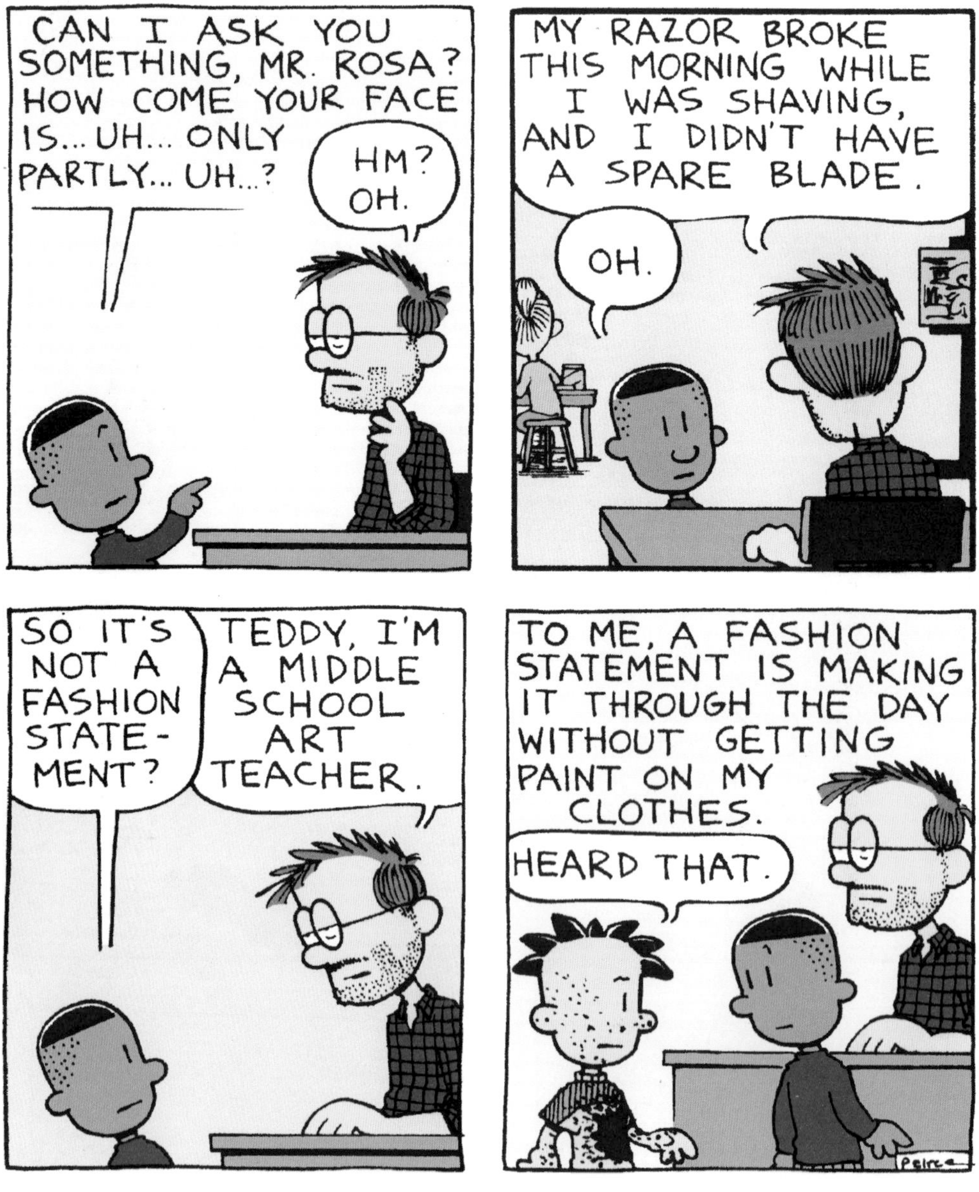
CAN I ASK YOU SOMETHING, MR. ROSA? HOW COME YOUR FACE IS... UH... ONLY PARTLY... UH...?
HM? OH.
MY RAZOR BROKE THIS MORNING WHILE I WAS SHAVING, AND I DIDN'T HAVE A SPARE BLADE.
OH.
SO IT'S NOT A FASHION STATE-MENT?
TEDDY, I'M A MIDDLE SCHOOL ART TEACHER.
TO ME, A FASHION STATEMENT IS MAKING IT THROUGH THE DAY WITHOUT GETTING PAINT ON MY CLOTHES.
HEARD THAT.
Peirce

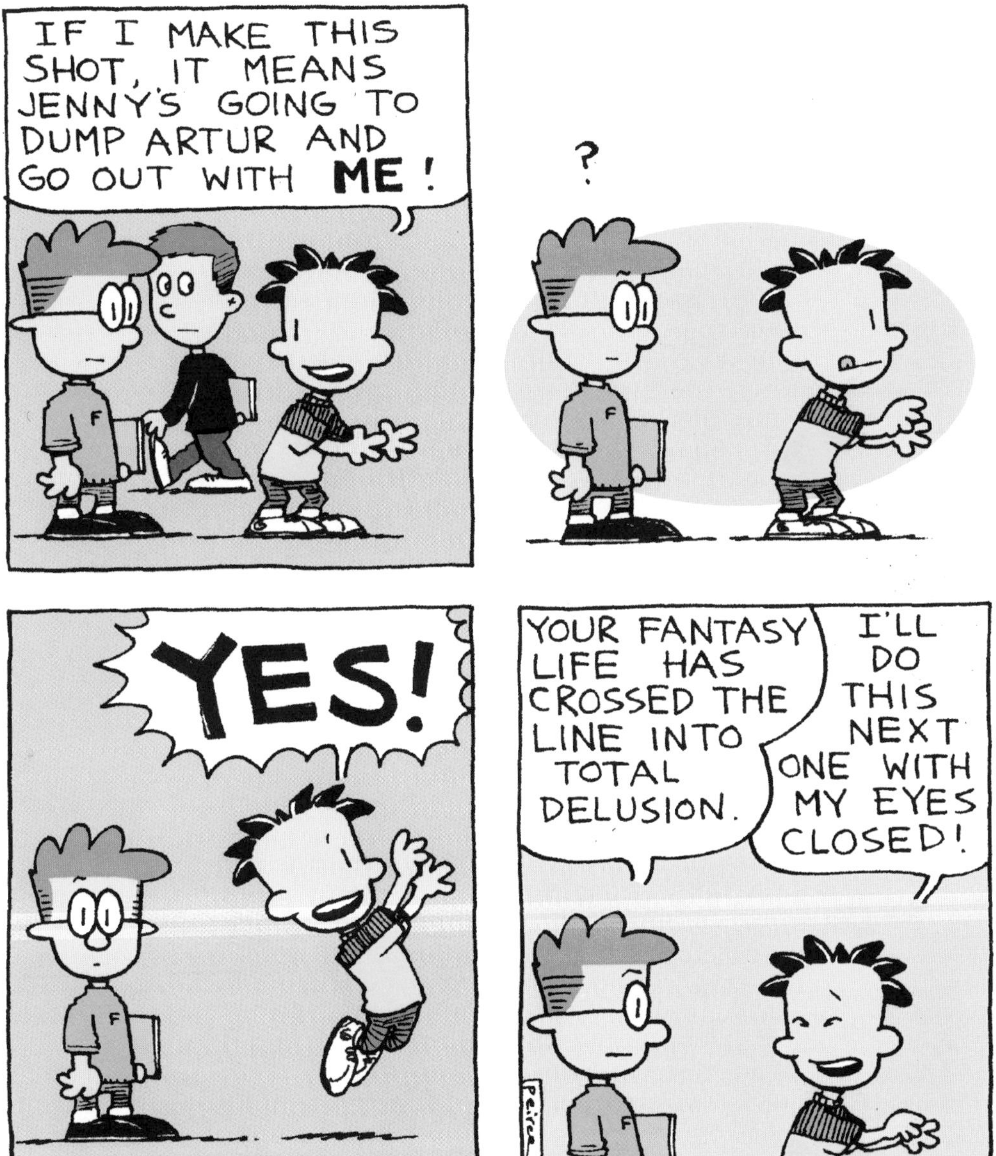
IF I MAKE THIS SHOT, IT MEANS JENNY'S GOING TO DUMP ARTUR AND GO OUT WITH **ME**!
?
YES!
YOUR FANTASY LIFE HAS CROSSED THE LINE INTO TOTAL DELUSION.
I'LL DO THIS NEXT ONE WITH MY EYES CLOSED!
Peirce

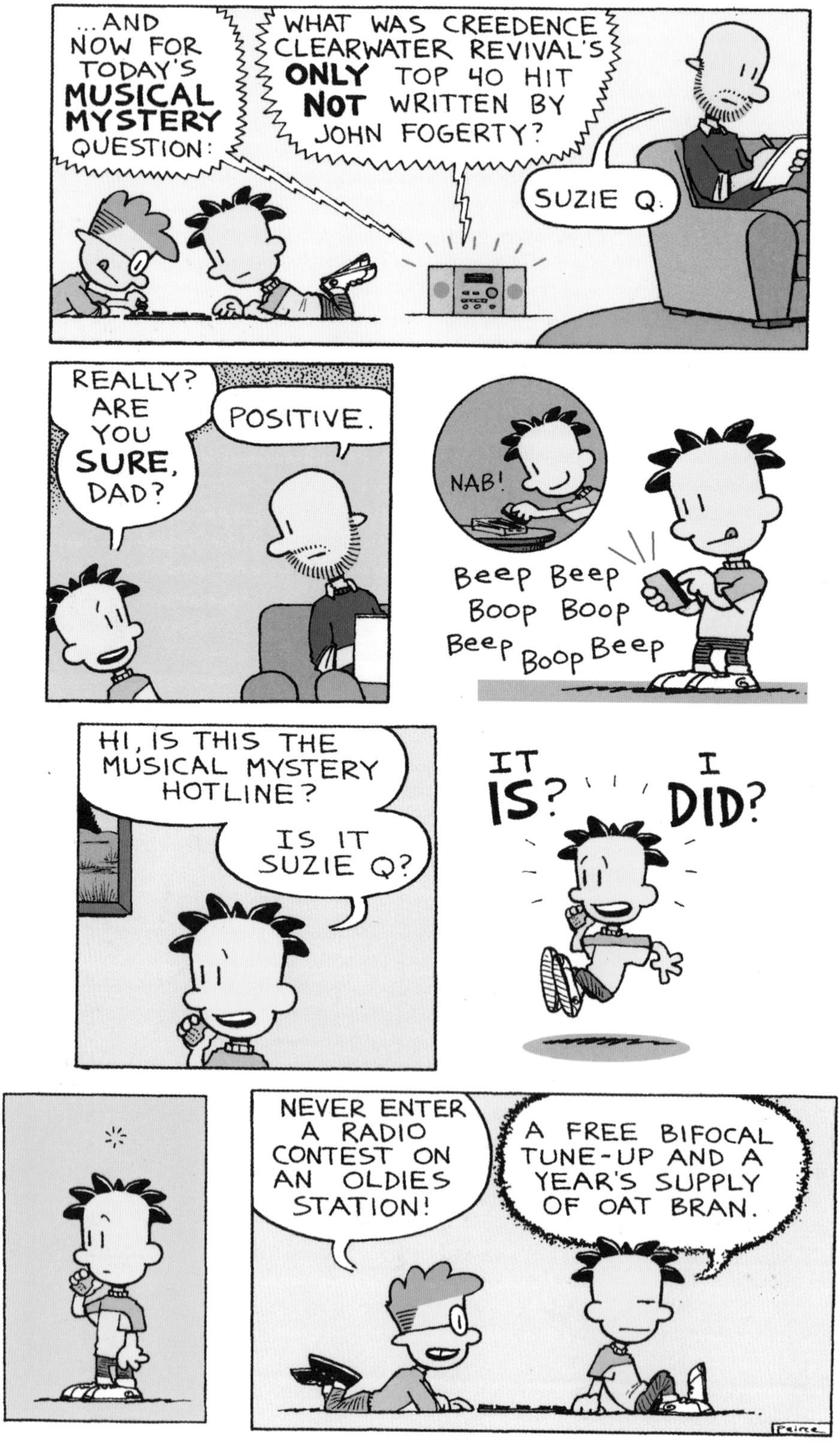
...AND NOW FOR TODAY'S MUSICAL MYSTERY QUESTION:
WHAT WAS CREEDENCE CLEARWATER REVIVAL'S ONLY TOP 40 HIT NOT WRITTEN BY JOHN FOGERTY?
SUZIE Q.
REALLY? ARE YOU SURE, DAD?
POSITIVE.
NAB!
Beep Beep Boop Boop Beep Boop Beep
HI, IS THIS THE MUSICAL MYSTERY HOTLINE?
IS IT SUZIE Q?
IT IS?
I DID?
NEVER ENTER A RADIO CONTEST ON AN OLDIES STATION!
A FREE BIFOCAL TUNE-UP AND A YEAR'S SUPPLY OF OAT BRAN.
Peirce

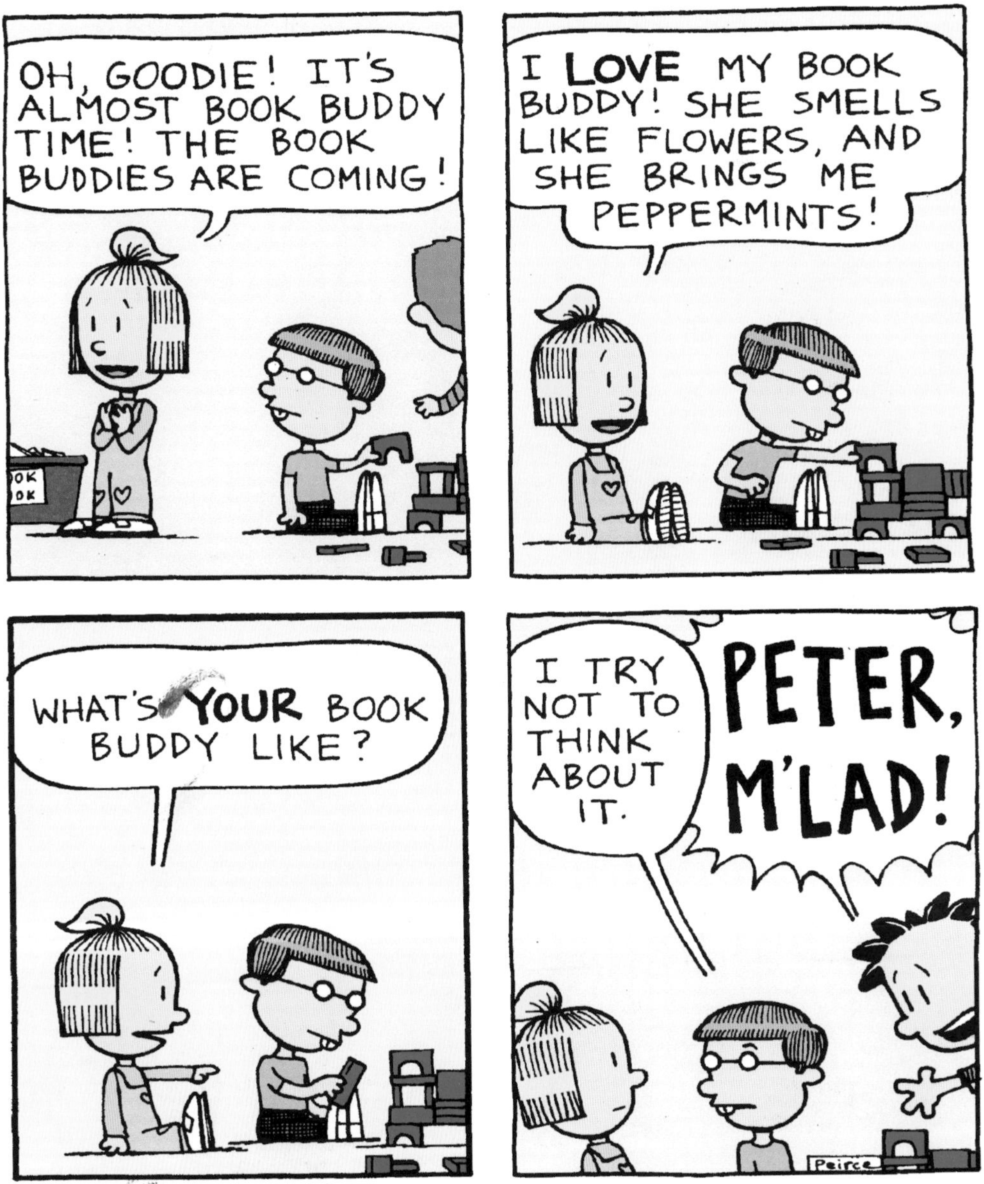
OH, GOODIE! IT'S ALMOST BOOK BUDDY TIME! THE BOOK BUDDIES ARE COMING!
I LOVE MY BOOK BUDDY! SHE SMELLS LIKE FLOWERS, AND SHE BRINGS ME PEPPERMINTS!
WHAT'S YOUR BOOK BUDDY LIKE?
I TRY NOT TO THINK ABOUT IT.
PETER, M'LAD!
Peirce

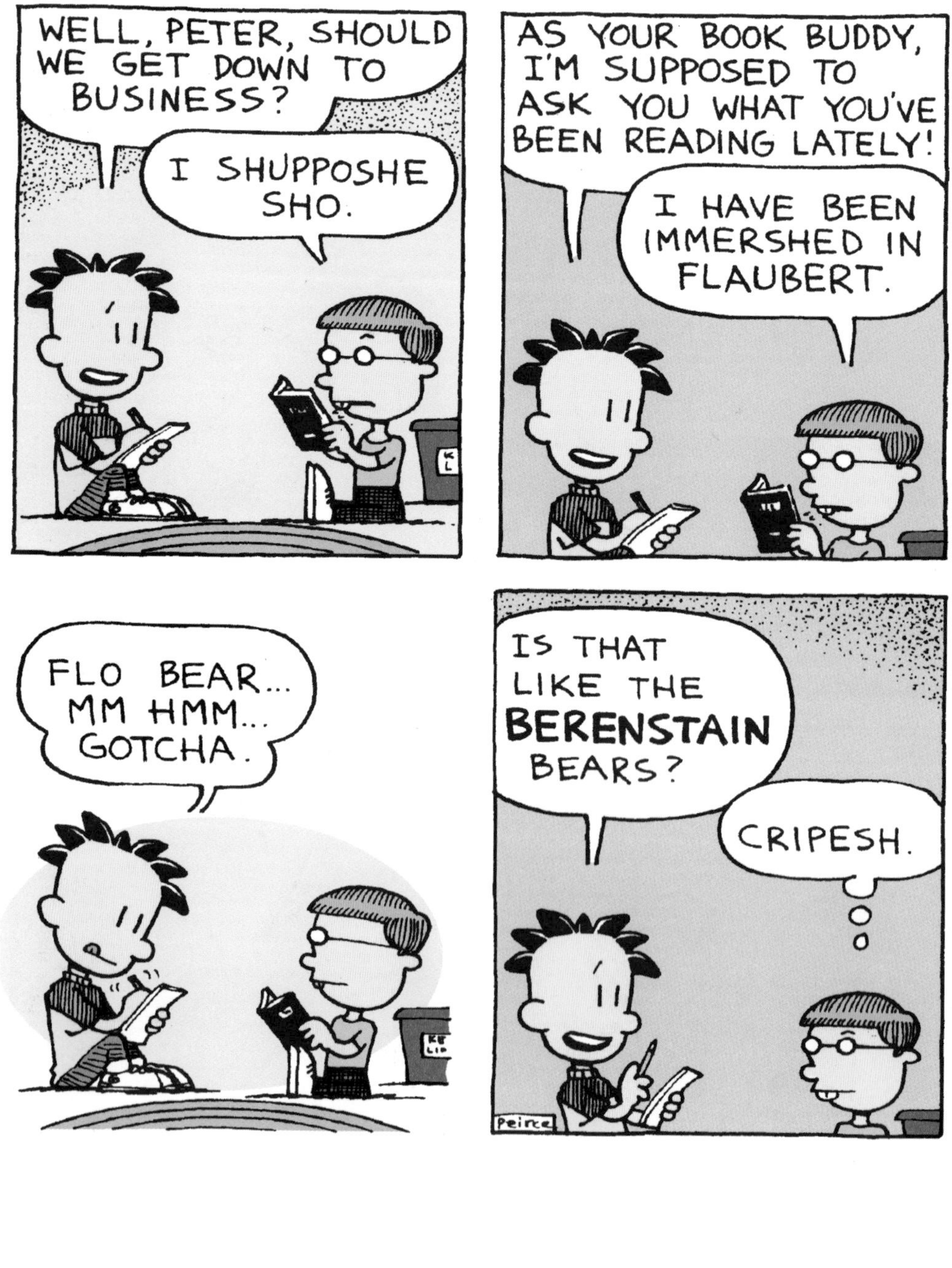
WELL, PETER, SHOULD WE GET DOWN TO BUSINESS?
I SHUPPOSHE SHO.
AS YOUR BOOK BUDDY, I'M SUPPOSED TO ASK YOU WHAT YOU'VE BEEN READING LATELY!
I HAVE BEEN IMMERSHED IN FLAUBERT.
FLO BEAR... MM HMM... GOTCHA.
IS THAT LIKE THE **BERENSTAIN** BEARS?
CRIPESH.
Peirce

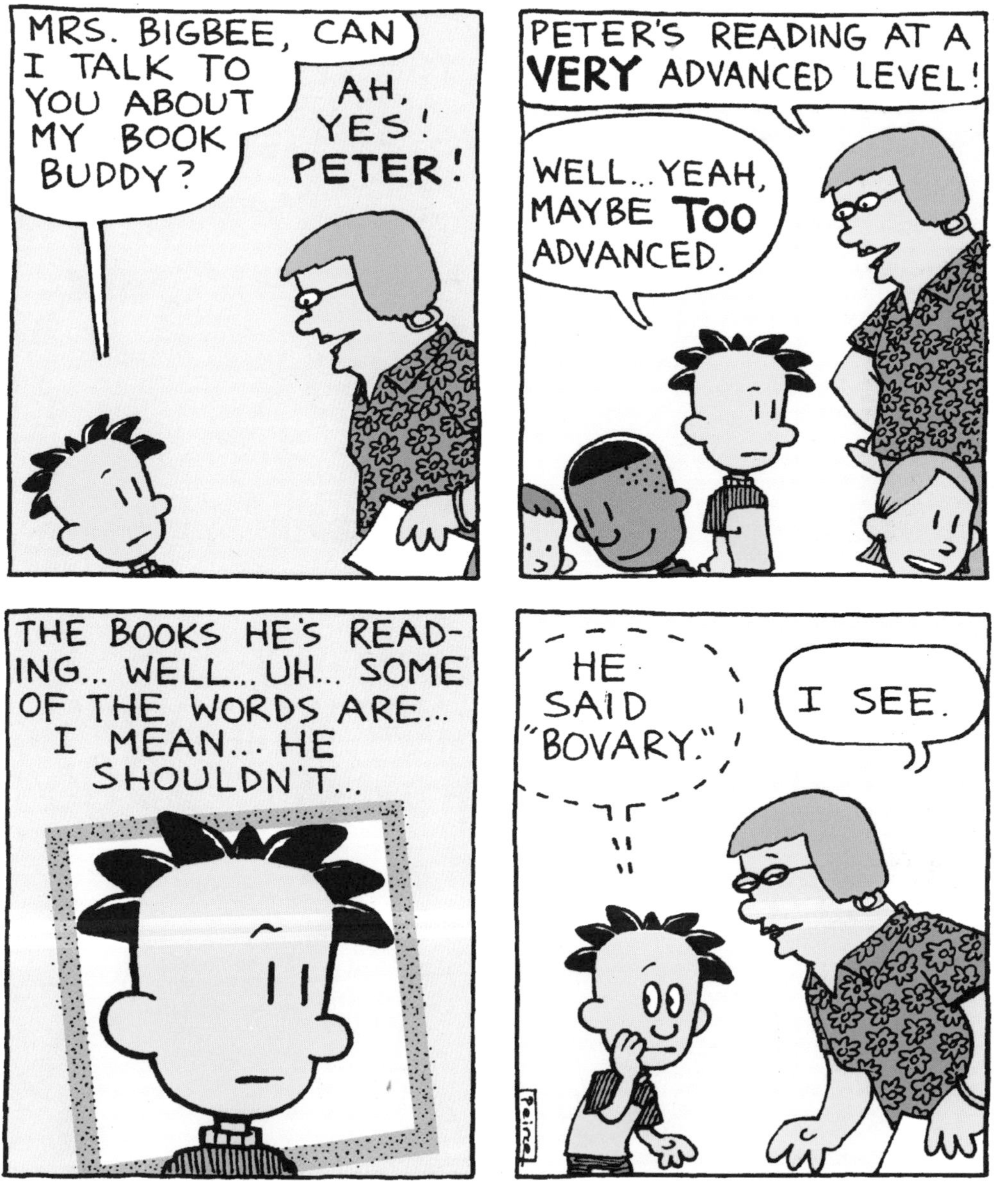
MRS. BIGBEE, CAN I TALK TO YOU ABOUT MY BOOK BUDDY?
AH, YES! PETER!
PETER'S READING AT A VERY ADVANCED LEVEL!
WELL...YEAH, MAYBE TOO ADVANCED.
THE BOOKS HE'S READING... WELL... UH... SOME OF THE WORDS ARE... I MEAN... HE SHOULDN'T...
HE SAID "BOVARY."
I SEE.
Peirce

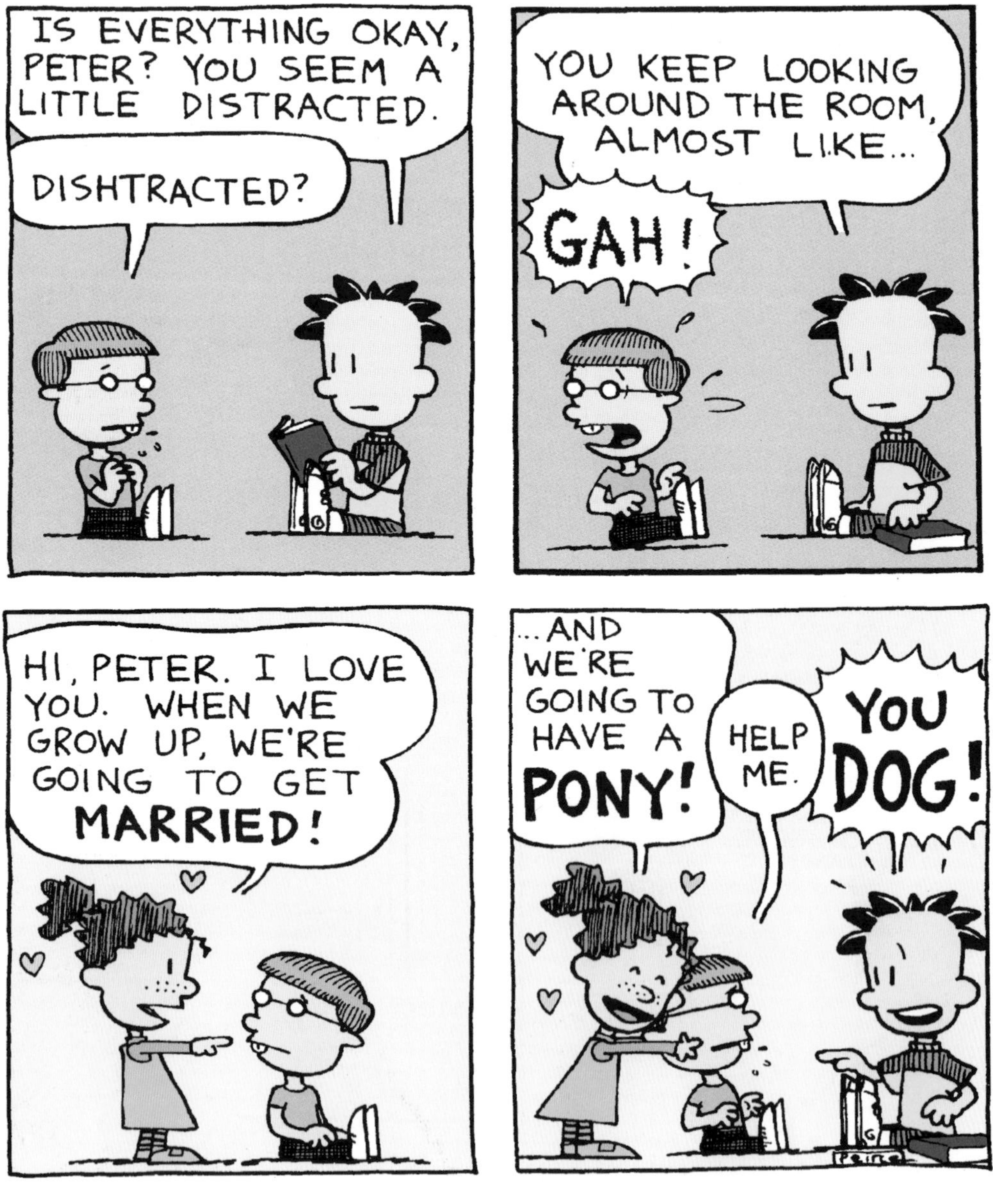
IS EVERYTHING OKAY, PETER? YOU SEEM A LITTLE DISTRACTED.
DISHTRACTED?
YOU KEEP LOOKING AROUND THE ROOM, ALMOST LIKE...
GAH!
HI, PETER. I LOVE YOU. WHEN WE GROW UP, WE'RE GOING TO GET MARRIED!
...AND WE'RE GOING TO HAVE A PONY!
HELP ME.
YOU DOG!

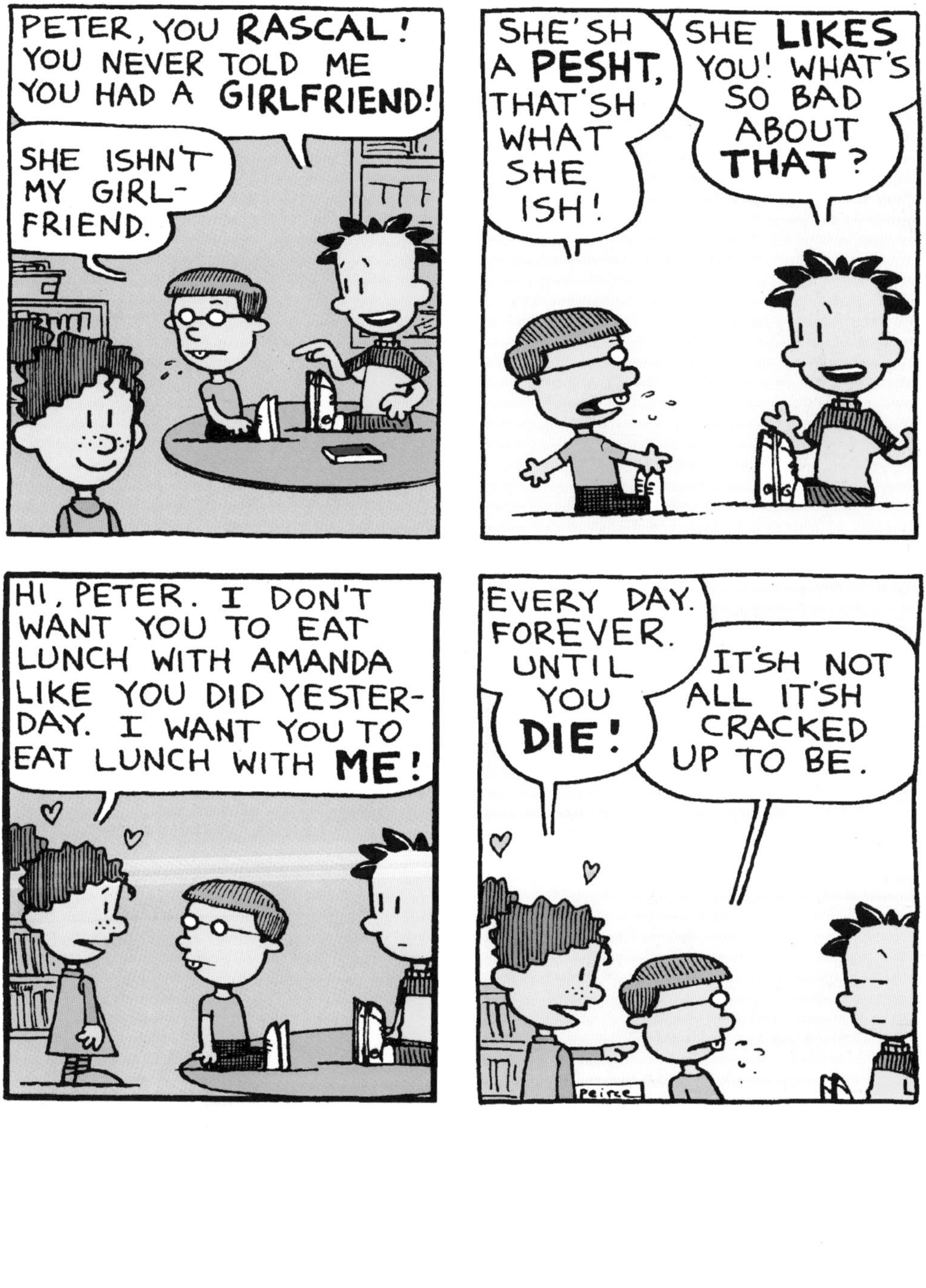
PETER, YOU RASCAL! YOU NEVER TOLD ME YOU HAD A GIRLFRIEND!
SHE ISHN'T MY GIRL-FRIEND.
SHE'SH A PESHT, THAT'SH WHAT SHE ISH!
SHE LIKES YOU! WHAT'S SO BAD ABOUT THAT?
HI, PETER. I DON'T WANT YOU TO EAT LUNCH WITH AMANDA LIKE YOU DID YESTER-DAY. I WANT YOU TO EAT LUNCH WITH ME!
EVERY DAY. FOREVER. UNTIL YOU DIE!
IT'SH NOT ALL IT'SH CRACKED UP TO BE.
peirce

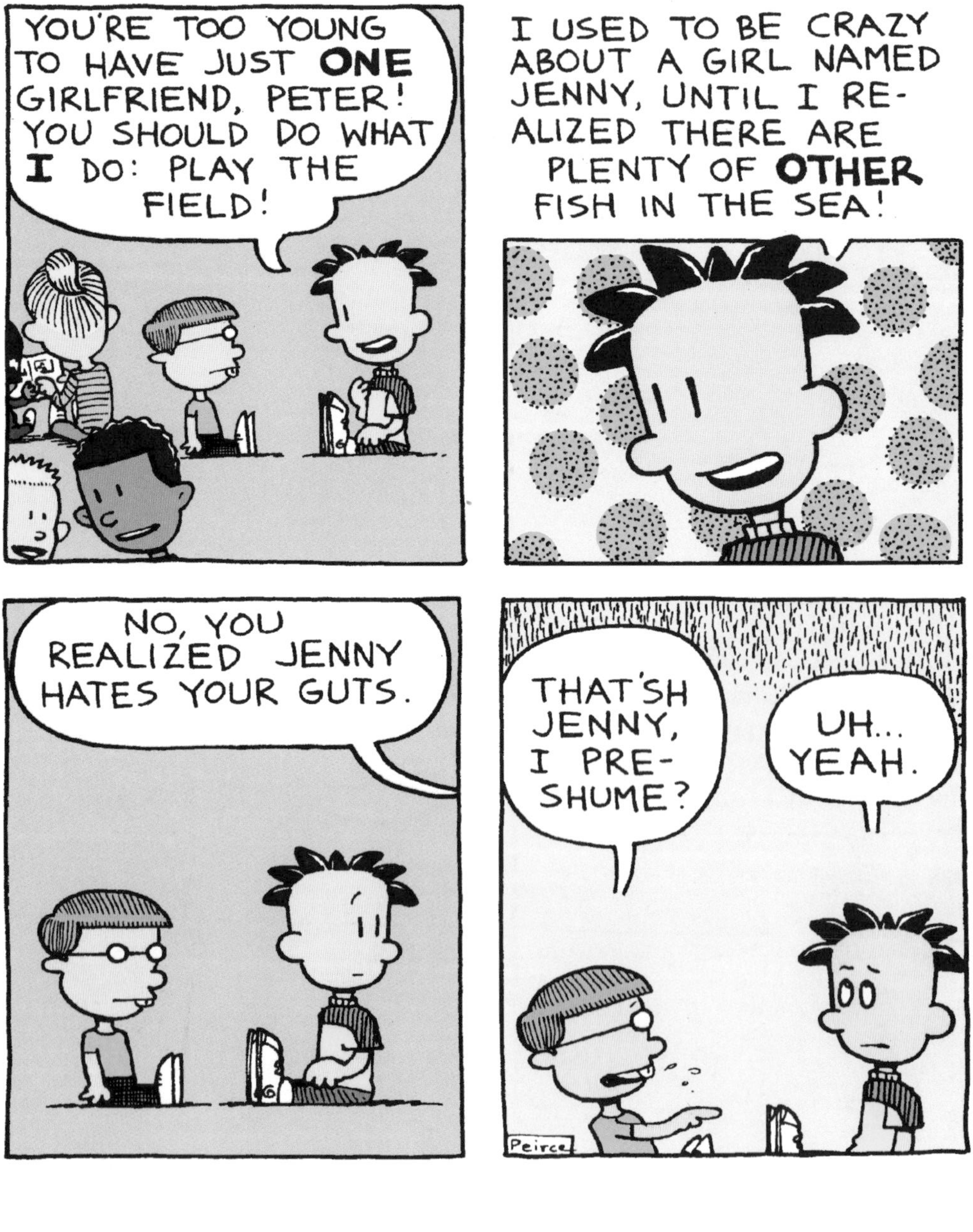
YOU'RE TOO YOUNG TO HAVE JUST **ONE** GIRLFRIEND, PETER! YOU SHOULD DO WHAT **I** DO: PLAY THE FIELD!
I USED TO BE CRAZY ABOUT A GIRL NAMED JENNY, UNTIL I RE-ALIZED THERE ARE PLENTY OF **OTHER** FISH IN THE SEA!
NO, YOU REALIZED JENNY HATES YOUR GUTS.
THAT'SH JENNY, I PRE-SHUME?
UH... YEAH.
Peirce

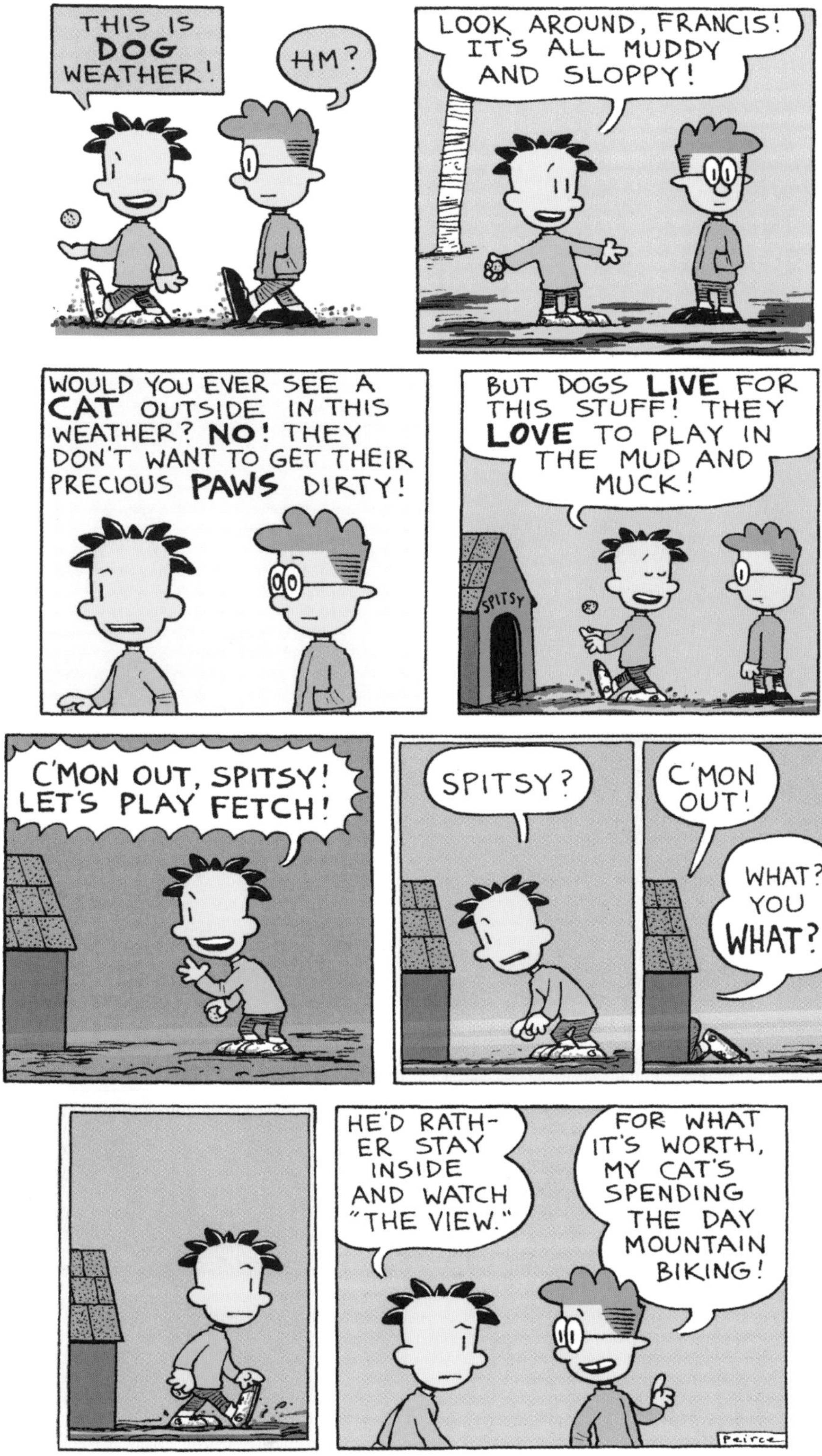
THIS IS DOG WEATHER!
HM?
LOOK AROUND, FRANCIS! IT'S ALL MUDDY AND SLOPPY!
WOULD YOU EVER SEE A CAT OUTSIDE IN THIS WEATHER? NO! THEY DON'T WANT TO GET THEIR PRECIOUS PAWS DIRTY!
BUT DOGS LIVE FOR THIS STUFF! THEY LOVE TO PLAY IN THE MUD AND MUCK!
SPITSY
C'MON OUT, SPITSY! LET'S PLAY FETCH!
SPITSY?
C'MON OUT!
WHAT? YOU WHAT?
HE'D RATH-ER STAY INSIDE AND WATCH "THE VIEW."
FOR WHAT IT'S WORTH, MY CAT'S SPENDING THE DAY MOUNTAIN BIKING!
Peirce

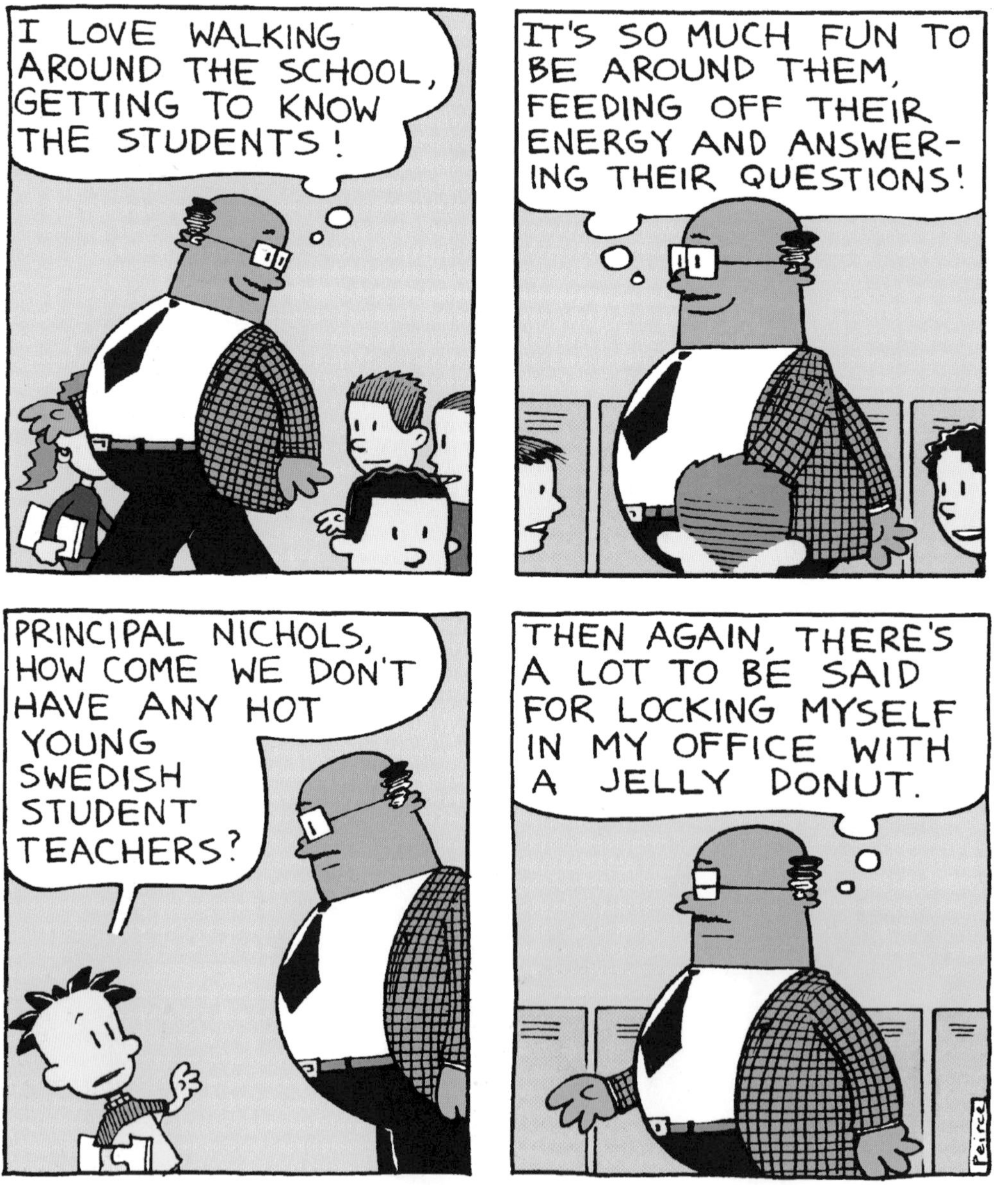
I LOVE WALKING AROUND THE SCHOOL, GETTING TO KNOW THE STUDENTS!
IT'S SO MUCH FUN TO BE AROUND THEM, FEEDING OFF THEIR ENERGY AND ANSWERING THEIR QUESTIONS!
PRINCIPAL NICHOLS, HOW COME WE DON'T HAVE ANY HOT YOUNG SWEDISH STUDENT TEACHERS?
THEN AGAIN, THERE'S A LOT TO BE SAID FOR LOCKING MYSELF IN MY OFFICE WITH A JELLY DONUT.
Peirce

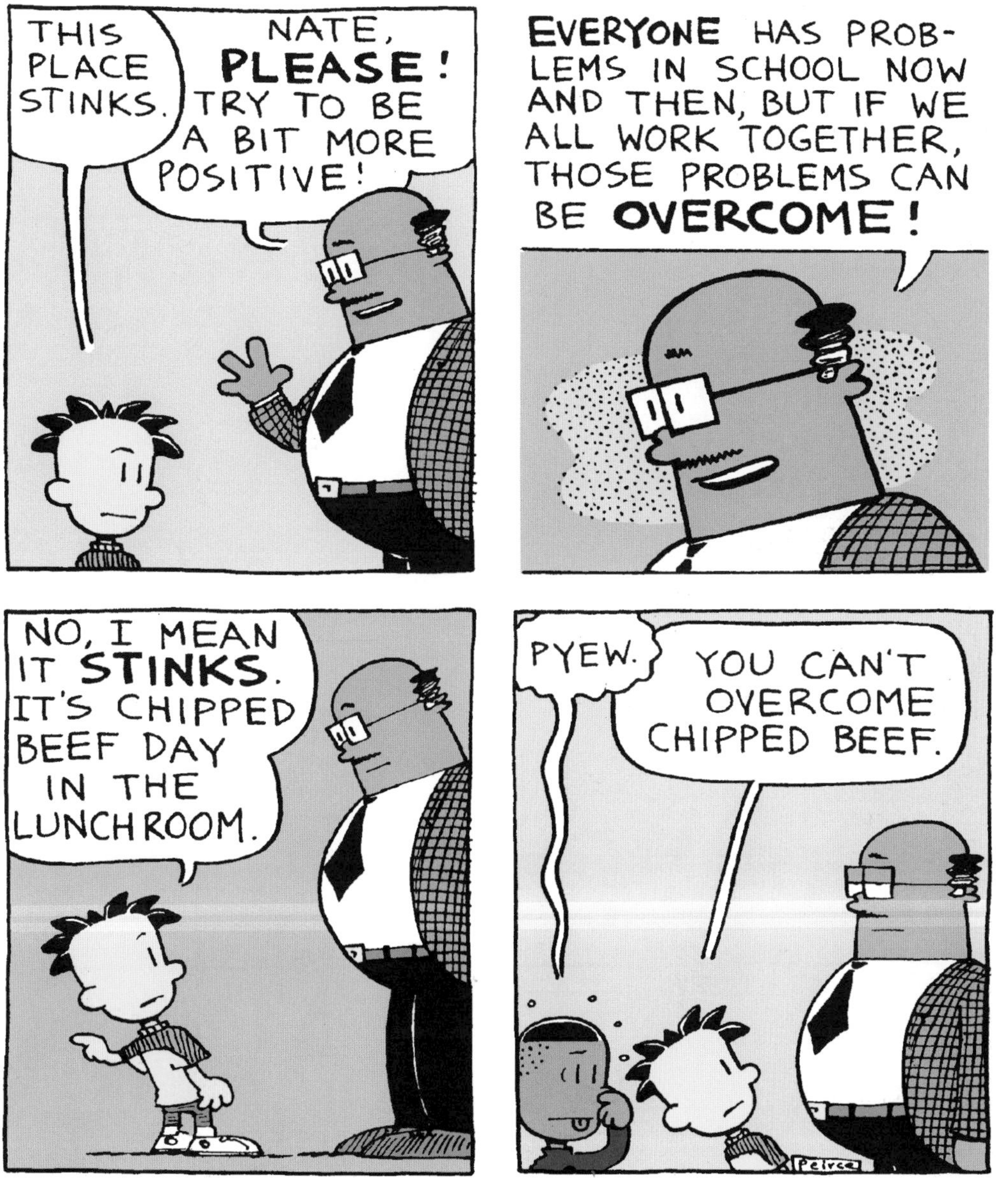
THIS PLACE STINKS.
NATE, **PLEASE**! TRY TO BE A BIT MORE POSITIVE!
EVERYONE HAS PROBLEMS IN SCHOOL NOW AND THEN, BUT IF WE ALL WORK TOGETHER, THOSE PROBLEMS CAN BE **OVERCOME**!
NO, I MEAN IT **STINKS**. IT'S CHIPPED BEEF DAY IN THE LUNCHROOM.
PYEW.
YOU CAN'T OVERCOME CHIPPED BEEF.
Peirce

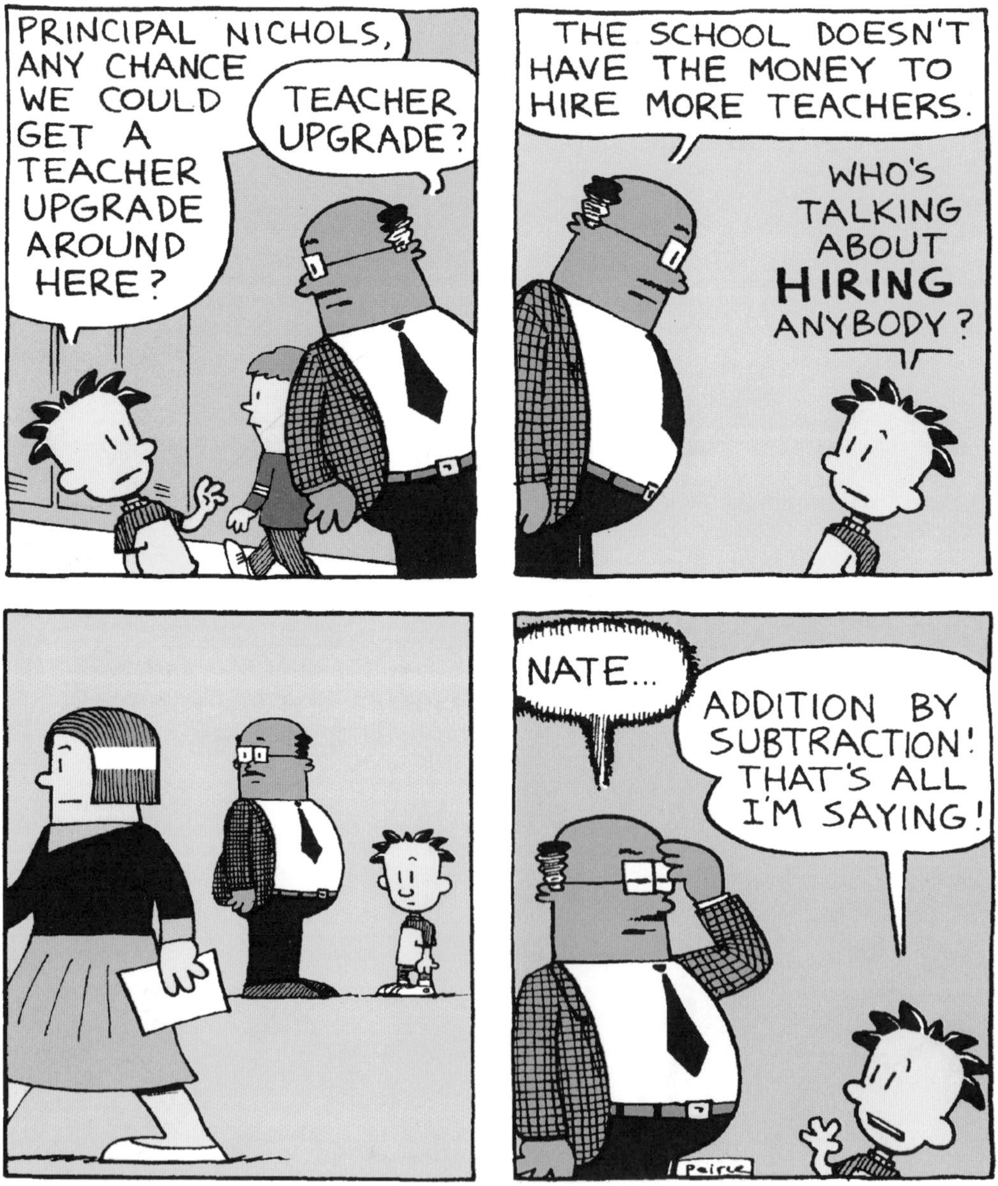
PRINCIPAL NICHOLS, ANY CHANCE WE COULD GET A TEACHER UPGRADE AROUND HERE?
TEACHER UPGRADE?
THE SCHOOL DOESN'T HAVE THE MONEY TO HIRE MORE TEACHERS.
WHO'S TALKING ABOUT **HIRING** ANYBODY?
NATE...
ADDITION BY SUBTRACTION! THAT'S ALL I'M SAYING!
Peirce

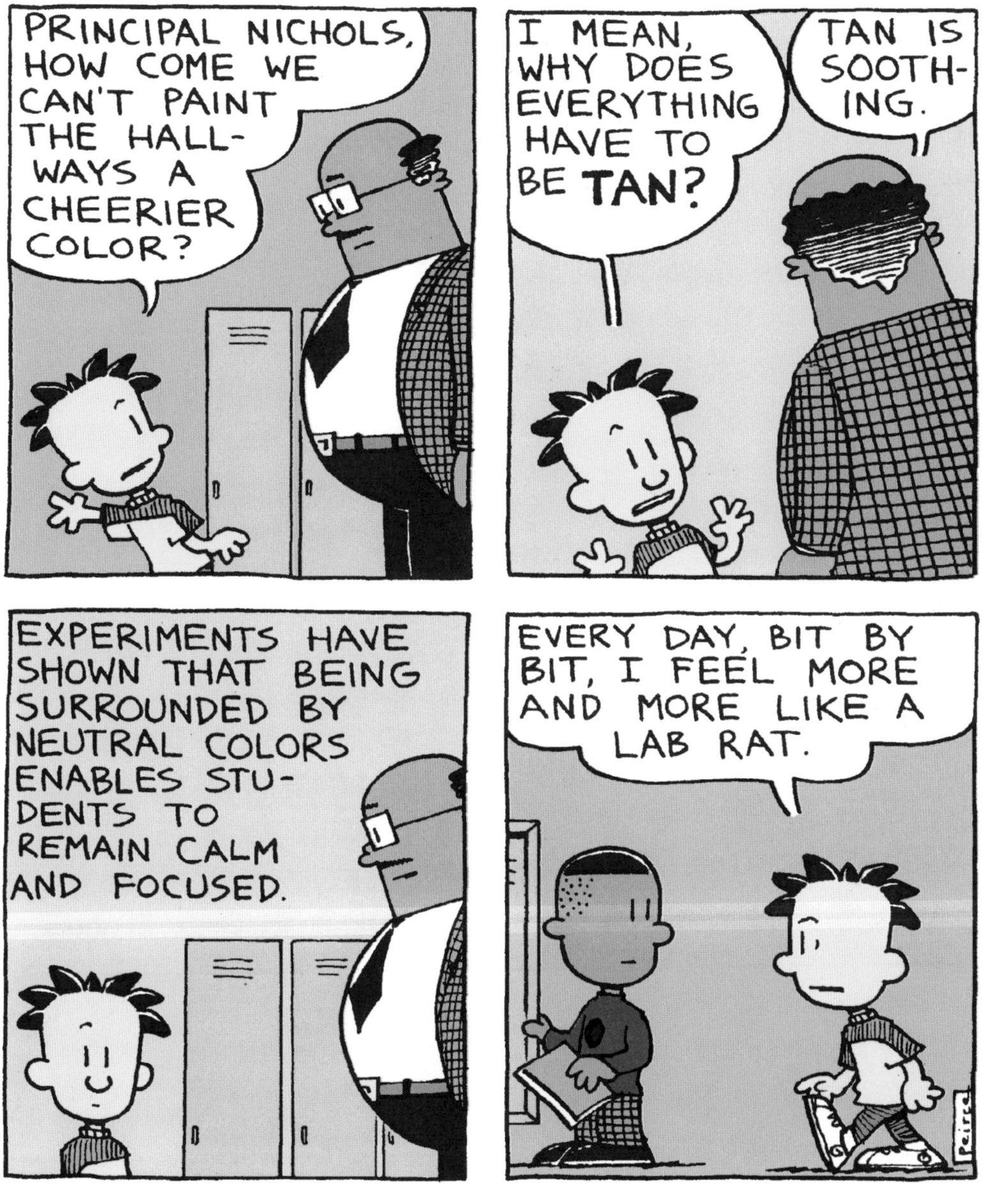
PRINCIPAL NICHOLS, HOW COME WE CAN'T PAINT THE HALLWAYS A CHEERIER COLOR?
I MEAN, WHY DOES EVERYTHING HAVE TO BE **TAN?**
TAN IS SOOTHING.
EXPERIMENTS HAVE SHOWN THAT BEING SURROUNDED BY NEUTRAL COLORS ENABLES STUDENTS TO REMAIN CALM AND FOCUSED.
EVERY DAY, BIT BY BIT, I FEEL MORE AND MORE LIKE A LAB RAT.
Peirce

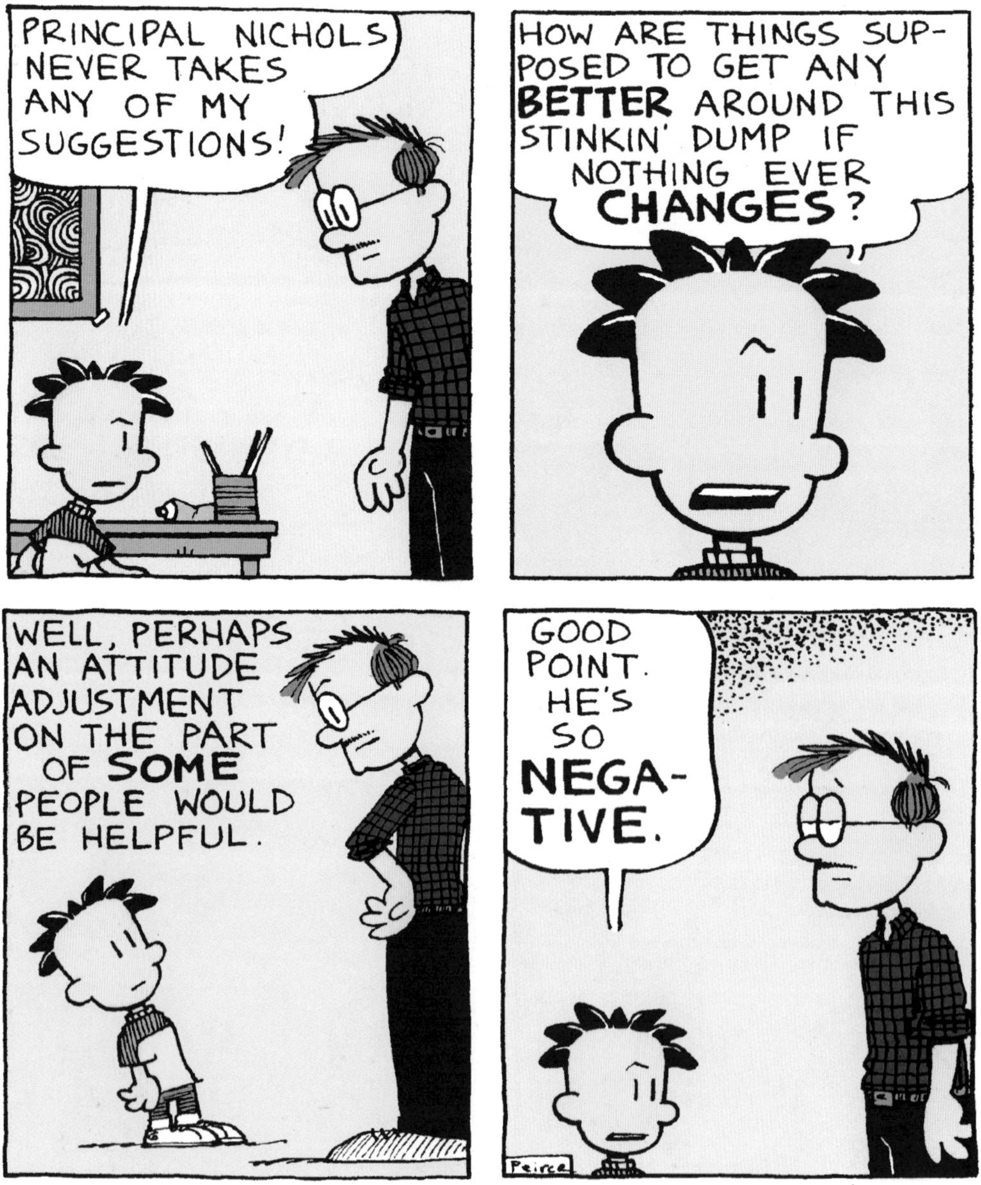
PRINCIPAL NICHOLS NEVER TAKES ANY OF MY SUGGESTIONS!
HOW ARE THINGS SUPPOSED TO GET ANY **BETTER** AROUND THIS STINKIN' DUMP IF NOTHING EVER **CHANGES**?
WELL, PERHAPS AN ATTITUDE ADJUSTMENT ON THE PART OF **SOME** PEOPLE WOULD BE HELPFUL.
GOOD POINT. HE'S SO **NEGATIVE.**
Peirce

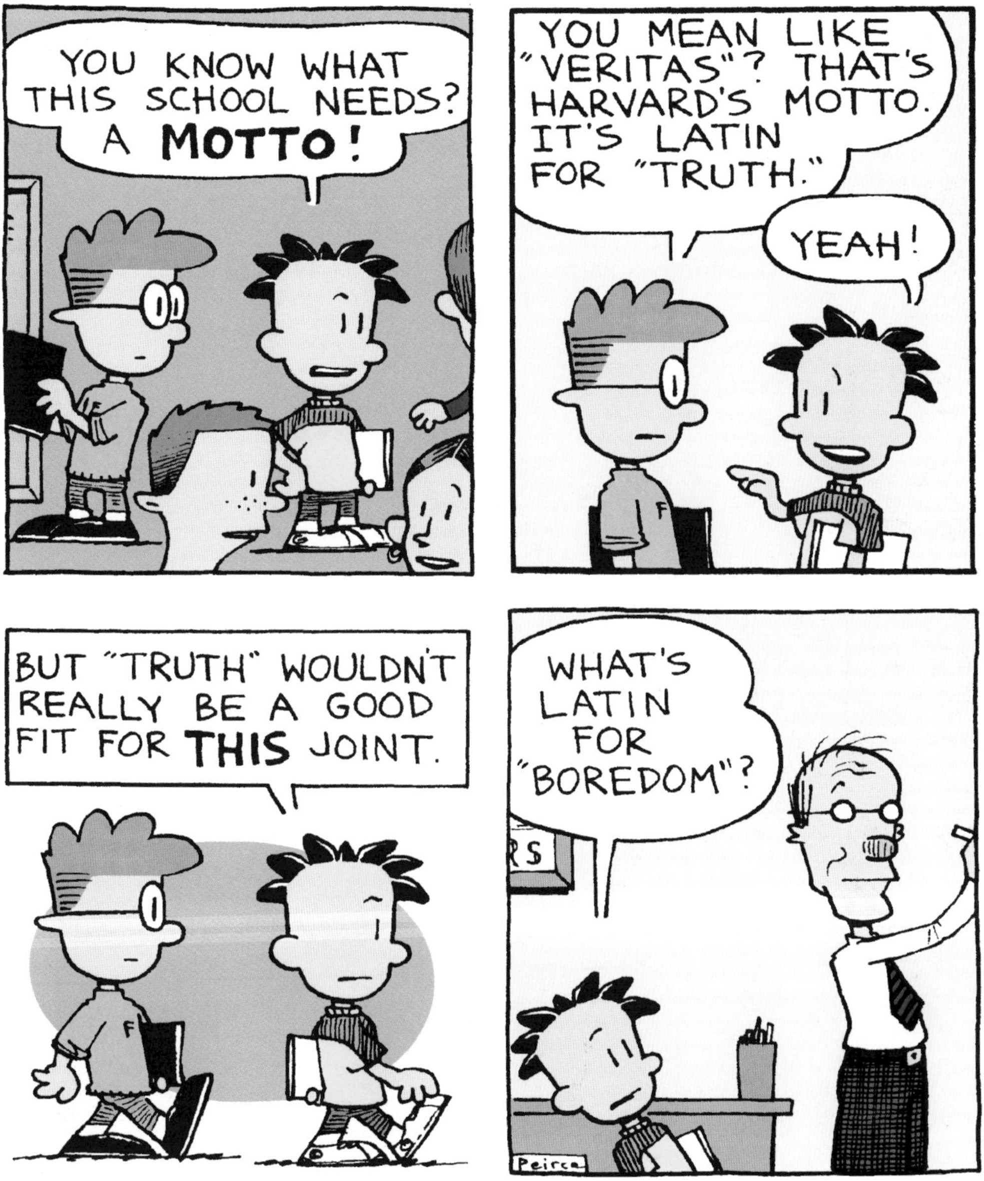
YOU KNOW WHAT THIS SCHOOL NEEDS? A **MOTTO**!
YOU MEAN LIKE "VERITAS"? THAT'S HARVARD'S MOTTO. IT'S LATIN FOR "TRUTH."
YEAH!
BUT "TRUTH" WOULDN'T REALLY BE A GOOD FIT FOR **THIS** JOINT.
WHAT'S LATIN FOR "BOREDOM"?
Peirce

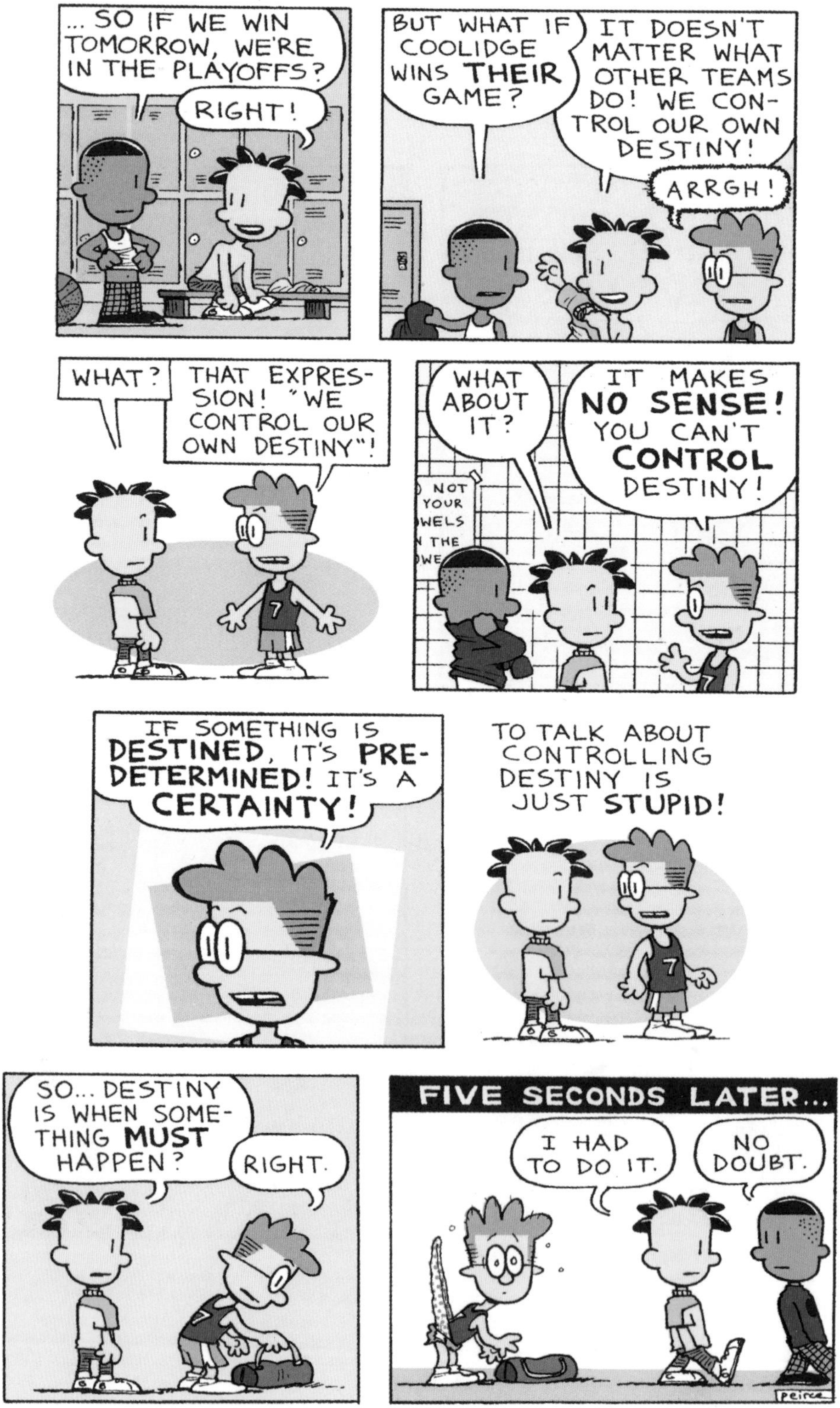
... SO IF WE WIN TOMORROW, WE'RE IN THE PLAYOFFS?
RIGHT!
BUT WHAT IF COOLIDGE WINS **THEIR** GAME?
IT DOESN'T MATTER WHAT OTHER TEAMS DO! WE CONTROL OUR OWN DESTINY!
ARRGH!
WHAT?
THAT EXPRESSION! "WE CONTROL OUR OWN DESTINY"!
WHAT ABOUT IT?
IT MAKES **NO SENSE!** YOU CAN'T **CONTROL** DESTINY!
IF SOMETHING IS **DESTINED**, IT'S **PREDETERMINED!** IT'S A **CERTAINTY!**
TO TALK ABOUT CONTROLLING DESTINY IS JUST **STUPID!**
SO... DESTINY IS WHEN SOMETHING **MUST** HAPPEN?
RIGHT.
FIVE SECONDS LATER...
I HAD TO DO IT.
NO DOUBT.
peirce

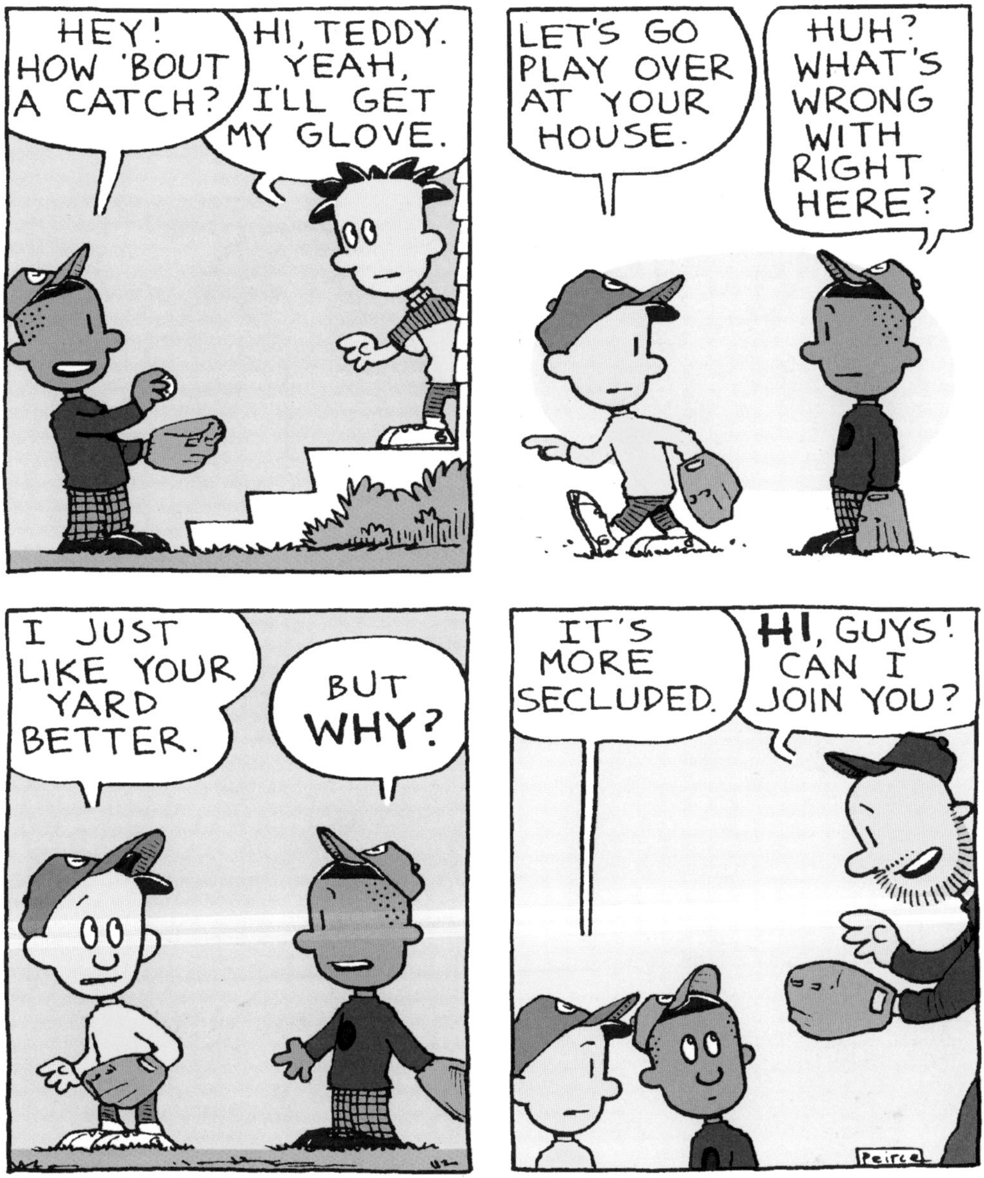
HEY! HOW 'BOUT A CATCH?
HI, TEDDY. YEAH, I'LL GET MY GLOVE.
LET'S GO PLAY OVER AT YOUR HOUSE.
HUH? WHAT'S WRONG WITH RIGHT HERE?
I JUST LIKE YOUR YARD BETTER.
BUT WHY?
IT'S MORE SECLUDED.
HI, GUYS! CAN I JOIN YOU?
Peirce

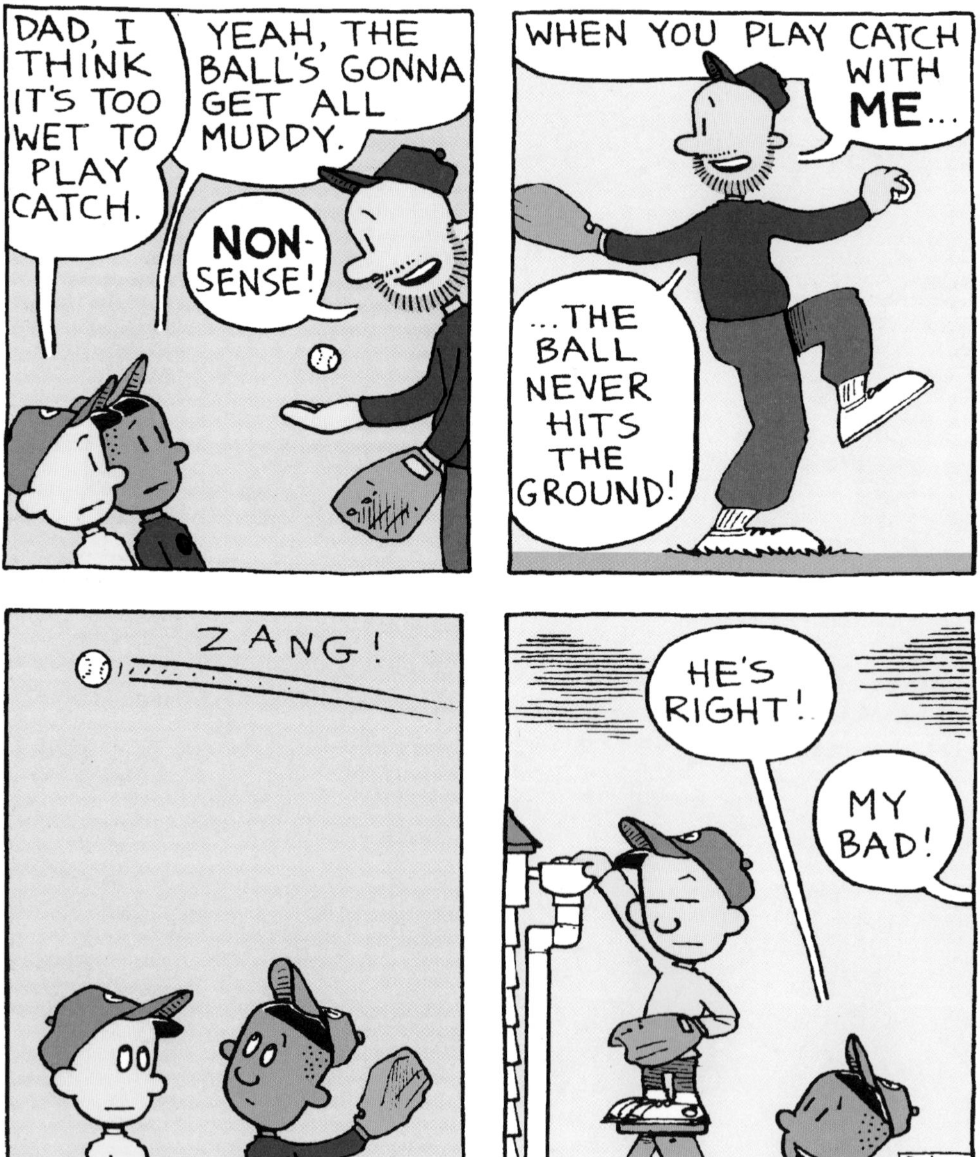
DAD, I THINK IT'S TOO WET TO PLAY CATCH.
YEAH, THE BALL'S GONNA GET ALL MUDDY.
NON-SENSE!
WHEN YOU PLAY CATCH WITH ME...
...THE BALL NEVER HITS THE GROUND!
ZANG!
HE'S RIGHT!
MY BAD!
Peirce

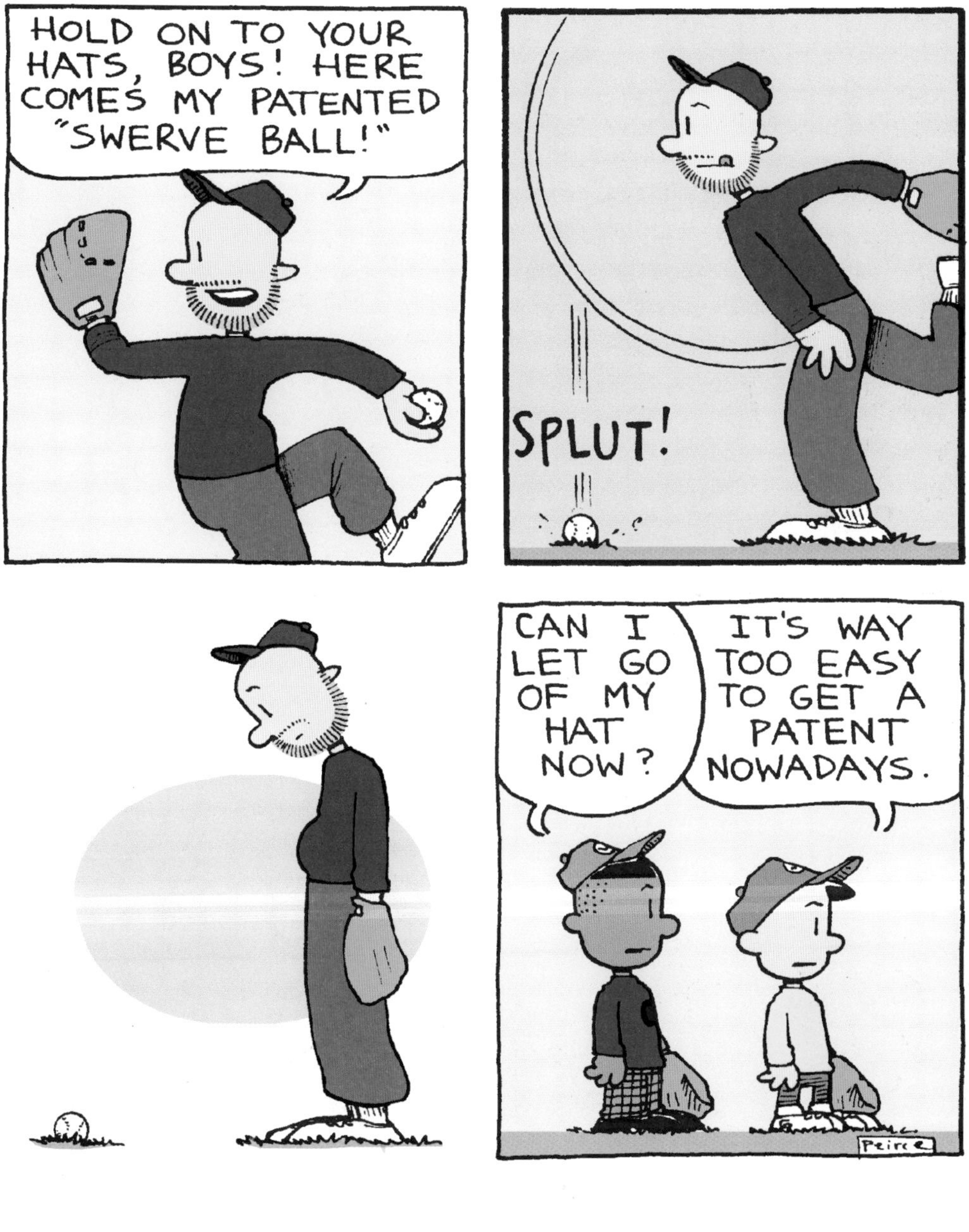
HOLD ON TO YOUR HATS, BOYS! HERE COMES MY PATENTED "SWERVE BALL!"
SPLUT!
CAN I LET GO OF MY HAT NOW?
IT'S WAY TOO EASY TO GET A PATENT NOWADAYS.
Peirce

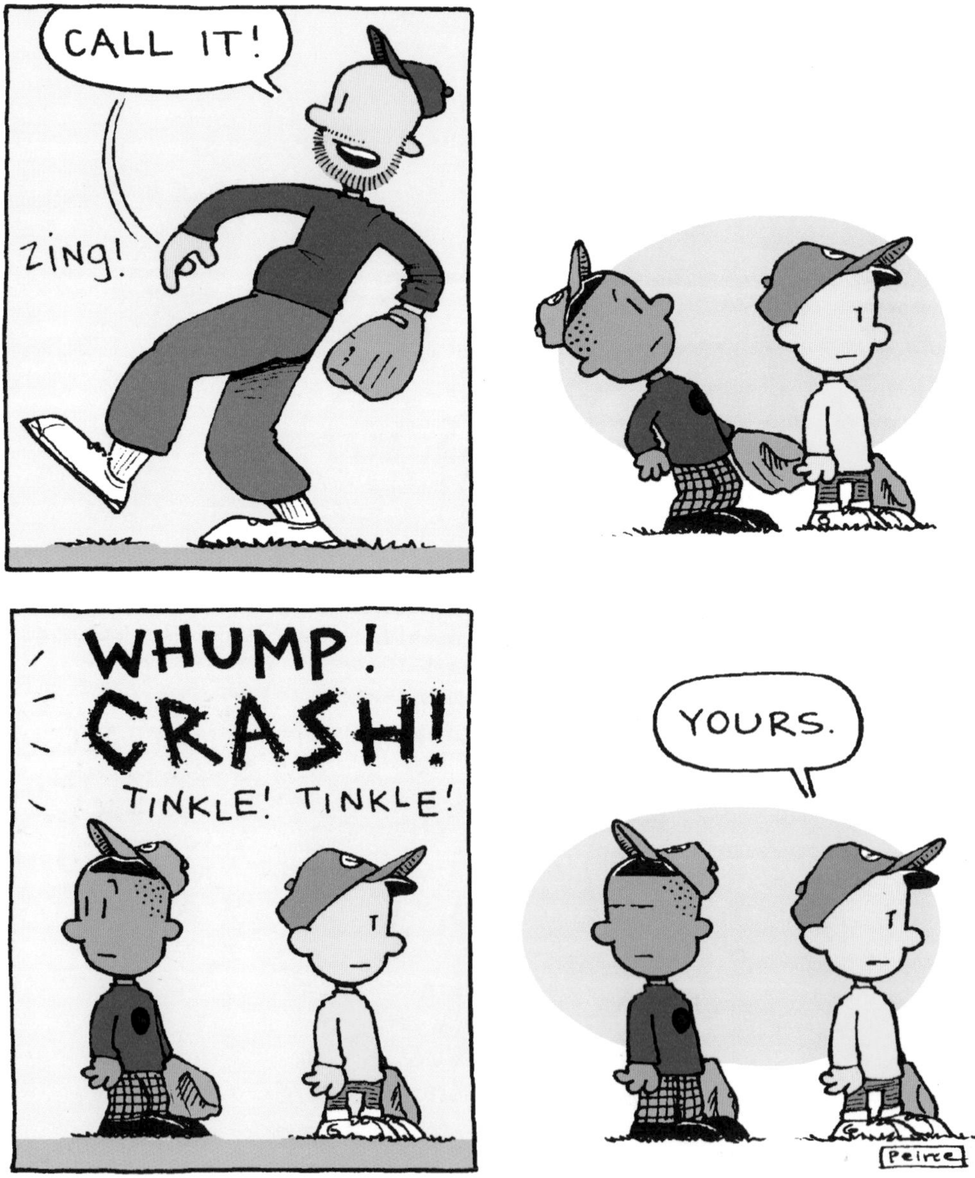
CALL IT!
ZING!
WHUMP!
CRASH!
TINKLE! TINKLE!
YOURS.
Peirce

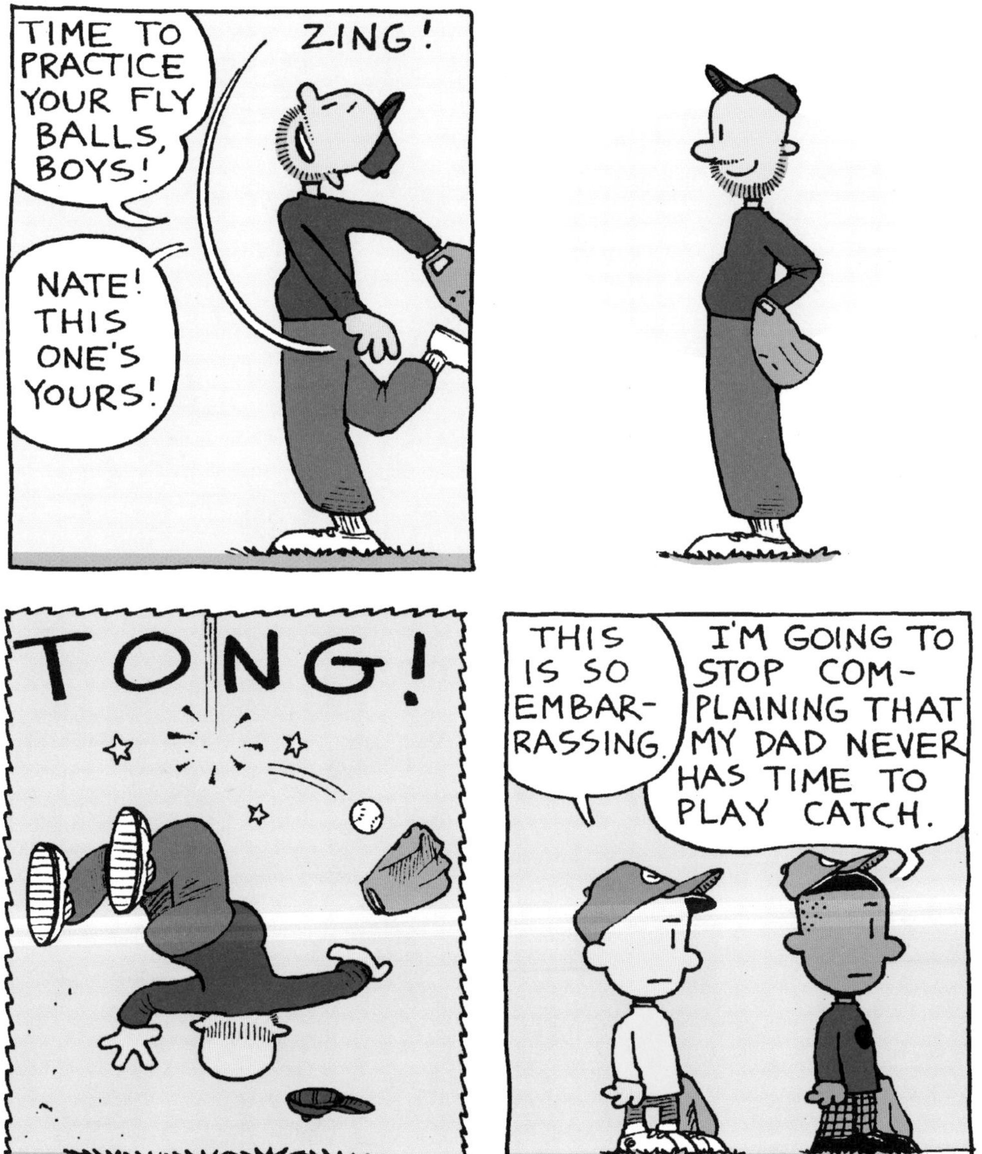
TIME TO PRACTICE YOUR FLY BALLS, BOYS!
ZING!
NATE! THIS ONE'S YOURS!
TONG!
THIS IS SO EMBAR-RASSING.
I'M GOING TO STOP COM-PLAINING THAT MY DAD NEVER HAS TIME TO PLAY CATCH.
peirce

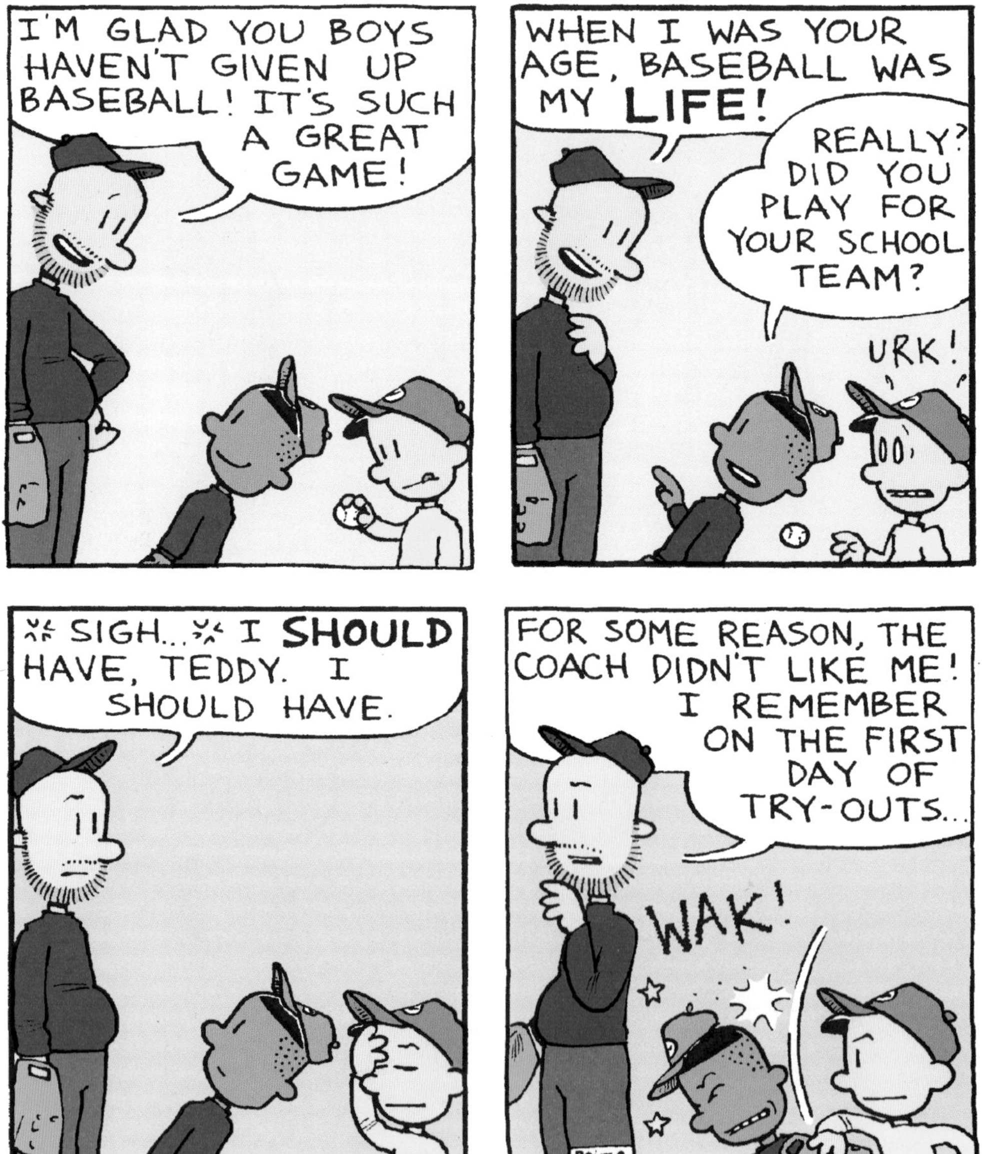
I'M GLAD YOU BOYS HAVEN'T GIVEN UP BASEBALL! IT'S SUCH A GREAT GAME!
WHEN I WAS YOUR AGE, BASEBALL WAS MY LIFE!
REALLY? DID YOU PLAY FOR YOUR SCHOOL TEAM?
URK!
SIGH... I SHOULD HAVE, TEDDY. I SHOULD HAVE.
FOR SOME REASON, THE COACH DIDN'T LIKE ME! I REMEMBER ON THE FIRST DAY OF TRY-OUTS...
WAK!
Peirce

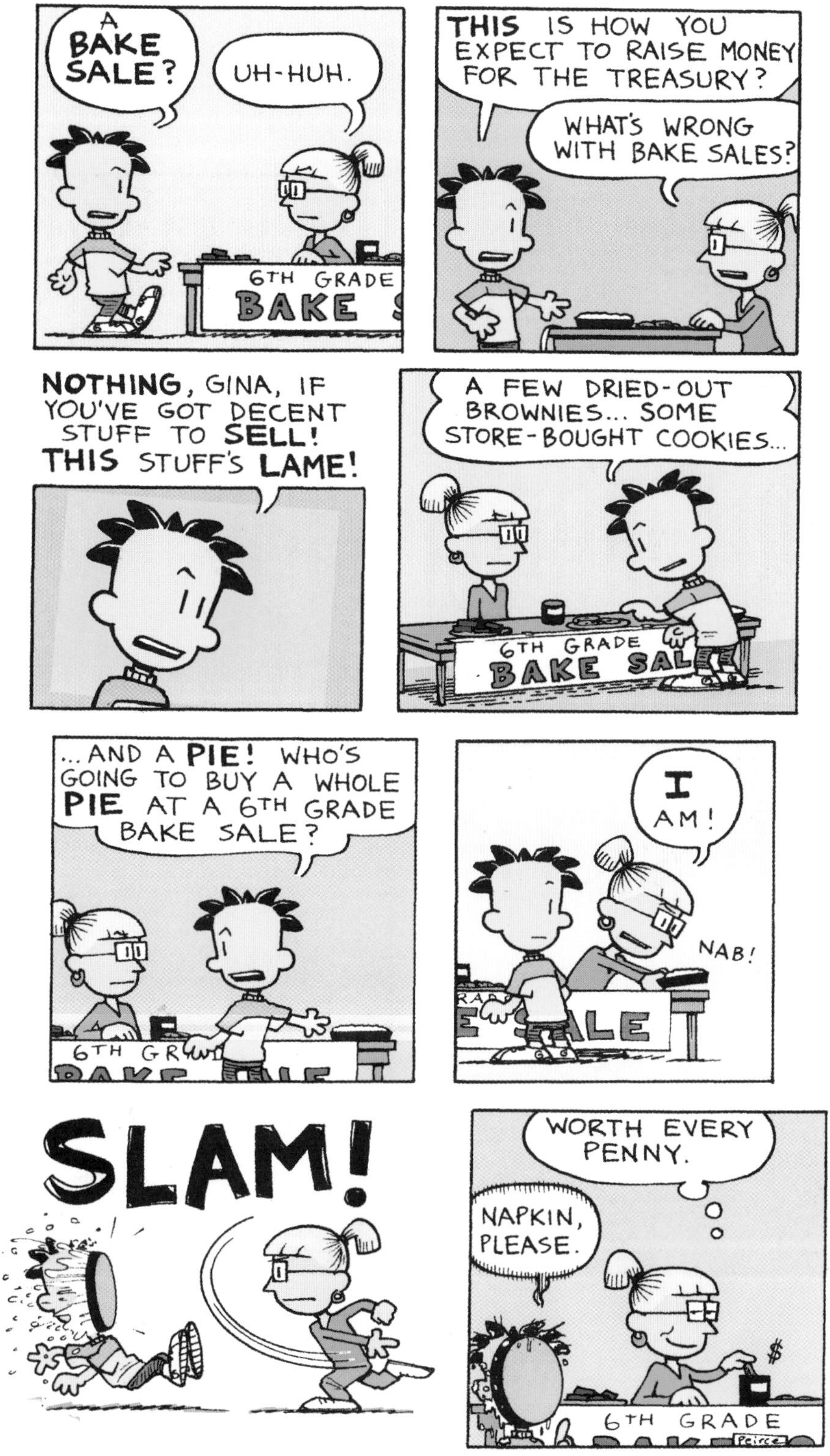
A BAKE SALE?
UH-HUH.
THIS IS HOW YOU EXPECT TO RAISE MONEY FOR THE TREASURY?
WHAT'S WRONG WITH BAKE SALES?
NOTHING, GINA, IF YOU'VE GOT DECENT STUFF TO SELL! THIS STUFF'S LAME!
A FEW DRIED-OUT BROWNIES... SOME STORE-BOUGHT COOKIES...
6TH GRADE BAKE SAL
...AND A PIE! WHO'S GOING TO BUY A WHOLE PIE AT A 6TH GRADE BAKE SALE?
I AM!
NAB!
SALE
SLAM!
WORTH EVERY PENNY.
NAPKIN, PLEASE.
6TH GRADE
Peirce

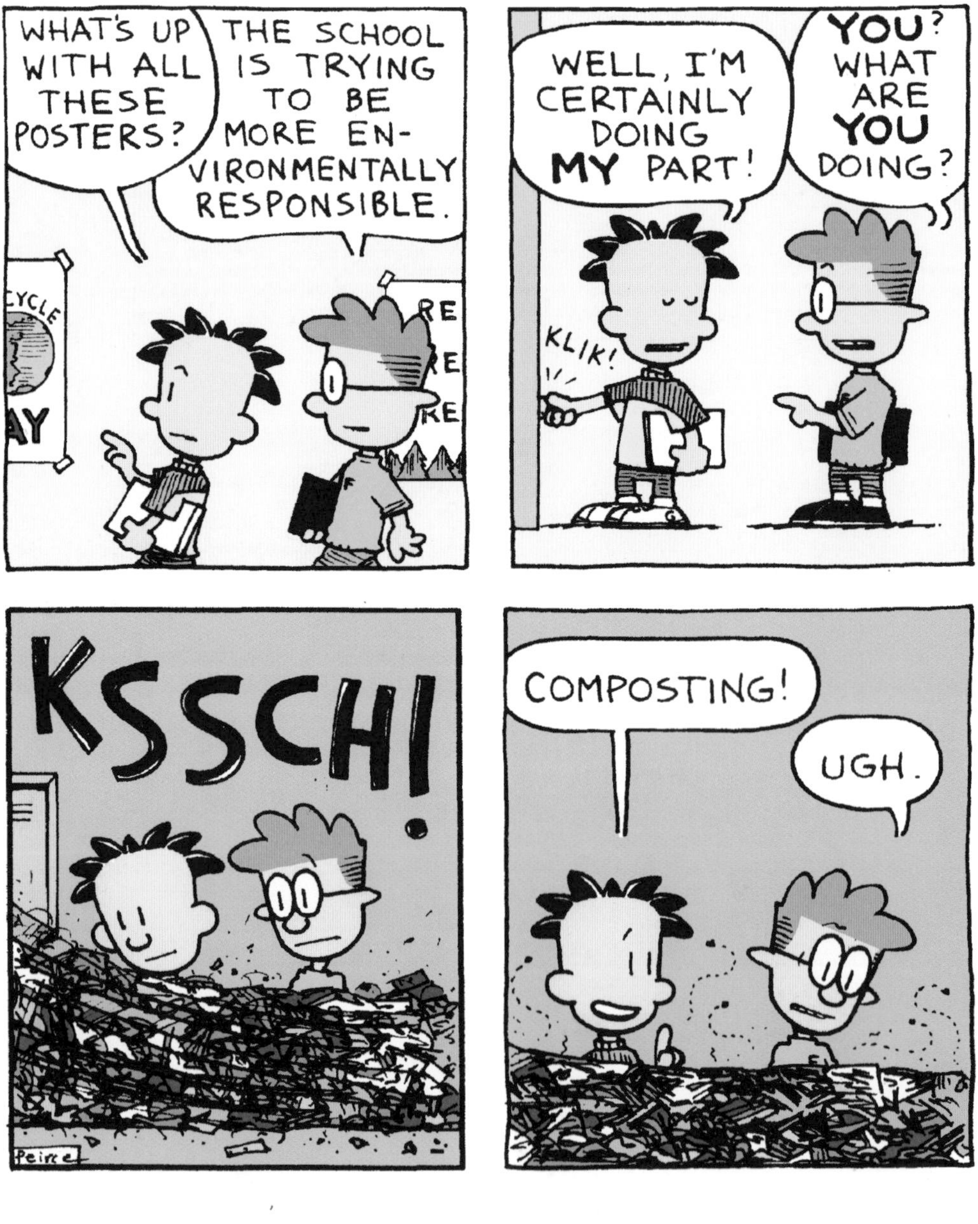
WHAT'S UP WITH ALL THESE POSTERS?
THE SCHOOL IS TRYING TO BE MORE EN-VIRONMENTALLY RESPONSIBLE.
WELL, I'M CERTAINLY DOING MY PART!
KLIK!
YOU? WHAT ARE YOU DOING?
KSSCH!
COMPOSTING!
UGH.
Peirce

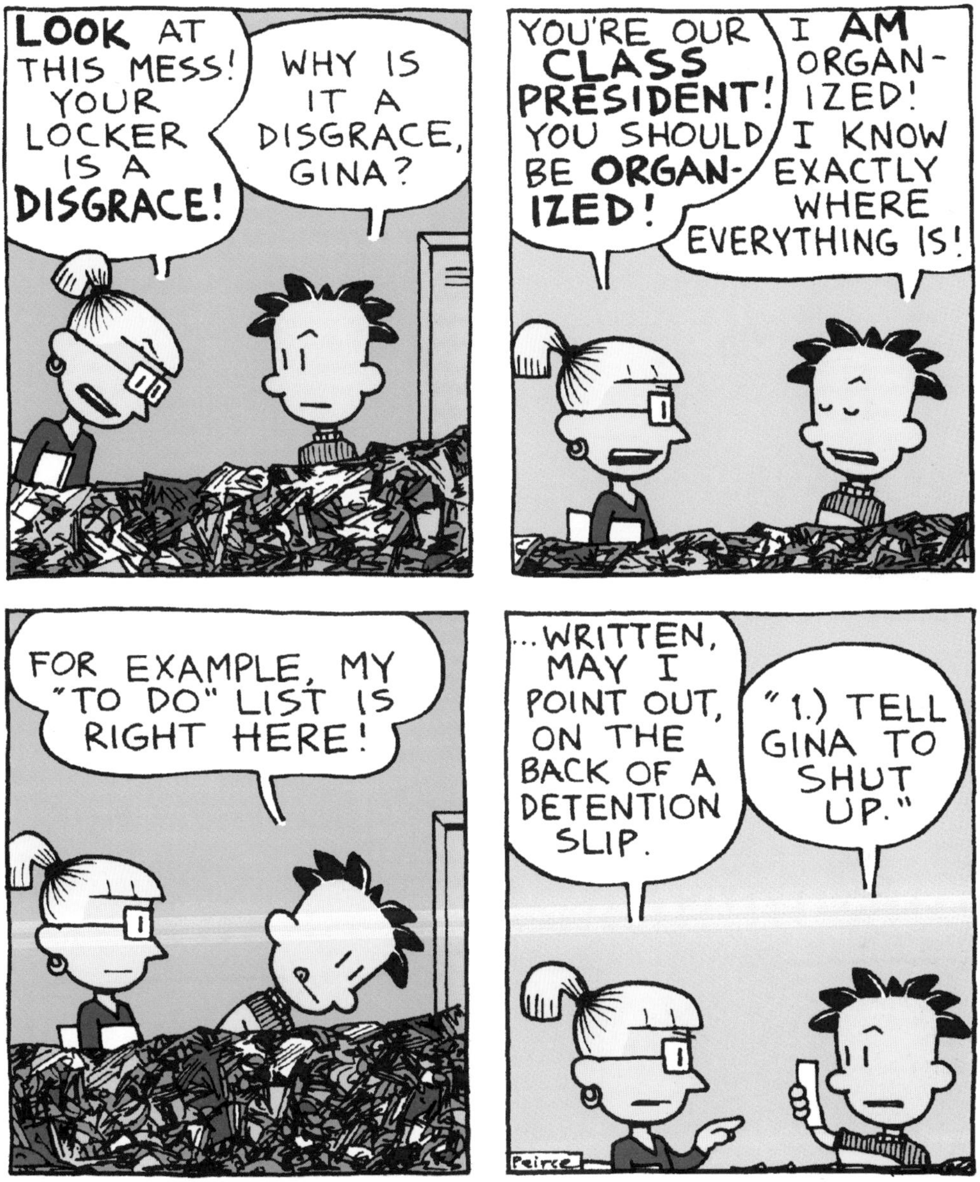
LOOK AT THIS MESS! YOUR LOCKER IS A DISGRACE!
WHY IS IT A DISGRACE, GINA?
YOU'RE OUR CLASS PRESIDENT! YOU SHOULD BE ORGANIZED!
I AM ORGANIZED! I KNOW EXACTLY WHERE EVERYTHING IS!
FOR EXAMPLE, MY "TO DO" LIST IS RIGHT HERE!
...WRITTEN, MAY I POINT OUT, ON THE BACK OF A DETENTION SLIP.
"1.) TELL GINA TO SHUT UP."
Peirce

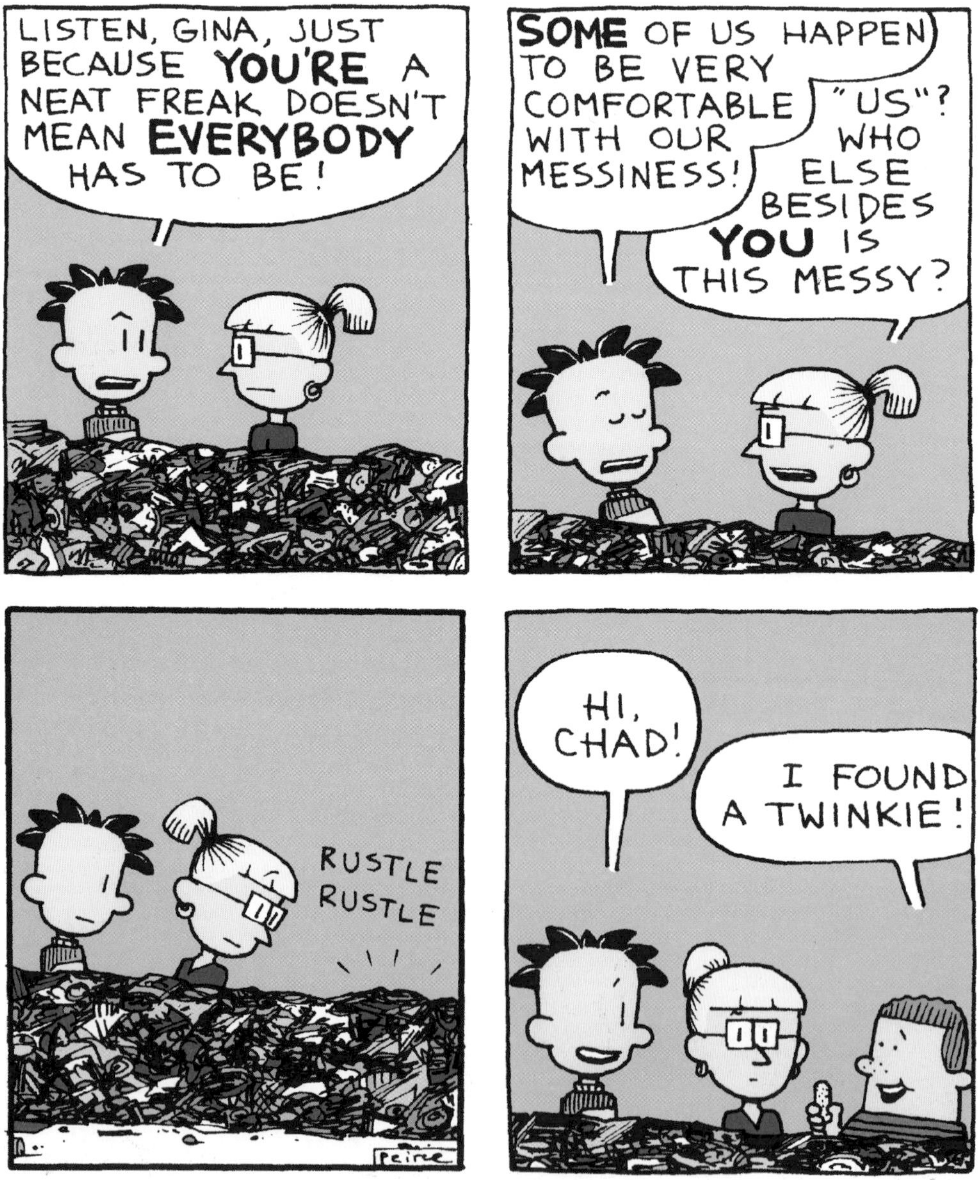

LISTEN, GINA, JUST BECAUSE YOU'RE A NEAT FREAK DOESN'T MEAN EVERYBODY HAS TO BE!
SOME OF US HAPPEN TO BE VERY COMFORTABLE WITH OUR MESSINESS!
"US"? WHO ELSE BESIDES YOU IS THIS MESSY?
RUSTLE RUSTLE
HI, CHAD!
I FOUND A TWINKIE!
PEIRCE

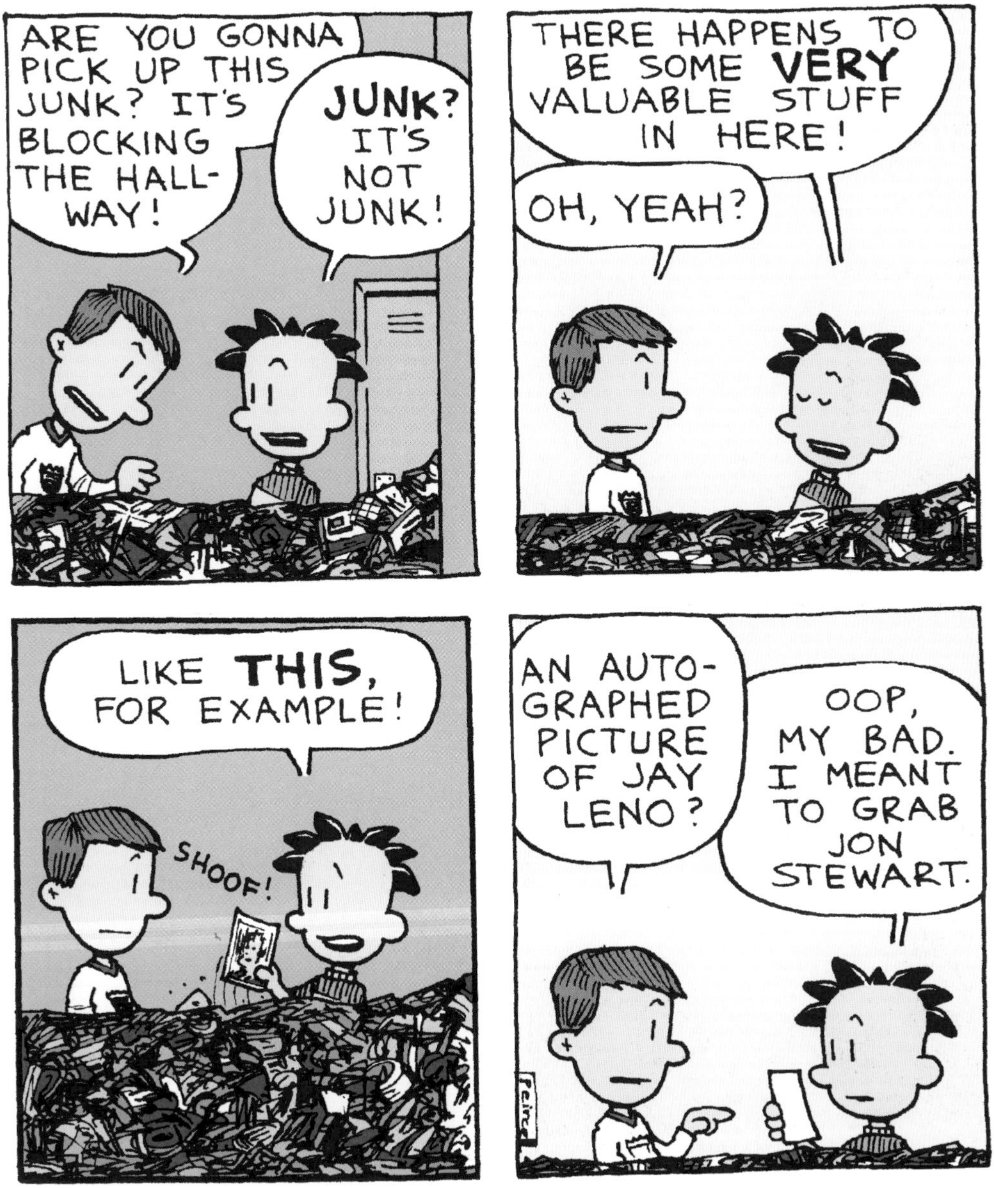
ARE YOU GONNA PICK UP THIS JUNK? IT'S BLOCKING THE HALL-WAY!
JUNK? IT'S NOT JUNK!
THERE HAPPENS TO BE SOME VERY VALUABLE STUFF IN HERE!
OH, YEAH?
LIKE THIS, FOR EXAMPLE!
SHOOF!
AN AUTO-GRAPHED PICTURE OF JAY LENO?
OOP, MY BAD. I MEANT TO GRAB JON STEWART.
Peirce

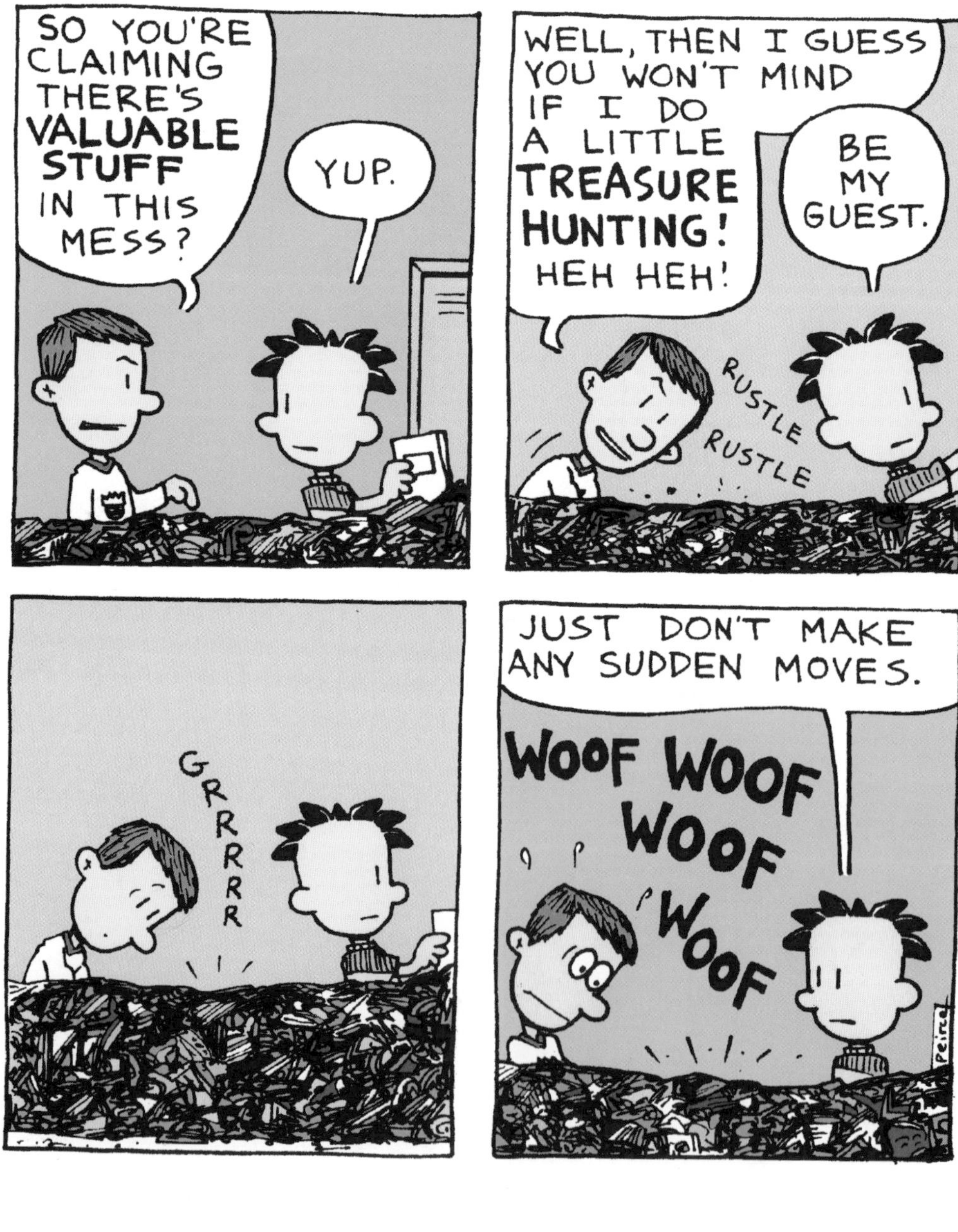

SO YOU'RE CLAIMING THERE'S **VALUABLE STUFF** IN THIS MESS?
YUP.
WELL, THEN I GUESS YOU WON'T MIND IF I DO A LITTLE **TREASURE HUNTING!** HEH HEH!
BE MY GUEST.
RUSTLE RUSTLE
GRRRRR
JUST DON'T MAKE ANY SUDDEN MOVES.
WOOF WOOF WOOF WOOF WOOF
Peirce

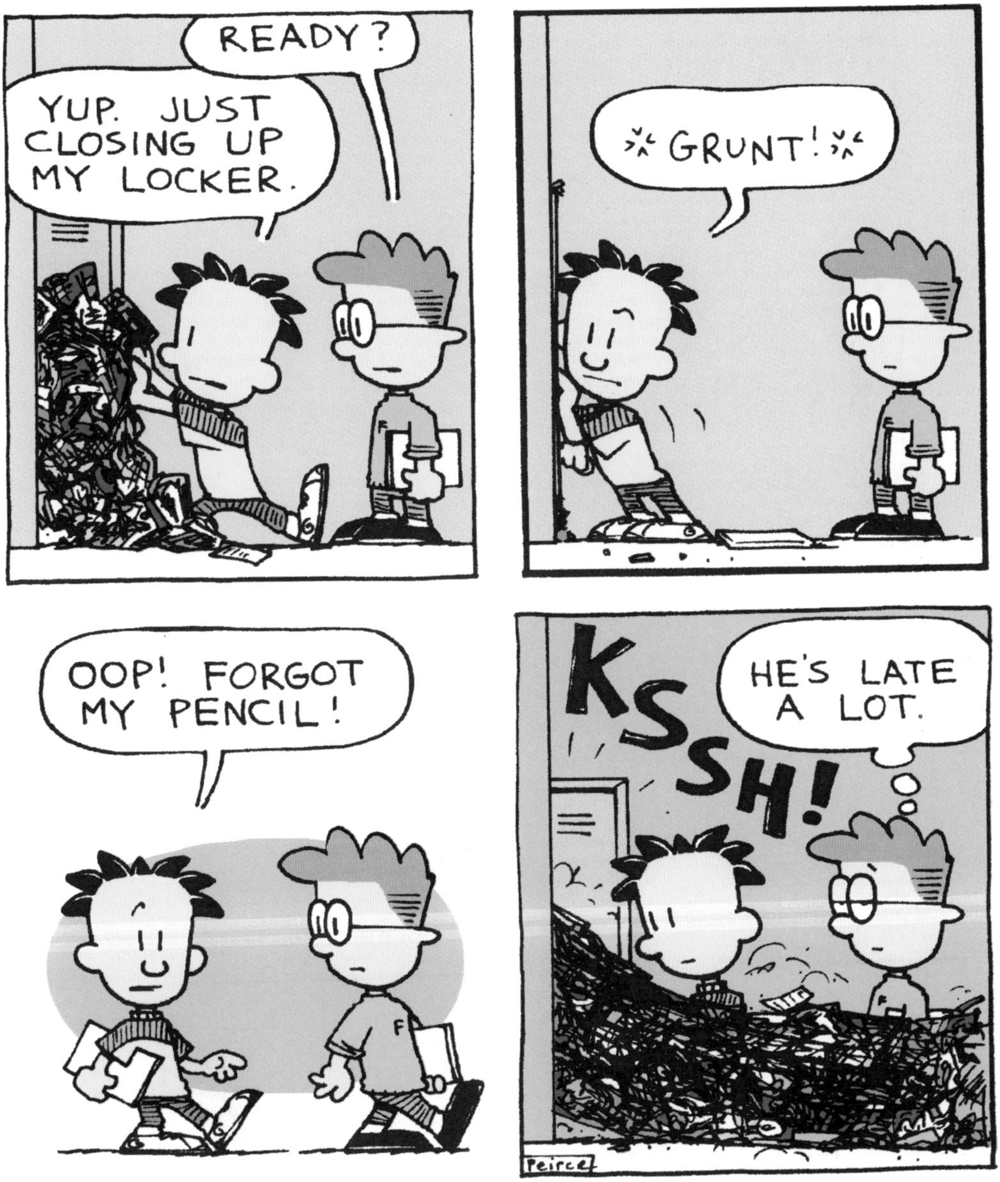
READY?
YUP. JUST CLOSING UP MY LOCKER.
GRUNT!
OOP! FORGOT MY PENCIL!
KSSH!
HE'S LATE A LOT.
Peirce

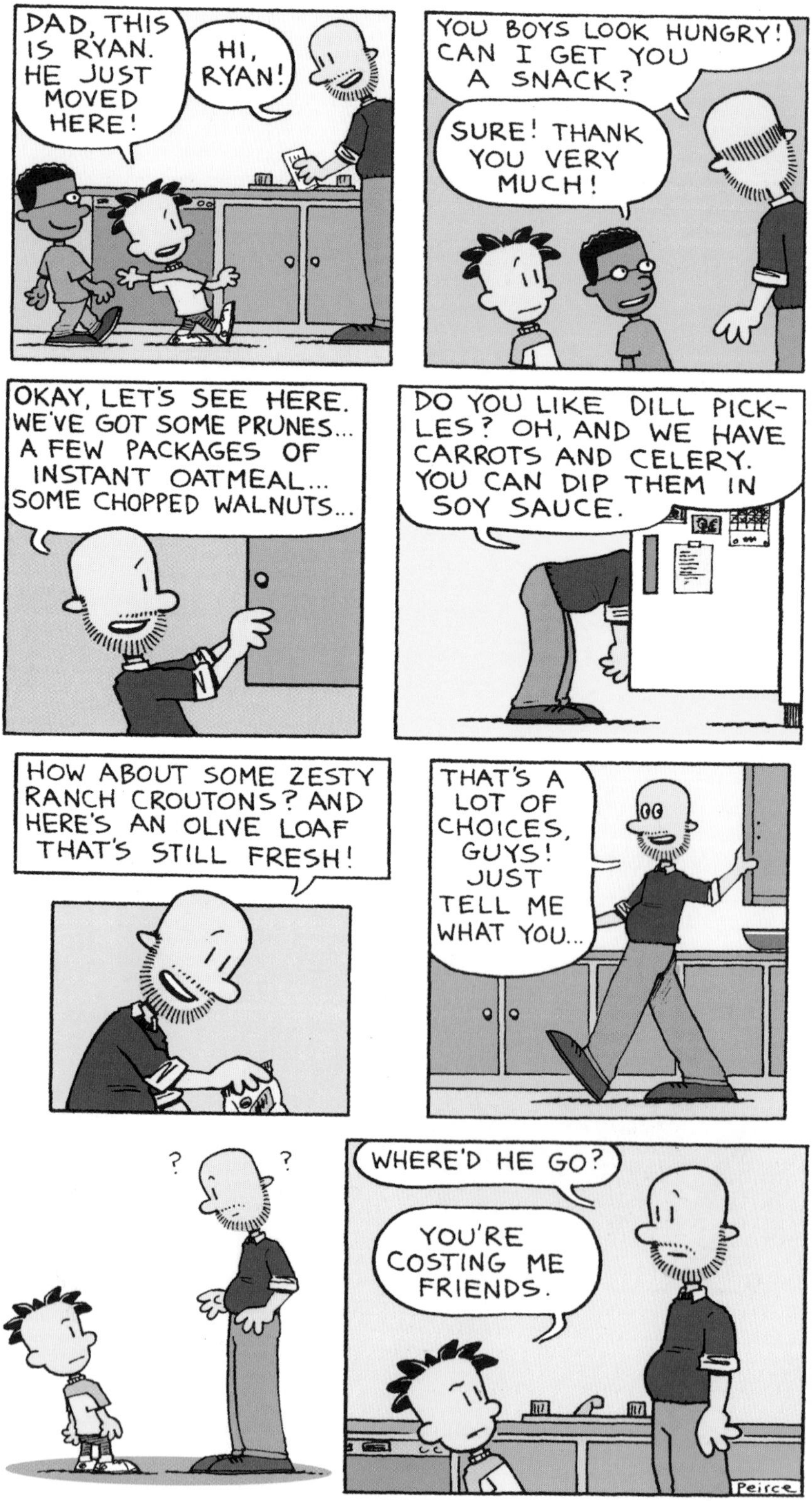
DAD, THIS IS RYAN. HE JUST MOVED HERE!
HI, RYAN!
YOU BOYS LOOK HUNGRY! CAN I GET YOU A SNACK?
SURE! THANK YOU VERY MUCH!
OKAY, LET'S SEE HERE. WE'VE GOT SOME PRUNES... A FEW PACKAGES OF INSTANT OATMEAL... SOME CHOPPED WALNUTS...
DO YOU LIKE DILL PICKLES? OH, AND WE HAVE CARROTS AND CELERY. YOU CAN DIP THEM IN SOY SAUCE.
HOW ABOUT SOME ZESTY RANCH CROUTONS? AND HERE'S AN OLIVE LOAF THAT'S STILL FRESH!
THAT'S A LOT OF CHOICES, GUYS! JUST TELL ME WHAT YOU...
? ?
WHERE'D HE GO?
YOU'RE COSTING ME FRIENDS.
Peirce

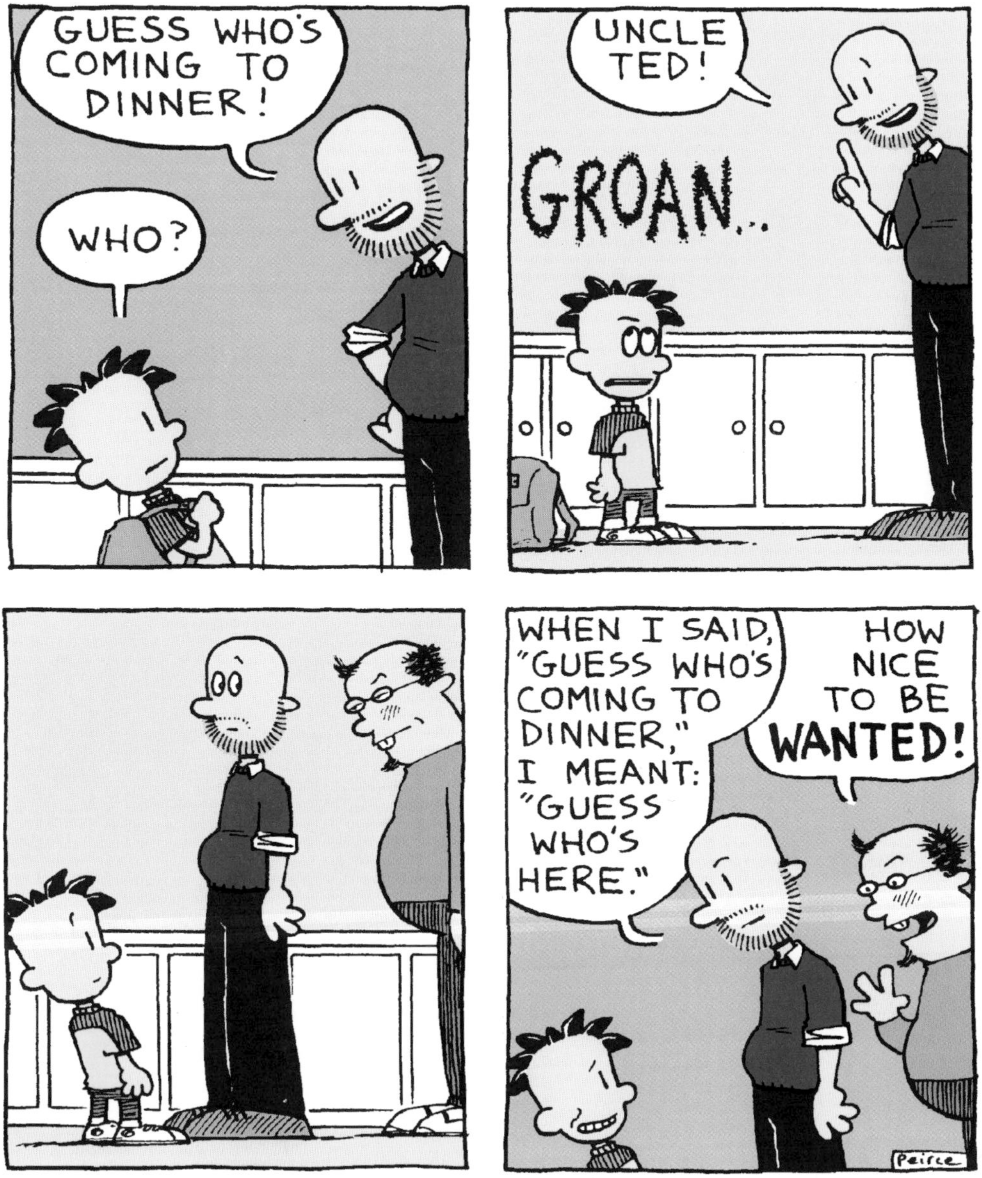
GUESS WHO'S COMING TO DINNER!
WHO?
UNCLE TED!
GROAN...
WHEN I SAID, "GUESS WHO'S COMING TO DINNER," I MEANT: "GUESS WHO'S HERE."
HOW NICE TO BE **WANTED!**
Peirce

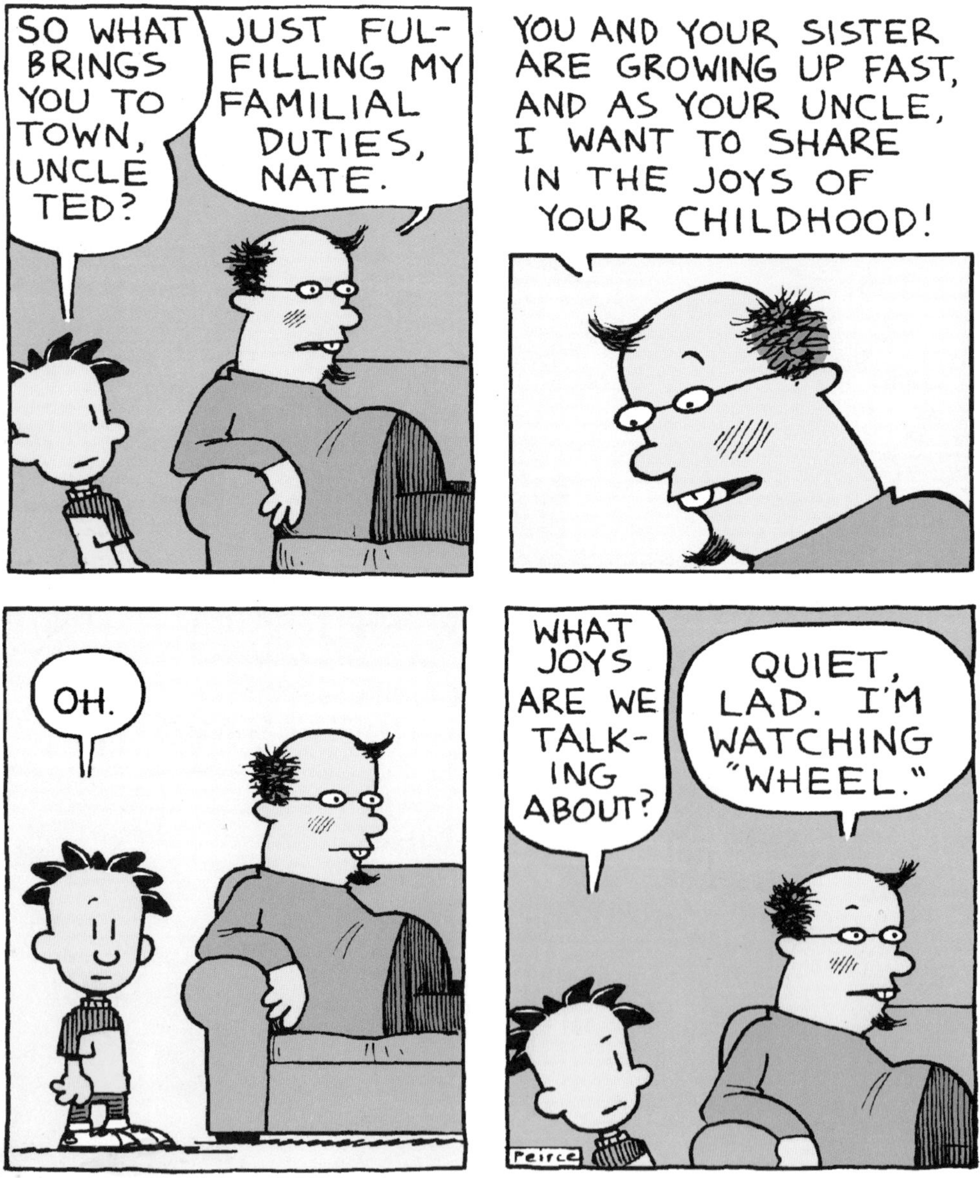
SO WHAT BRINGS YOU TO TOWN, UNCLE TED?
JUST FULFILLING MY FAMILIAL DUTIES, NATE.
YOU AND YOUR SISTER ARE GROWING UP FAST, AND AS YOUR UNCLE, I WANT TO SHARE IN THE JOYS OF YOUR CHILDHOOD!
OH.
WHAT JOYS ARE WE TALKING ABOUT?
QUIET, LAD. I'M WATCHING "WHEEL."
Peirce

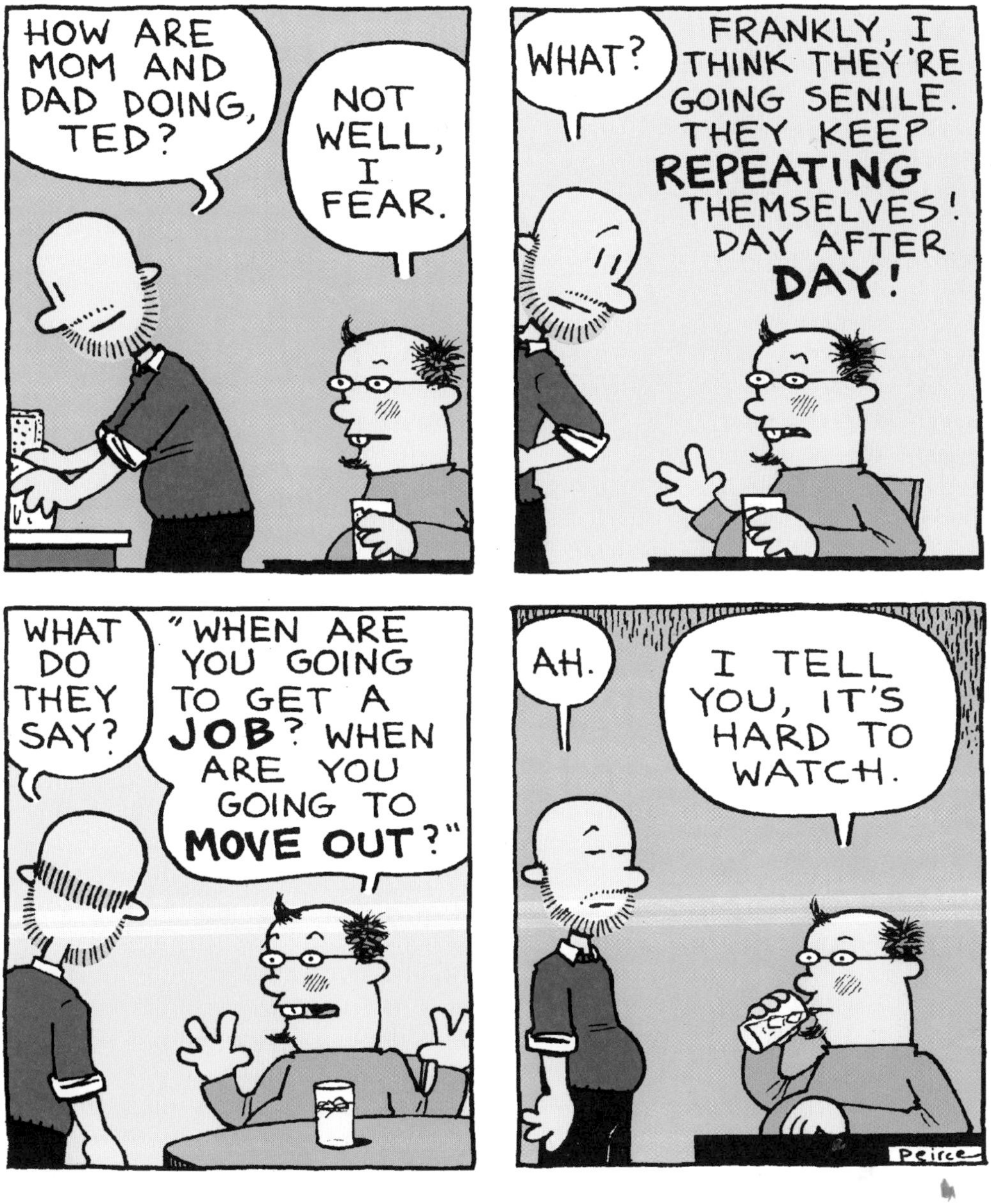
HOW ARE MOM AND DAD DOING, TED?
NOT WELL, I FEAR.
WHAT?
FRANKLY, I THINK THEY'RE GOING SENILE. THEY KEEP **REPEATING** THEMSELVES! DAY AFTER **DAY**!
WHAT DO THEY SAY?
"WHEN ARE YOU GOING TO GET A **JOB**? WHEN ARE YOU GOING TO **MOVE OUT**?"
AH.
I TELL YOU, IT'S HARD TO WATCH.
Peirce

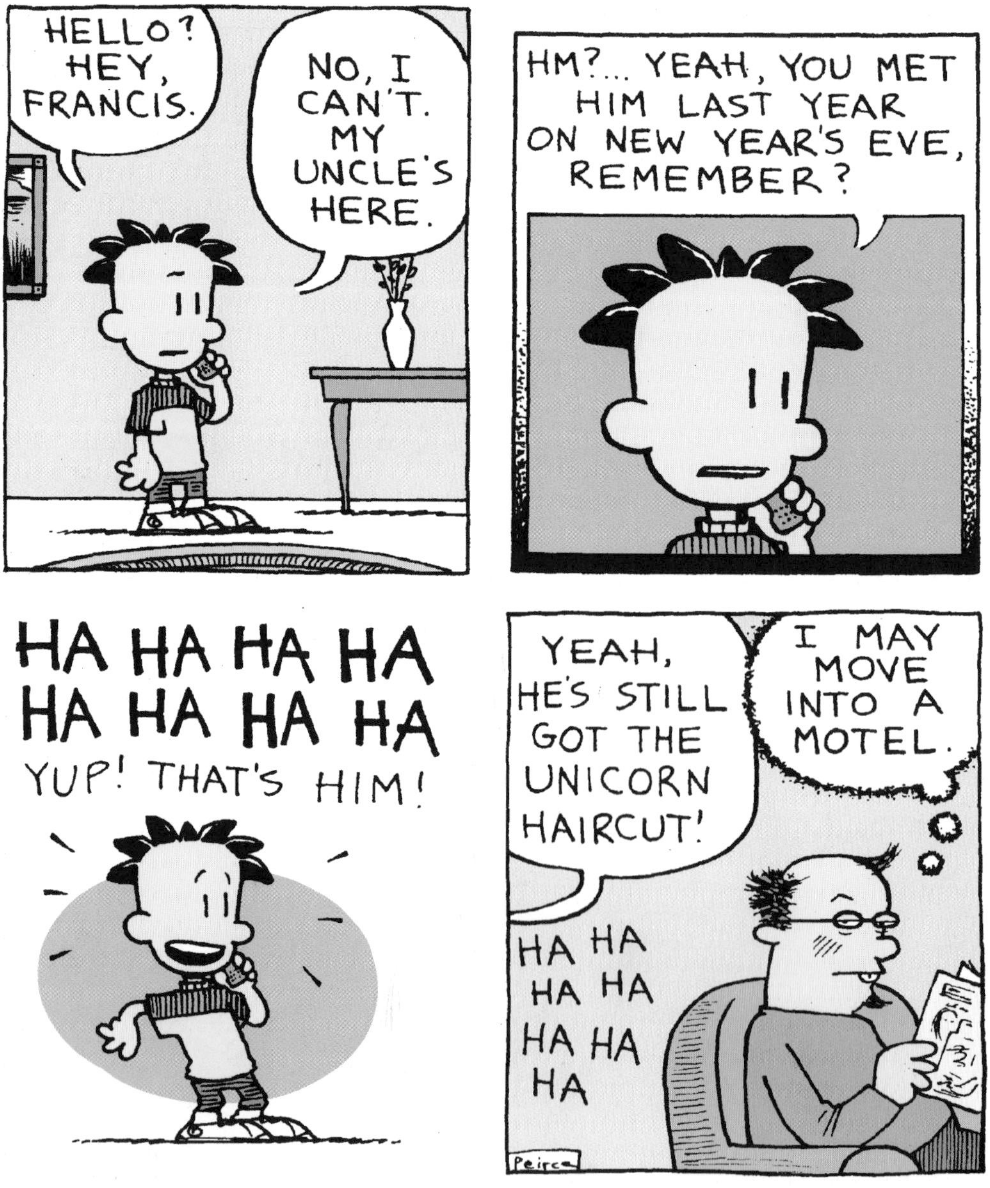

HELLO? HEY, FRANCIS.
NO, I CAN'T. MY UNCLE'S HERE.
HM?... YEAH, YOU MET HIM LAST YEAR ON NEW YEAR'S EVE, REMEMBER?
HA HA HA HA HA HA HA HA
YUP! THAT'S HIM!
YEAH, HE'S STILL GOT THE UNICORN HAIRCUT!
I MAY MOVE INTO A MOTEL.
HA HA HA HA HA HA HA
Peirce

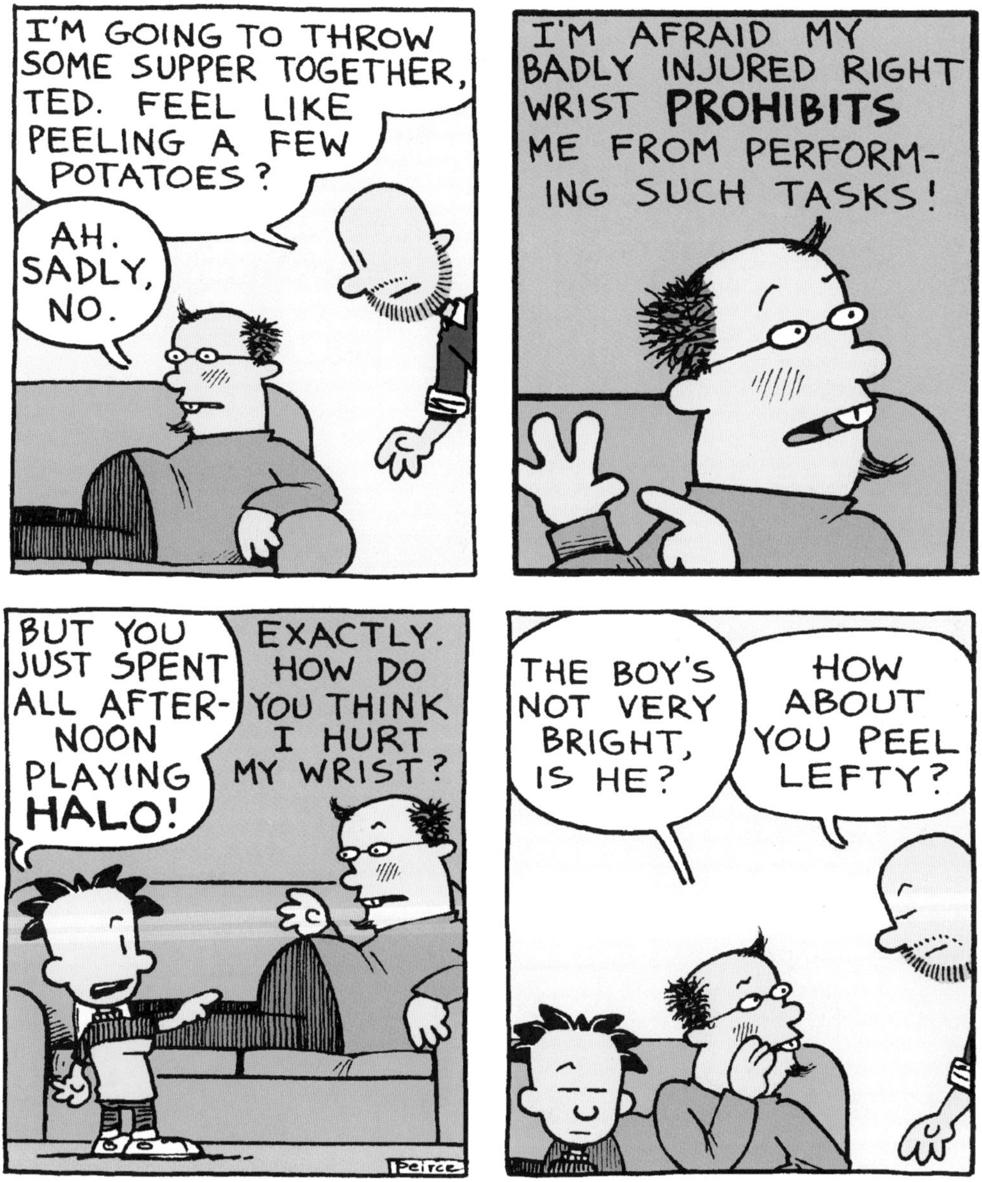
I'M GOING TO THROW SOME SUPPER TOGETHER, TED. FEEL LIKE PEELING A FEW POTATOES?
AH. SADLY, NO.
I'M AFRAID MY BADLY INJURED RIGHT WRIST **PROHIBITS** ME FROM PERFORMING SUCH TASKS!
BUT YOU JUST SPENT ALL AFTERNOON PLAYING **HALO!**
EXACTLY. HOW DO YOU THINK I HURT MY WRIST?
Peirce
THE BOY'S NOT VERY BRIGHT, IS HE?
HOW ABOUT YOU PEEL LEFTY?

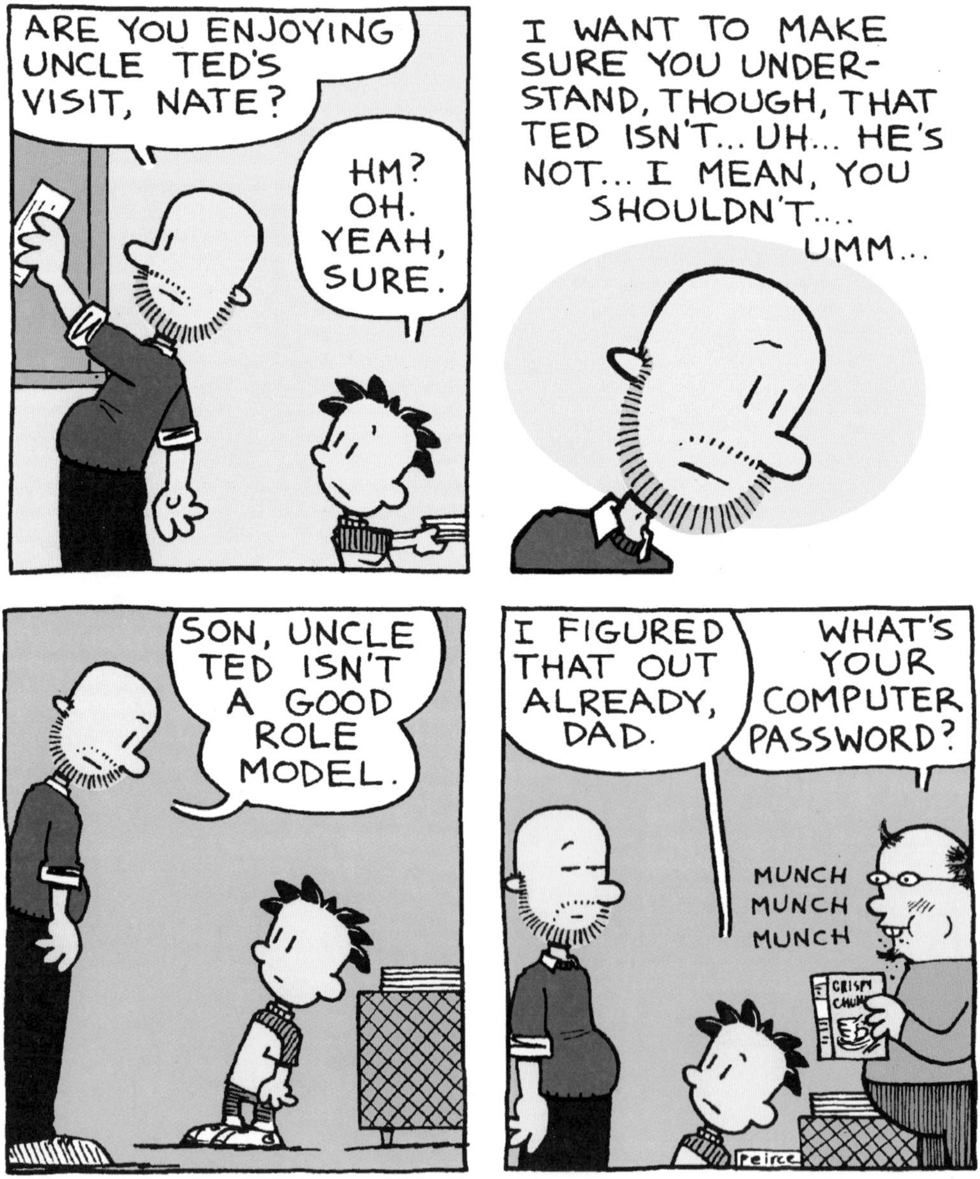
ARE YOU ENJOYING UNCLE TED'S VISIT, NATE?
HM? OH. YEAH, SURE.
I WANT TO MAKE SURE YOU UNDER-STAND, THOUGH, THAT TED ISN'T... UH... HE'S NOT... I MEAN, YOU SHOULDN'T.... UMM...
SON, UNCLE TED ISN'T A GOOD ROLE MODEL.
I FIGURED THAT OUT ALREADY, DAD.
WHAT'S YOUR COMPUTER PASSWORD?
MUNCH MUNCH MUNCH
CRISPY CHUN
Peirce

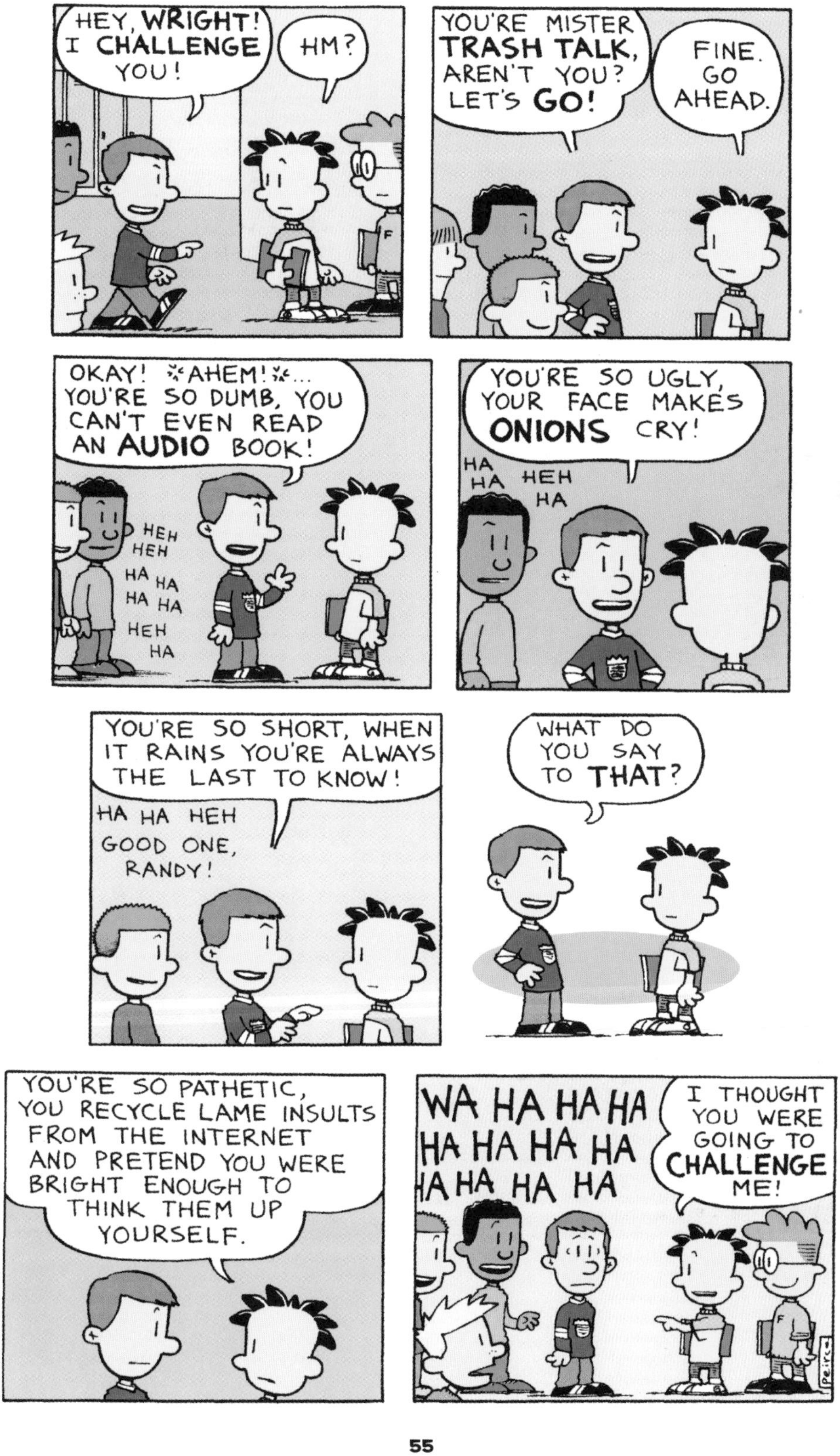
HEY, WRIGHT! I CHALLENGE YOU!
HM?
YOU'RE MISTER TRASH TALK, AREN'T YOU? LET'S GO!
FINE. GO AHEAD.
OKAY! *AHEM!*... YOU'RE SO DUMB, YOU CAN'T EVEN READ AN AUDIO BOOK!
HEH HEH HA HA HA HA HEH HA
YOU'RE SO UGLY, YOUR FACE MAKES ONIONS CRY!
HA HA HEH HA
YOU'RE SO SHORT, WHEN IT RAINS YOU'RE ALWAYS THE LAST TO KNOW!
HA HA HEH GOOD ONE, RANDY!
WHAT DO YOU SAY TO THAT?
YOU'RE SO PATHETIC, YOU RECYCLE LAME INSULTS FROM THE INTERNET AND PRETEND YOU WERE BRIGHT ENOUGH TO THINK THEM UP YOURSELF.
WA HA HA HA HA HA HA HA HA HA HA HA
I THOUGHT YOU WERE GOING TO CHALLENGE ME!
PEIRCE

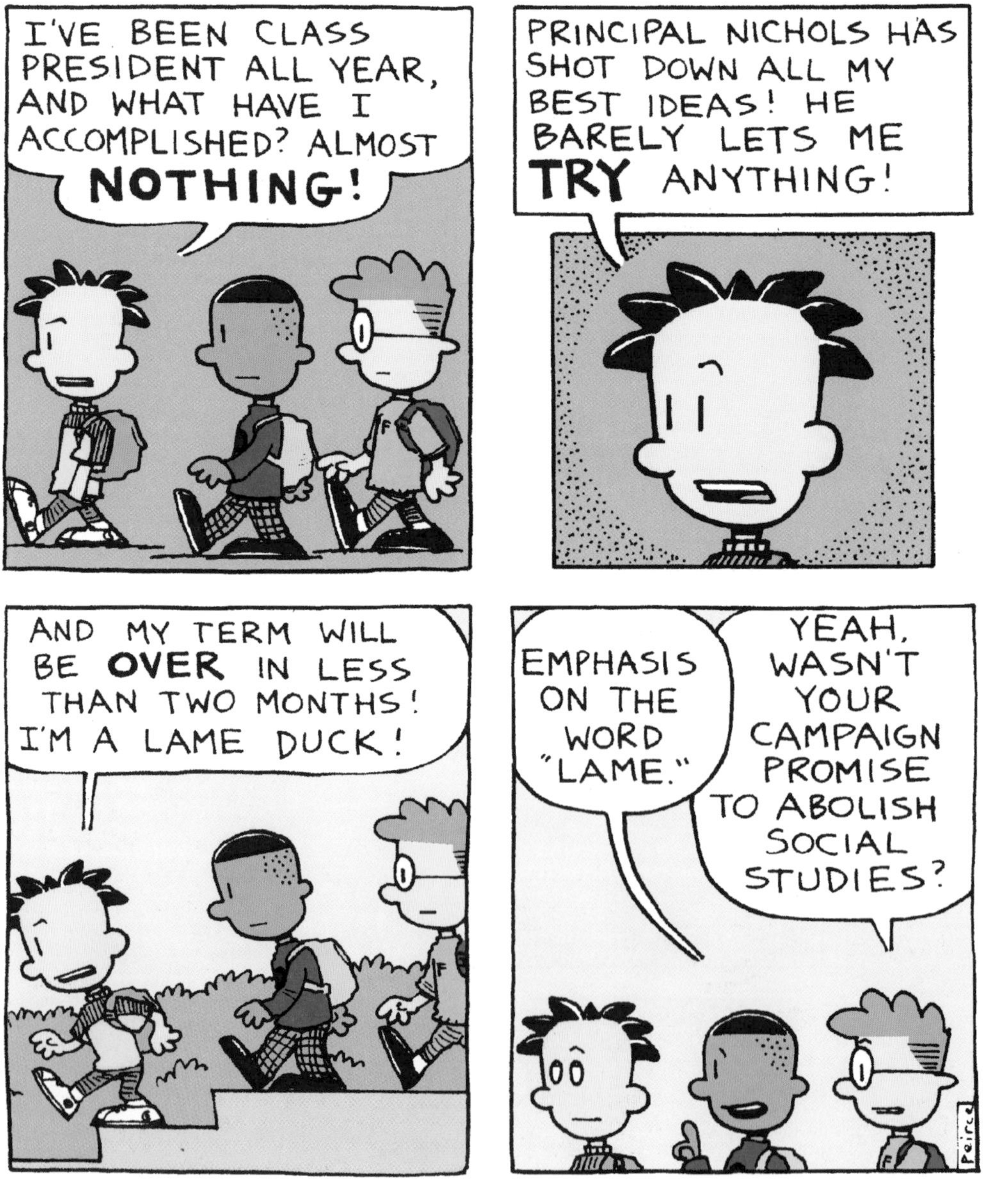
I'VE BEEN CLASS PRESIDENT ALL YEAR, AND WHAT HAVE I ACCOMPLISHED? ALMOST **NOTHING**!
PRINCIPAL NICHOLS HAS SHOT DOWN ALL MY BEST IDEAS! HE BARELY LETS ME **TRY** ANYTHING!
AND MY TERM WILL BE **OVER** IN LESS THAN TWO MONTHS! I'M A LAME DUCK!
YEAH, WASN'T YOUR CAMPAIGN PROMISE TO ABOLISH SOCIAL STUDIES?
EMPHASIS ON THE WORD "LAME."
Peirce

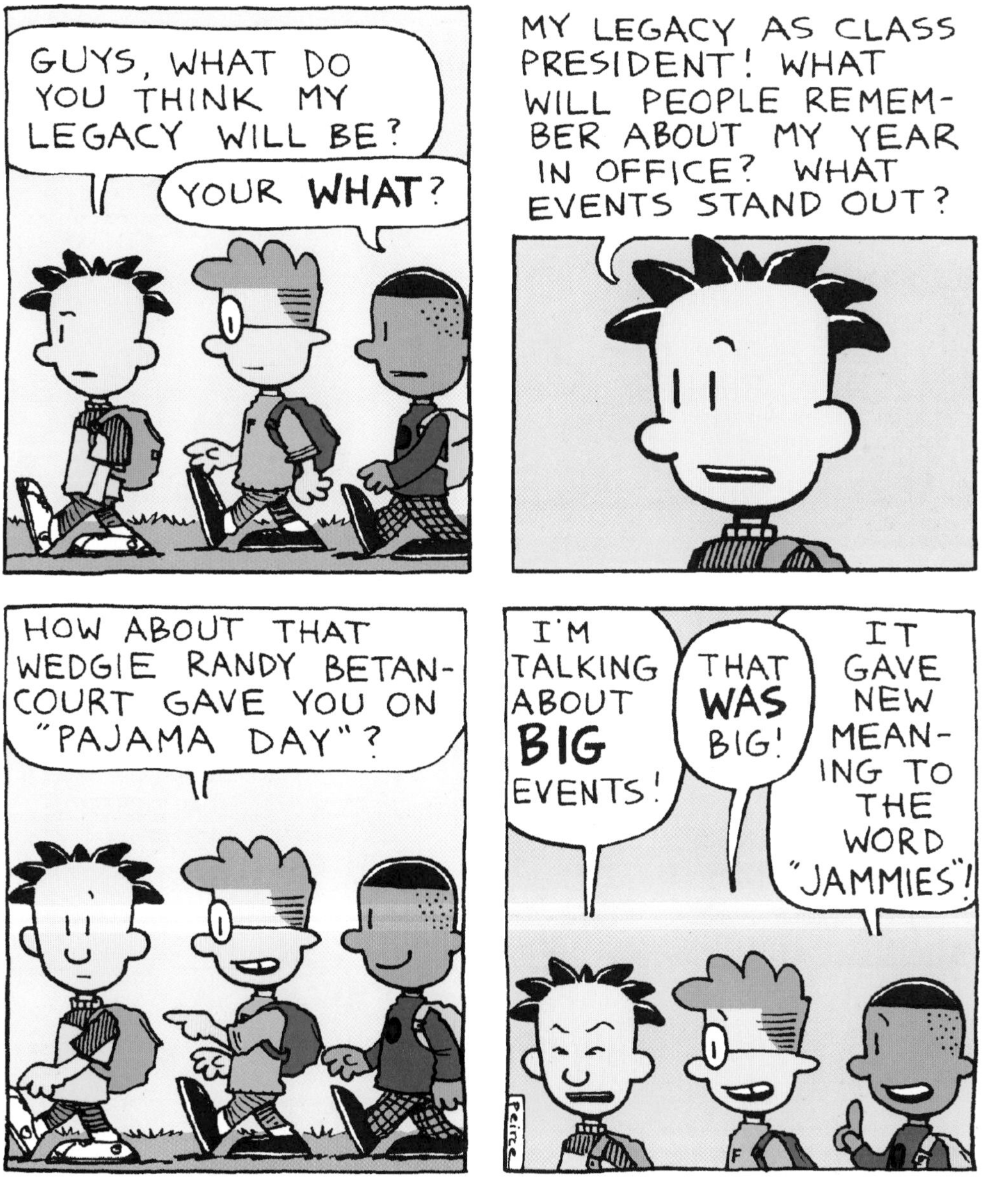
GUYS, WHAT DO YOU THINK MY LEGACY WILL BE?
YOUR **WHAT**?
MY LEGACY AS CLASS PRESIDENT! WHAT WILL PEOPLE REMEMBER ABOUT MY YEAR IN OFFICE? WHAT EVENTS STAND OUT?
HOW ABOUT THAT WEDGIE RANDY BETANCOURT GAVE YOU ON "PAJAMA DAY"?
I'M TALKING ABOUT **BIG** EVENTS!
THAT **WAS** BIG!
IT GAVE NEW MEANING TO THE WORD "JAMMIES"!
Peirce

PRINCIPAL NICHOLS! CAN I TALK TO YOU ABOUT SOMETHING?
IF YOU CAN BE BRIEF, NATE. I HAVE A MEETING.
YEAH, OKAY.
IT'S ABOUT MY LEGACY AS CLASS PRESIDENT. WHEN PEOPLE ANALYZE MY ADMINISTRATION IN FUTURE YEARS...
THE SECRET IS TO NEVER STOP WALKING.
SEEMS REASON-ABLE TO ME THAT SOME SORT OF COMMEMOR-ATIVE PLAQUE IS IN ORDER.
Peirce

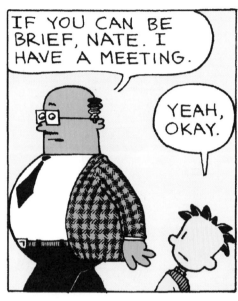

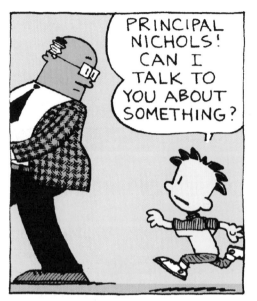

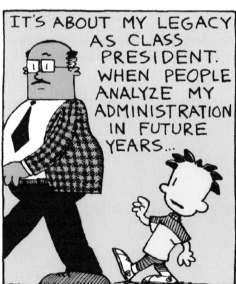

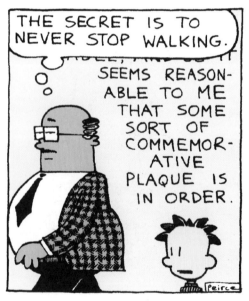

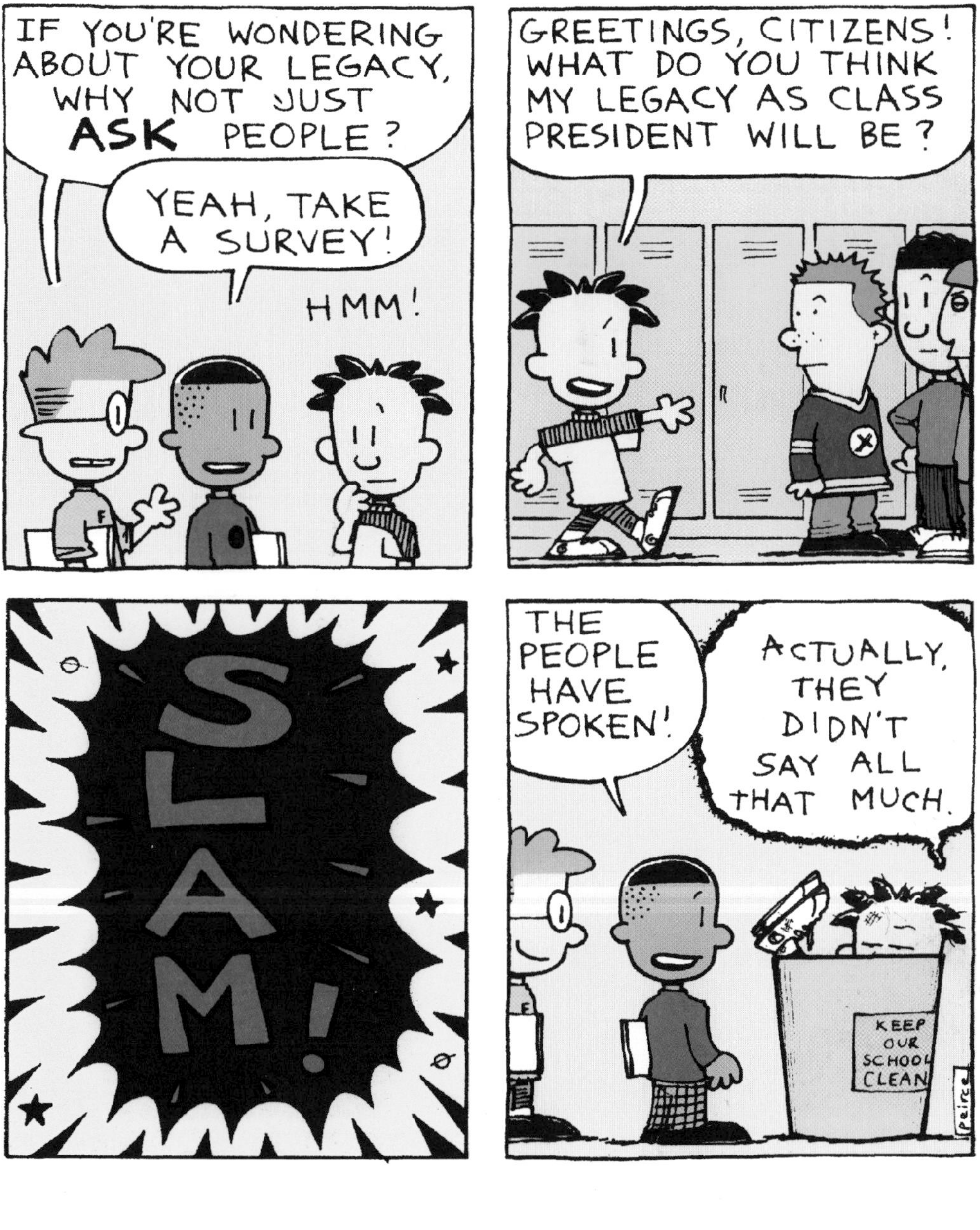
IF YOU'RE WONDERING ABOUT YOUR LEGACY, WHY NOT JUST **ASK** PEOPLE?
YEAH, TAKE A SURVEY!
HMM!
GREETINGS, CITIZENS! WHAT DO YOU THINK MY LEGACY AS CLASS PRESIDENT WILL BE?
SLAM!
THE PEOPLE HAVE SPOKEN!
ACTUALLY, THEY DIDN'T SAY ALL THAT MUCH.
KEEP OUR SCHOOL CLEAN
peirce

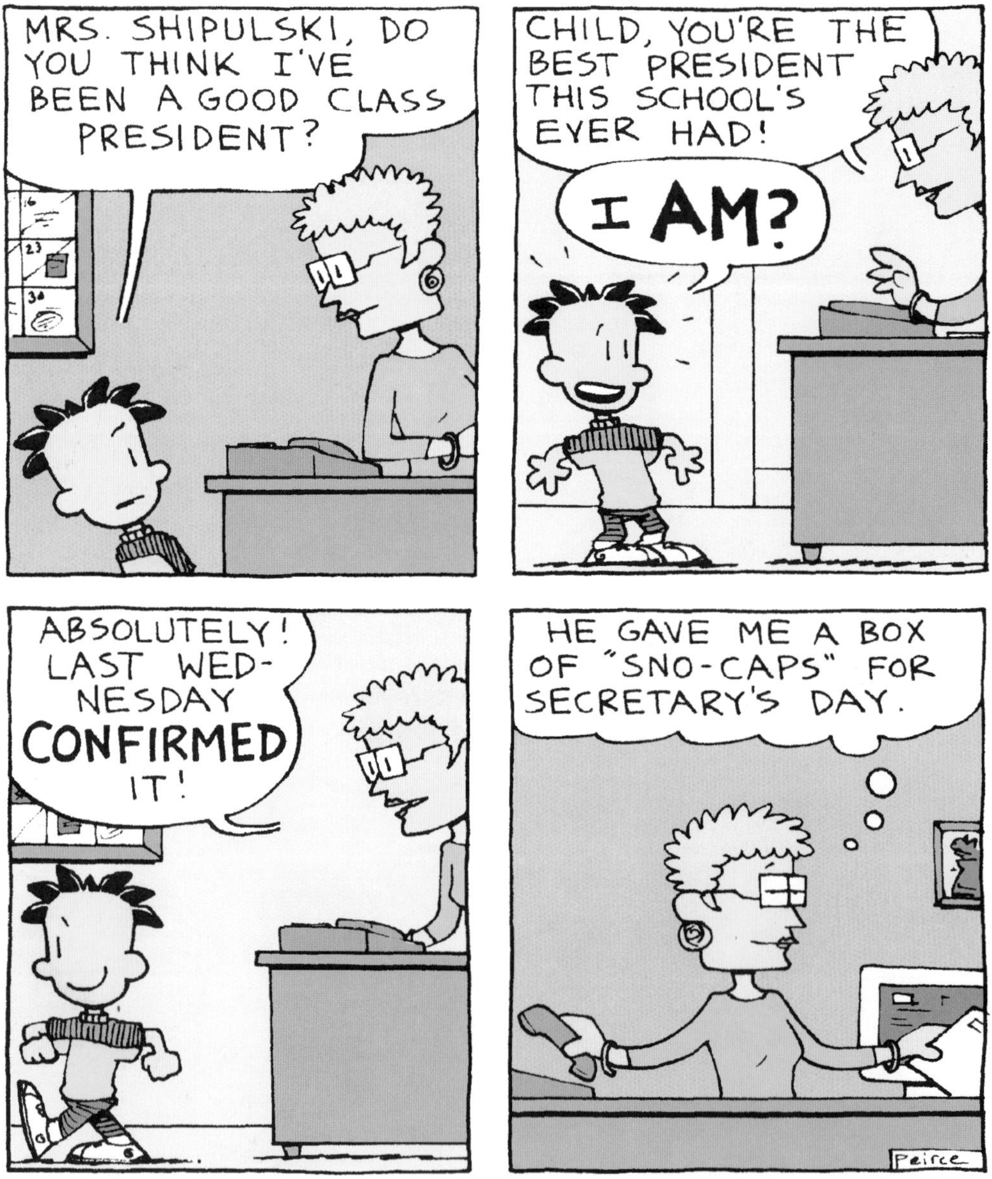
MRS. SHIPULSKI, DO YOU THINK I'VE BEEN A GOOD CLASS PRESIDENT?
CHILD, YOU'RE THE BEST PRESIDENT THIS SCHOOL'S EVER HAD!
I AM?
ABSOLUTELY! LAST WED-NESDAY CONFIRMED IT!
HE GAVE ME A BOX OF "SNO-CAPS" FOR SECRETARY'S DAY.
Peirce

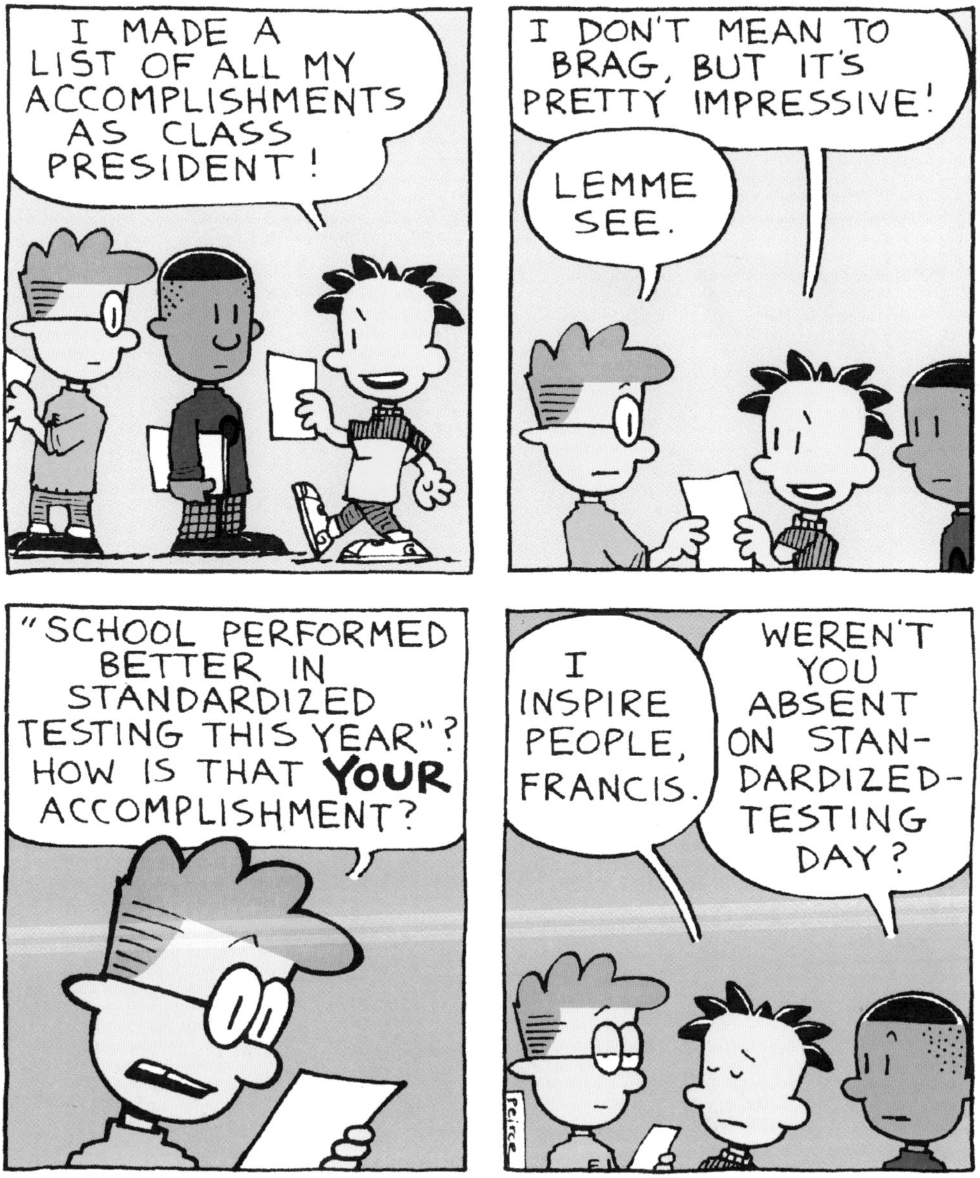
I MADE A LIST OF ALL MY ACCOMPLISHMENTS AS CLASS PRESIDENT!
I DON'T MEAN TO BRAG, BUT IT'S PRETTY IMPRESSIVE!
LEMME SEE.
"SCHOOL PERFORMED BETTER IN STANDARDIZED TESTING THIS YEAR"? HOW IS THAT **YOUR** ACCOMPLISHMENT?
WEREN'T YOU ABSENT ON STANDARDIZED-TESTING DAY?
I INSPIRE PEOPLE, FRANCIS.
Peirce

LET'S GO TEDDY COME ON BABY PITCH IT RIGHT IN THERE IN THERE RIGHT DOWN THE PIKE KID RIGHT DOWN BROADWAY **SWING** BATTER!

ATTA BOY ATTA BABY I'VE SEEN BETTER LOOKING SWINGS IN MY BACKYARD HE CAN'T HE CAN'T HE CAN'T HIT HE'S WAY BEHIND YOU KID C'MON NOW TEDDY PUT IT RIGHT PAST HIM HE'S NO BATTER NO BATTER **SWING** BATTER!

THAT'S ALL RIGHT TEDDY THAT'S ALL RIGHT KID YOU GOT THIS GUY JUST THROW STRIKES BABY JUST ROCK AND FIRE KID ROCK AND FIRE HE'S LOOKIN FOR A WALK HE CAN'T HIT HE'S NO BATTER NO BATTER NO BATTER C'MON BABY HIT THE MITT JUST HIT THE MITT FOCUS ON THE MITT KID ATTA BOY LET'S GET THIS KID NOW LET'S PUT HIM IN THE BOOKS SIT HIM DOWN TEDDY SIT HIM DOWN HE'S AFRAID OF YOU TEDDY HE CAN'T HIT HE'S NO BATTER NO BATTER NO BATTER NO BATTER **SWING** BATTER!

FEEL THE BREEZE FEEL THE BREEZE HE'S BEHIND YOU TEDDY HE'S WAY BEHIND YOU JUST ONE MORE BABY JUST ONE MORE PUT IT RIGHT PAST HIM TEDDY PUT IT RIGHT PAST HIM YOU AND THE GLOVE KID JUST YOU AND THE GLOVE HE'S NO BATTER NO BATTER NO BATTER HE CAN'T HIT

WILL YOU **SHUT UP!**

JUST FOR THIS BATTER, OR FOR THE WHOLE INNING?

FOREVER!

HE'S HAVING A ROUGH DAY.

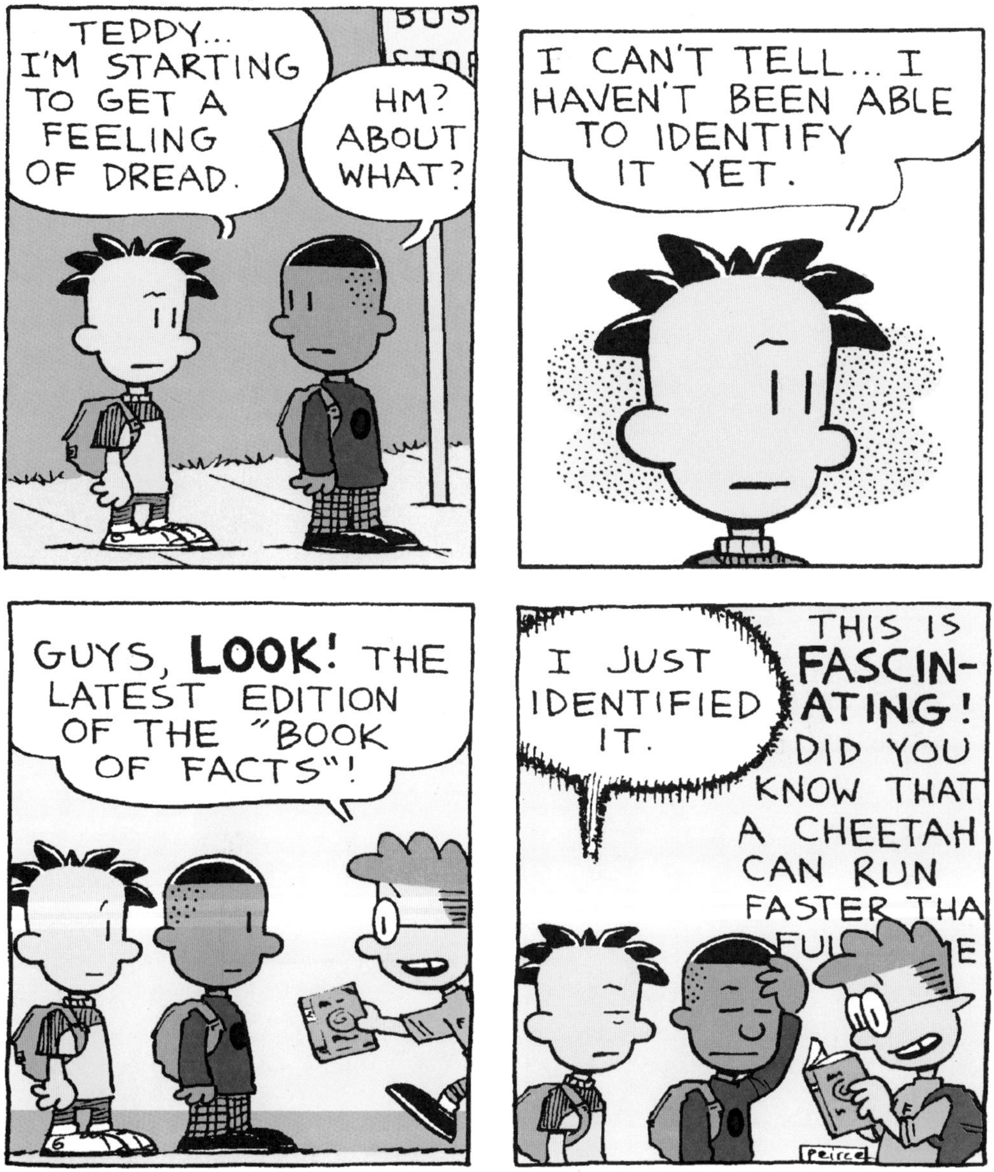
BUS STOP
TEDDY... I'M STARTING TO GET A FEELING OF DREAD.
HM? ABOUT WHAT?
I CAN'T TELL... I HAVEN'T BEEN ABLE TO IDENTIFY IT YET.
GUYS, **LOOK!** THE LATEST EDITION OF THE "BOOK OF FACTS"!
I JUST IDENTIFIED IT.
THIS IS **FASCINATING!** DID YOU KNOW THAT A CHEETAH CAN RUN FASTER THA
peirce

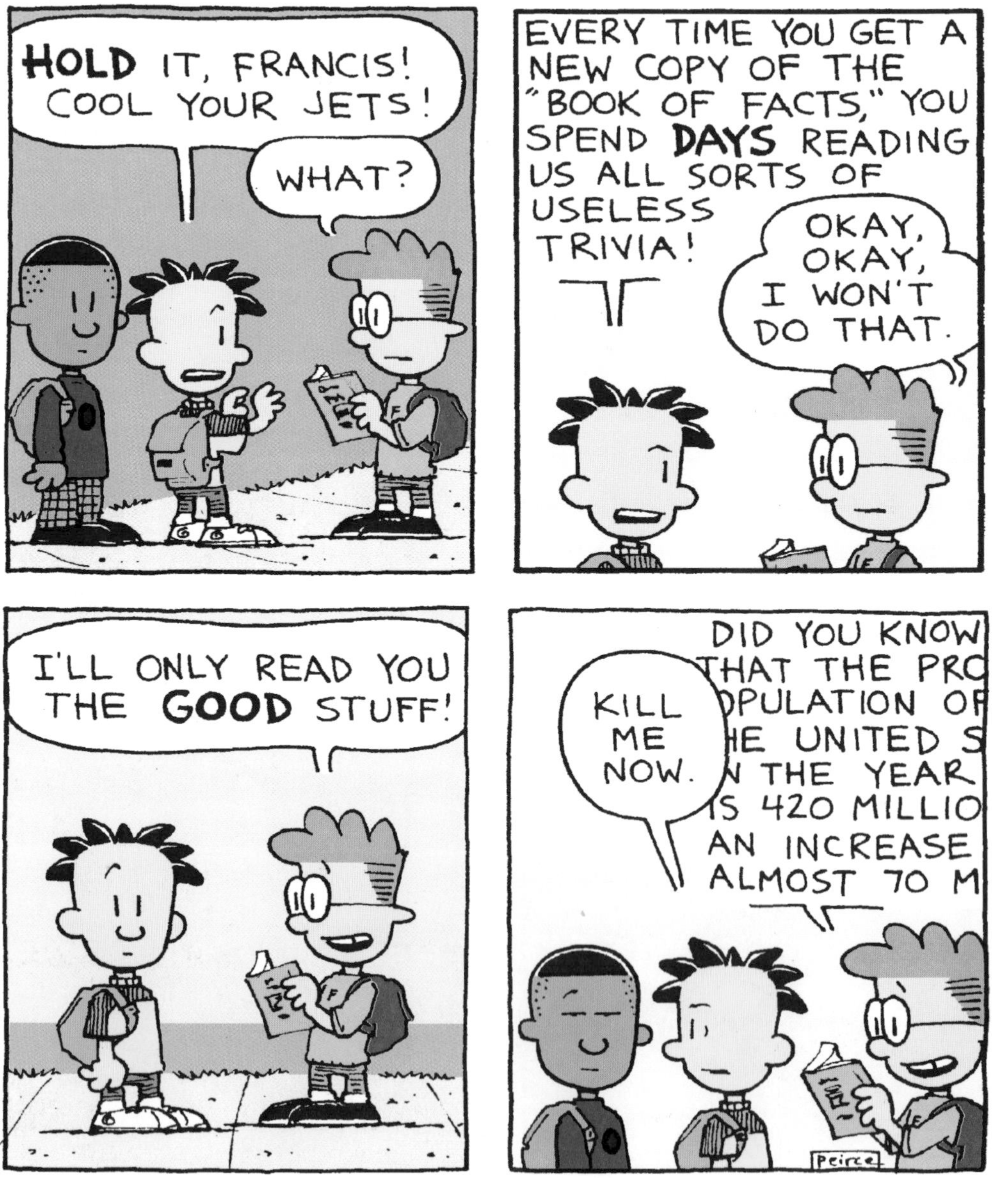
HOLD IT, FRANCIS! COOL YOUR JETS!
WHAT?
EVERY TIME YOU GET A NEW COPY OF THE "BOOK OF FACTS," YOU SPEND DAYS READING US ALL SORTS OF USELESS TRIVIA!
OKAY, OKAY, I WON'T DO THAT.
I'LL ONLY READ YOU THE GOOD STUFF!
DID YOU KNOW THAT THE PRO OPULATION OF HE UNITED S N THE YEAR IS 420 MILLIO AN INCREASE ALMOST 70 M
KILL ME NOW.
Peirce

[redacted]

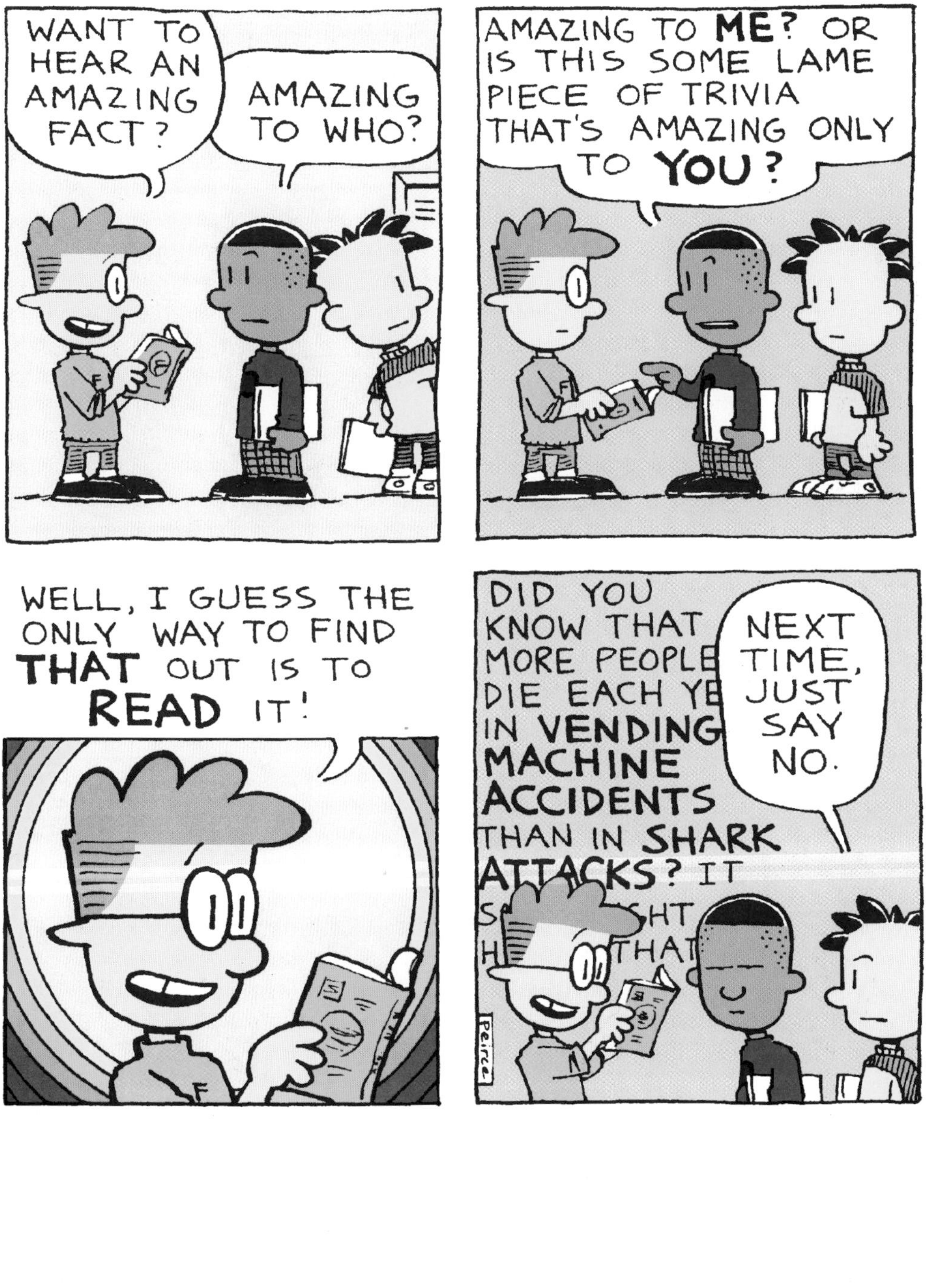
WANT TO HEAR AN AMAZING FACT?
AMAZING TO WHO?
AMAZING TO **ME**? OR IS THIS SOME LAME PIECE OF TRIVIA THAT'S AMAZING ONLY TO **YOU**?
WELL, I GUESS THE ONLY WAY TO FIND **THAT** OUT IS TO **READ** IT!
DID YOU KNOW THAT MORE PEOPLE DIE EACH YE IN **VENDING MACHINE ACCIDENTS** THAN IN **SHARK ATTACKS**? IT
NEXT TIME, JUST SAY NO.
Peirce

DO YOU KNOW WHEN THE NEXT TOTAL SOLAR ECLIPSE IN THE U.S. WILL OCCUR?

AUGUST 21ST, 2017! DO YOU KNOW WHO WON THE NOBEL PRIZE FOR PHYSICS IN 1949?

HIDEKI YUKAWA! DO YOU KNOW WHAT COUNTRY RANKS FIFTH IN RENEWABLE WATER RESOURCES PER CAPITA?

PAPUA NEW AND DO WHICH COMPL PATIEN VISITIN EMERG ROOMS

THE "JUST IGNORE HIM" STRATEGY ISN'T WORKING.

LET'S EXPLORE THE WEDGIE OPTION.

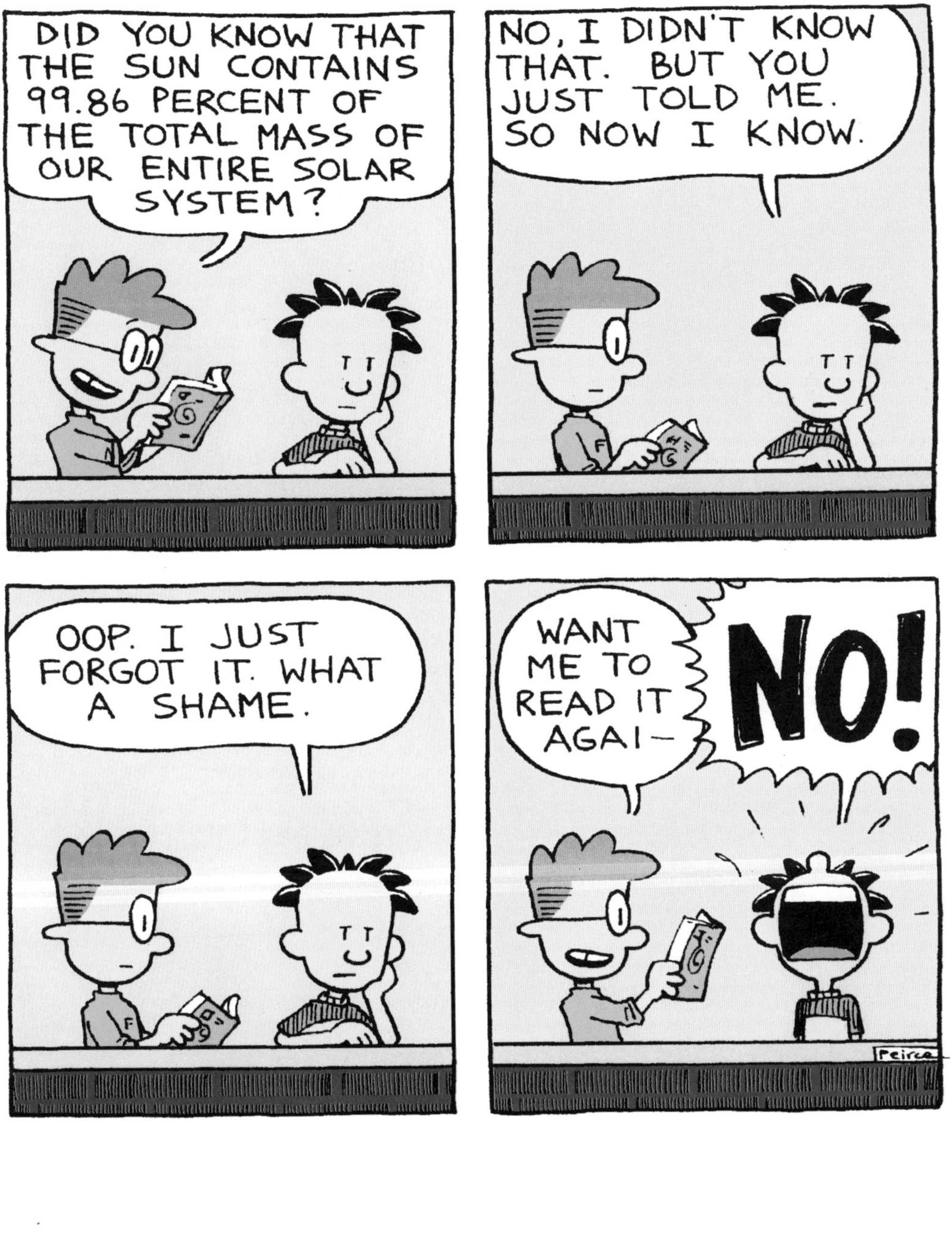
DID YOU KNOW THAT THE SUN CONTAINS 99.86 PERCENT OF THE TOTAL MASS OF OUR ENTIRE SOLAR SYSTEM?
NO, I DIDN'T KNOW THAT. BUT YOU JUST TOLD ME. SO NOW I KNOW.
OOP. I JUST FORGOT IT. WHAT A SHAME.
WANT ME TO READ IT AGAI–
NO!
Peirce

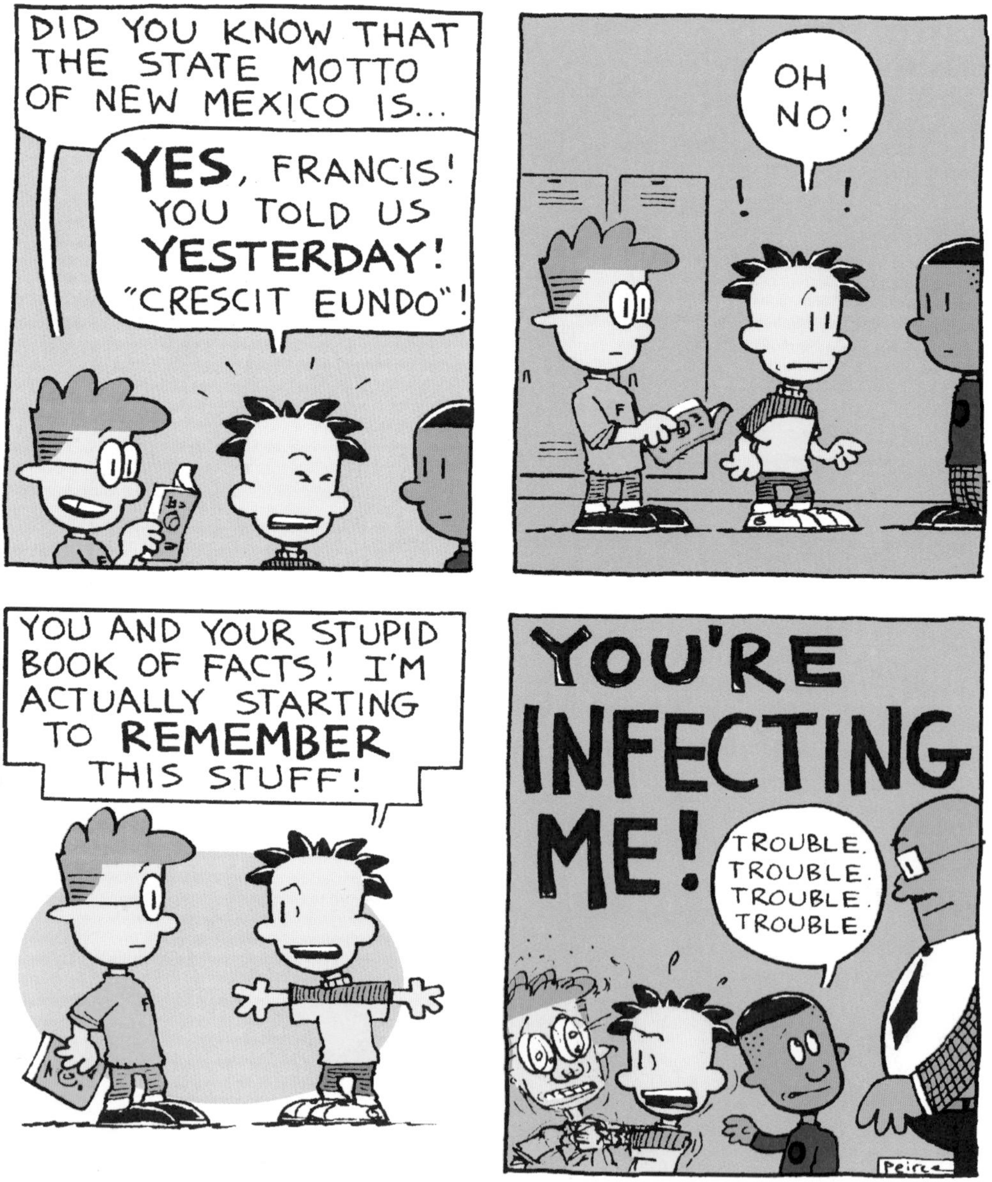
DID YOU KNOW THAT THE STATE MOTTO OF NEW MEXICO IS...
YES, FRANCIS! YOU TOLD US YESTERDAY! "CRESCIT EUNDO"!
OH NO!
YOU AND YOUR STUPID BOOK OF FACTS! I'M ACTUALLY STARTING TO REMEMBER THIS STUFF!
YOU'RE INFECTING ME!
TROUBLE. TROUBLE. TROUBLE. TROUBLE.
Peirce

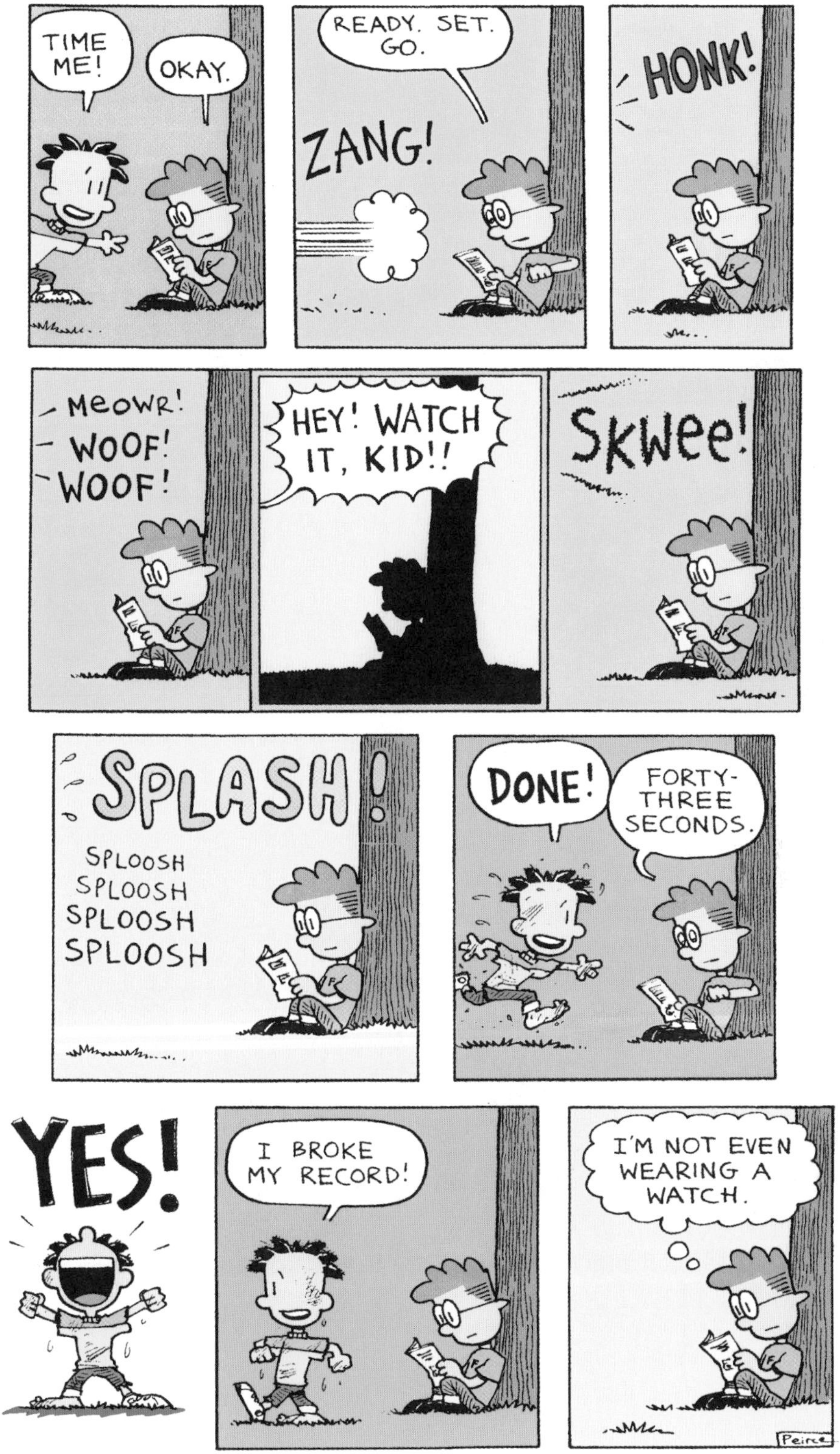
TIME ME!
OKAY.
READY. SET. GO.
ZANG!
HONK!
MEOWR!
WOOF! WOOF!
HEY! WATCH IT, KID!!
SKWEE!
SPLASH!
SPLOOSH
SPLOOSH
SPLOOSH
SPLOOSH
DONE!
FORTY-THREE SECONDS.
YES!
I BROKE MY RECORD!
I'M NOT EVEN WEARING A WATCH.
Peirce

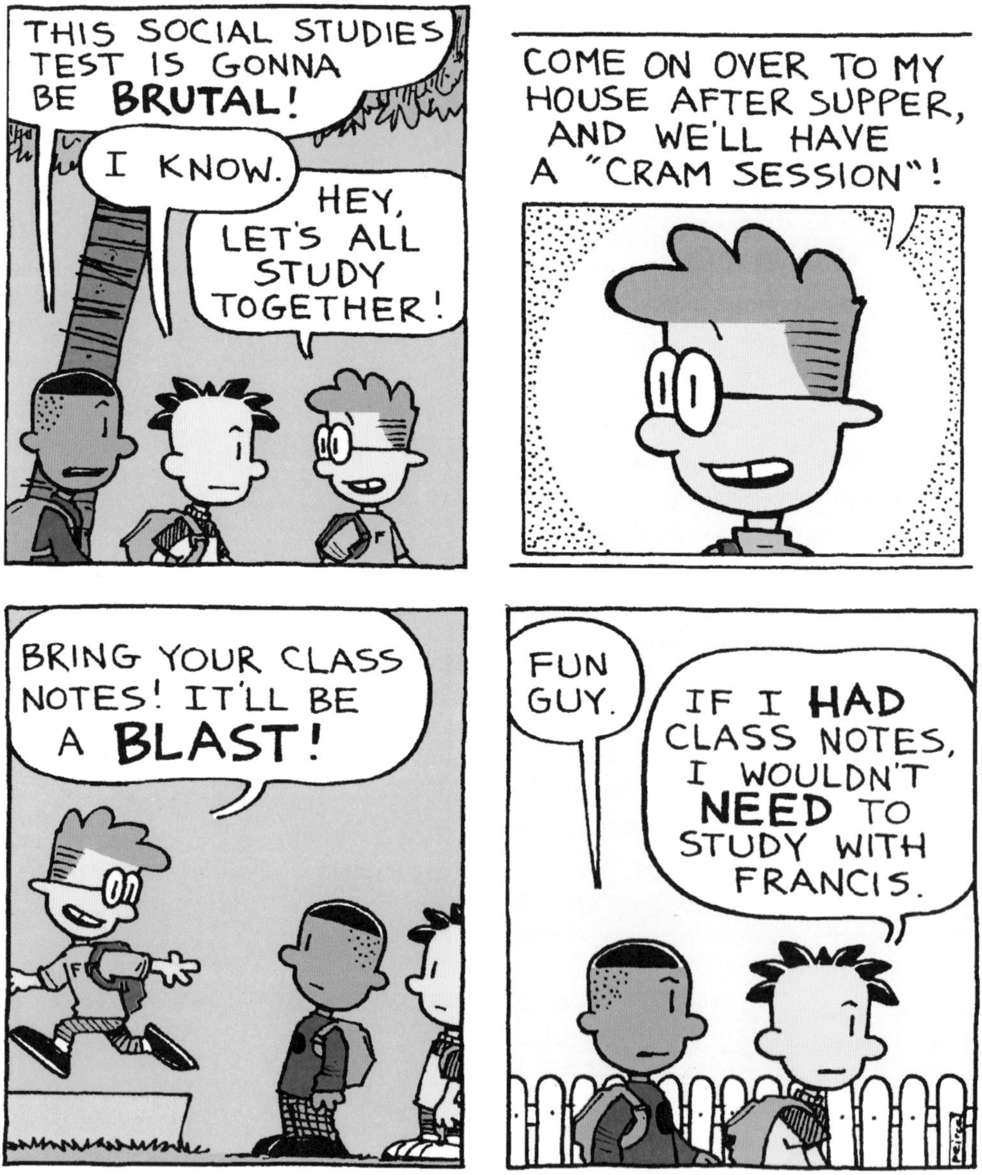
THIS SOCIAL STUDIES TEST IS GONNA BE BRUTAL!
I KNOW.
HEY, LET'S ALL STUDY TOGETHER!
COME ON OVER TO MY HOUSE AFTER SUPPER, AND WE'LL HAVE A "CRAM SESSION"!
BRING YOUR CLASS NOTES! IT'LL BE A BLAST!
FUN GUY.
IF I HAD CLASS NOTES, I WOULDN'T NEED TO STUDY WITH FRANCIS.
PEIRCE

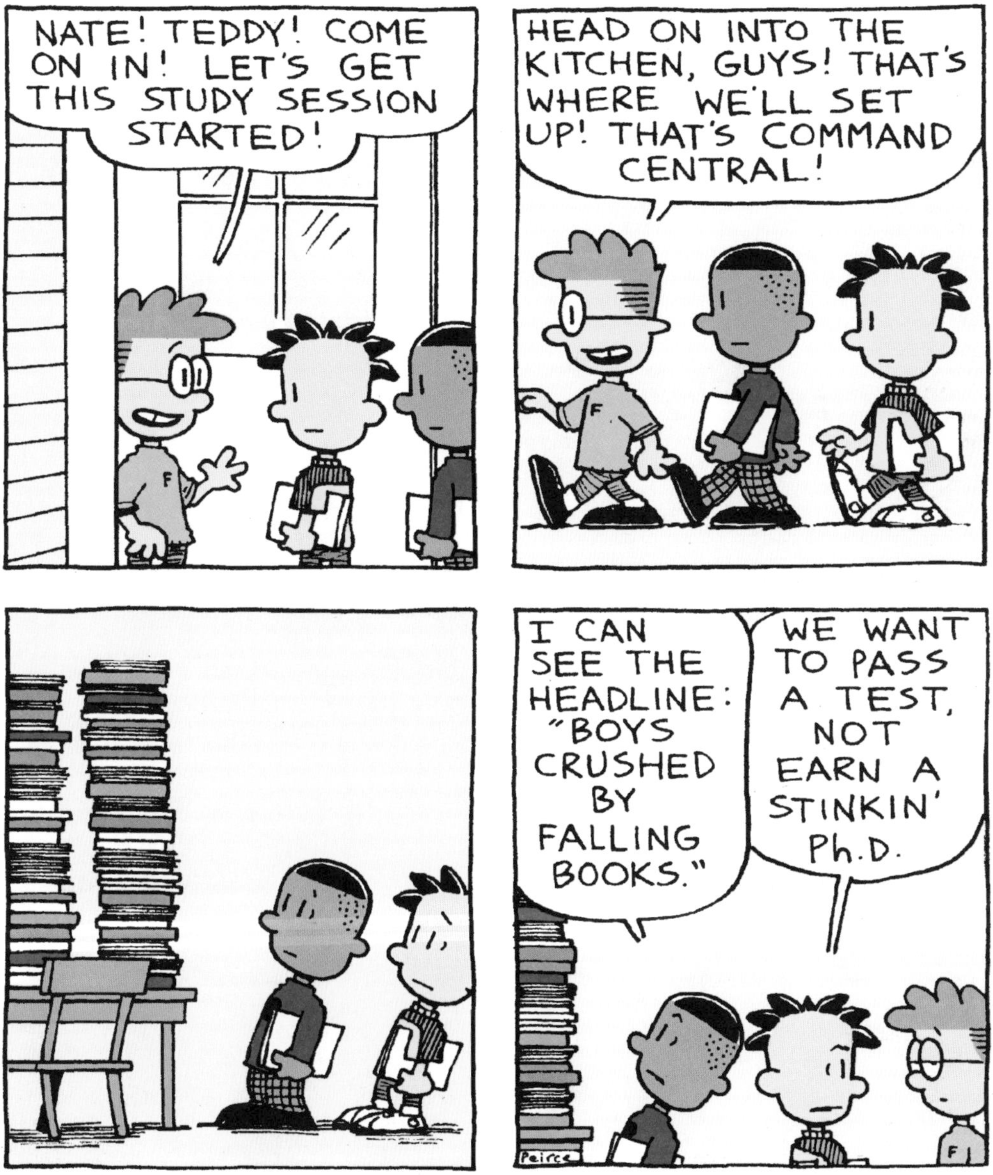
NATE! TEDDY! COME ON IN! LET'S GET THIS STUDY SESSION STARTED!
HEAD ON INTO THE KITCHEN, GUYS! THAT'S WHERE WE'LL SET UP! THAT'S COMMAND CENTRAL!
I CAN SEE THE HEADLINE: "BOYS CRUSHED BY FALLING BOOKS."
WE WANT TO PASS A TEST, NOT EARN A STINKIN' Ph.D.
Peirce

OKAY, GUYS, WE'VE GOT A LOT TO COVER HERE, SO LET'S GET STARTED.

I'VE CREATED A TIMELINE DETAILING ALL THE EVENTS THAT ARE GOING TO BE COVERED ON THE TEST! HERE ARE YOUR COPIES!

LOOK AT THEM CARE-FULLY AND TELL ME IF YOU HAVE ANY QUESTIONS.

YES?

WHEN YOU SAID WE WERE GOING TO STUDY IN THE KITCHEN, I ASSUMED THERE'D BE SNACKS.

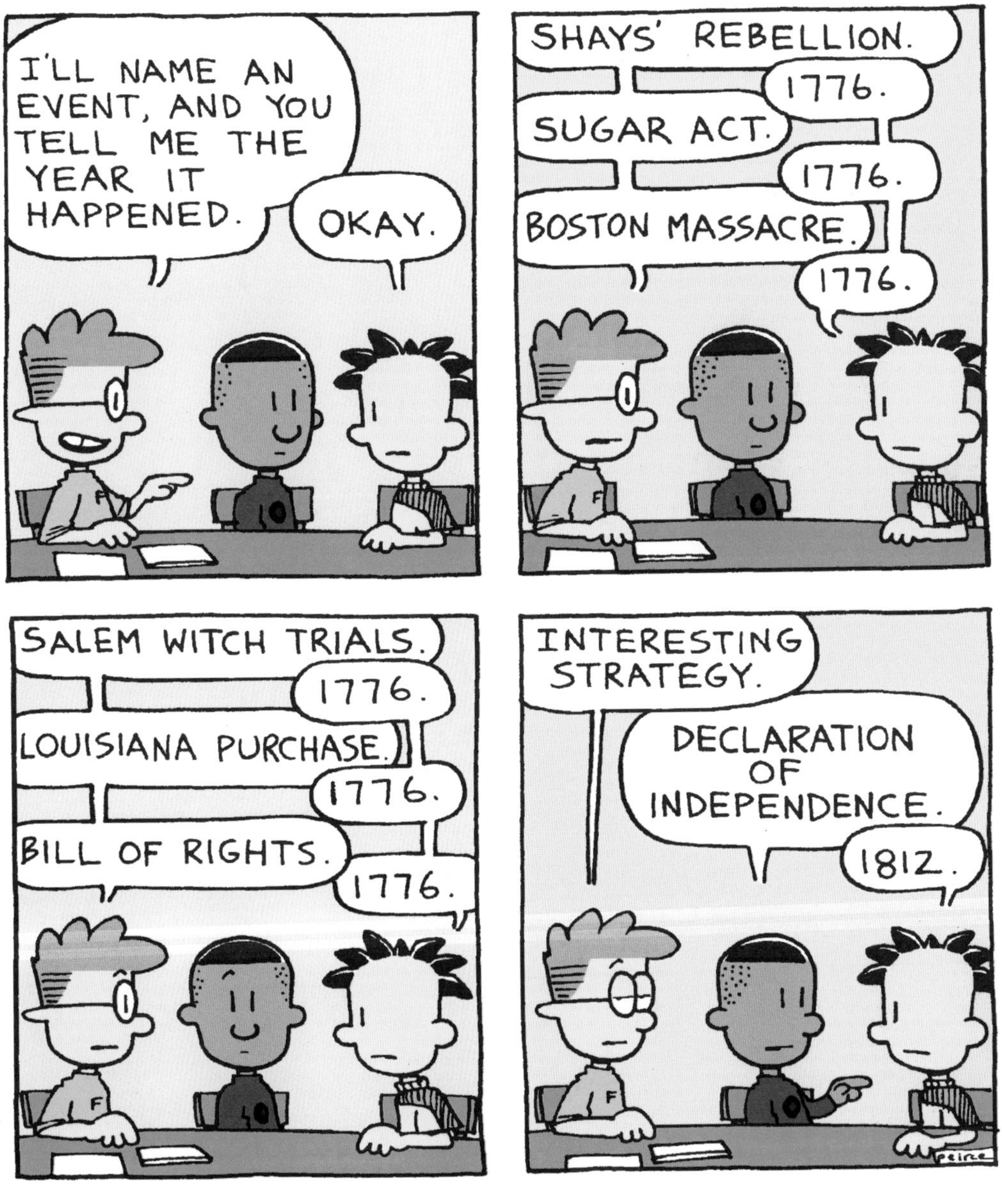
I'LL NAME AN EVENT, AND YOU TELL ME THE YEAR IT HAPPENED.
OKAY.
SHAYS' REBELLION.
1776.
SUGAR ACT.
1776.
BOSTON MASSACRE.
1776.
SALEM WITCH TRIALS.
1776.
LOUISIANA PURCHASE.
1776.
BILL OF RIGHTS.
1776.
INTERESTING STRATEGY.
DECLARATION OF INDEPENDENCE.
1812.
peirce

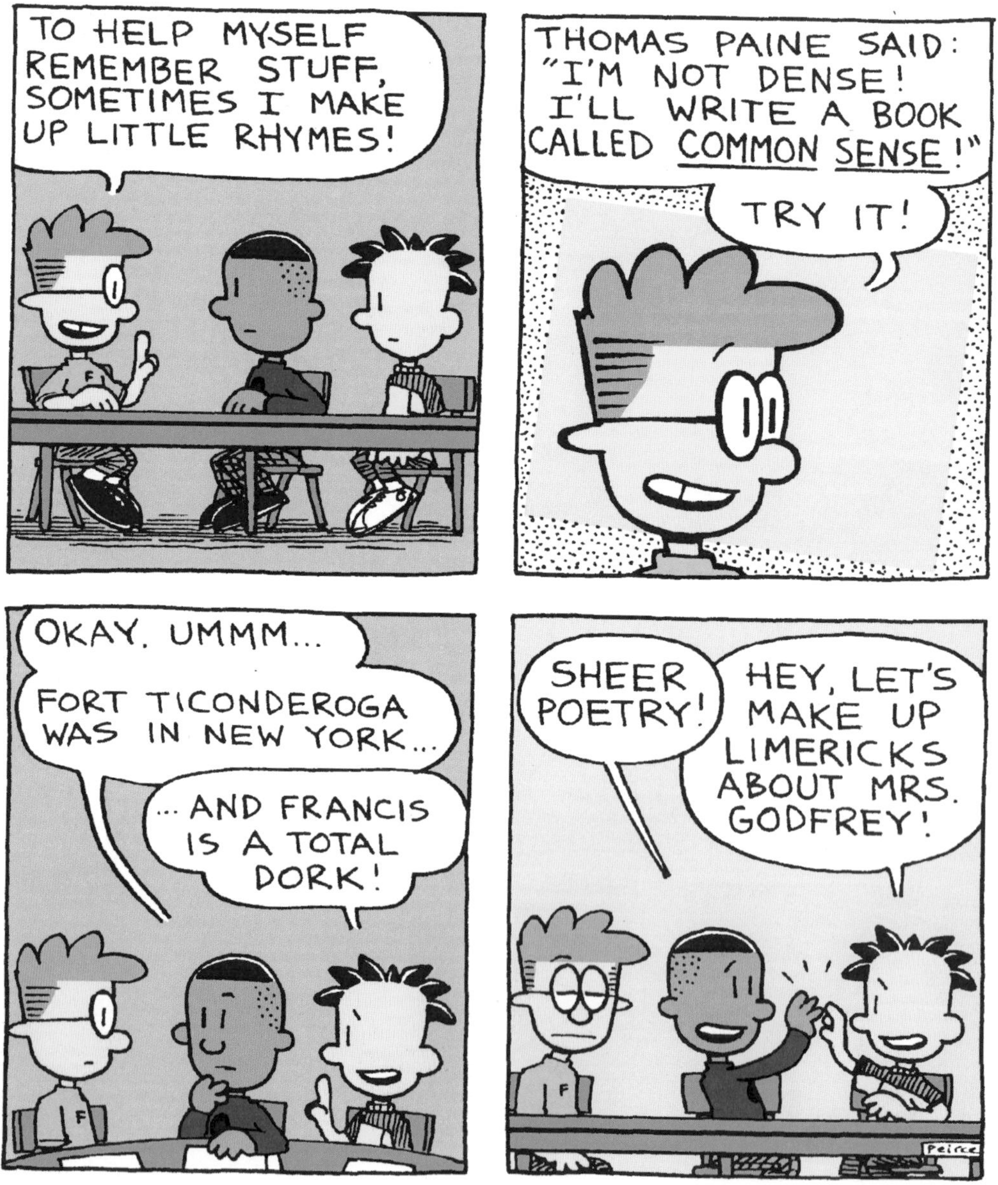
TO HELP MYSELF REMEMBER STUFF, SOMETIMES I MAKE UP LITTLE RHYMES!
THOMAS PAINE SAID: "I'M NOT DENSE! I'LL WRITE A BOOK CALLED COMMON SENSE!"
TRY IT!
OKAY. UMMM...
FORT TICONDEROGA WAS IN NEW YORK...
...AND FRANCIS IS A TOTAL DORK!
SHEER POETRY!
HEY, LET'S MAKE UP LIMERICKS ABOUT MRS. GODFREY!
Peirce

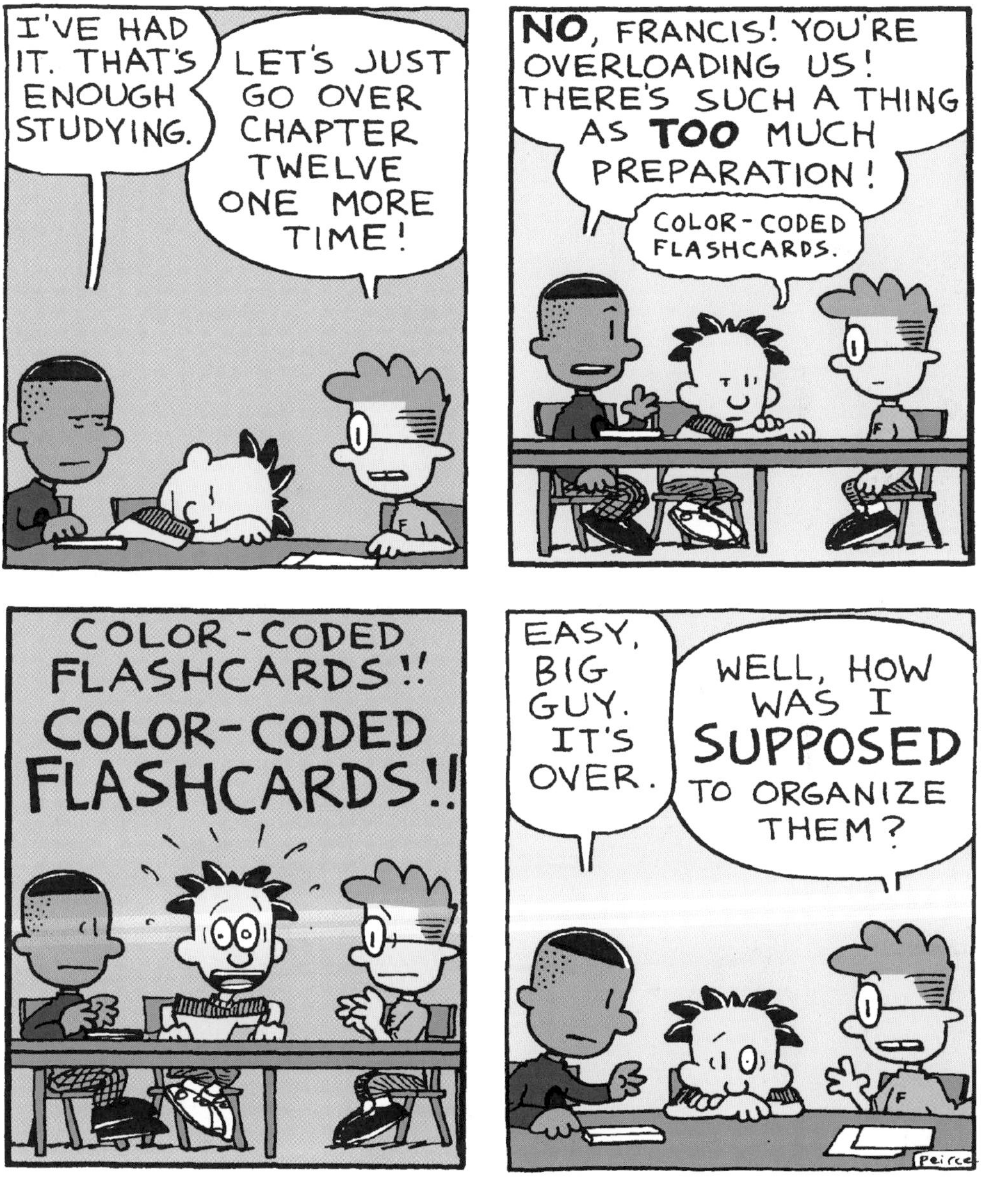
I'VE HAD IT. THAT'S ENOUGH STUDYING.
LET'S JUST GO OVER CHAPTER TWELVE ONE MORE TIME!
NO, FRANCIS! YOU'RE OVERLOADING US! THERE'S SUCH A THING AS TOO MUCH PREPARATION!
COLOR-CODED FLASHCARDS.
COLOR-CODED FLASHCARDS!!
COLOR-CODED FLASHCARDS!!
EASY, BIG GUY. IT'S OVER.
WELL, HOW WAS I SUPPOSED TO ORGANIZE THEM?
Peirce

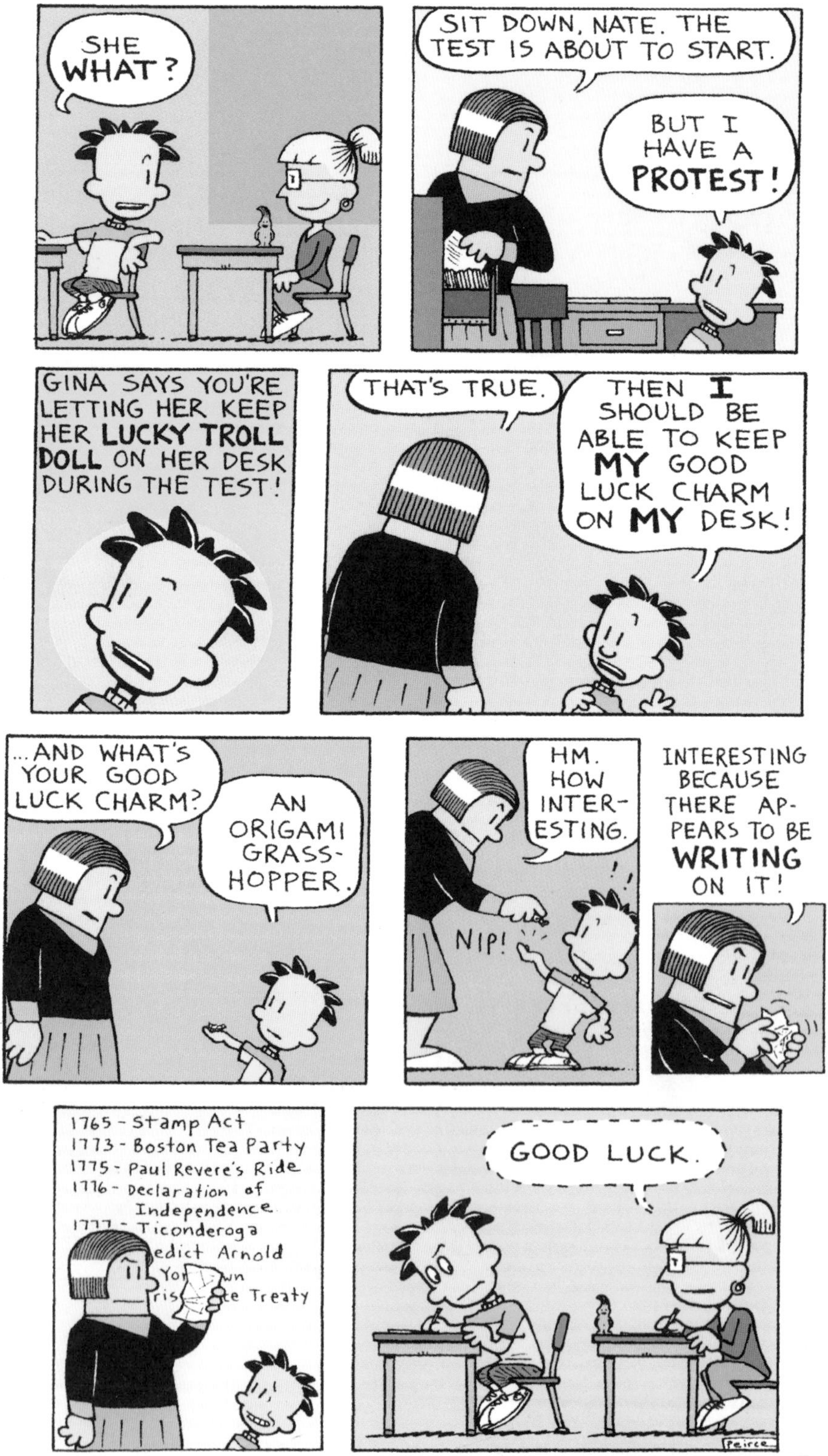
SHE WHAT?
SIT DOWN, NATE. THE TEST IS ABOUT TO START.
BUT I HAVE A PROTEST!
GINA SAYS YOU'RE LETTING HER KEEP HER LUCKY TROLL DOLL ON HER DESK DURING THE TEST!
THAT'S TRUE.
THEN I SHOULD BE ABLE TO KEEP MY GOOD LUCK CHARM ON MY DESK!
...AND WHAT'S YOUR GOOD LUCK CHARM?
AN ORIGAMI GRASS-HOPPER.
HM. HOW INTER-ESTING.
NIP!
INTERESTING BECAUSE THERE AP-PEARS TO BE WRITING ON IT!
1765 - Stamp Act
1773 - Boston Tea Party
1775 - Paul Revere's Ride
1776 - Declaration of Independence
1777 - Ticonderoga
GOOD LUCK.
Peirce

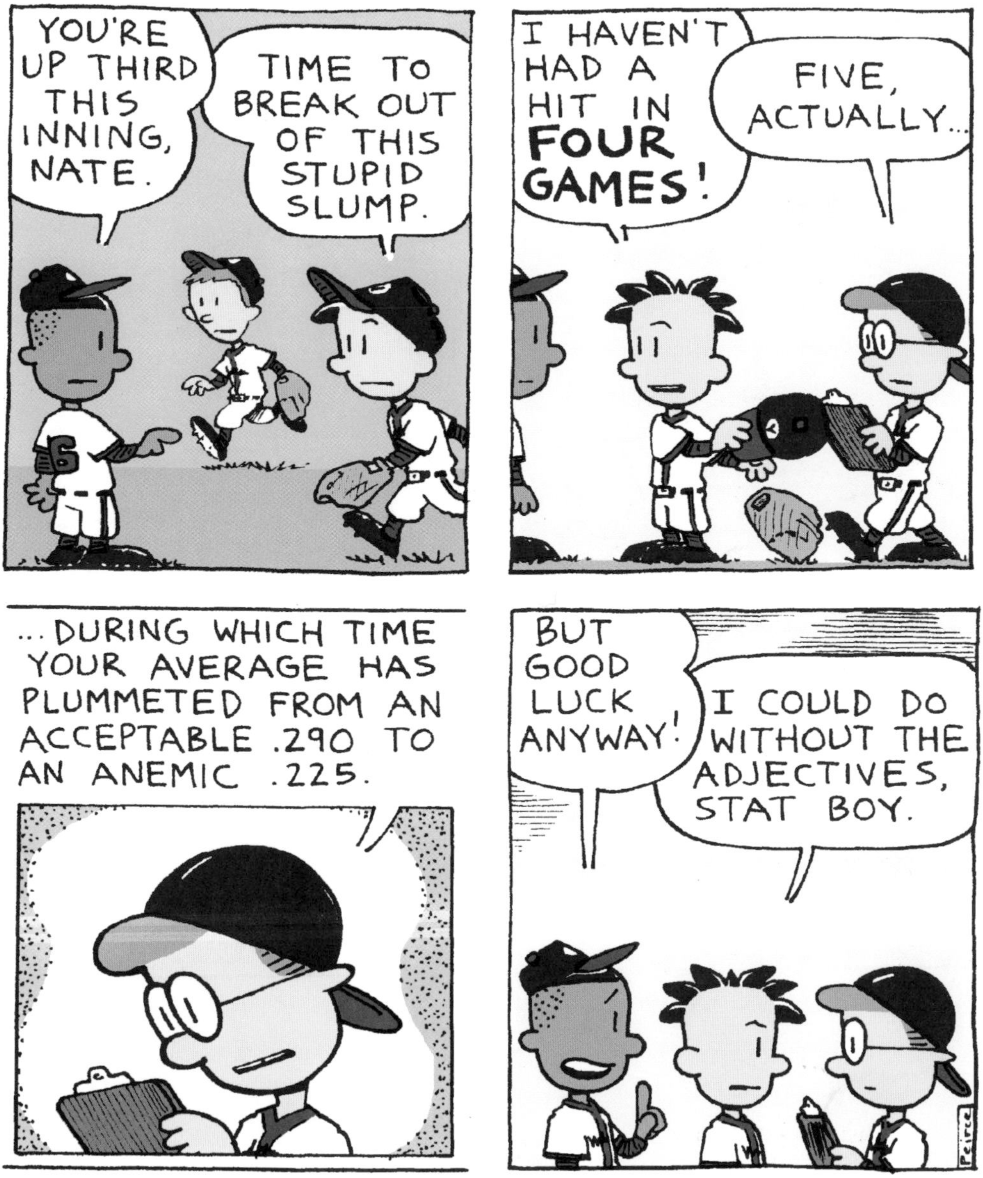
YOU'RE UP THIRD THIS INNING, NATE.
TIME TO BREAK OUT OF THIS STUPID SLUMP.
I HAVEN'T HAD A HIT IN **FOUR GAMES**!
FIVE, ACTUALLY...
...DURING WHICH TIME YOUR AVERAGE HAS PLUMMETED FROM AN ACCEPTABLE .290 TO AN ANEMIC .225.
BUT GOOD LUCK ANYWAY!
I COULD DO WITHOUT THE ADJECTIVES, STAT BOY.
Peirce

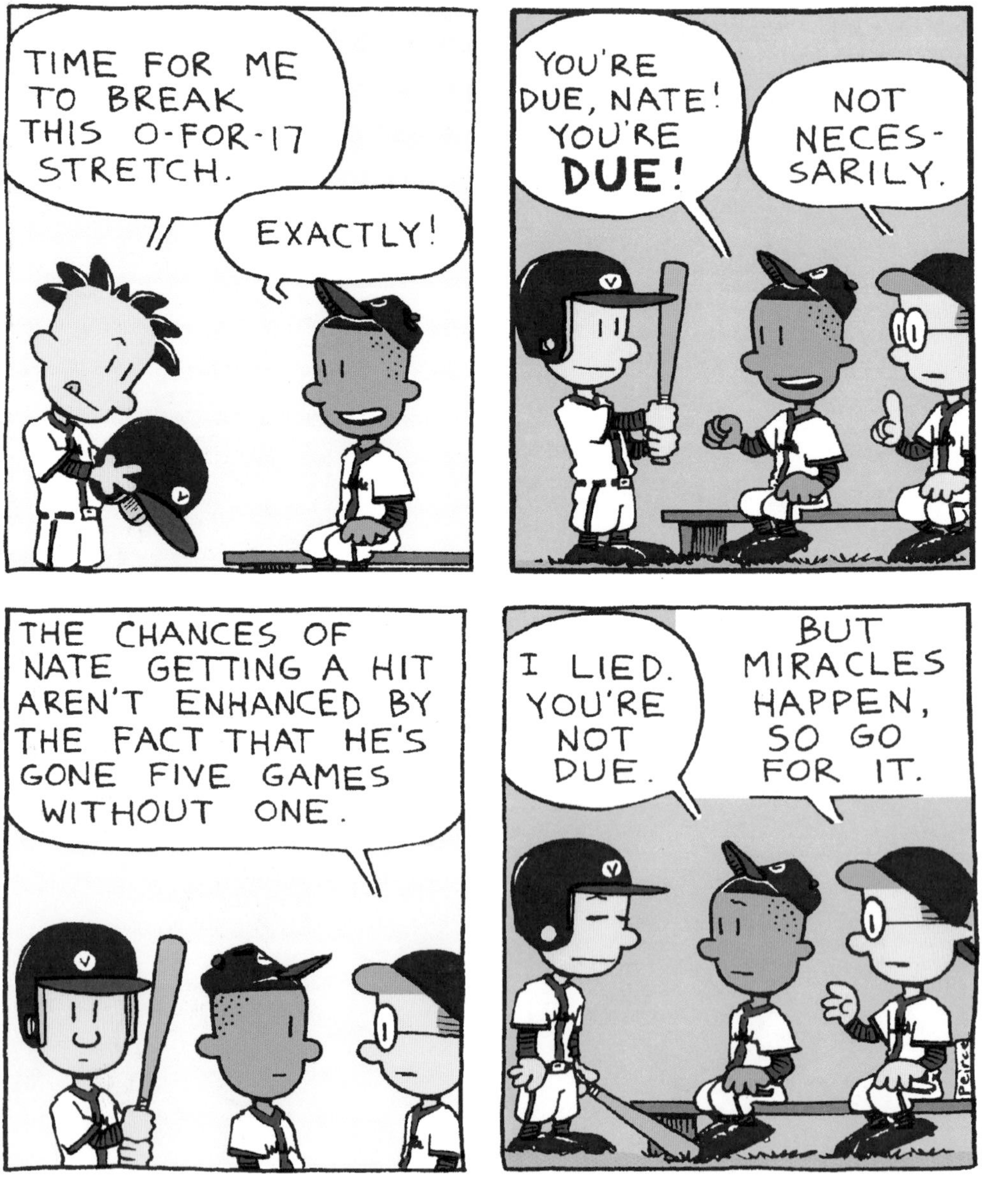
TIME FOR ME TO BREAK THIS 0-FOR-17 STRETCH.
EXACTLY!
YOU'RE DUE, NATE! YOU'RE **DUE**!
NOT NECES-SARILY.
THE CHANCES OF NATE GETTING A HIT AREN'T ENHANCED BY THE FACT THAT HE'S GONE FIVE GAMES WITHOUT ONE.
I LIED. YOU'RE NOT DUE.
BUT MIRACLES HAPPEN, SO GO FOR IT.
Peirce

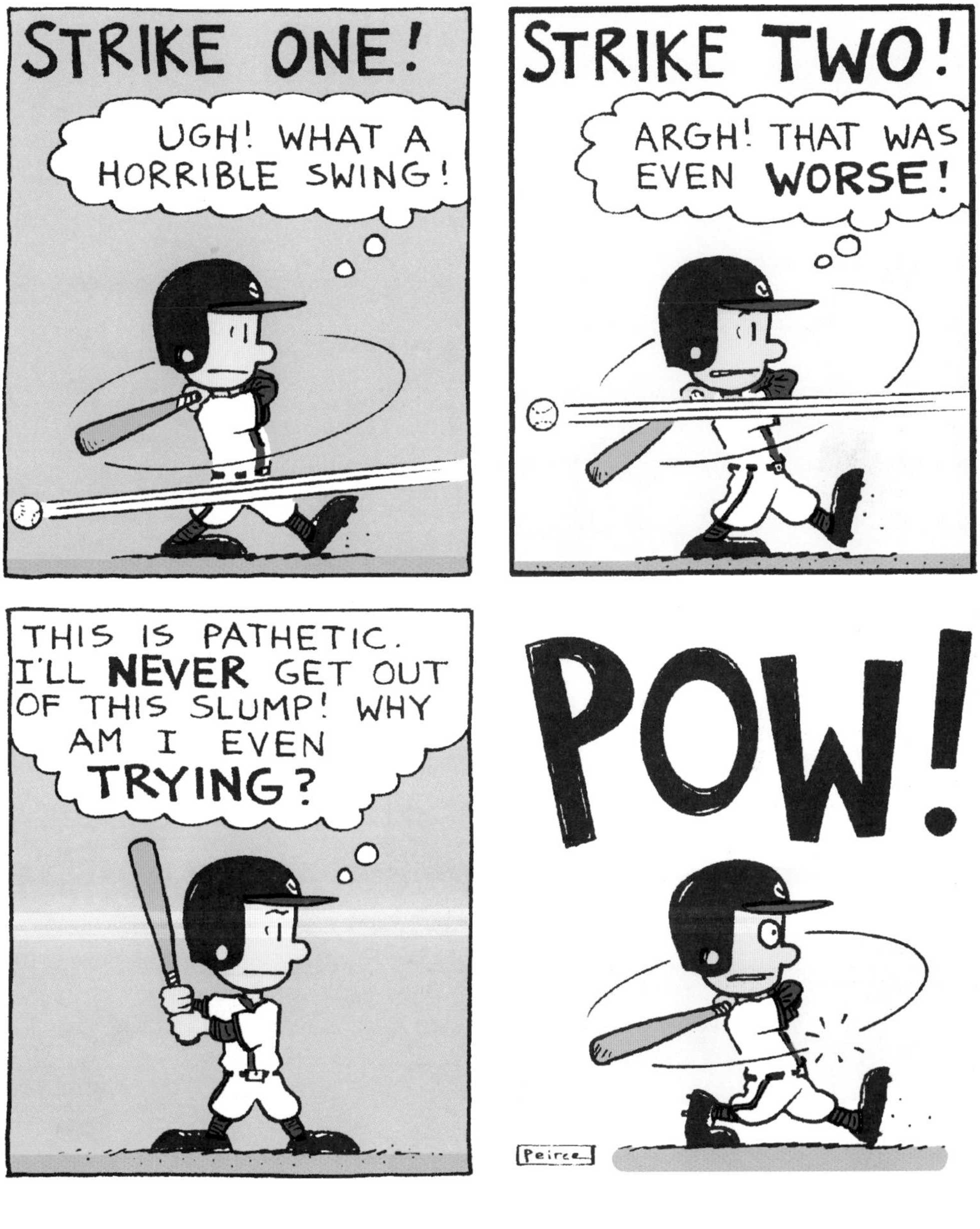
STRIKE ONE!
UGH! WHAT A HORRIBLE SWING!
STRIKE TWO!
ARGH! THAT WAS EVEN WORSE!
THIS IS PATHETIC. I'LL NEVER GET OUT OF THIS SLUMP! WHY AM I EVEN TRYING?
POW!
Peirce

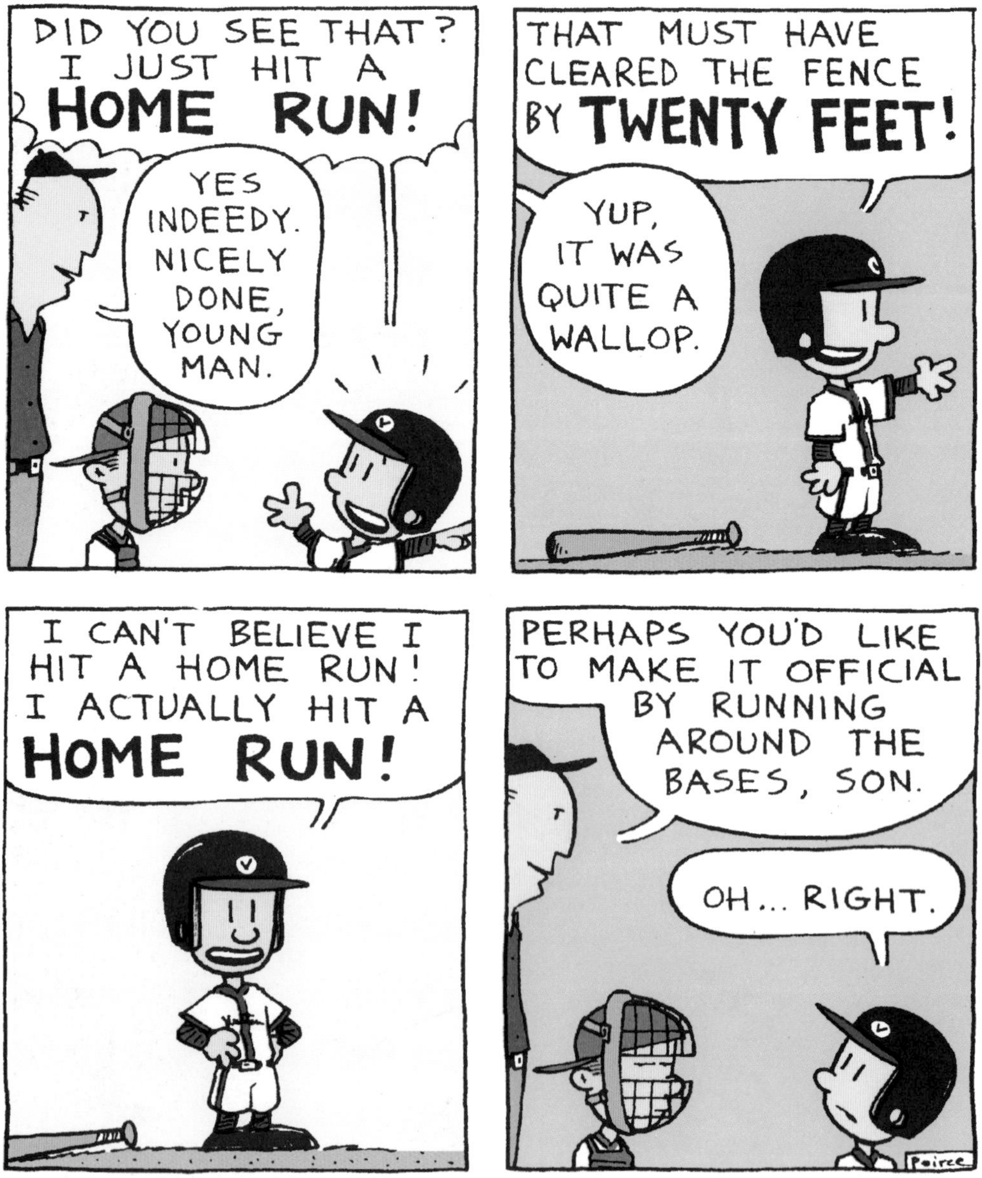
DID YOU SEE THAT? I JUST HIT A HOME RUN!
YES INDEEDY. NICELY DONE, YOUNG MAN.
THAT MUST HAVE CLEARED THE FENCE BY TWENTY FEET!
YUP, IT WAS QUITE A WALLOP.
I CAN'T BELIEVE I HIT A HOME RUN! I ACTUALLY HIT A HOME RUN!
PERHAPS YOU'D LIKE TO MAKE IT OFFICIAL BY RUNNING AROUND THE BASES, SON.
OH... RIGHT.
Peirce

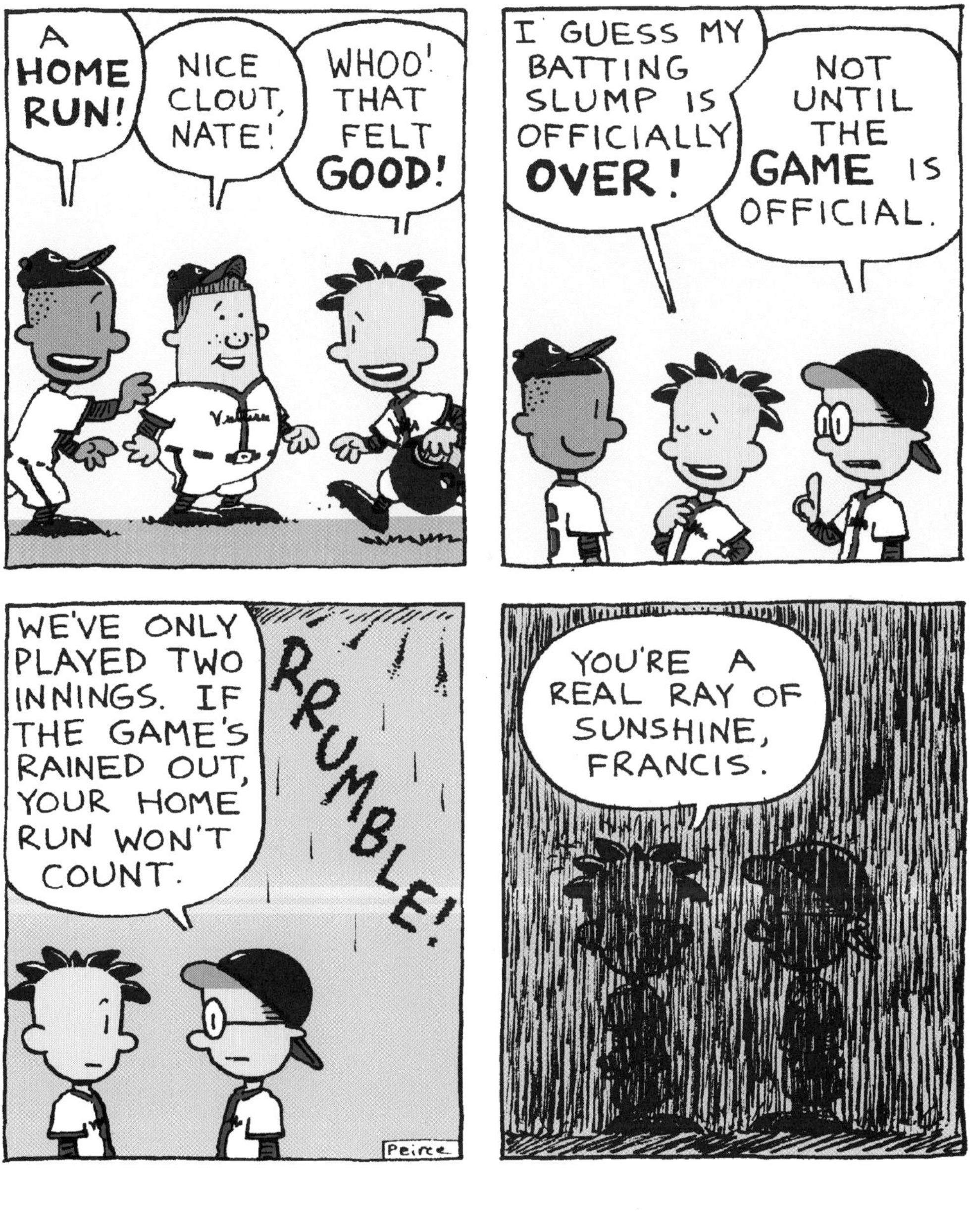
A HOME RUN!
NICE CLOUT, NATE!
WHOO! THAT FELT GOOD!
I GUESS MY BATTING SLUMP IS OFFICIALLY OVER!
NOT UNTIL THE GAME IS OFFICIAL.
WE'VE ONLY PLAYED TWO INNINGS. IF THE GAME'S RAINED OUT, YOUR HOME RUN WON'T COUNT.
RRUMBLE!
Peirce
YOU'RE A REAL RAY OF SUNSHINE, FRANCIS.

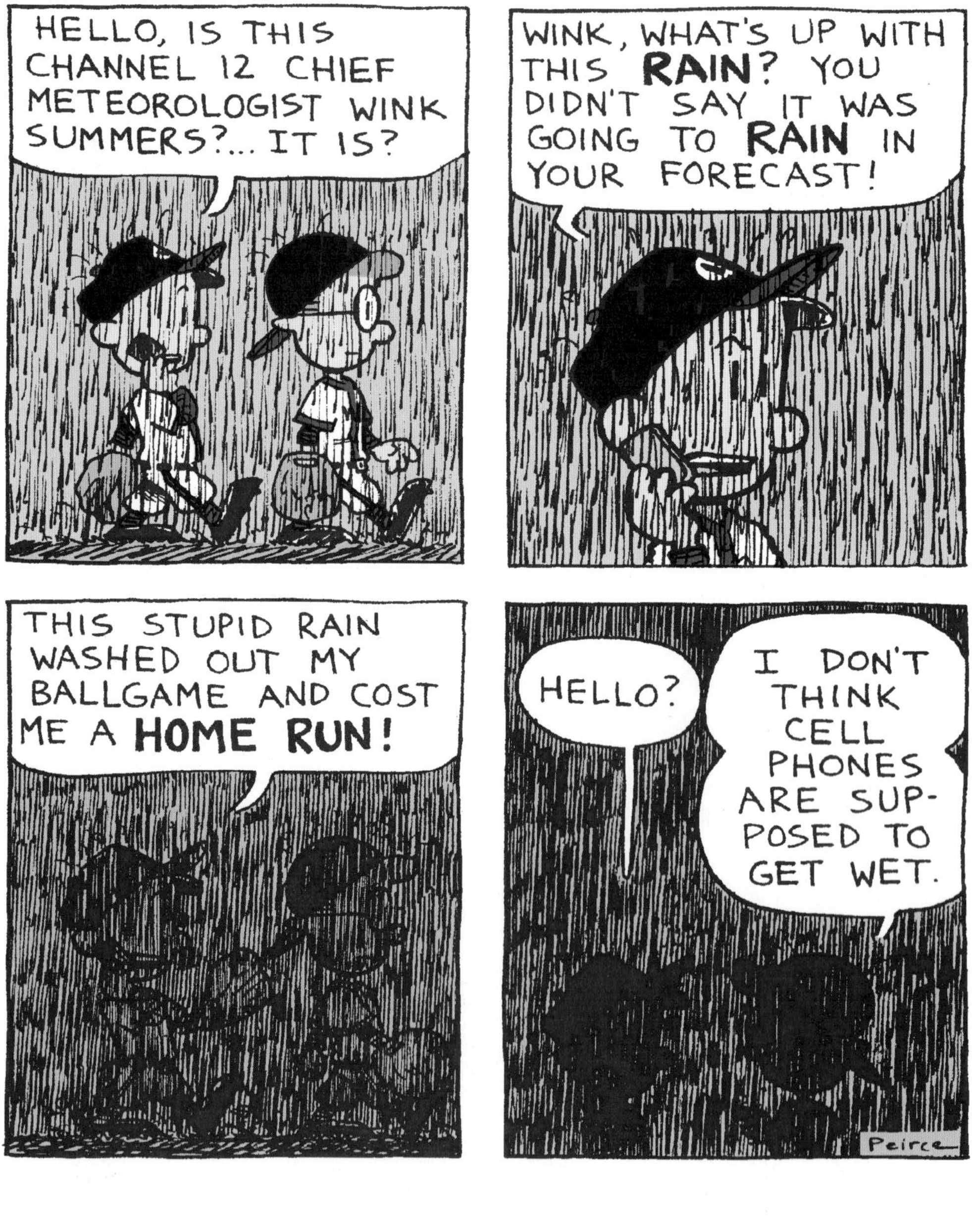
HELLO, IS THIS CHANNEL 12 CHIEF METEOROLOGIST WINK SUMMERS?... IT IS?
WINK, WHAT'S UP WITH THIS RAIN? YOU DIDN'T SAY IT WAS GOING TO RAIN IN YOUR FORECAST!
THIS STUPID RAIN WASHED OUT MY BALLGAME AND COST ME A HOME RUN!
HELLO?
I DON'T THINK CELL PHONES ARE SUP-POSED TO GET WET.
Peirce

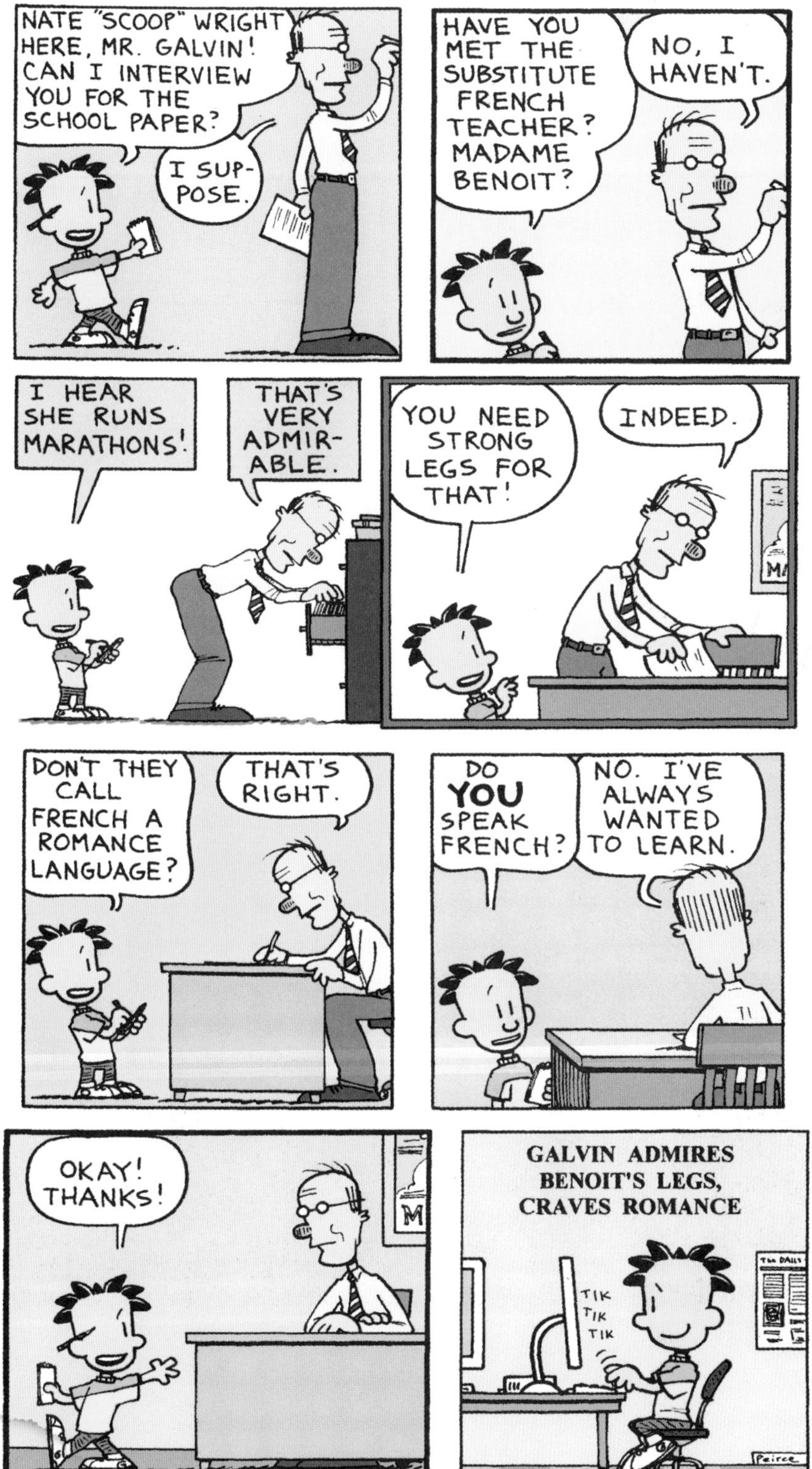
NATE "SCOOP" WRIGHT HERE, MR. GALVIN! CAN I INTERVIEW YOU FOR THE SCHOOL PAPER?
I SUPPOSE.
HAVE YOU MET THE SUBSTITUTE FRENCH TEACHER? MADAME BENOIT?
NO, I HAVEN'T.
I HEAR SHE RUNS MARATHONS!
THAT'S VERY ADMIRABLE.
YOU NEED STRONG LEGS FOR THAT!
INDEED.
DON'T THEY CALL FRENCH A ROMANCE LANGUAGE?
THAT'S RIGHT.
DO YOU SPEAK FRENCH?
NO. I'VE ALWAYS WANTED TO LEARN.
OKAY! THANKS!
GALVIN ADMIRES BENOIT'S LEGS, CRAVES ROMANCE
TIK TIK TIK
Peirce

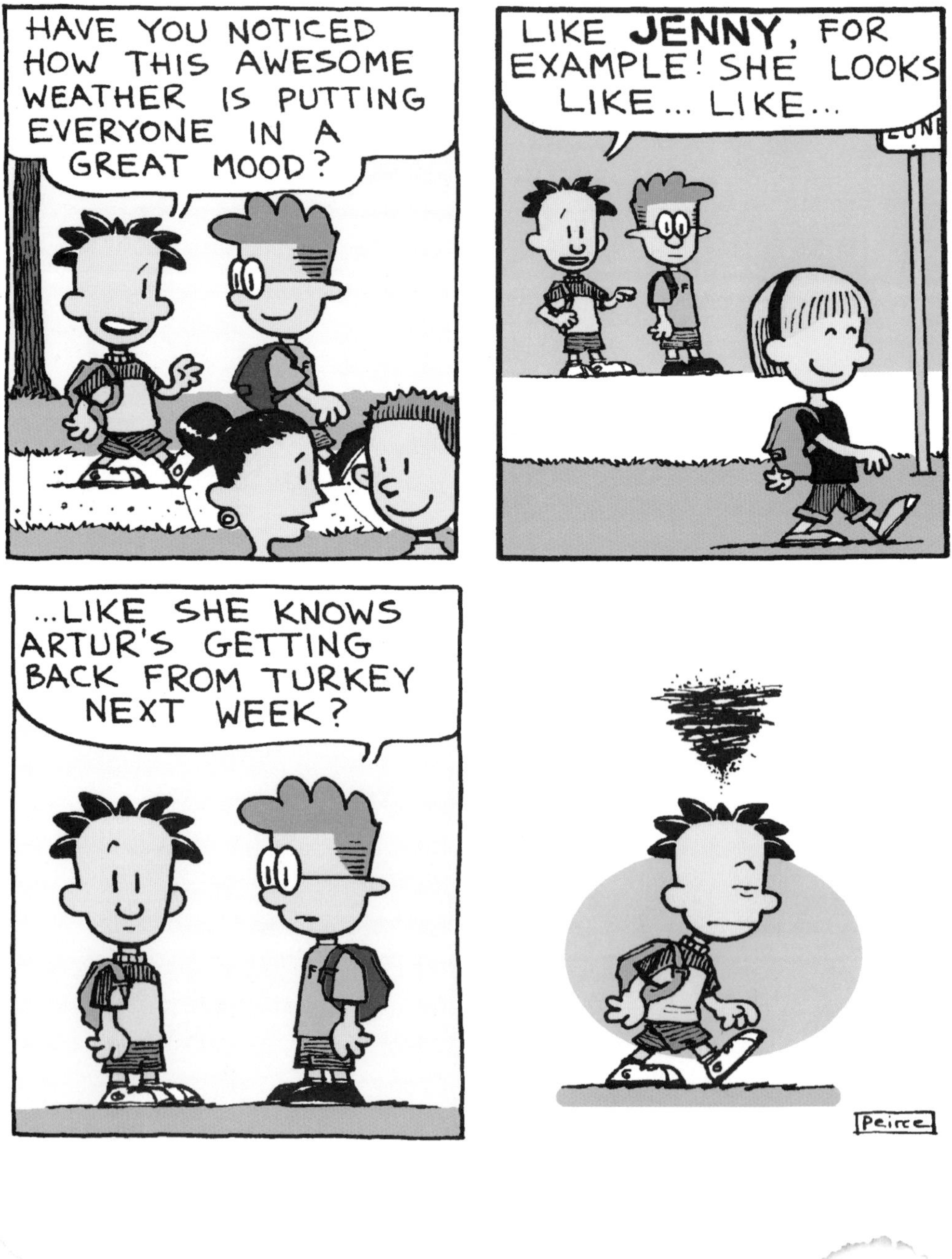
HAVE YOU NOTICED HOW THIS AWESOME WEATHER IS PUTTING EVERYONE IN A GREAT MOOD?
LIKE JENNY, FOR EXAMPLE! SHE LOOKS LIKE... LIKE...
...LIKE SHE KNOWS ARTUR'S GETTING BACK FROM TURKEY NEXT WEEK?
Peirce

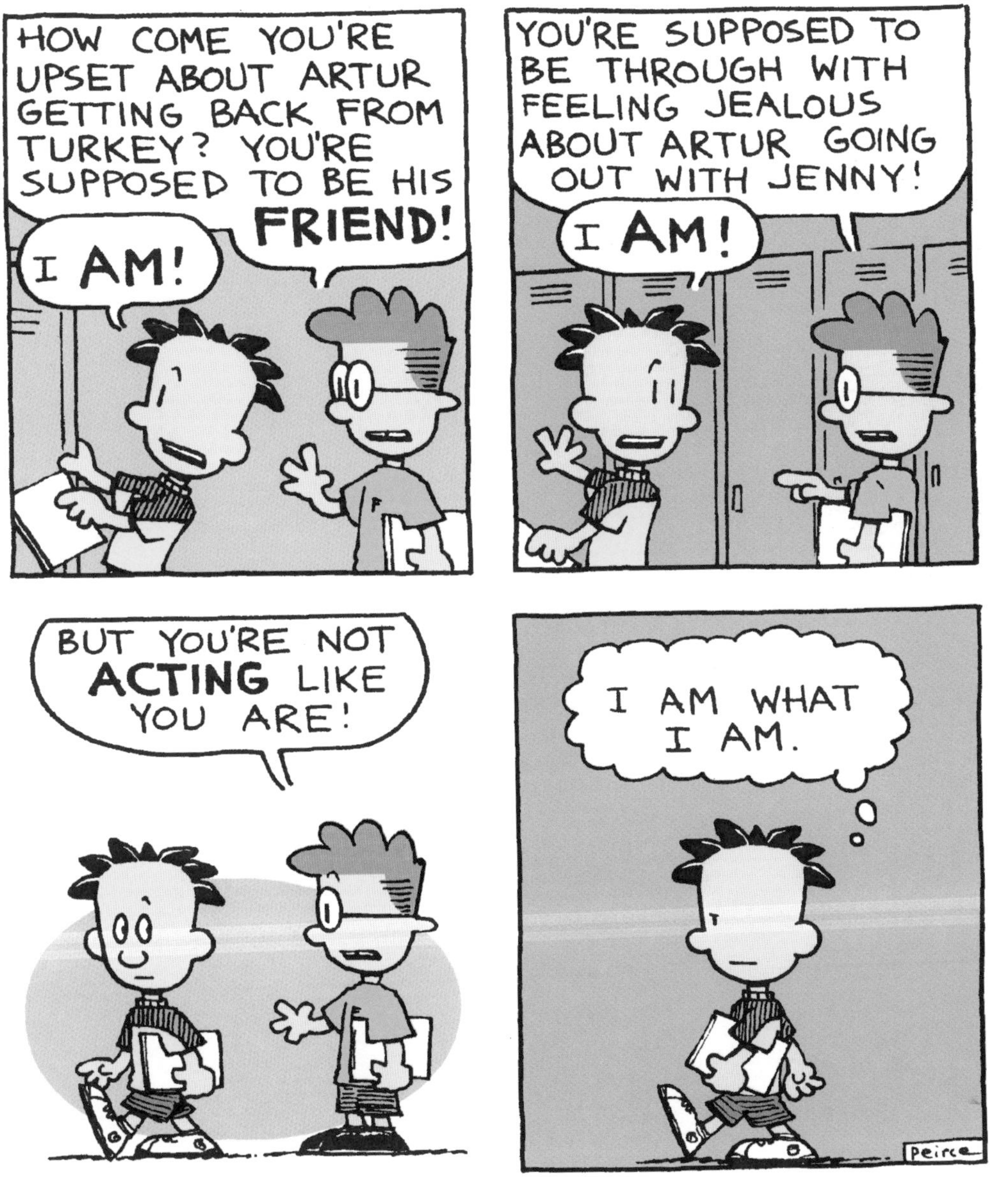
HOW COME YOU'RE UPSET ABOUT ARTUR GETTING BACK FROM TURKEY? YOU'RE SUPPOSED TO BE HIS FRIEND!
I AM!
YOU'RE SUPPOSED TO BE THROUGH WITH FEELING JEALOUS ABOUT ARTUR GOING OUT WITH JENNY!
I AM!
BUT YOU'RE NOT ACTING LIKE YOU ARE!
I AM WHAT I AM.
Peirce

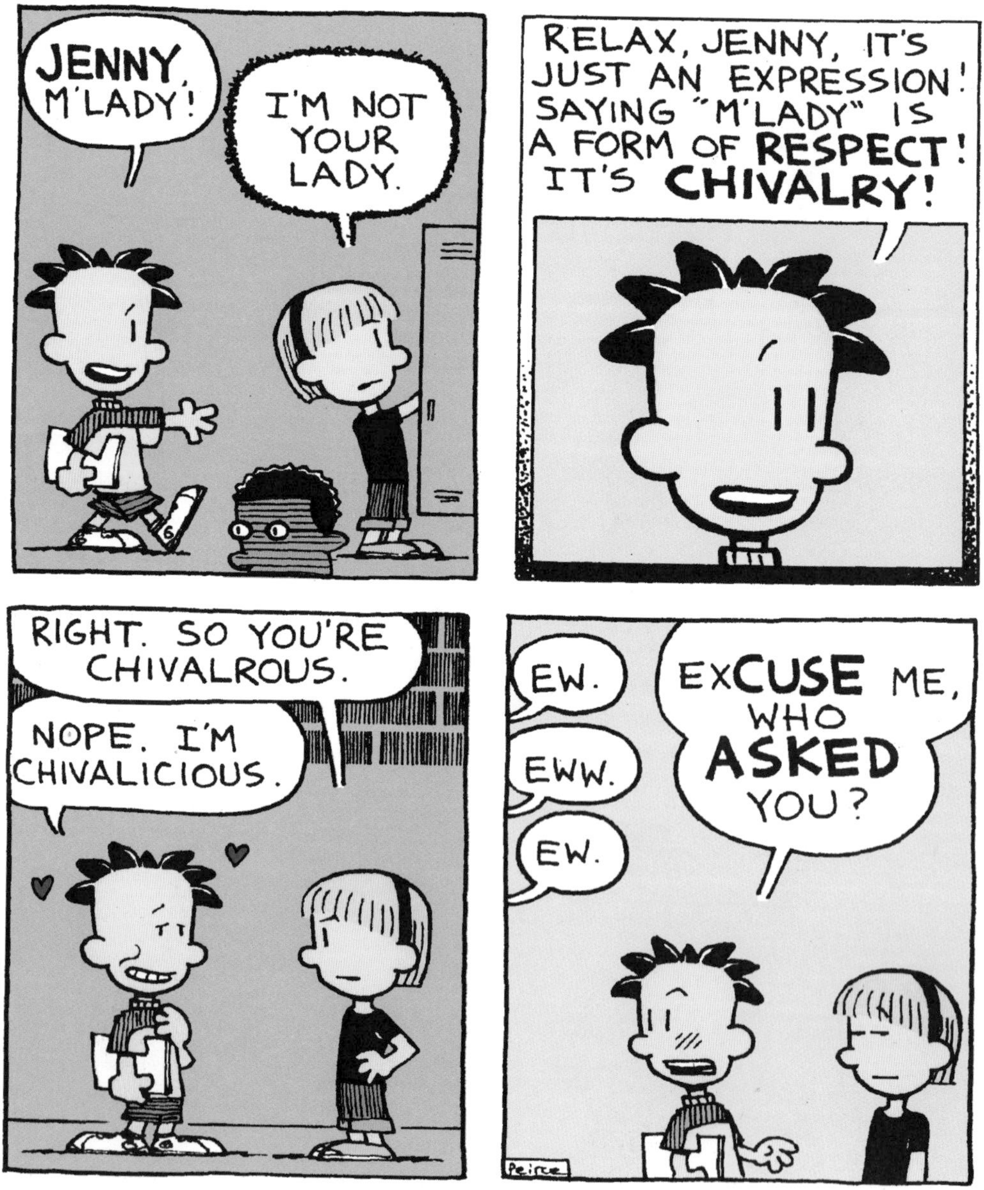
JENNY, M'LADY!
I'M NOT YOUR LADY.
RELAX, JENNY, IT'S JUST AN EXPRESSION! SAYING "M'LADY" IS A FORM OF RESPECT! IT'S CHIVALRY!
RIGHT. SO YOU'RE CHIVALROUS.
NOPE. I'M CHIVALICIOUS.
EW.
EWW.
EW.
EXCUSE ME, WHO ASKED YOU?
Peirce

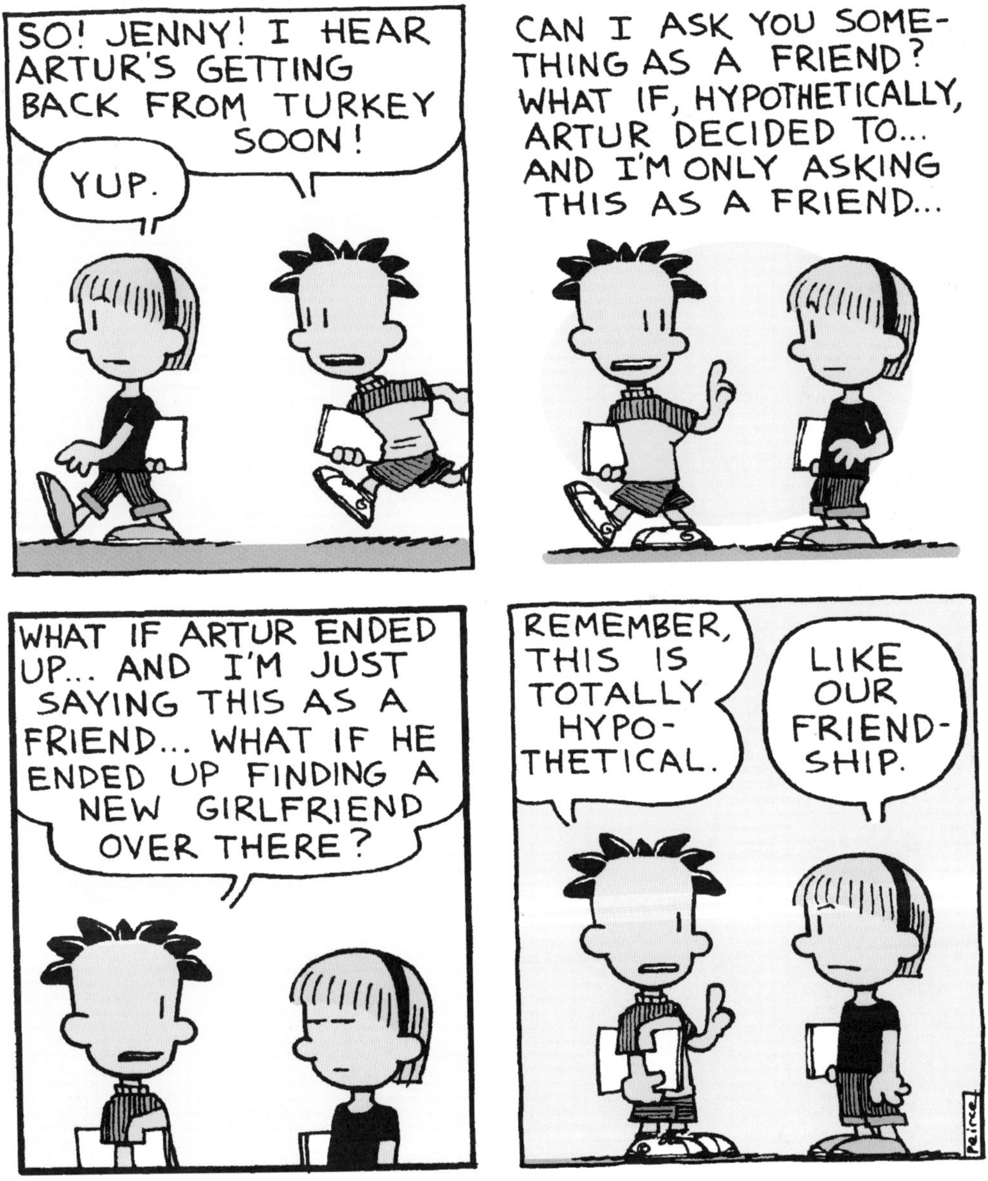
SO! JENNY! I HEAR ARTUR'S GETTING BACK FROM TURKEY SOON!
YUP.
CAN I ASK YOU SOMETHING AS A FRIEND? WHAT IF, HYPOTHETICALLY, ARTUR DECIDED TO... AND I'M ONLY ASKING THIS AS A FRIEND...
WHAT IF ARTUR ENDED UP... AND I'M JUST SAYING THIS AS A FRIEND... WHAT IF HE ENDED UP FINDING A NEW GIRLFRIEND OVER THERE?
REMEMBER, THIS IS TOTALLY HYPOTHETICAL.
LIKE OUR FRIENDSHIP.
Peirce

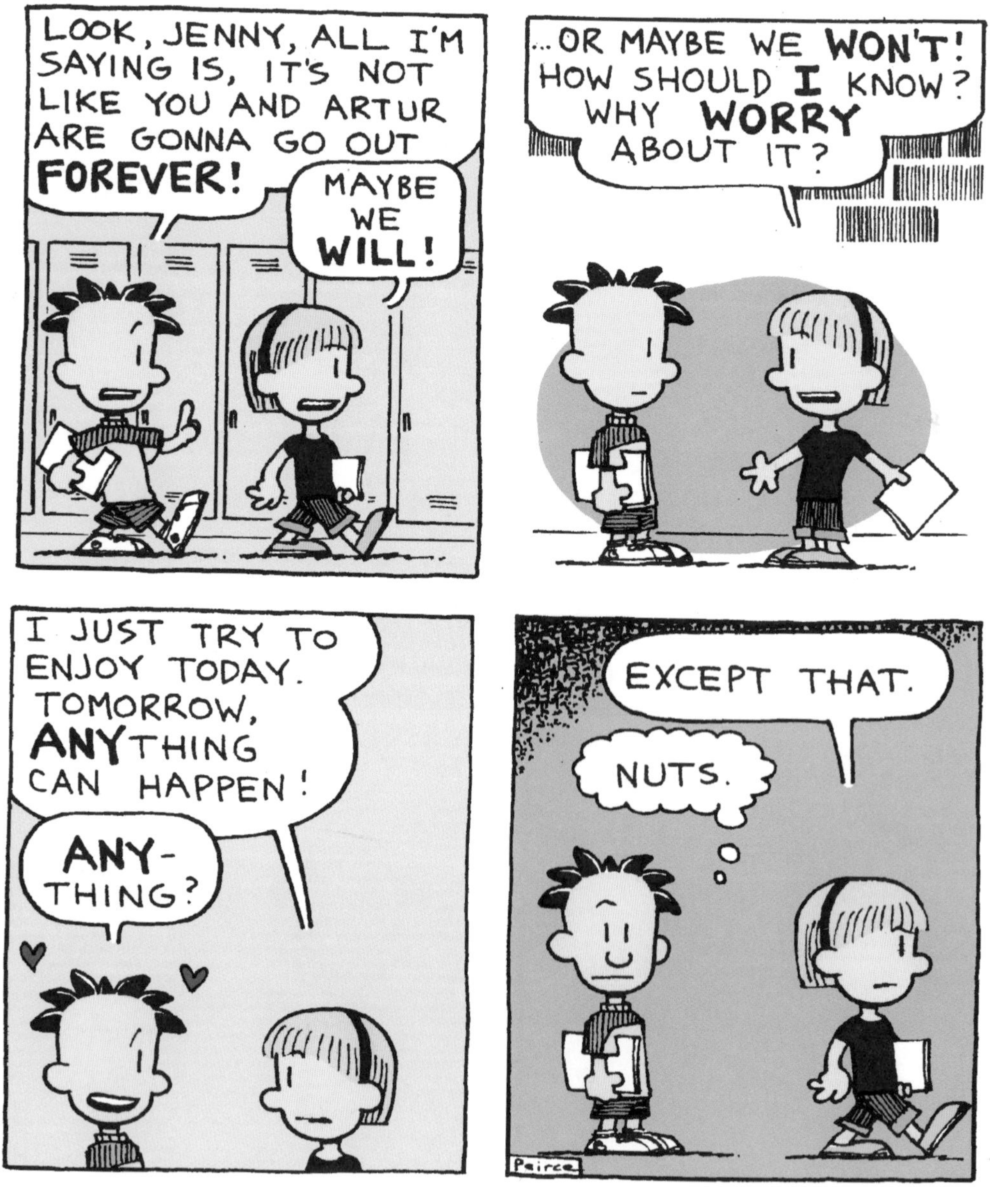
LOOK, JENNY, ALL I'M SAYING IS, IT'S NOT LIKE YOU AND ARTUR ARE GONNA GO OUT **FOREVER!**
MAYBE WE **WILL!**
...OR MAYBE WE **WON'T!** HOW SHOULD **I** KNOW? WHY **WORRY** ABOUT IT?
I JUST TRY TO ENJOY TODAY. TOMORROW, **ANY**THING CAN HAPPEN!
ANY-THING?
EXCEPT THAT.
NUTS.
Peirce

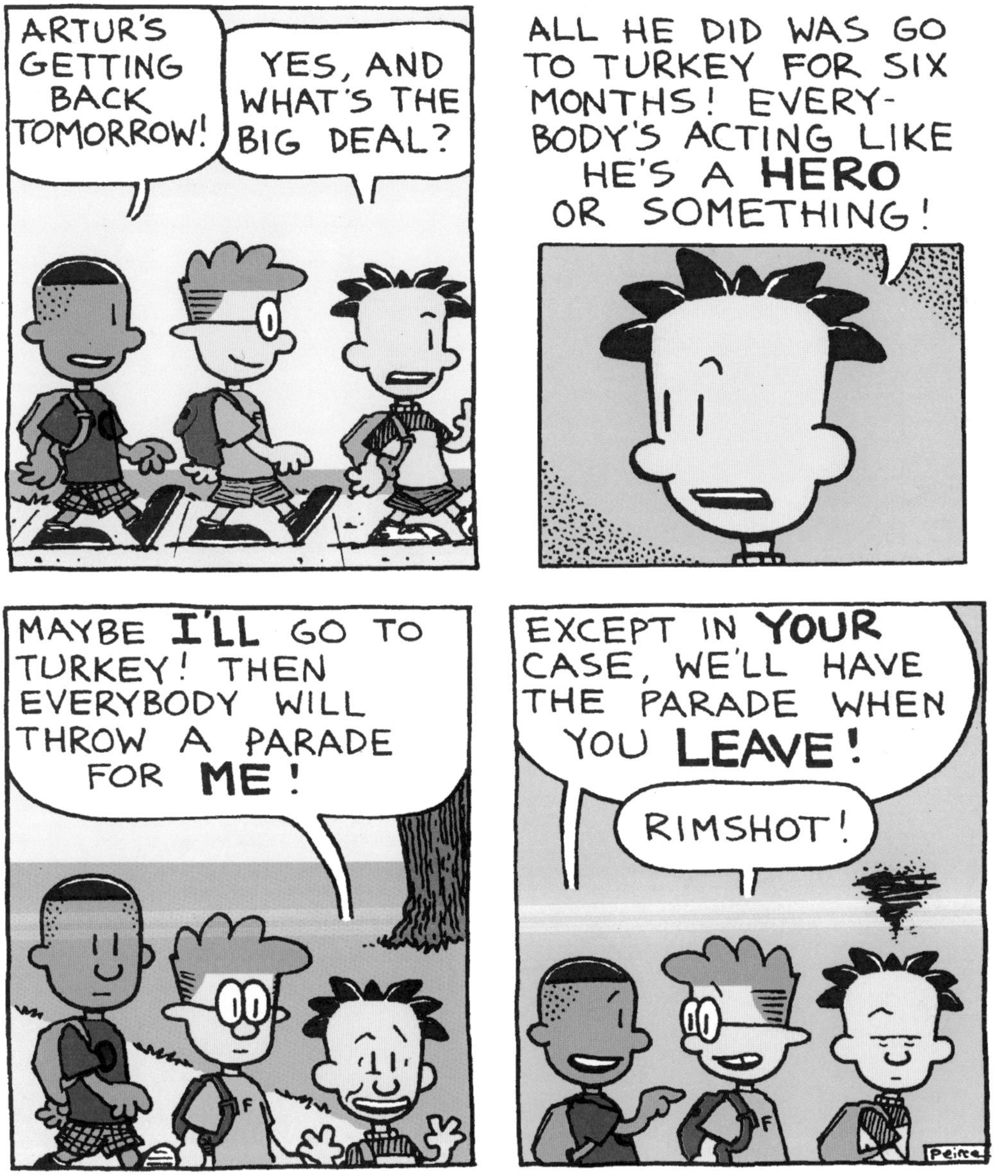
ARTUR'S GETTING BACK TOMORROW!
YES, AND WHAT'S THE BIG DEAL?
ALL HE DID WAS GO TO TURKEY FOR SIX MONTHS! EVERYBODY'S ACTING LIKE HE'S A **HERO** OR SOMETHING!
MAYBE **I'LL** GO TO TURKEY! THEN EVERYBODY WILL THROW A PARADE FOR **ME**!
EXCEPT IN **YOUR** CASE, WE'LL HAVE THE PARADE WHEN YOU **LEAVE**!
RIMSHOT!
Peirce

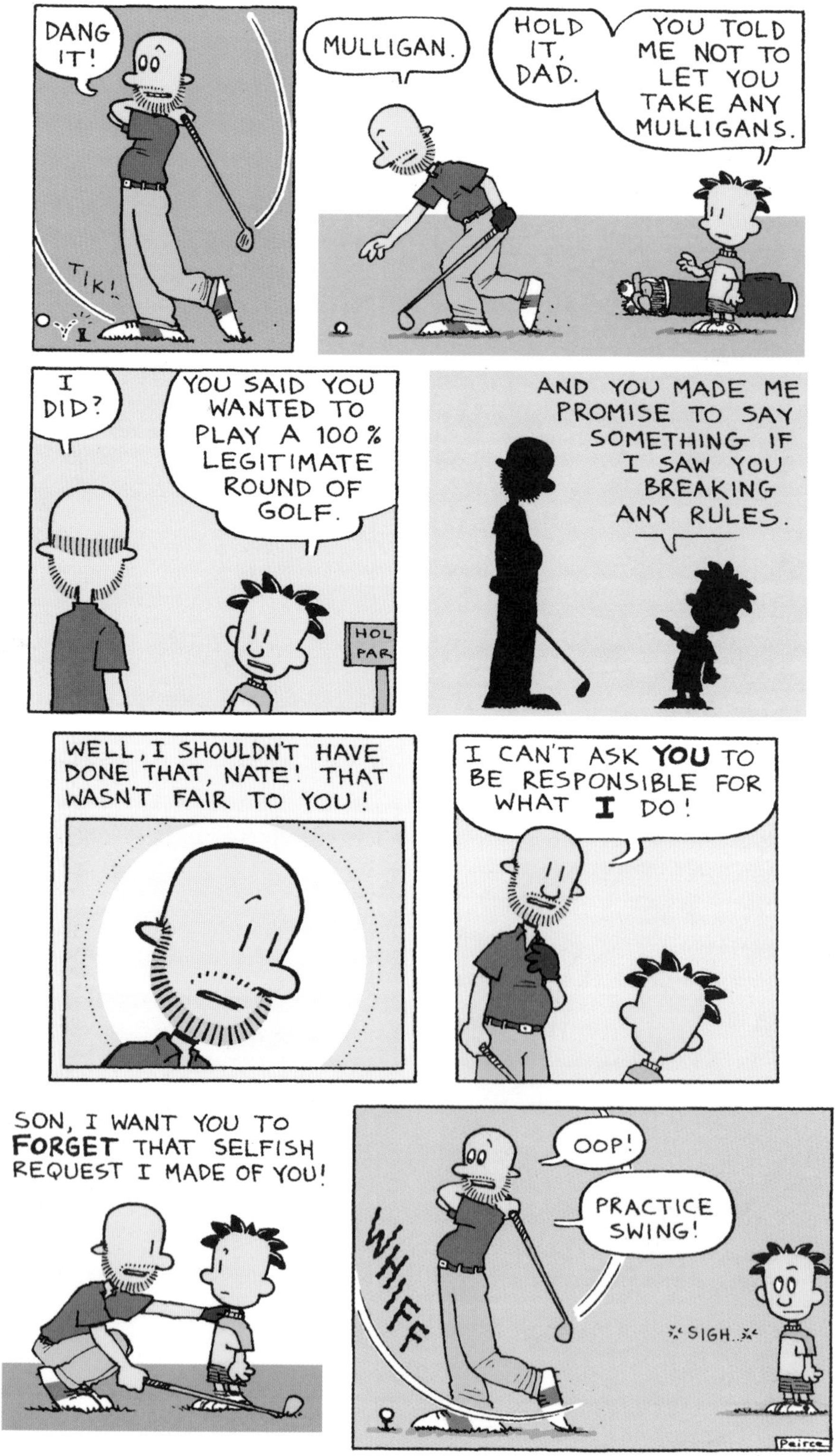
DANG IT!
TIK!
MULLIGAN.
HOLD IT, DAD.
YOU TOLD ME NOT TO LET YOU TAKE ANY MULLIGANS.
I DID?
YOU SAID YOU WANTED TO PLAY A 100% LEGITIMATE ROUND OF GOLF.
HOL
PAR
AND YOU MADE ME PROMISE TO SAY SOMETHING IF I SAW YOU BREAKING ANY RULES.
WELL, I SHOULDN'T HAVE DONE THAT, NATE! THAT WASN'T FAIR TO YOU!
I CAN'T ASK YOU TO BE RESPONSIBLE FOR WHAT I DO!
SON, I WANT YOU TO FORGET THAT SELFISH REQUEST I MADE OF YOU!
OOP!
PRACTICE SWING!
WHIFF
SIGH..
Peirce

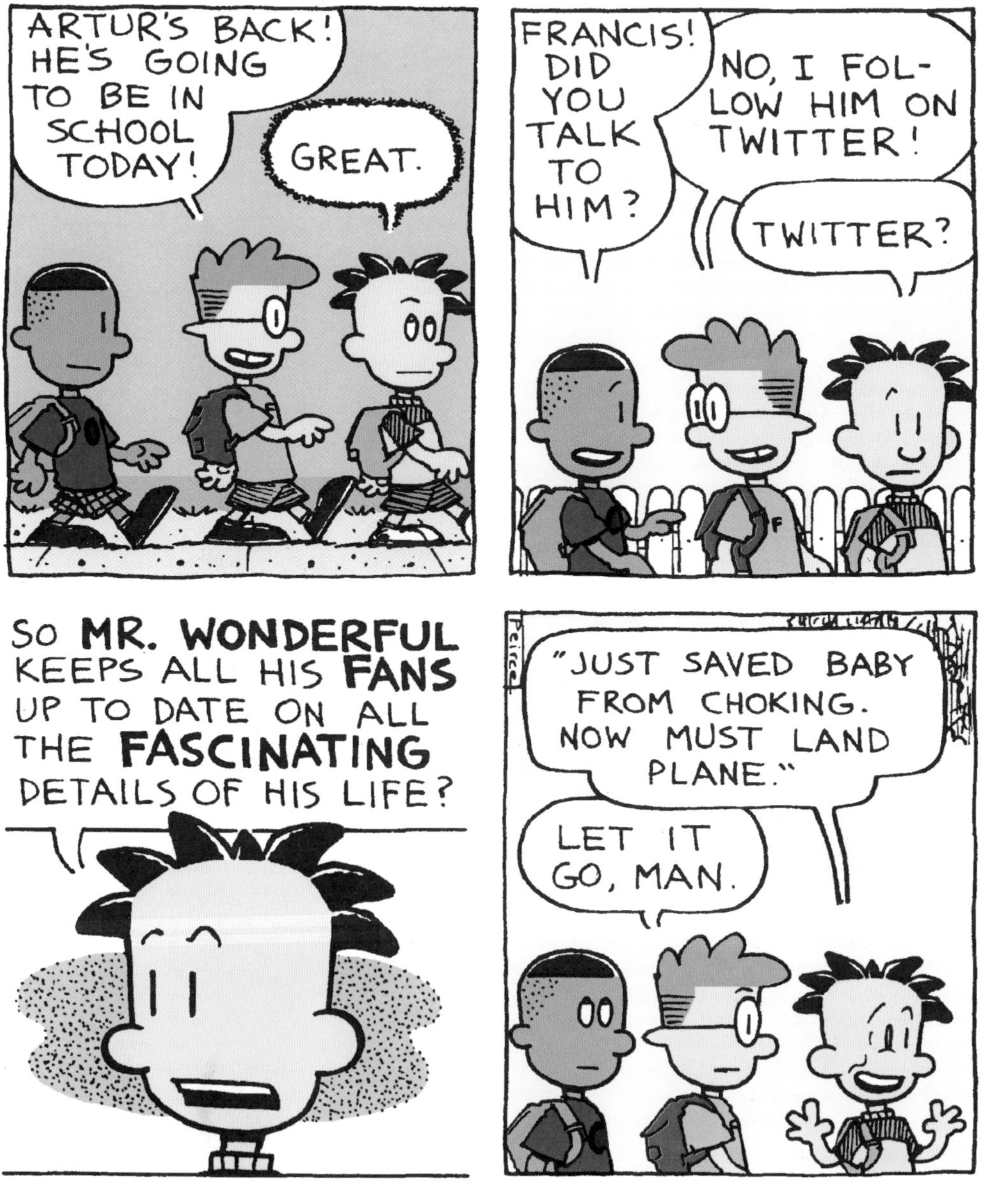
ARTUR'S BACK! HE'S GOING TO BE IN SCHOOL TODAY!
GREAT.
FRANCIS! DID YOU TALK TO HIM?
NO, I FOL-LOW HIM ON TWITTER!
TWITTER?
SO MR. WONDERFUL KEEPS ALL HIS FANS UP TO DATE ON ALL THE FASCINATING DETAILS OF HIS LIFE?
"JUST SAVED BABY FROM CHOKING. NOW MUST LAND PLANE."
LET IT GO, MAN.
Peirce

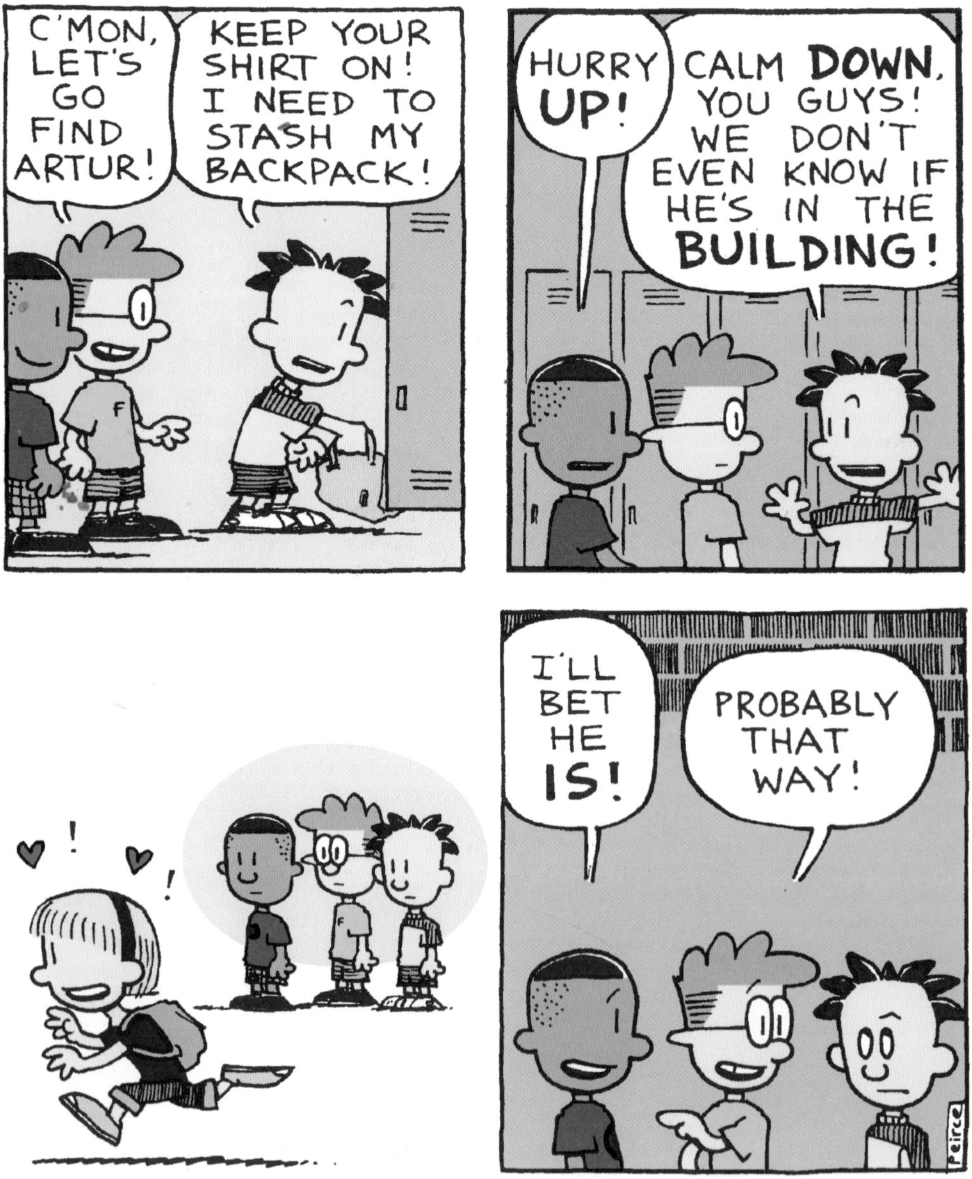
C'MON, LET'S GO FIND ARTUR!
KEEP YOUR SHIRT ON! I NEED TO STASH MY BACKPACK!
HURRY UP!
CALM DOWN, YOU GUYS! WE DON'T EVEN KNOW IF HE'S IN THE BUILDING!
I'LL BET HE IS!
PROBABLY THAT WAY!
Peirce

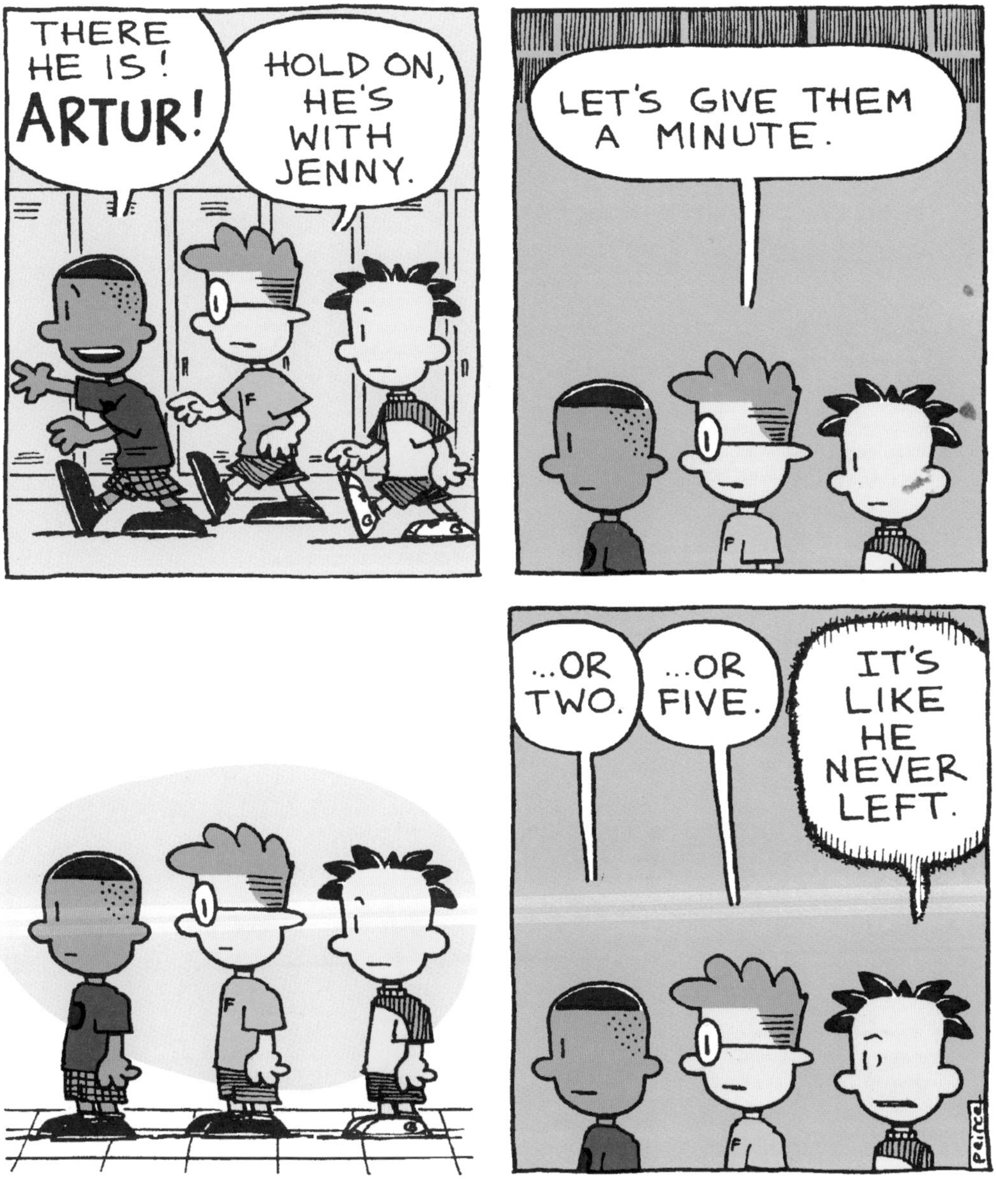
THERE HE IS! ARTUR!
HOLD ON, HE'S WITH JENNY.
LET'S GIVE THEM A MINUTE.
...OR TWO.
...OR FIVE.
IT'S LIKE HE NEVER LEFT.
peirce

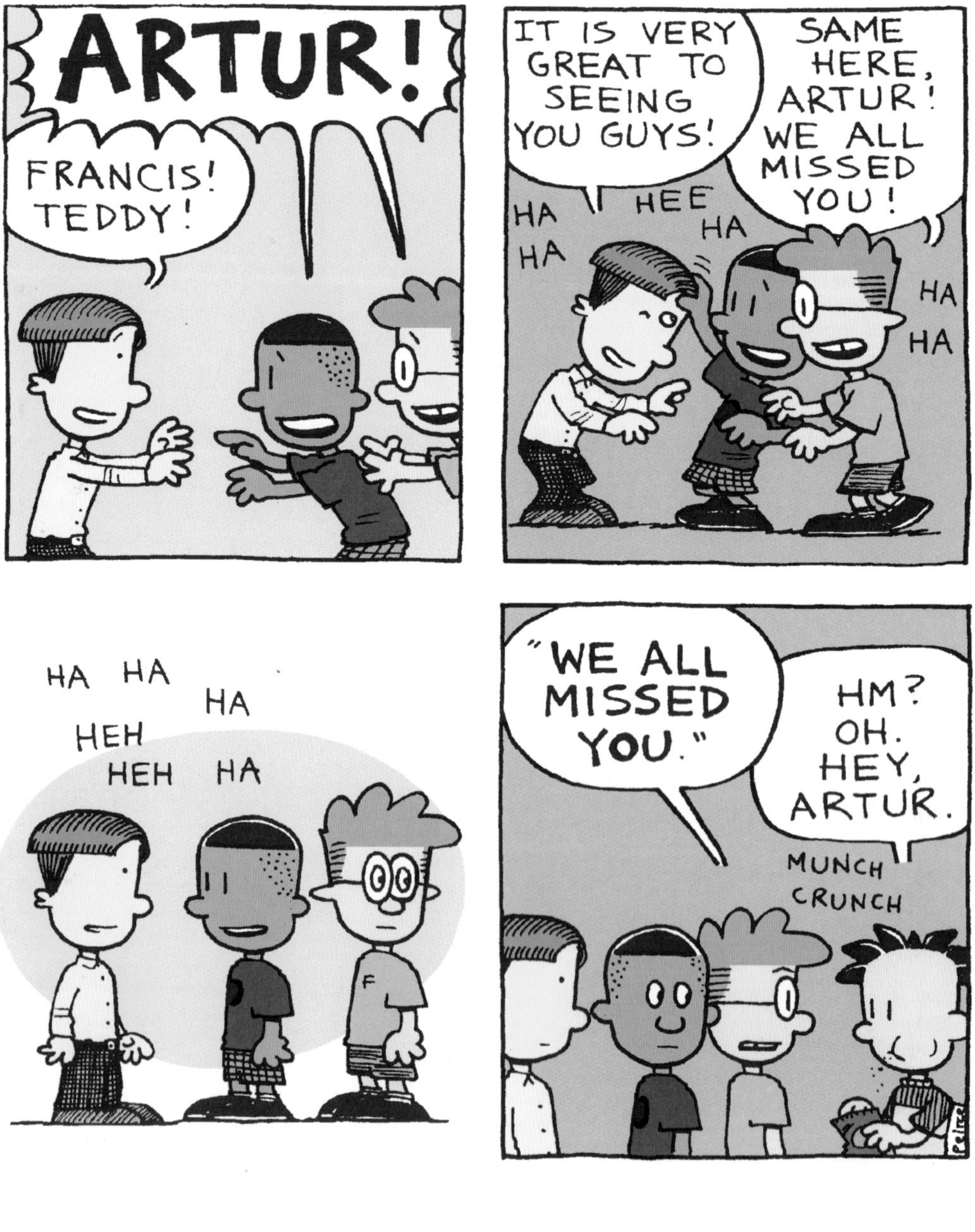
ARTUR!
FRANCIS! TEDDY!
IT IS VERY GREAT TO SEEING YOU GUYS!
SAME HERE, ARTUR! WE ALL MISSED YOU!
HA HA
HEE HA
HA HA
HA HA HA
HEH HEH HA
"WE ALL MISSED YOU."
HM? OH. HEY, ARTUR.
MUNCH CRUNCH

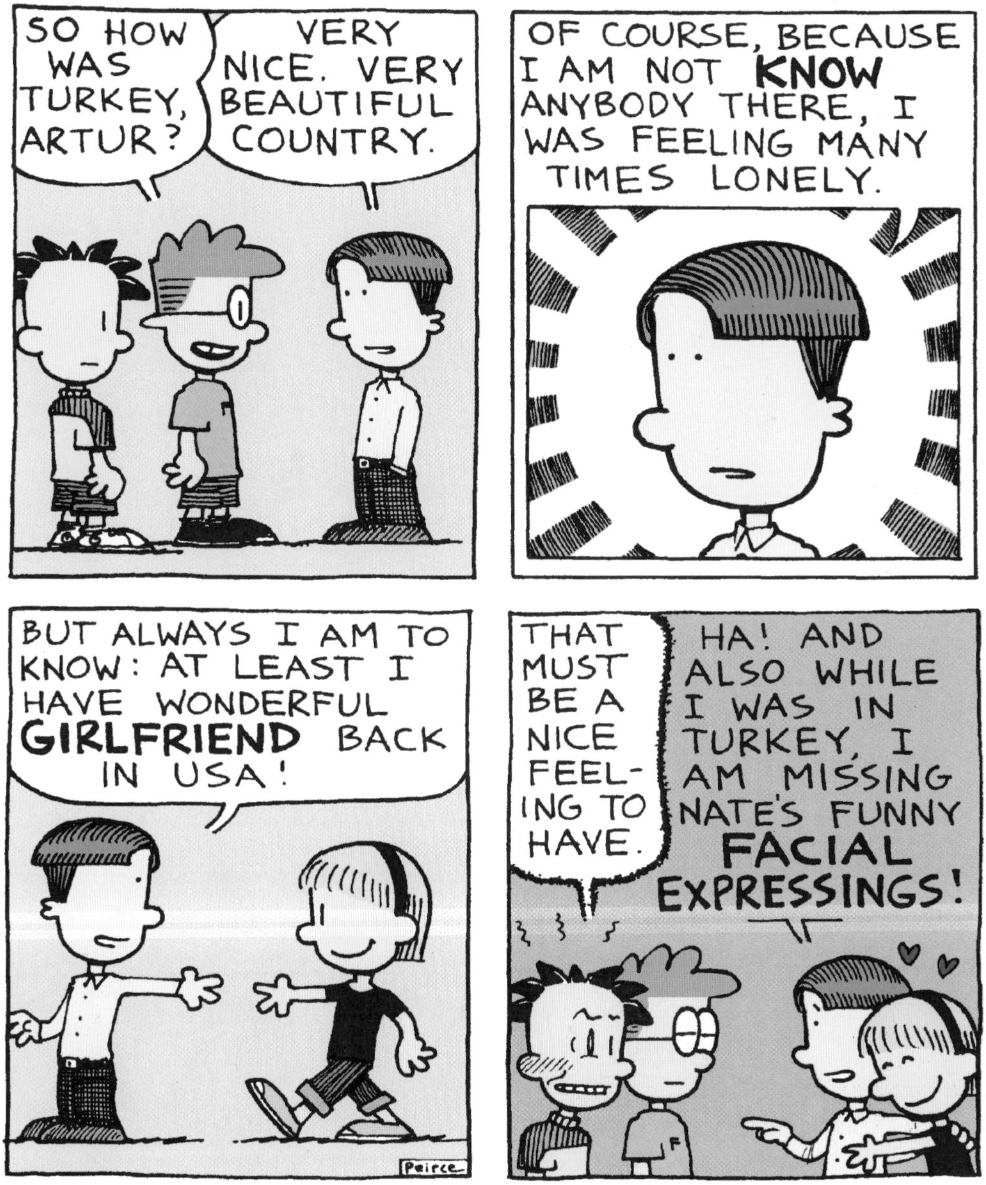
SO HOW WAS TURKEY, ARTUR?
VERY NICE. VERY BEAUTIFUL COUNTRY.
OF COURSE, BECAUSE I AM NOT KNOW ANYBODY THERE, I WAS FEELING MANY TIMES LONELY.
BUT ALWAYS I AM TO KNOW: AT LEAST I HAVE WONDERFUL GIRLFRIEND BACK IN USA!
Peirce
THAT MUST BE A NICE FEEL-ING TO HAVE.
HA! AND ALSO WHILE I WAS IN TURKEY, I AM MISSING NATE'S FUNNY FACIAL EXPRESSINGS!
F

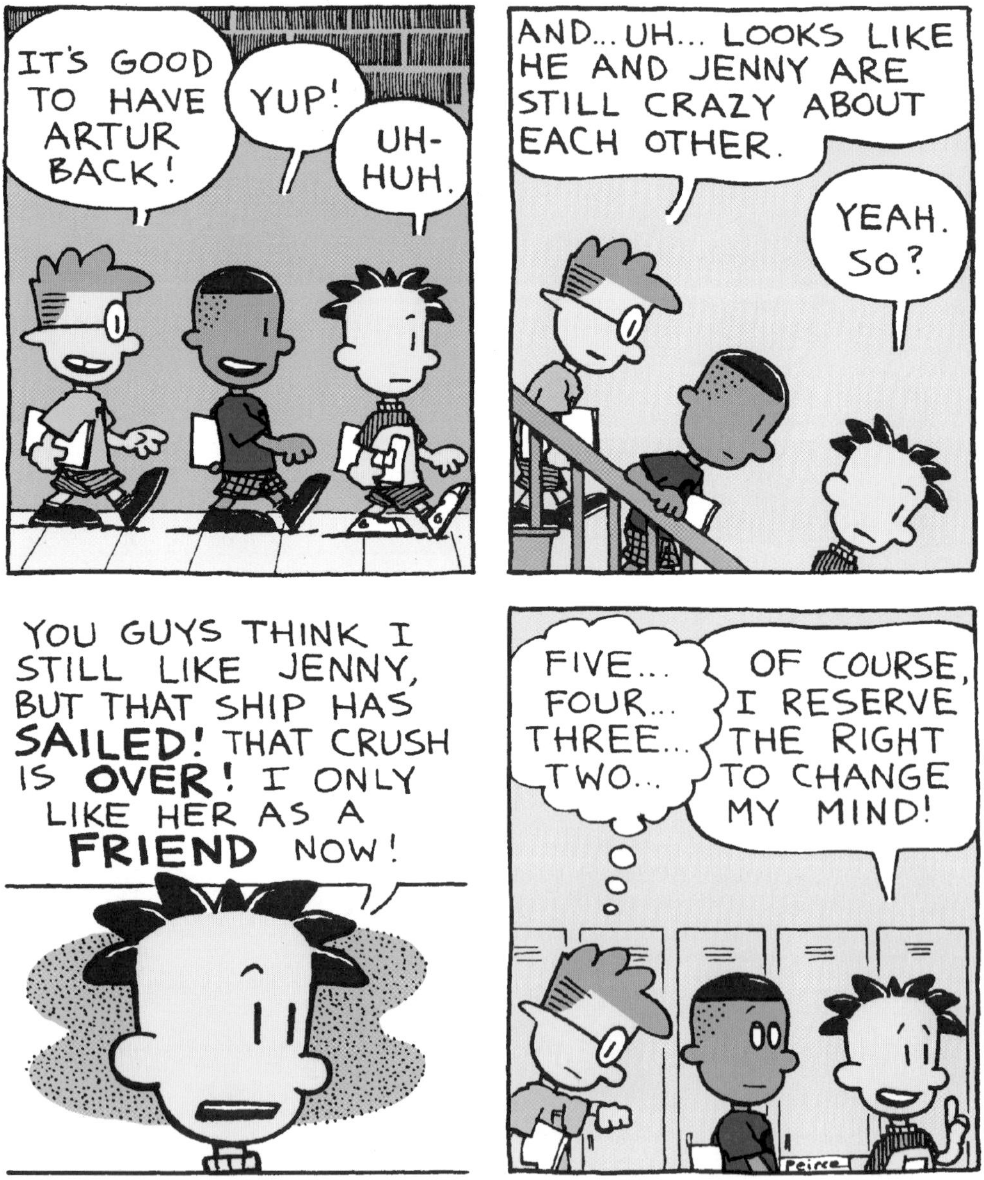
IT'S GOOD TO HAVE ARTUR BACK!
YUP!
UH-HUH.
AND... UH... LOOKS LIKE HE AND JENNY ARE STILL CRAZY ABOUT EACH OTHER.
YEAH. SO?
YOU GUYS THINK I STILL LIKE JENNY, BUT THAT SHIP HAS SAILED! THAT CRUSH IS OVER! I ONLY LIKE HER AS A FRIEND NOW!
FIVE... FOUR... THREE... TWO...
OF COURSE, I RESERVE THE RIGHT TO CHANGE MY MIND!
Peirce

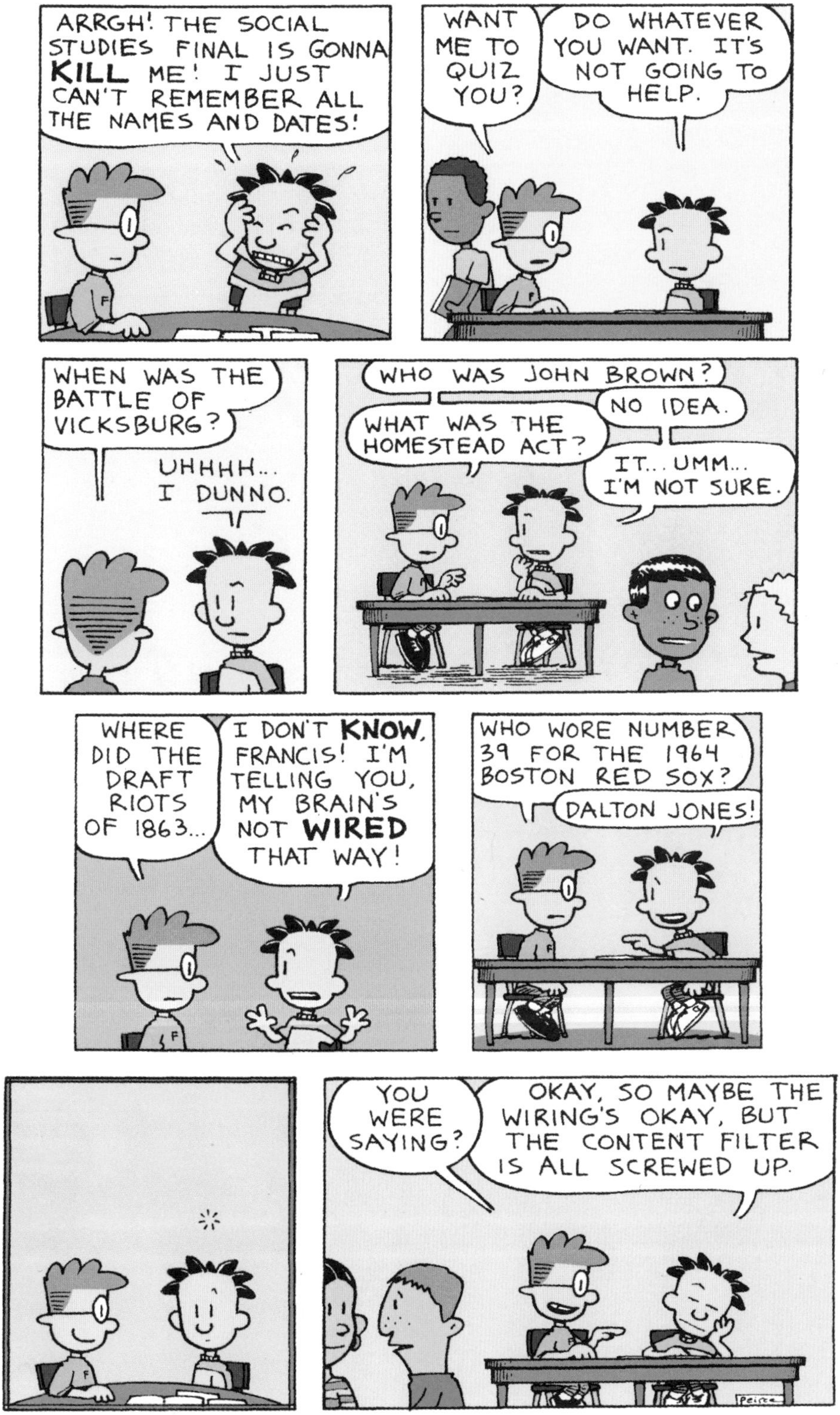
ARRGH! THE SOCIAL STUDIES FINAL IS GONNA **KILL** ME! I JUST CAN'T REMEMBER ALL THE NAMES AND DATES!
WANT ME TO QUIZ YOU?
DO WHATEVER YOU WANT. IT'S NOT GOING TO HELP.
WHEN WAS THE BATTLE OF VICKSBURG?
UHHHH... I DUNNO.
WHO WAS JOHN BROWN?
WHAT WAS THE HOMESTEAD ACT?
NO IDEA.
IT... UMM... I'M NOT SURE.
WHERE DID THE DRAFT RIOTS OF 1863...
I DON'T **KNOW**, FRANCIS! I'M TELLING YOU, MY BRAIN'S NOT **WIRED** THAT WAY!
WHO WORE NUMBER 39 FOR THE 1964 BOSTON RED SOX?
DALTON JONES!
YOU WERE SAYING?
OKAY, SO MAYBE THE WIRING'S OKAY, BUT THE CONTENT FILTER IS ALL SCREWED UP.

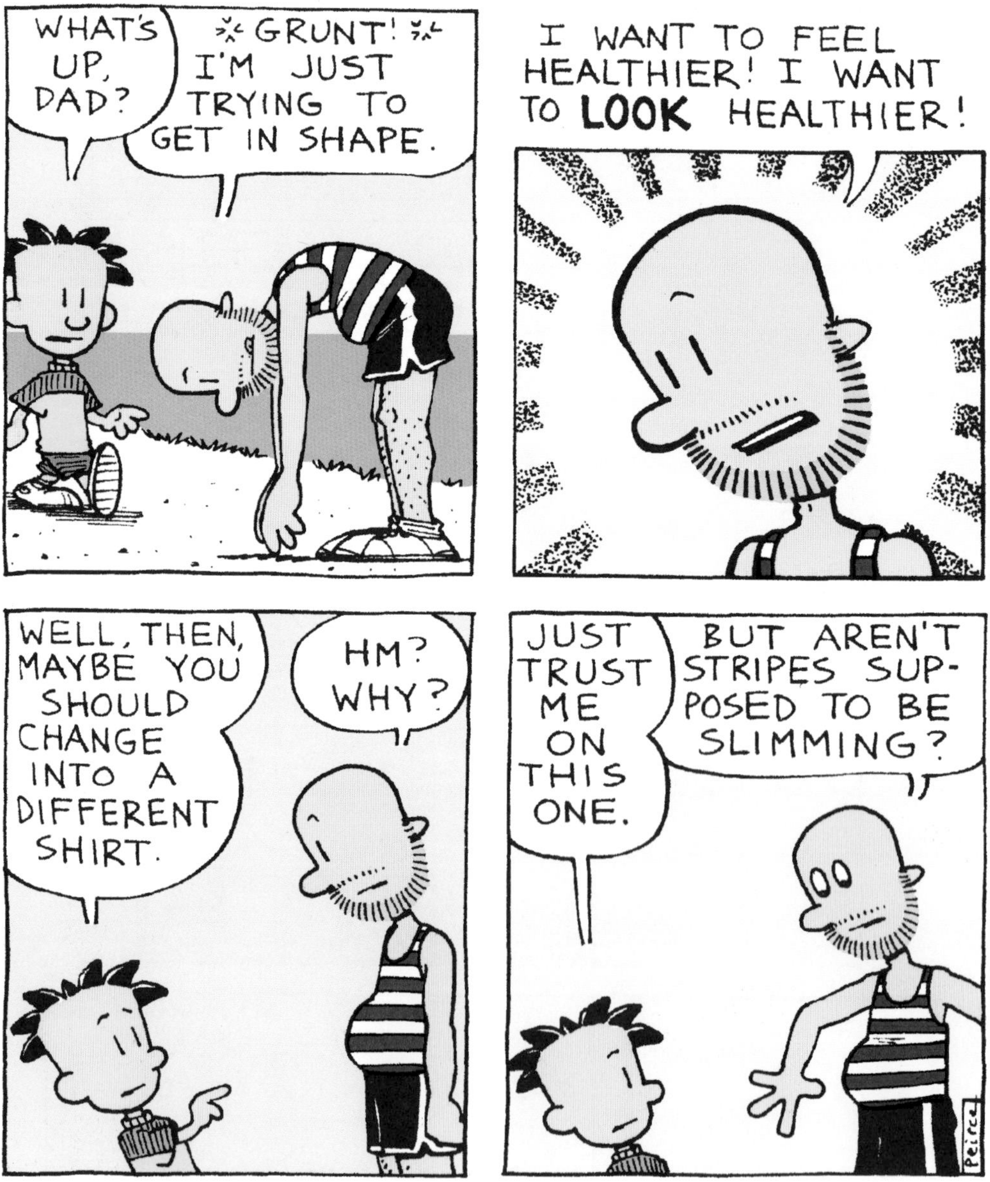
WHAT'S UP, DAD?
GRUNT! I'M JUST TRYING TO GET IN SHAPE.
I WANT TO FEEL HEALTHIER! I WANT TO **LOOK** HEALTHIER!
WELL, THEN, MAYBE YOU SHOULD CHANGE INTO A DIFFERENT SHIRT.
HM? WHY?
BUT AREN'T STRIPES SUPPOSED TO BE SLIMMING?
JUST TRUST ME ON THIS ONE.
Peirce

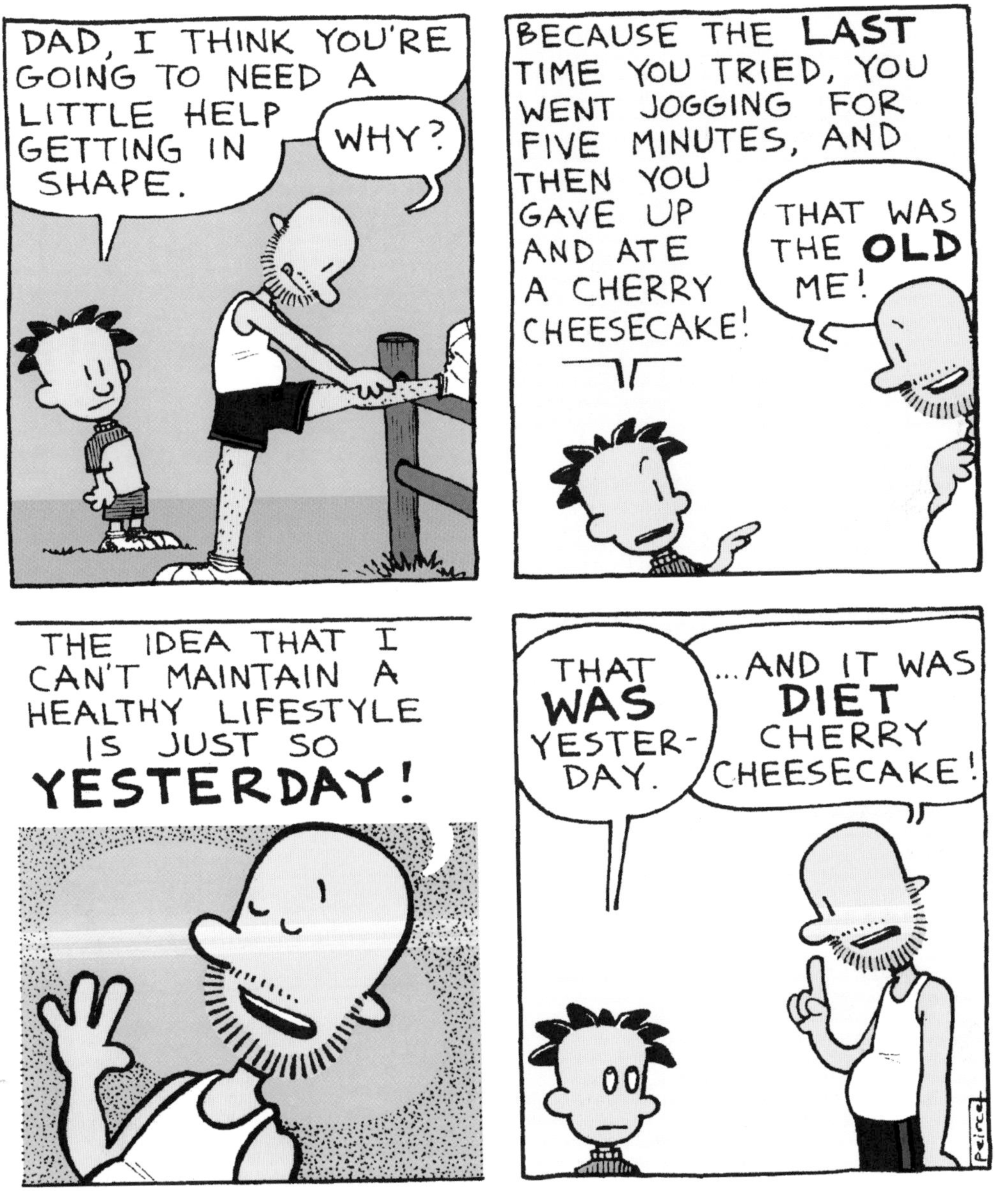
DAD, I THINK YOU'RE GOING TO NEED A LITTLE HELP GETTING IN SHAPE.
WHY?
BECAUSE THE LAST TIME YOU TRIED, YOU WENT JOGGING FOR FIVE MINUTES, AND THEN YOU GAVE UP AND ATE A CHERRY CHEESECAKE!
THAT WAS THE OLD ME!
THE IDEA THAT I CAN'T MAINTAIN A HEALTHY LIFESTYLE IS JUST SO YESTERDAY!
THAT WAS YESTER-DAY.
...AND IT WAS DIET CHERRY CHEESECAKE!
peirce

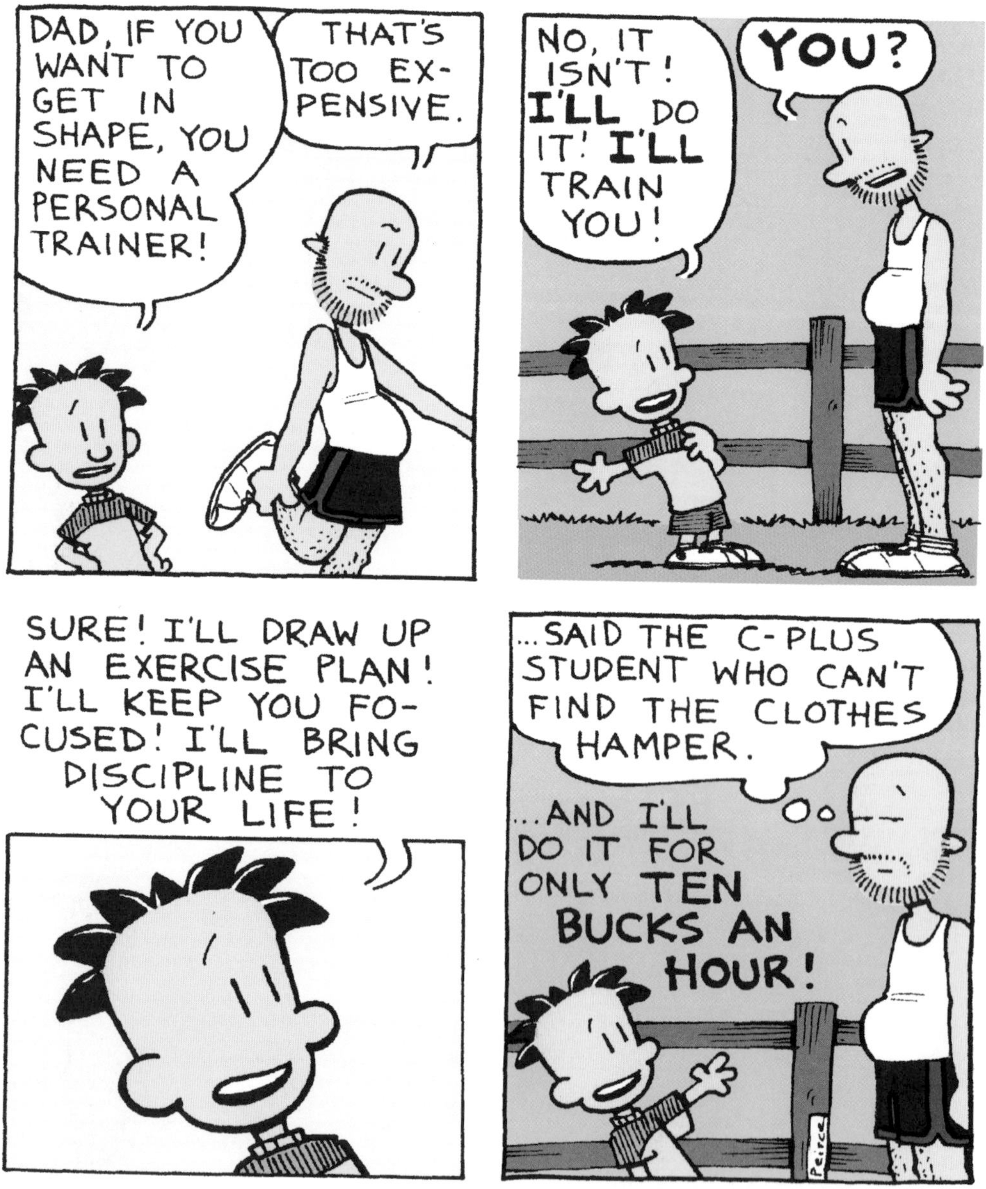
DAD, IF YOU WANT TO GET IN SHAPE, YOU NEED A PERSONAL TRAINER!
THAT'S TOO EX-PENSIVE.
NO, IT ISN'T! I'LL DO IT! I'LL TRAIN YOU!
YOU?
SURE! I'LL DRAW UP AN EXERCISE PLAN! I'LL KEEP YOU FO-CUSED! I'LL BRING DISCIPLINE TO YOUR LIFE!
...SAID THE C-PLUS STUDENT WHO CAN'T FIND THE CLOTHES HAMPER.
...AND I'LL DO IT FOR ONLY TEN BUCKS AN HOUR!
Peirce

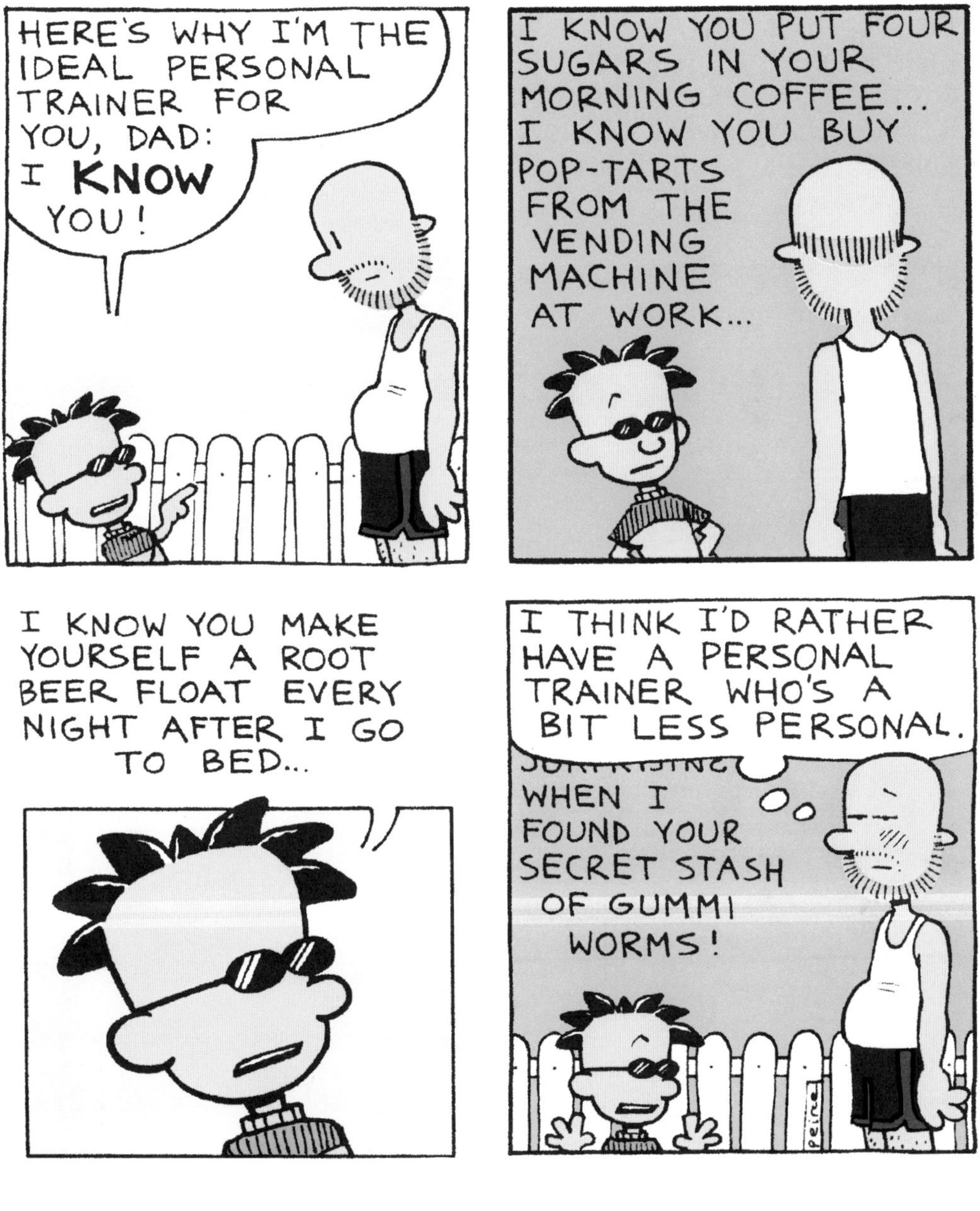
HERE'S WHY I'M THE IDEAL PERSONAL TRAINER FOR YOU, DAD: I **KNOW** YOU!
I KNOW YOU PUT FOUR SUGARS IN YOUR MORNING COFFEE... I KNOW YOU BUY POP-TARTS FROM THE VENDING MACHINE AT WORK...
I KNOW YOU MAKE YOURSELF A ROOT BEER FLOAT EVERY NIGHT AFTER I GO TO BED...
I THINK I'D RATHER HAVE A PERSONAL TRAINER WHO'S A BIT LESS PERSONAL.
WHEN I FOUND YOUR SECRET STASH OF GUMMI WORMS!
peirce

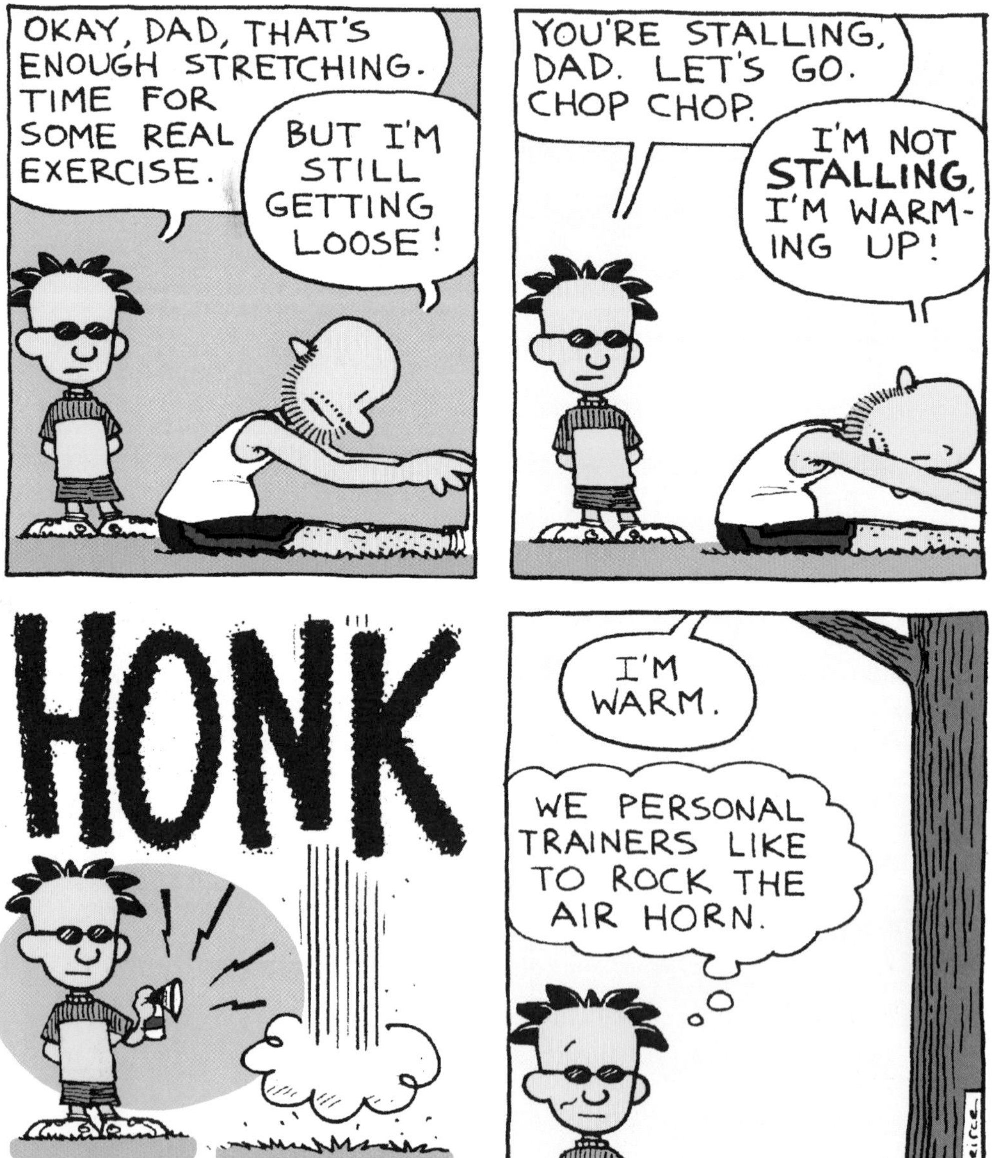
OKAY, DAD, THAT'S ENOUGH STRETCHING. TIME FOR SOME REAL EXERCISE.
BUT I'M STILL GETTING LOOSE!
YOU'RE STALLING, DAD. LET'S GO. CHOP CHOP.
I'M NOT **STALLING**, I'M WARMING UP!
HONK
I'M WARM.
WE PERSONAL TRAINERS LIKE TO ROCK THE AIR HORN.
PRICE

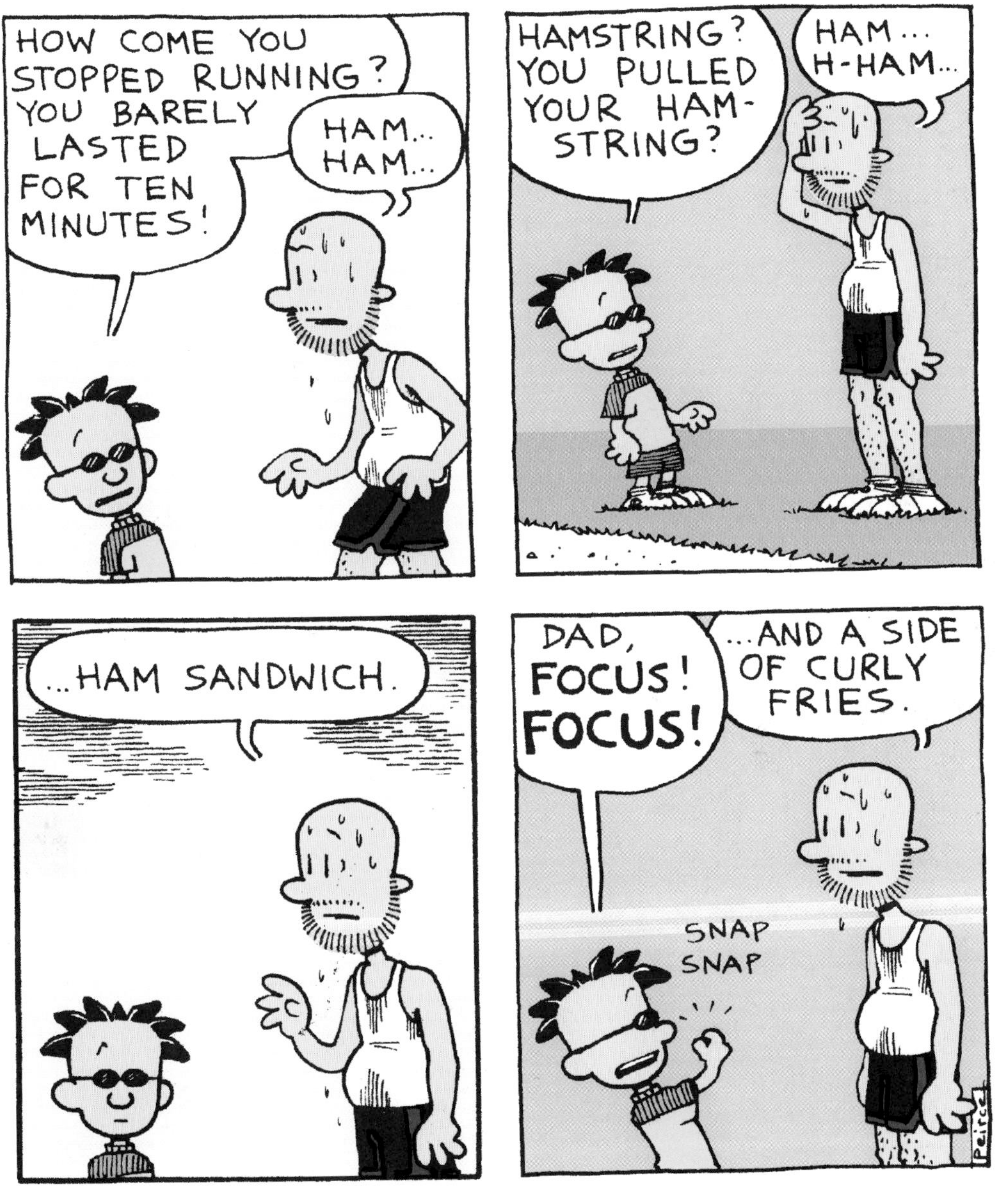
HOW COME YOU STOPPED RUNNING? YOU BARELY LASTED FOR TEN MINUTES!
HAM... HAM...
HAMSTRING? YOU PULLED YOUR HAM-STRING?
HAM... H-HAM...
...HAM SANDWICH.
DAD, FOCUS! FOCUS!
...AND A SIDE OF CURLY FRIES.
SNAP SNAP
Peirce

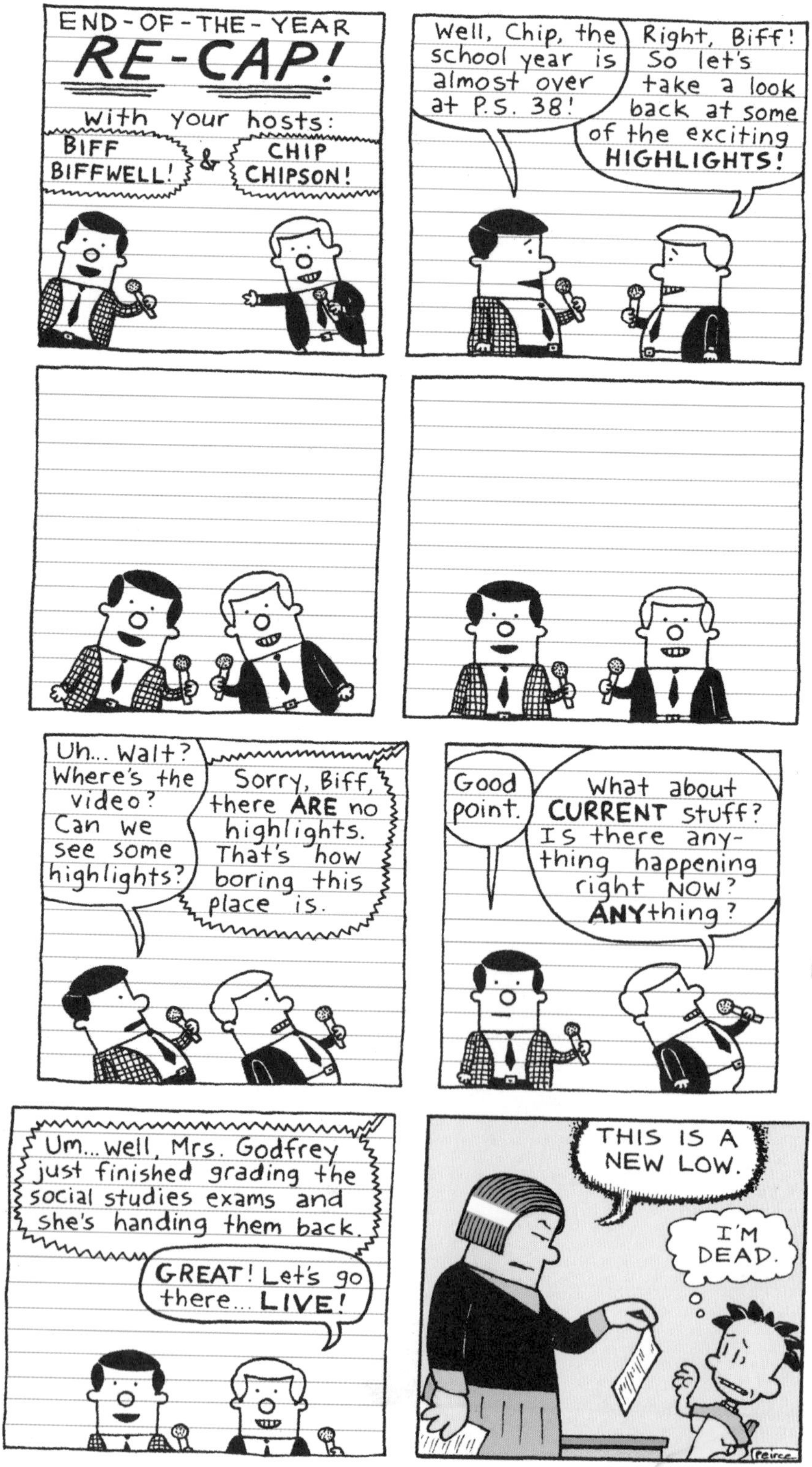

END-OF-THE-YEAR
RE-CAP!
with your hosts:
BIFF BIFFWELL!
&
CHIP CHIPSON!
Well, Chip, the school year is almost over at P.S. 38!
Right, Biff! So let's take a look back at some of the exciting HIGHLIGHTS!
Uh... Walt? Where's the video? Can we see some highlights?
Sorry, Biff, there ARE no highlights. That's how boring this place is.
Good point.
What about CURRENT stuff? Is there anything happening right NOW? ANYthing?
Um... well, Mrs. Godfrey just finished grading the social studies exams and she's handing them back.
GREAT! Let's go there... LIVE!
THIS IS A NEW LOW.
I'M DEAD.
Peirce

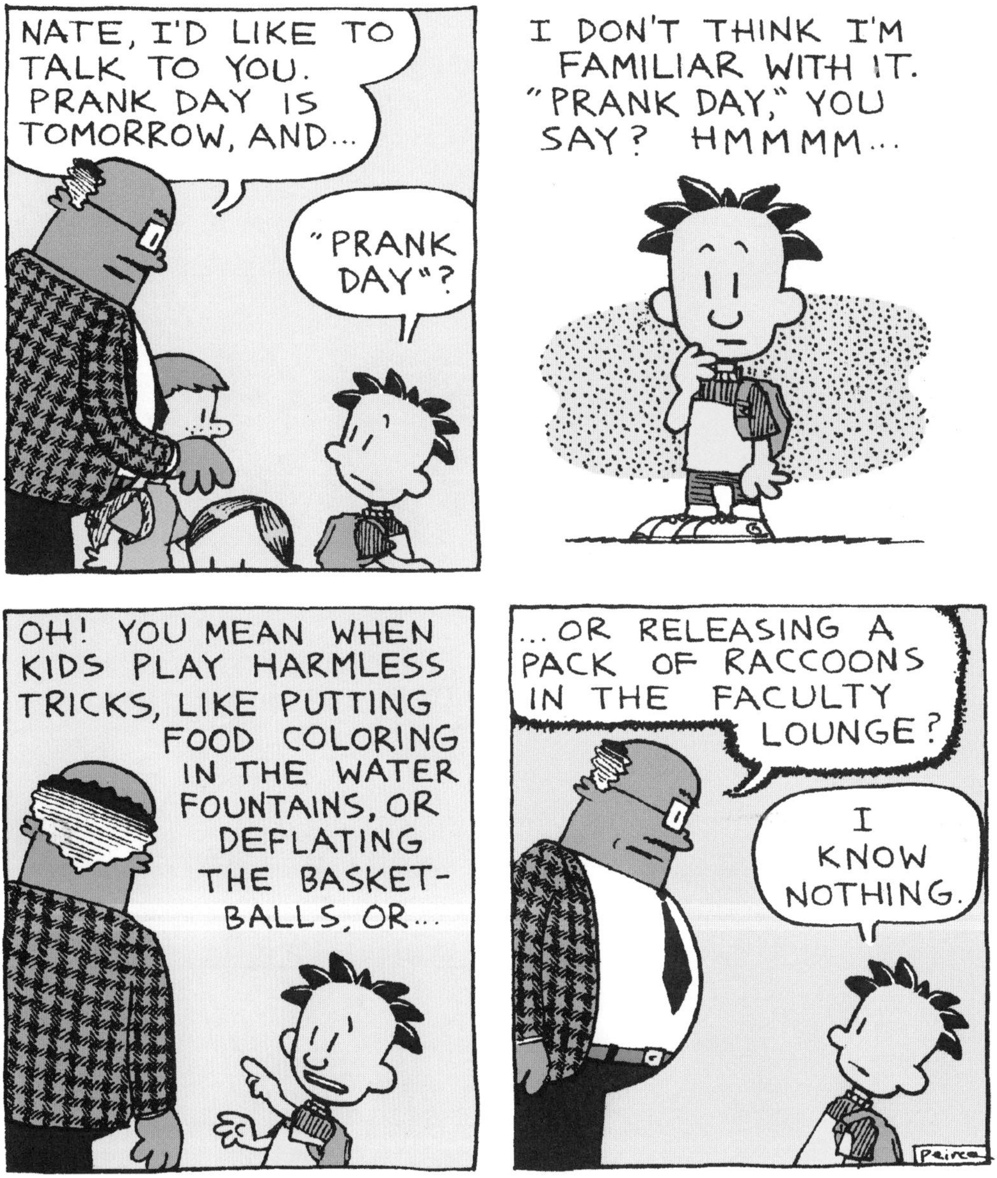
NATE, I'D LIKE TO TALK TO YOU. PRANK DAY IS TOMORROW, AND...
"PRANK DAY"?
I DON'T THINK I'M FAMILIAR WITH IT. "PRANK DAY," YOU SAY? HMMMM...
OH! YOU MEAN WHEN KIDS PLAY HARMLESS TRICKS, LIKE PUTTING FOOD COLORING IN THE WATER FOUNTAINS, OR DEFLATING THE BASKET-BALLS, OR...
...OR RELEASING A PACK OF RACCOONS IN THE FACULTY LOUNGE?
I KNOW NOTHING.
Peirce

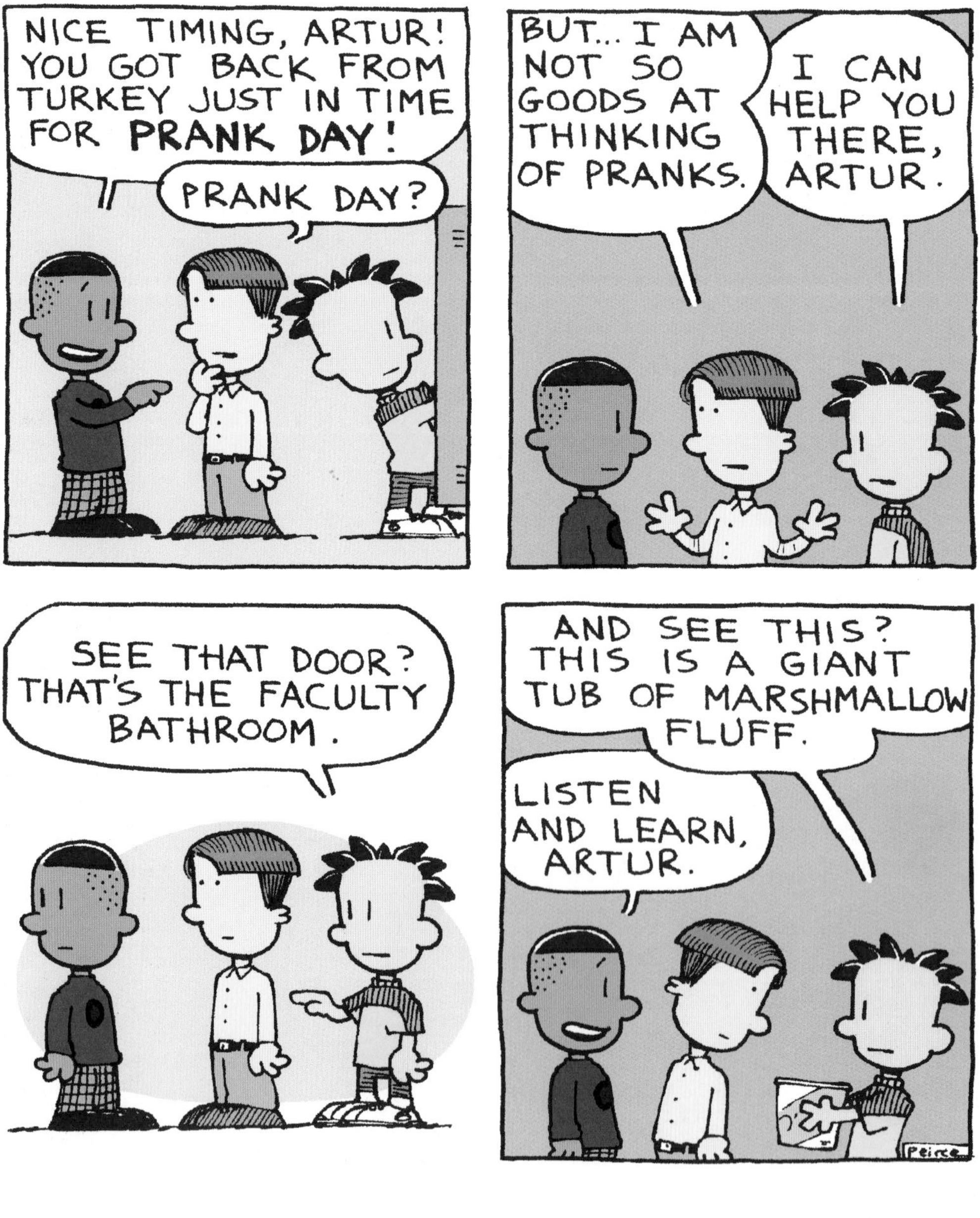

NICE TIMING, ARTUR! YOU GOT BACK FROM TURKEY JUST IN TIME FOR PRANK DAY!
PRANK DAY?
BUT... I AM NOT SO GOODS AT THINKING OF PRANKS.
I CAN HELP YOU THERE, ARTUR.
SEE THAT DOOR? THAT'S THE FACULTY BATHROOM.
AND SEE THIS? THIS IS A GIANT TUB OF MARSHMALLOW FLUFF.
LISTEN AND LEARN, ARTUR.
Peirce

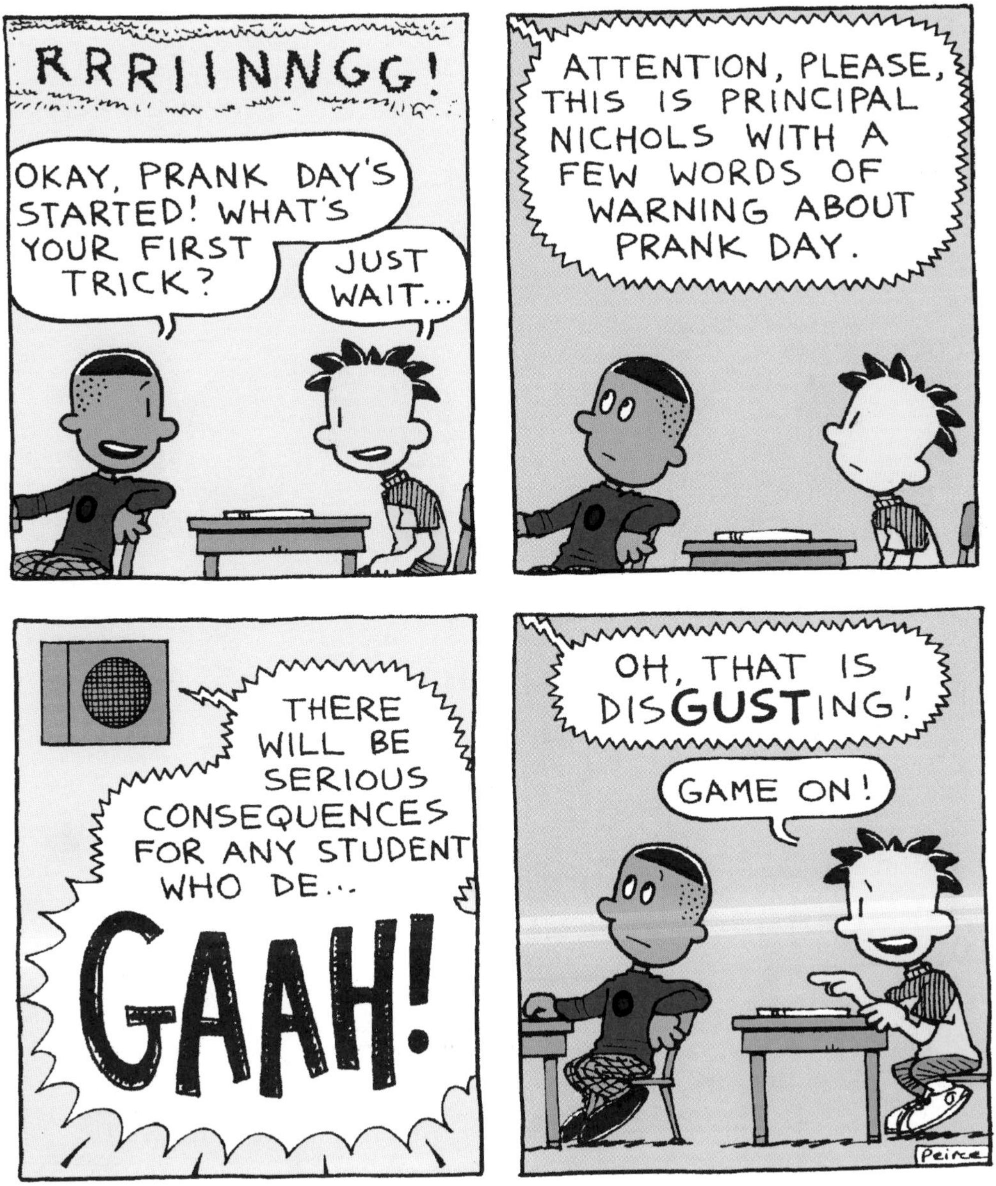
RRRIINNGG!
OKAY, PRANK DAY'S STARTED! WHAT'S YOUR FIRST TRICK?
JUST WAIT...
ATTENTION, PLEASE, THIS IS PRINCIPAL NICHOLS WITH A FEW WORDS OF WARNING ABOUT PRANK DAY.
THERE WILL BE SERIOUS CONSEQUENCES FOR ANY STUDENT WHO DE...
GAAH!
OH, THAT IS DIS**GUST**ING!
GAME ON!
Peirce

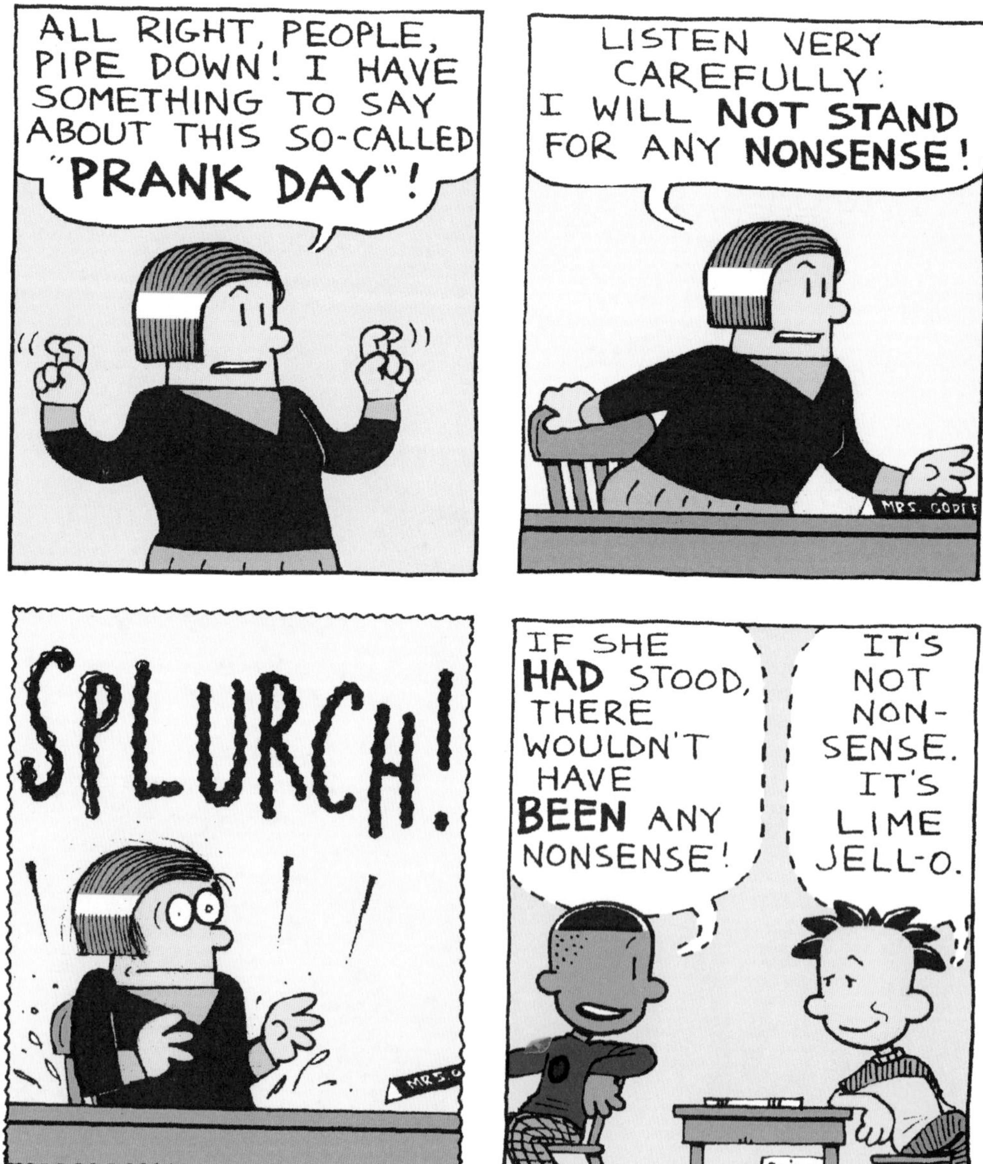
ALL RIGHT, PEOPLE, PIPE DOWN! I HAVE SOMETHING TO SAY ABOUT THIS SO-CALLED "PRANK DAY"!
LISTEN VERY CAREFULLY: I WILL NOT STAND FOR ANY NONSENSE!
MRS. GODFE
SPLURCH!
MRS. G
IF SHE HAD STOOD, THERE WOULDN'T HAVE BEEN ANY NONSENSE!
IT'S NOT NON-SENSE. IT'S LIME JELL-O.
Peirce

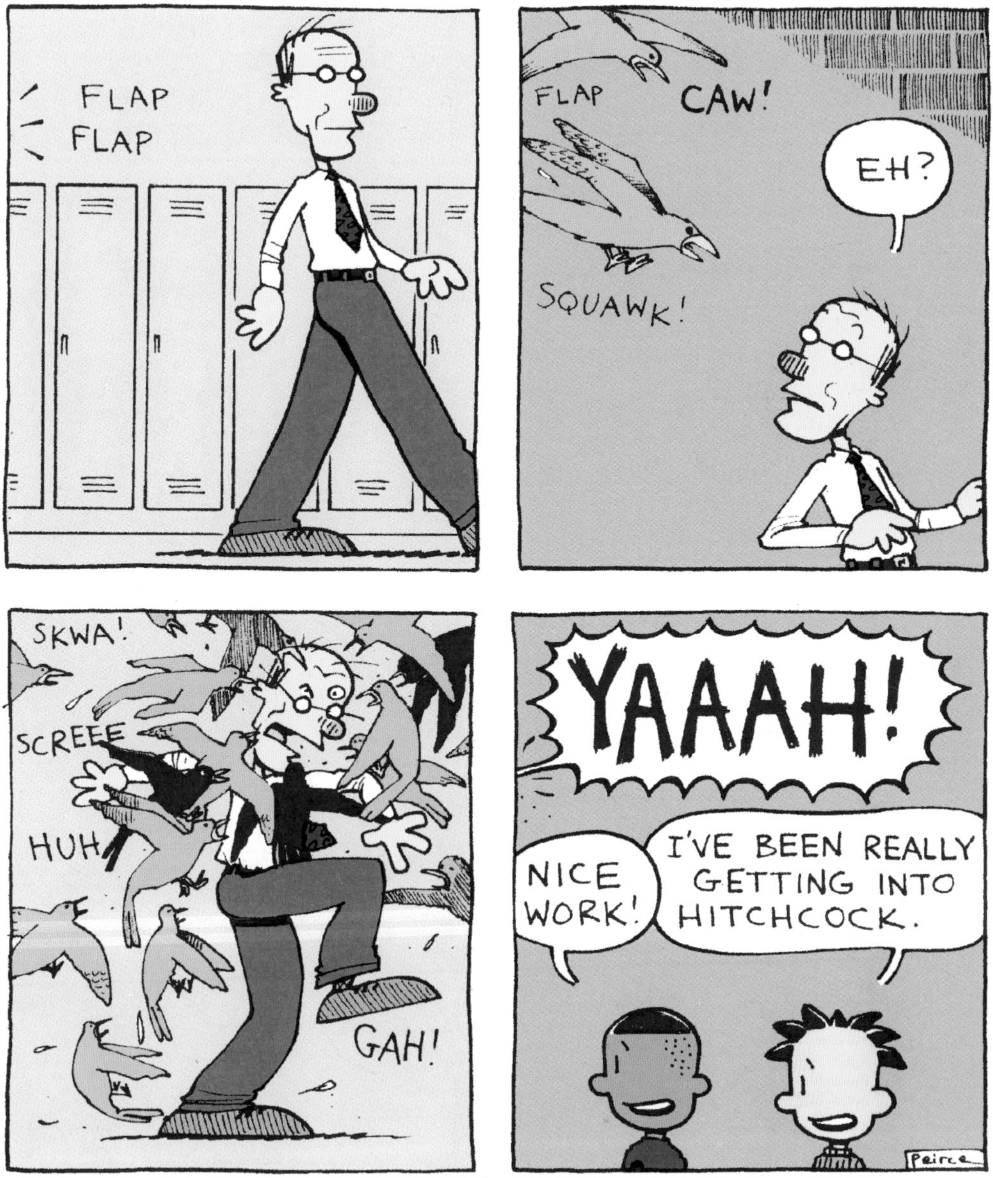
FLAP
FLAP
FLAP
CAW!
SQUAWK!
EH?
SKWA!
SCREEE
HUH
GAH!
YAAAH!
NICE WORK!
I'VE BEEN REALLY GETTING INTO HITCHCOCK.
Peirce

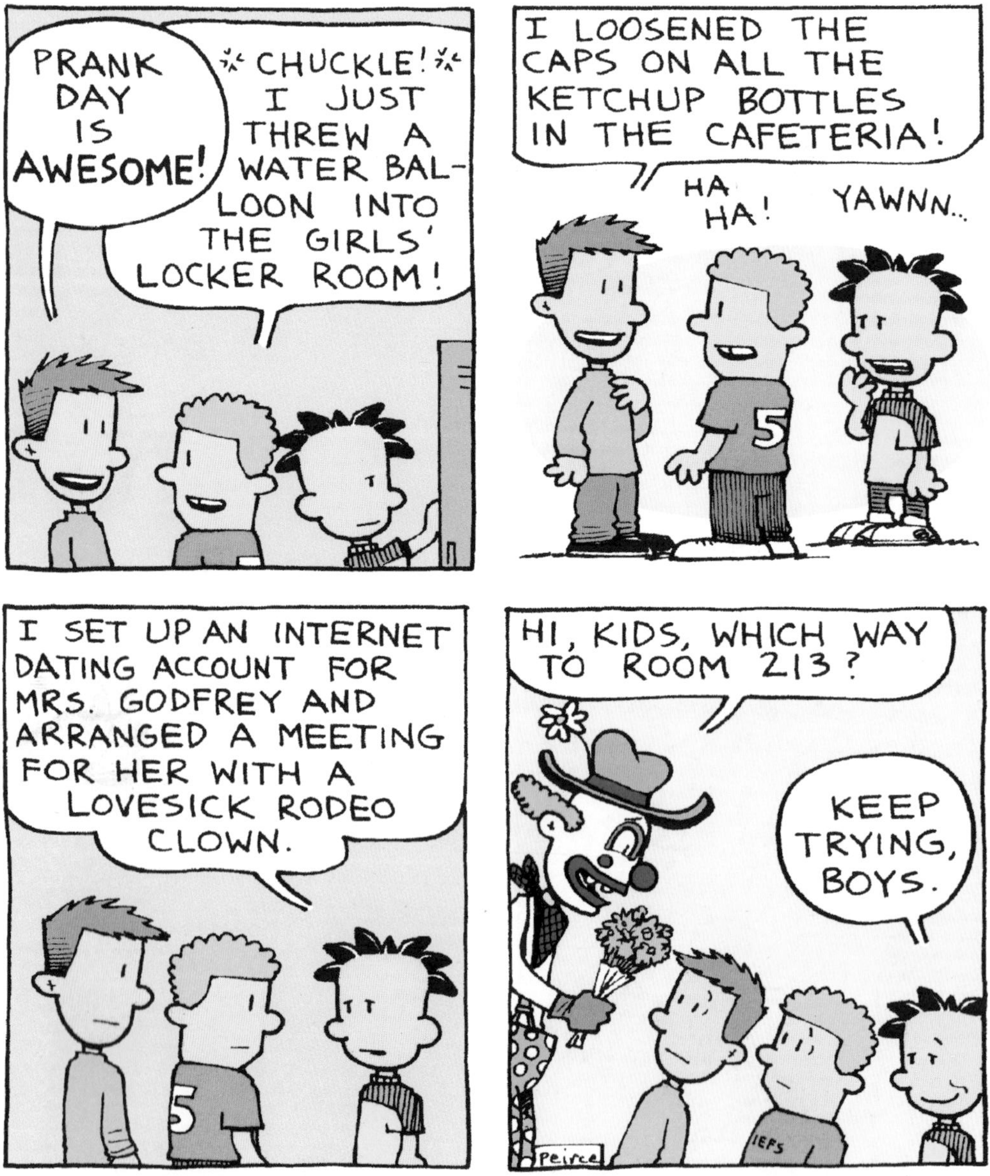
PRANK DAY IS AWESOME!
CHUCKLE! I JUST THREW A WATER BAL-LOON INTO THE GIRLS' LOCKER ROOM!
I LOOSENED THE CAPS ON ALL THE KETCHUP BOTTLES IN THE CAFETERIA!
HA HA!
YAWNN...
I SET UP AN INTERNET DATING ACCOUNT FOR MRS. GODFREY AND ARRANGED A MEETING FOR HER WITH A LOVESICK RODEO CLOWN.
HI, KIDS, WHICH WAY TO ROOM 213?
KEEP TRYING, BOYS.
Peirce

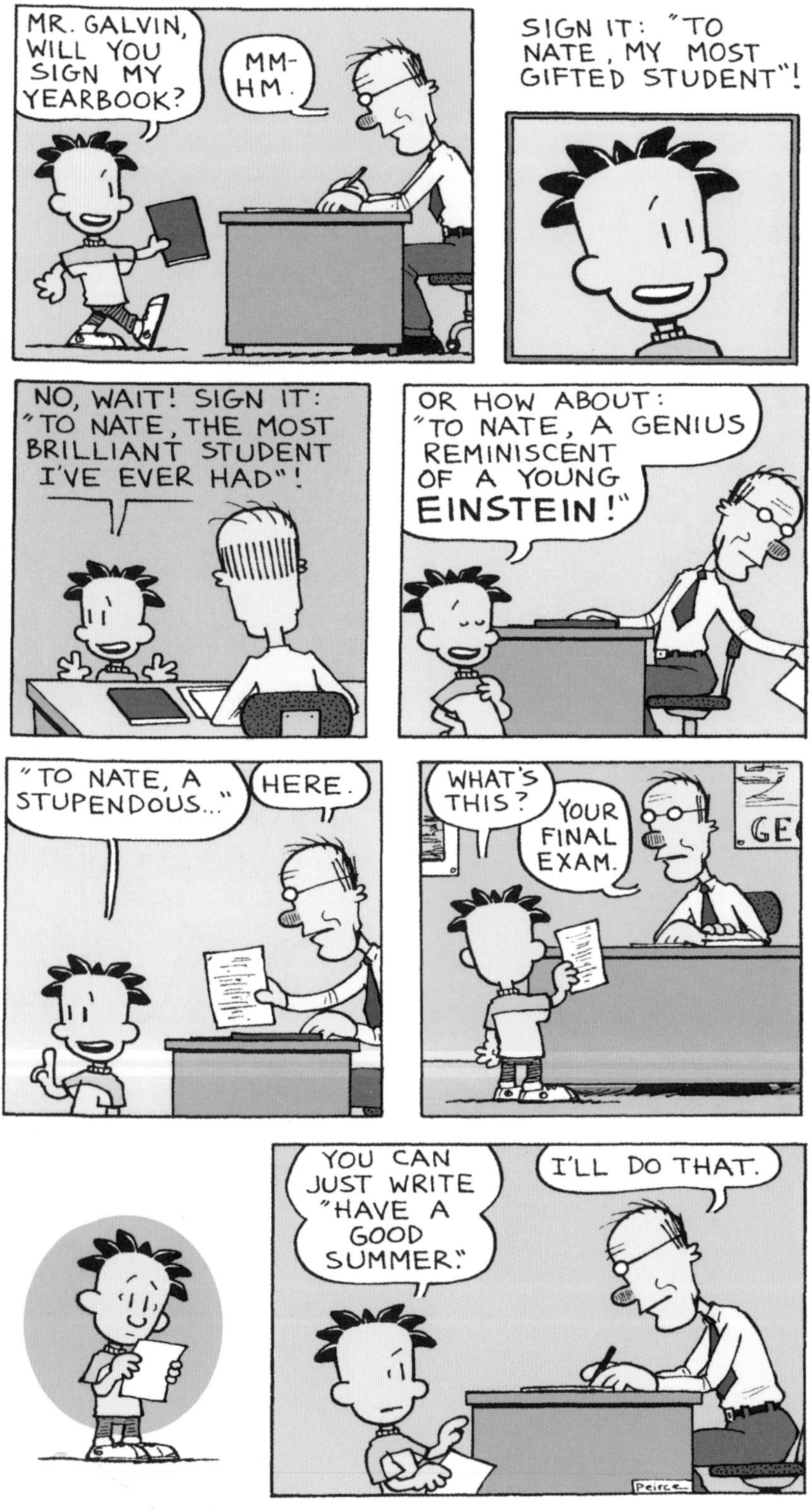
MR. GALVIN, WILL YOU SIGN MY YEARBOOK?
MM-HM.
SIGN IT: "TO NATE, MY MOST GIFTED STUDENT"!
NO, WAIT! SIGN IT: "TO NATE, THE MOST BRILLIANT STUDENT I'VE EVER HAD"!
OR HOW ABOUT: "TO NATE, A GENIUS REMINISCENT OF A YOUNG EINSTEIN!"
"TO NATE, A STUPENDOUS..."
HERE.
WHAT'S THIS?
YOUR FINAL EXAM.
YOU CAN JUST WRITE "HAVE A GOOD SUMMER."
I'LL DO THAT.
Peirce

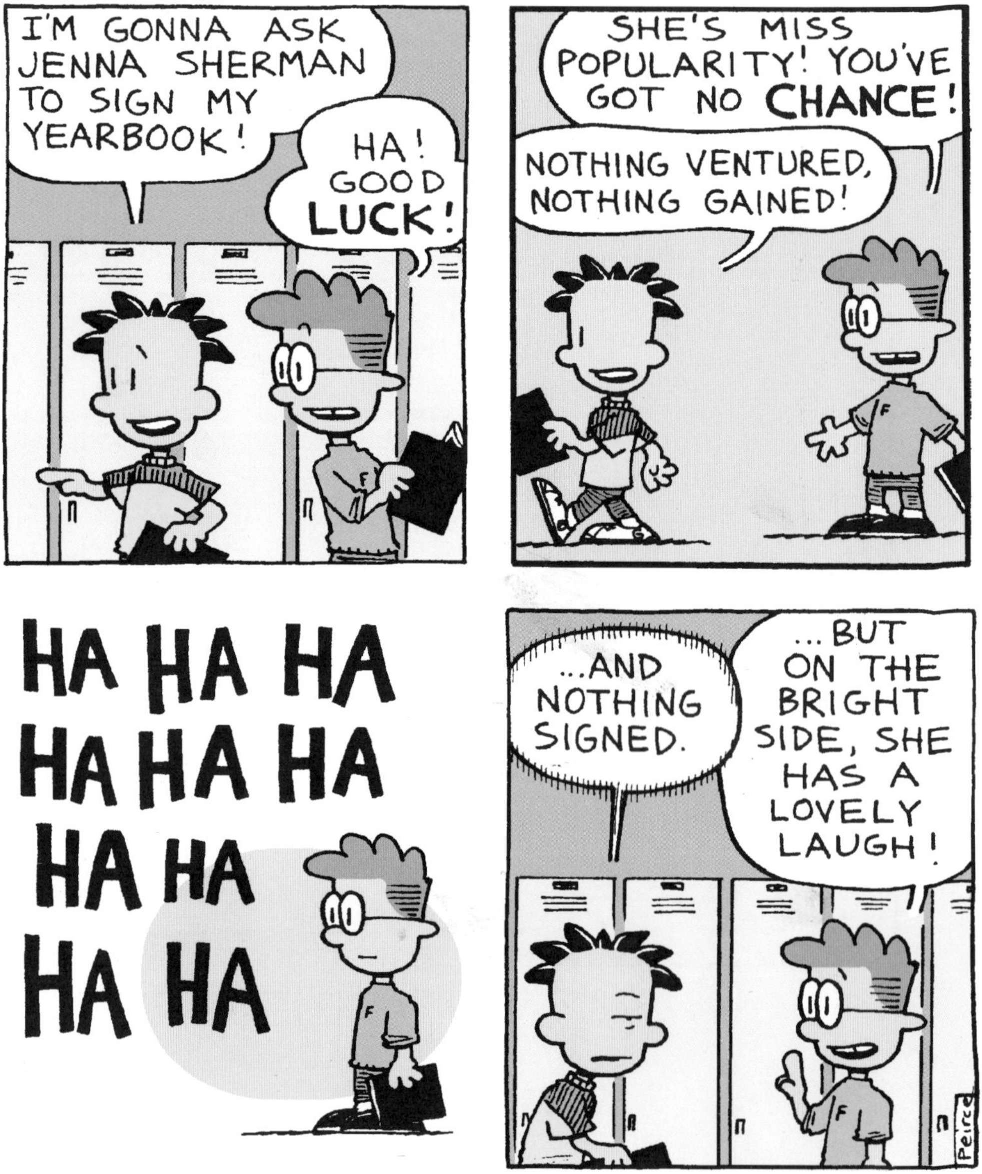
I'M GONNA ASK JENNA SHERMAN TO SIGN MY YEARBOOK!
HA! GOOD LUCK!
SHE'S MISS POPULARITY! YOU'VE GOT NO CHANCE!
NOTHING VENTURED, NOTHING GAINED!
HA HA HA HA HA HA HA HA HA HA HA HA
...AND NOTHING SIGNED.
...BUT ON THE BRIGHT SIDE, SHE HAS A LOVELY LAUGH!
Peirce

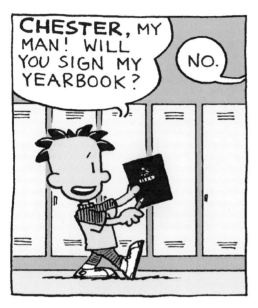

CHESTER, MY MAN! WILL YOU SIGN MY YEARBOOK?

NO.

I HATE SIGNING YEARBOOKS, AND I HATE YOU. SO HERE'S WHAT I'LL DO INSTEAD:

I'LL WRITE MY NAME ON YOUR FACE WITH A "SHARPIE." AND IF YOU HOLD STILL WHILE I'M DOING IT, I WON'T PUNCH YOU.

UNDER THE CIRCUMSTANCES, I FEEL LUCKY HE DIDN'T WRITE IT USING MY OWN BLOOD.

Peirce

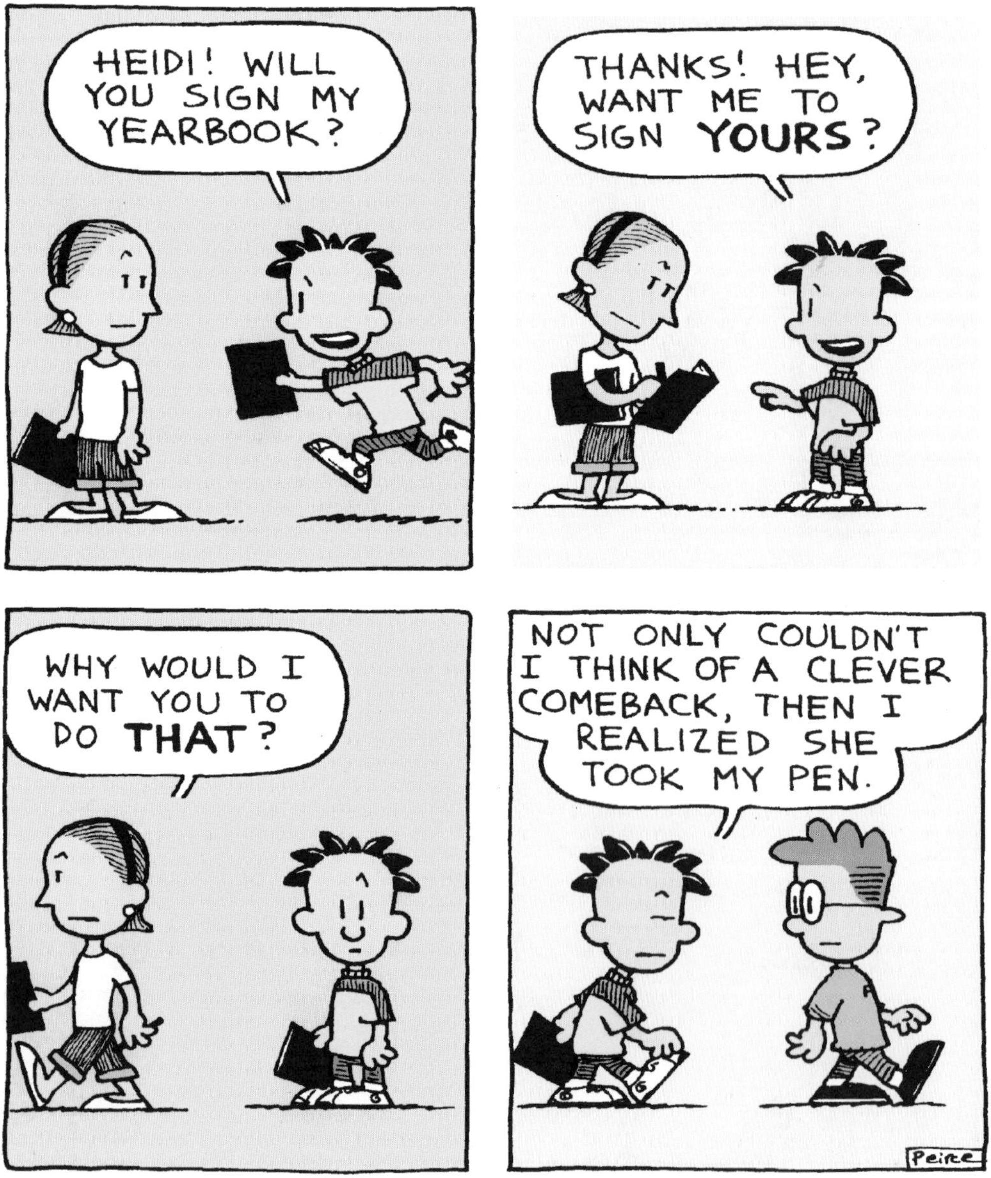
HEIDI! WILL YOU SIGN MY YEARBOOK?
THANKS! HEY, WANT ME TO SIGN YOURS?
WHY WOULD I WANT YOU TO DO THAT?
NOT ONLY COULDN'T I THINK OF A CLEVER COMEBACK, THEN I REALIZED SHE TOOK MY PEN.
Peirce

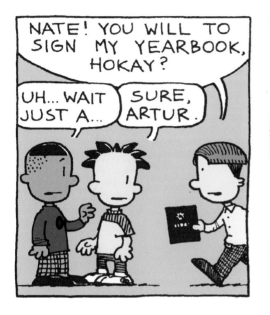

NATE! YOU WILL TO SIGN MY YEARBOOK, HOKAY?

UH... WAIT JUST A...

SURE, ARTUR.

Artur,
  You're a good kid. Have a great summer. I'm sure you've already got a lot of plans to hang out with Jenny, assuming you guys don't break up over the summer. Ha Ha, just kidding.

All I'm saying is, you never know what can happen. You could be an awesome couple one day, and the next day it's Dump City. Don't be surprised if Jenny decides to move i   a different directi   ember, A 've k   onger an you   and s knows   ecause th you ne   ll. That' I I'm tr   to say, if

I TRIED TO WARN YOU, ARTUR.

I'M GOING TO NEED SOME MORE PAPER.

115

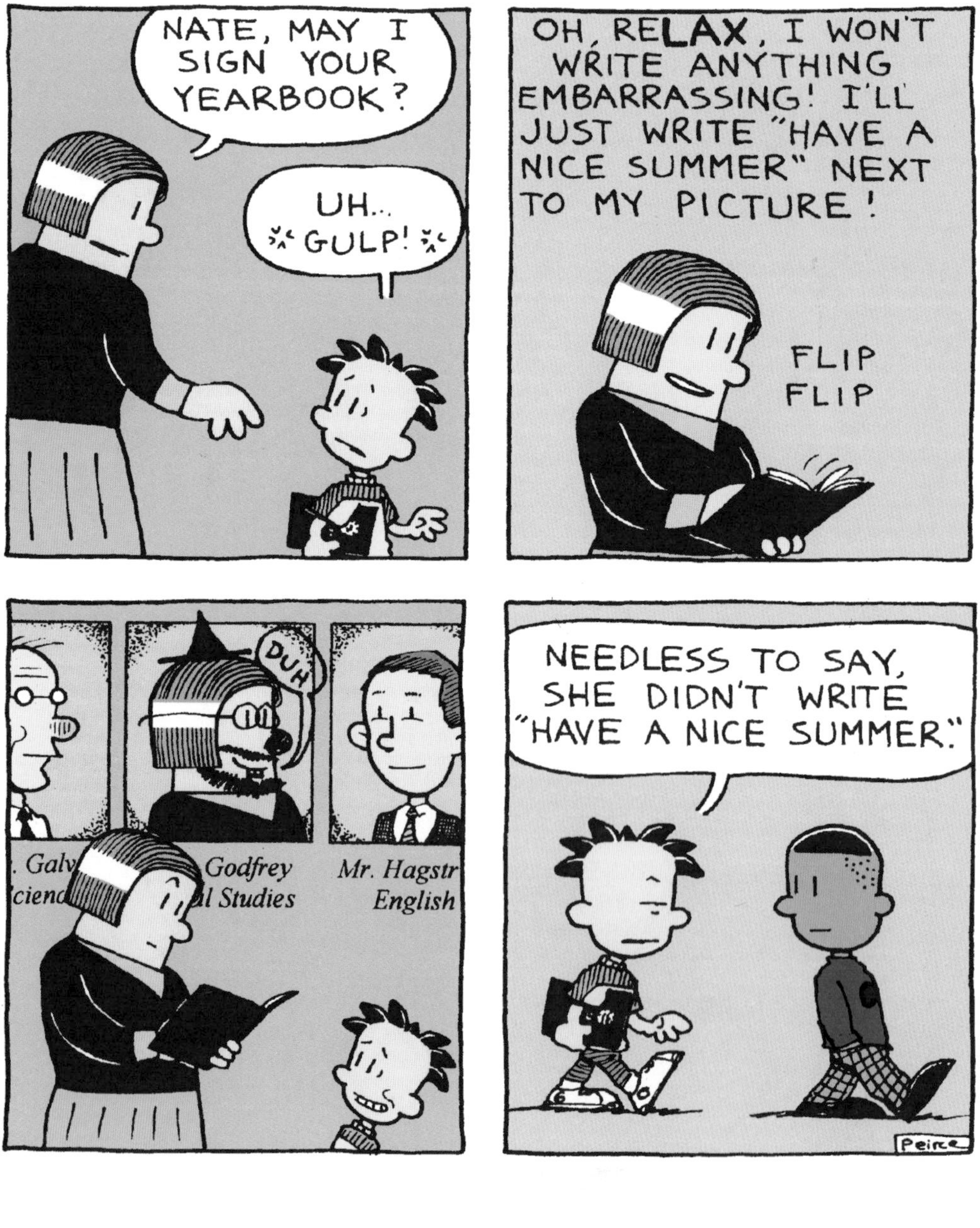
NATE, MAY I SIGN YOUR YEARBOOK?
UH... GULP!
OH, RELAX, I WON'T WRITE ANYTHING EMBARRASSING! I'LL JUST WRITE "HAVE A NICE SUMMER" NEXT TO MY PICTURE!
FLIP FLIP
DUH
Godfrey
Mr. Hagstr
English
NEEDLESS TO SAY, SHE DIDN'T WRITE "HAVE A NICE SUMMER."
Peirce

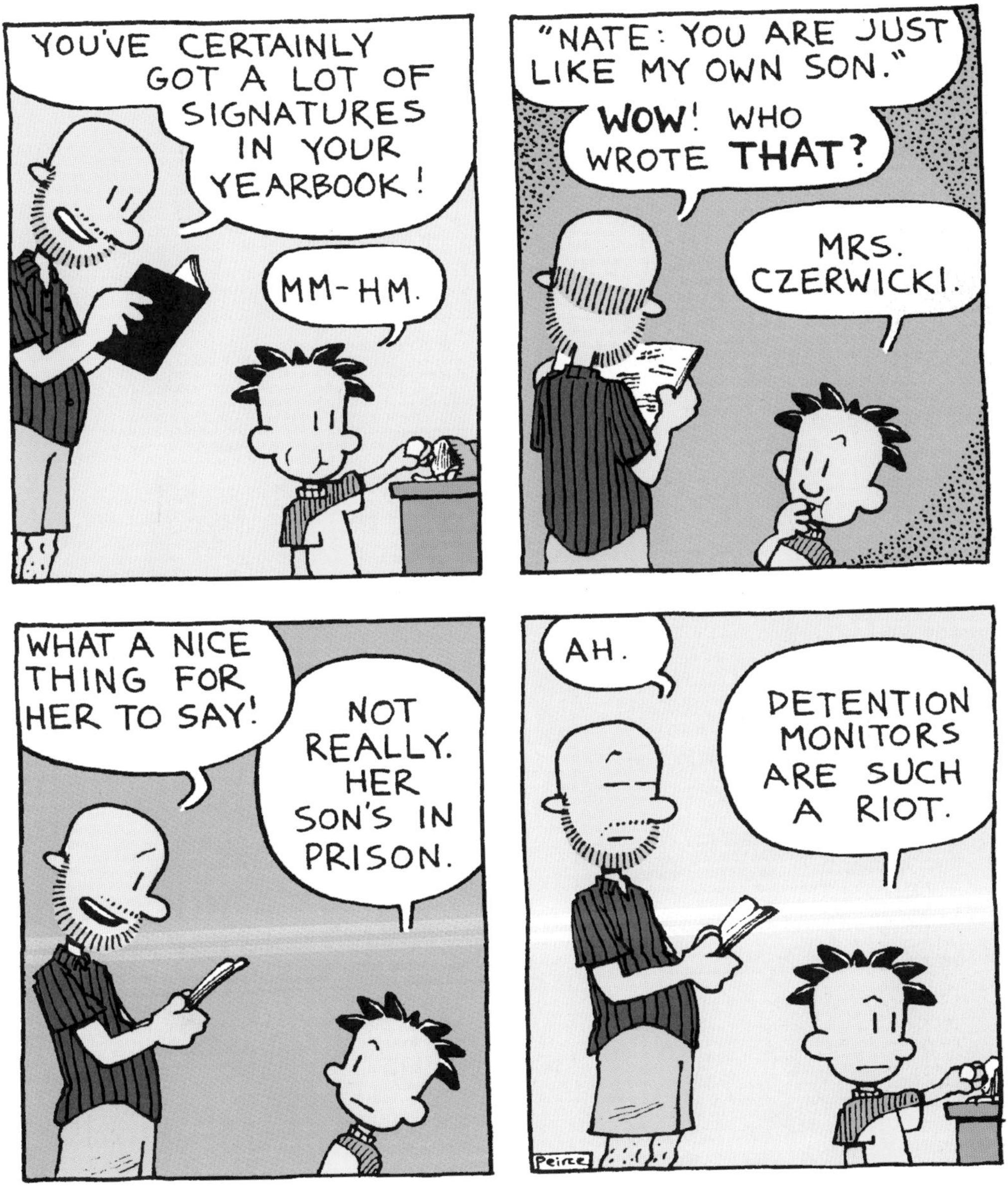
YOU'VE CERTAINLY GOT A LOT OF SIGNATURES IN YOUR YEARBOOK!
MM-HM.
"NATE: YOU ARE JUST LIKE MY OWN SON."
WOW! WHO WROTE **THAT?**
MRS. CZERWICKI.
WHAT A NICE THING FOR HER TO SAY!
NOT REALLY. HER SON'S IN PRISON.
AH.
DETENTION MONITORS ARE SUCH A RIOT.
Peirce

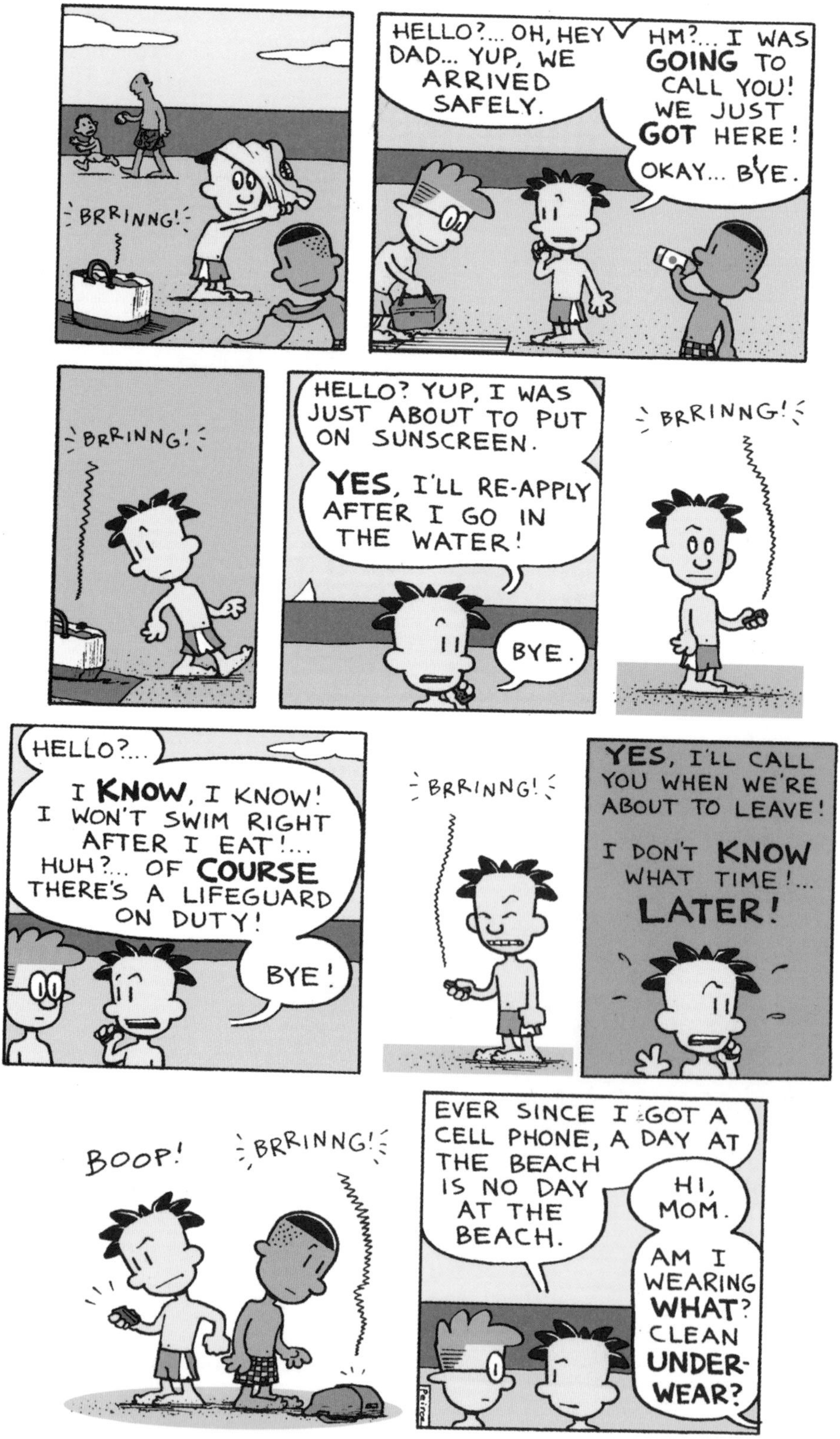
BRRINNG!
HELLO?... OH, HEY DAD... YUP, WE ARRIVED SAFELY.
HM?... I WAS GOING TO CALL YOU! WE JUST GOT HERE!
OKAY... BYE.
BRRINNG!
HELLO? YUP, I WAS JUST ABOUT TO PUT ON SUNSCREEN.
YES, I'LL RE-APPLY AFTER I GO IN THE WATER!
BYE.
BRRINNG!
HELLO?...
I KNOW, I KNOW! I WON'T SWIM RIGHT AFTER I EAT!... HUH?... OF COURSE THERE'S A LIFEGUARD ON DUTY!
BYE!
BRRINNG!
YES, I'LL CALL YOU WHEN WE'RE ABOUT TO LEAVE!
I DON'T KNOW WHAT TIME!... LATER!
BOOP!
BRRINNG!
EVER SINCE I GOT A CELL PHONE, A DAY AT THE BEACH IS NO DAY AT THE BEACH.
HI, MOM.
AM I WEARING WHAT? CLEAN UNDER-WEAR?
Peirce

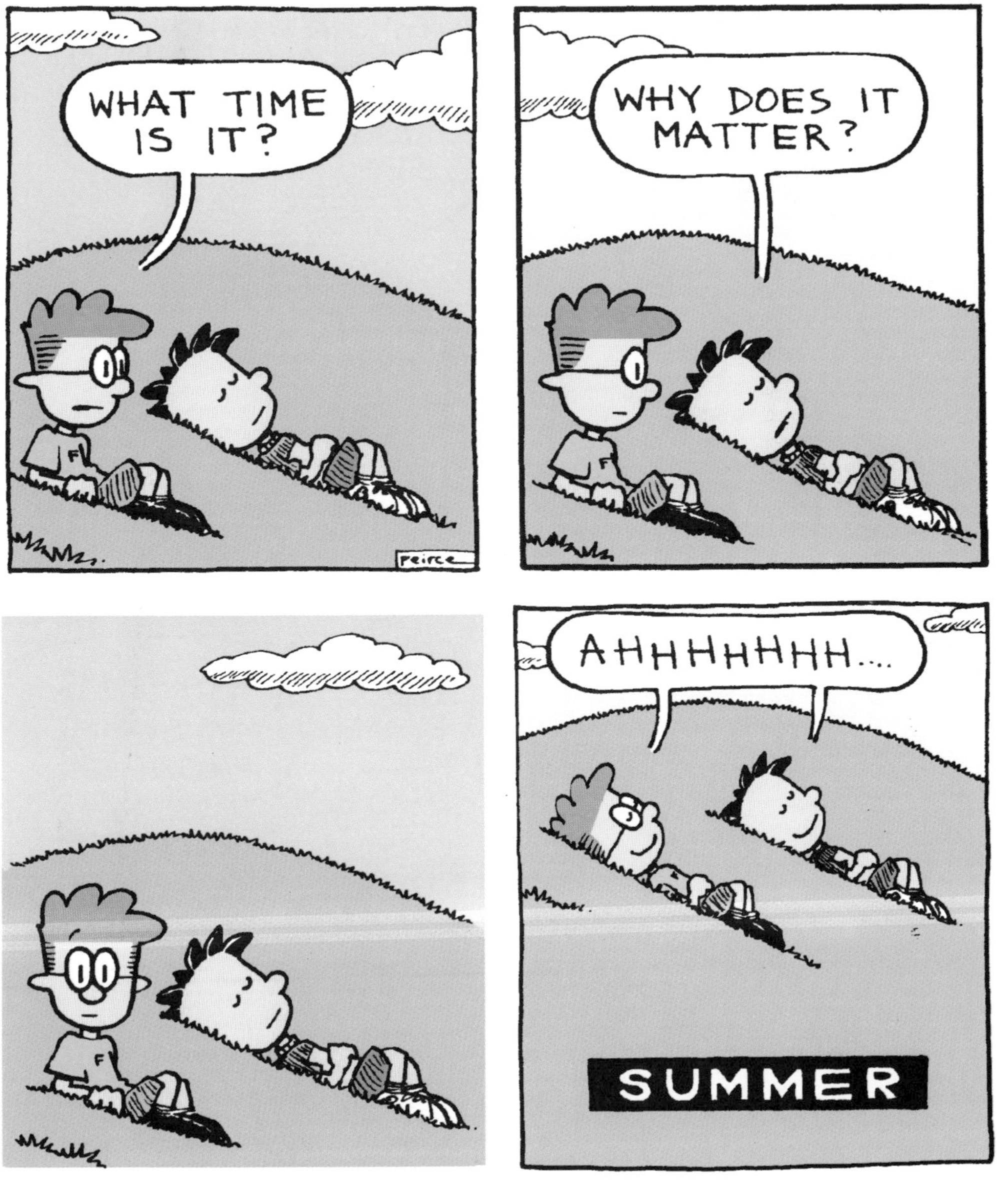
WHAT TIME IS IT?
WHY DOES IT MATTER?
AHHHHHHH....
SUMMER
peirce

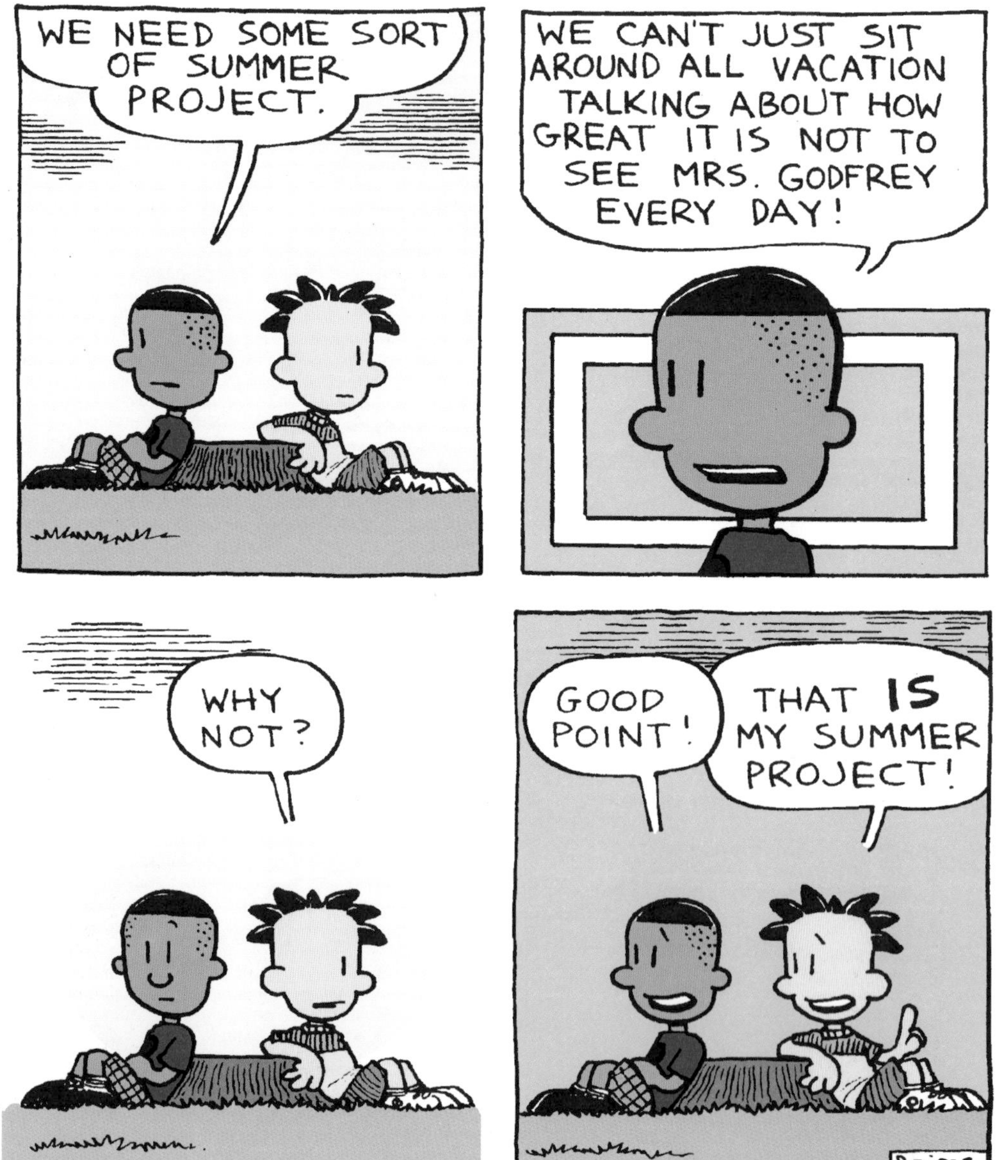
WE NEED SOME SORT OF SUMMER PROJECT.
WE CAN'T JUST SIT AROUND ALL VACATION TALKING ABOUT HOW GREAT IT IS NOT TO SEE MRS. GODFREY EVERY DAY!
WHY NOT?
GOOD POINT!
THAT **IS** MY SUMMER PROJECT!
Peirce

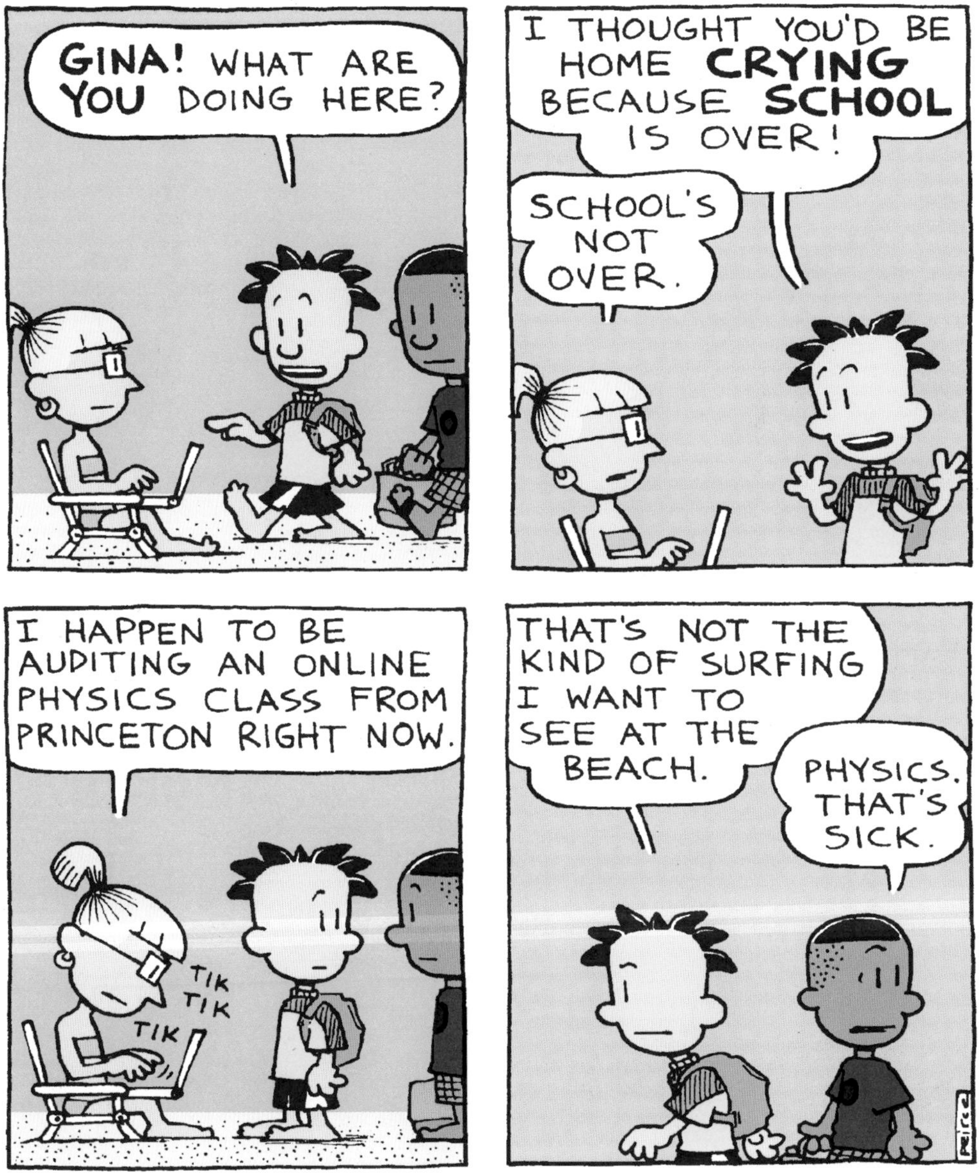
GINA! WHAT ARE YOU DOING HERE?
I THOUGHT YOU'D BE HOME CRYING BECAUSE SCHOOL IS OVER!
SCHOOL'S NOT OVER.
I HAPPEN TO BE AUDITING AN ONLINE PHYSICS CLASS FROM PRINCETON RIGHT NOW.
TIK TIK TIK
THAT'S NOT THE KIND OF SURFING I WANT TO SEE AT THE BEACH.
PHYSICS. THAT'S SICK.
PEIRCE

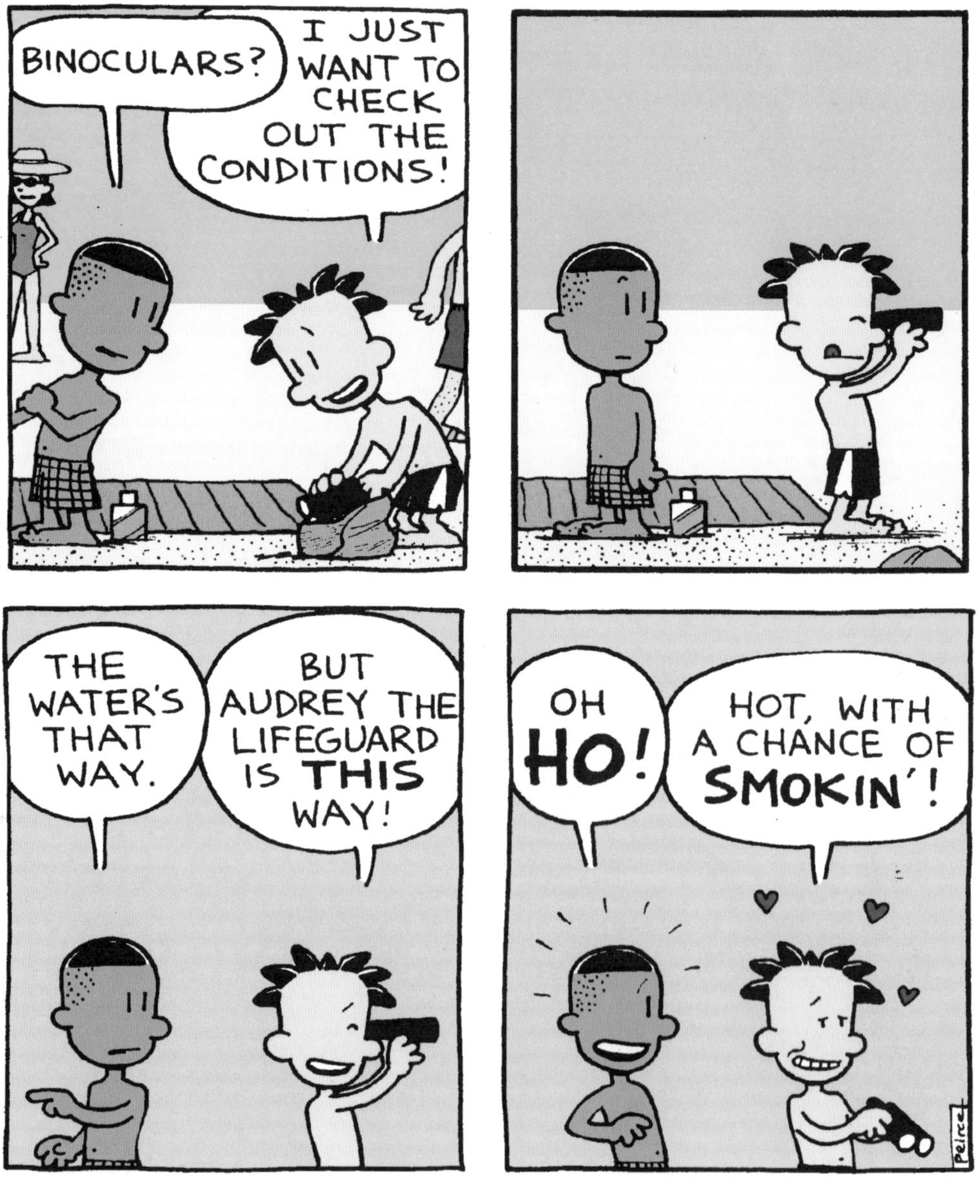
BINOCULARS?
I JUST WANT TO CHECK OUT THE CONDITIONS!
THE WATER'S THAT WAY.
BUT AUDREY THE LIFEGUARD IS THIS WAY!
OH HO!
HOT, WITH A CHANCE OF SMOKIN'!
Peirce

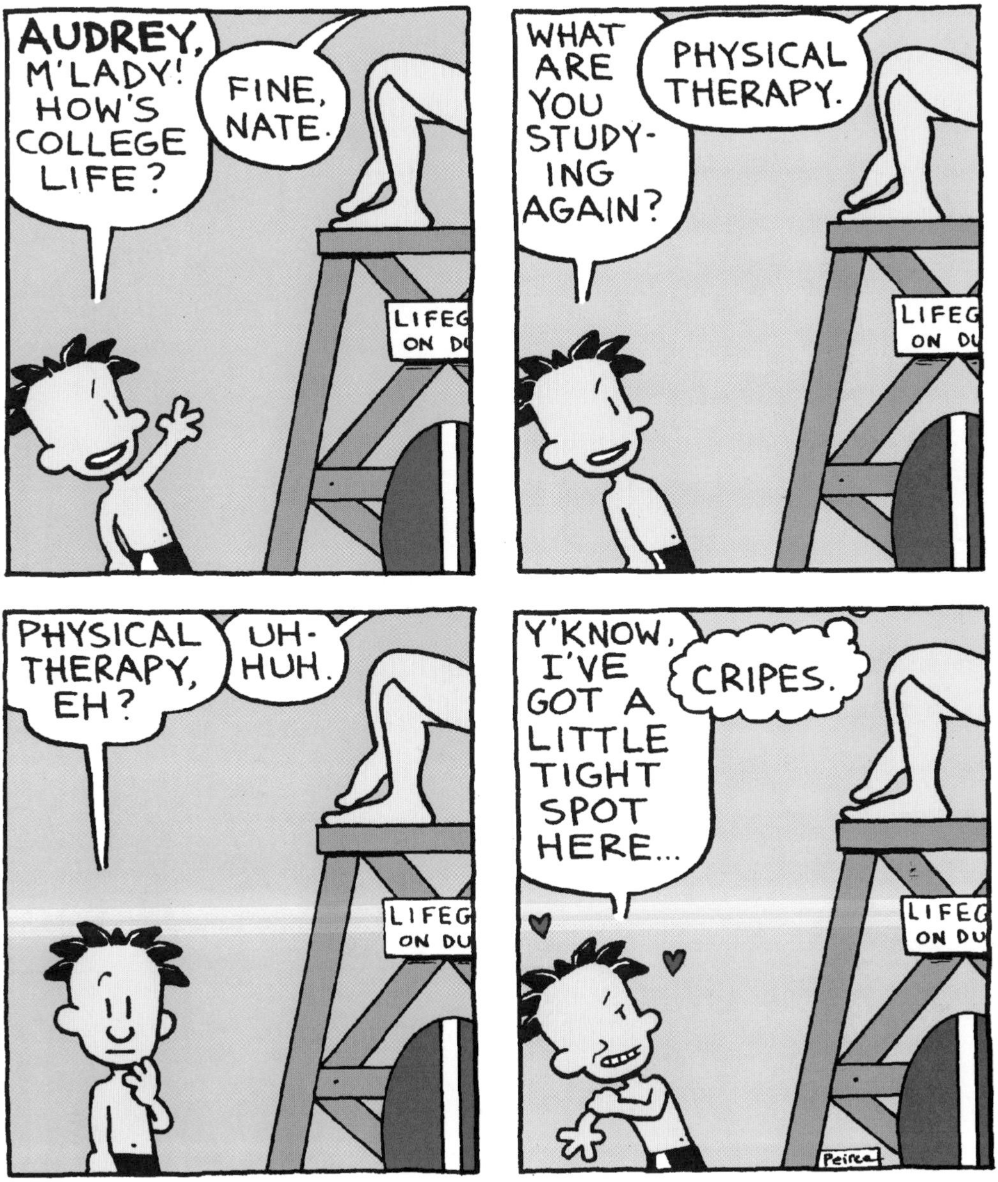
AUDREY, M'LADY! HOW'S COLLEGE LIFE?
FINE, NATE.
LIFEG ON DU
WHAT ARE YOU STUDYING AGAIN?
PHYSICAL THERAPY.
LIFEG ON DU
PHYSICAL THERAPY, EH?
UH-HUH.
LIFEG ON DU
Y'KNOW, I'VE GOT A LITTLE TIGHT SPOT HERE...
CRIPES.
LIFEG ON DU
Peirce

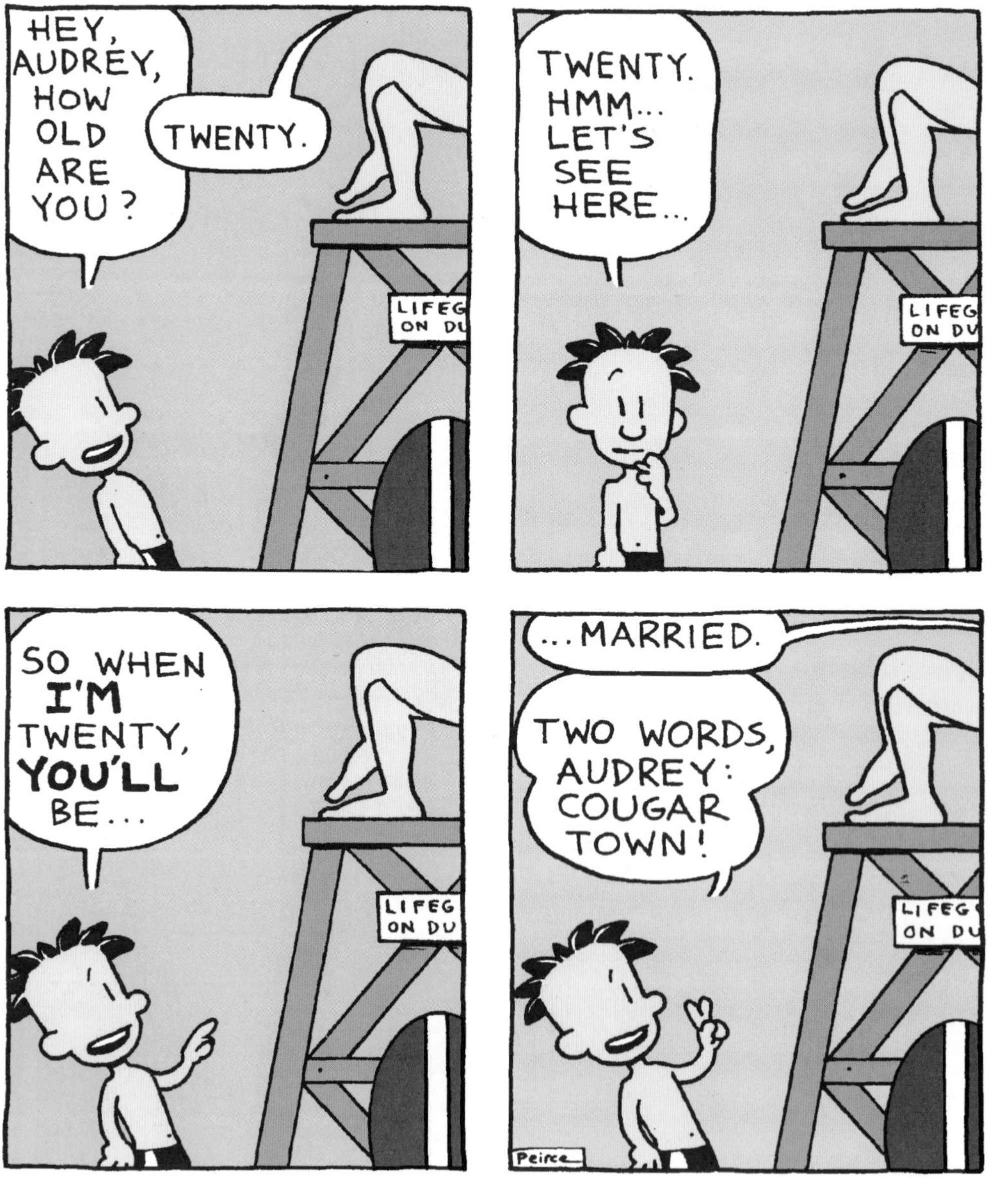
HEY, AUDREY, HOW OLD ARE YOU?
TWENTY.
TWENTY. HMM... LET'S SEE HERE...
SO WHEN **I'M** TWENTY, **YOU'LL** BE...
...MARRIED.
TWO WORDS, AUDREY: COUGAR TOWN!
LIFEG
ON DU
Peirce

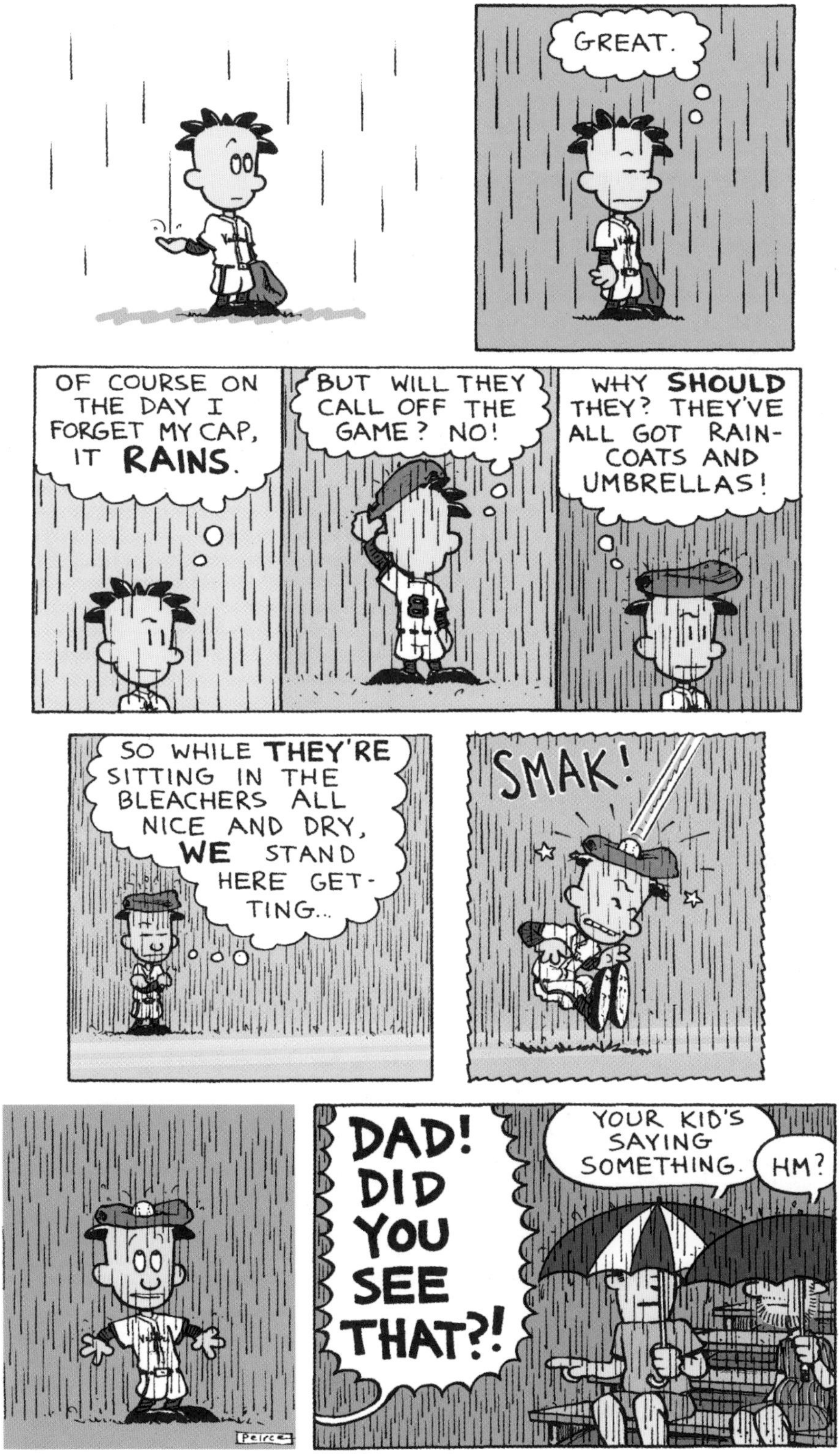
GREAT.
OF COURSE ON THE DAY I FORGET MY CAP, IT **RAINS**.
BUT WILL THEY CALL OFF THE GAME? NO!
WHY **SHOULD** THEY? THEY'VE ALL GOT RAIN-COATS AND UMBRELLAS!
SO WHILE **THEY'RE** SITTING IN THE BLEACHERS ALL NICE AND DRY, **WE** STAND HERE GET-TING...
SMAK!
DAD! DID YOU SEE THAT?!
YOUR KID'S SAYING SOMETHING.
HM?
Peirce

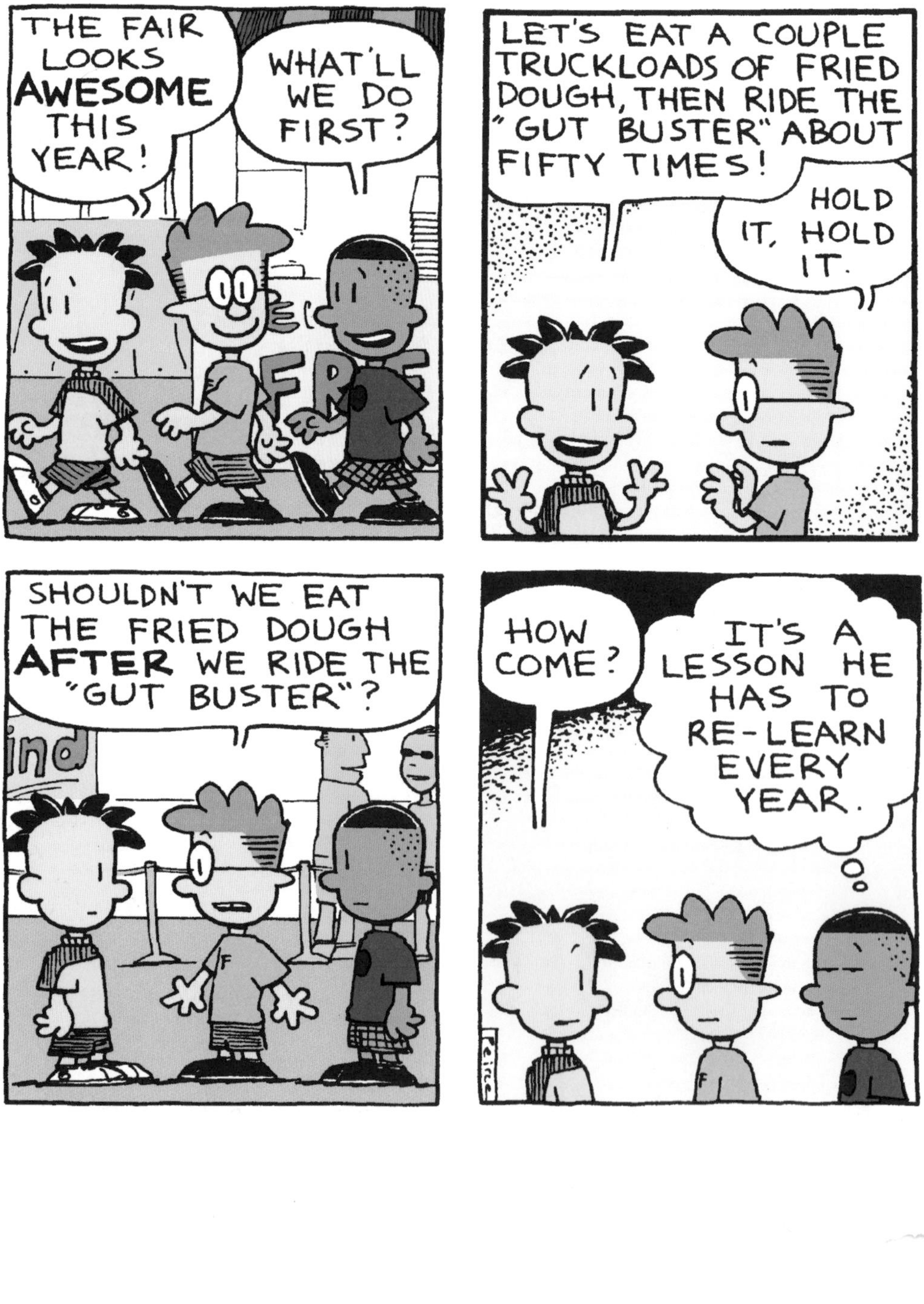
THE FAIR LOOKS AWESOME THIS YEAR!
WHAT'LL WE DO FIRST?
LET'S EAT A COUPLE TRUCKLOADS OF FRIED DOUGH, THEN RIDE THE "GUT BUSTER" ABOUT FIFTY TIMES!
HOLD IT, HOLD IT.
SHOULDN'T WE EAT THE FRIED DOUGH AFTER WE RIDE THE "GUT BUSTER"?
HOW COME?
IT'S A LESSON HE HAS TO RE-LEARN EVERY YEAR.

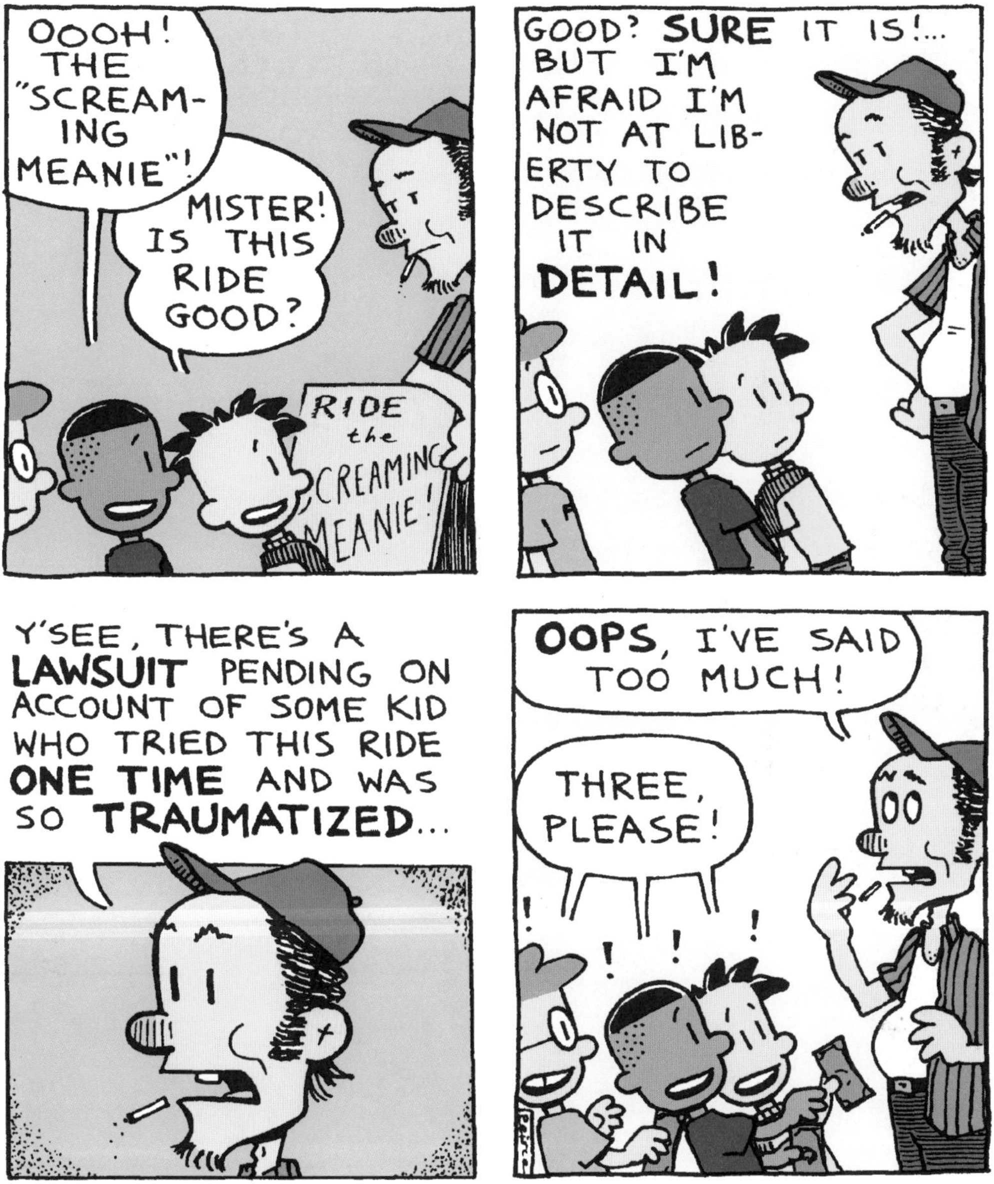

OOOH! THE "SCREAMING MEANIE"!
MISTER! IS THIS RIDE GOOD?
RIDE the SCREAMING MEANIE!
GOOD? SURE IT IS!... BUT I'M AFRAID I'M NOT AT LIBERTY TO DESCRIBE IT IN DETAIL!
Y'SEE, THERE'S A LAWSUIT PENDING ON ACCOUNT OF SOME KID WHO TRIED THIS RIDE ONE TIME AND WAS SO TRAUMATIZED...
OOPS, I'VE SAID TOO MUCH!
THREE, PLEASE!
! ! ! !

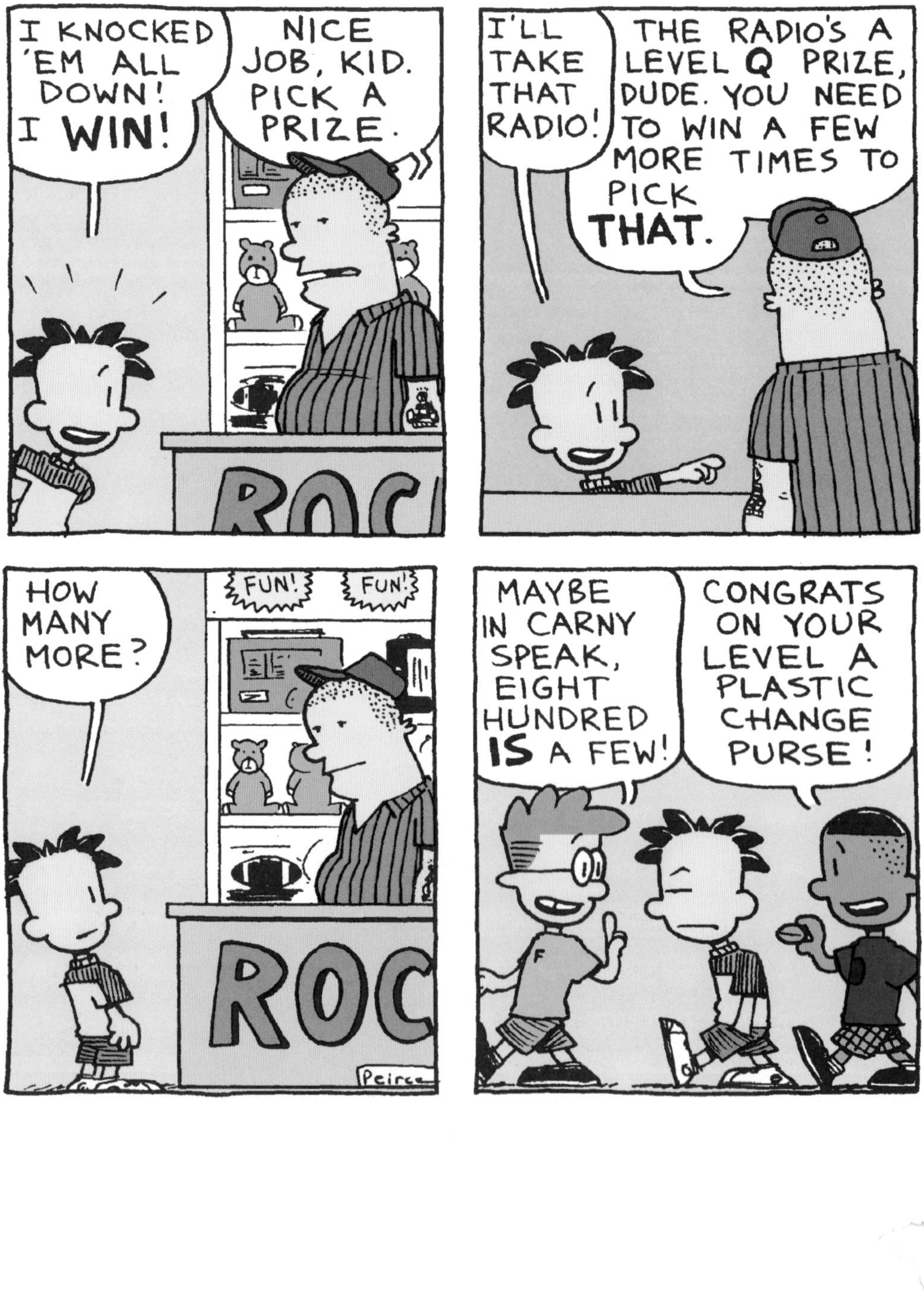
I KNOCKED 'EM ALL DOWN! I WIN!
NICE JOB, KID. PICK A PRIZE.
I'LL TAKE THAT RADIO!
THE RADIO'S A LEVEL Q PRIZE, DUDE. YOU NEED TO WIN A FEW MORE TIMES TO PICK THAT.
FUN!
FUN!
HOW MANY MORE?
MAYBE IN CARNY SPEAK, EIGHT HUNDRED IS A FEW!
CONGRATS ON YOUR LEVEL A PLASTIC CHANGE PURSE!
Peirce

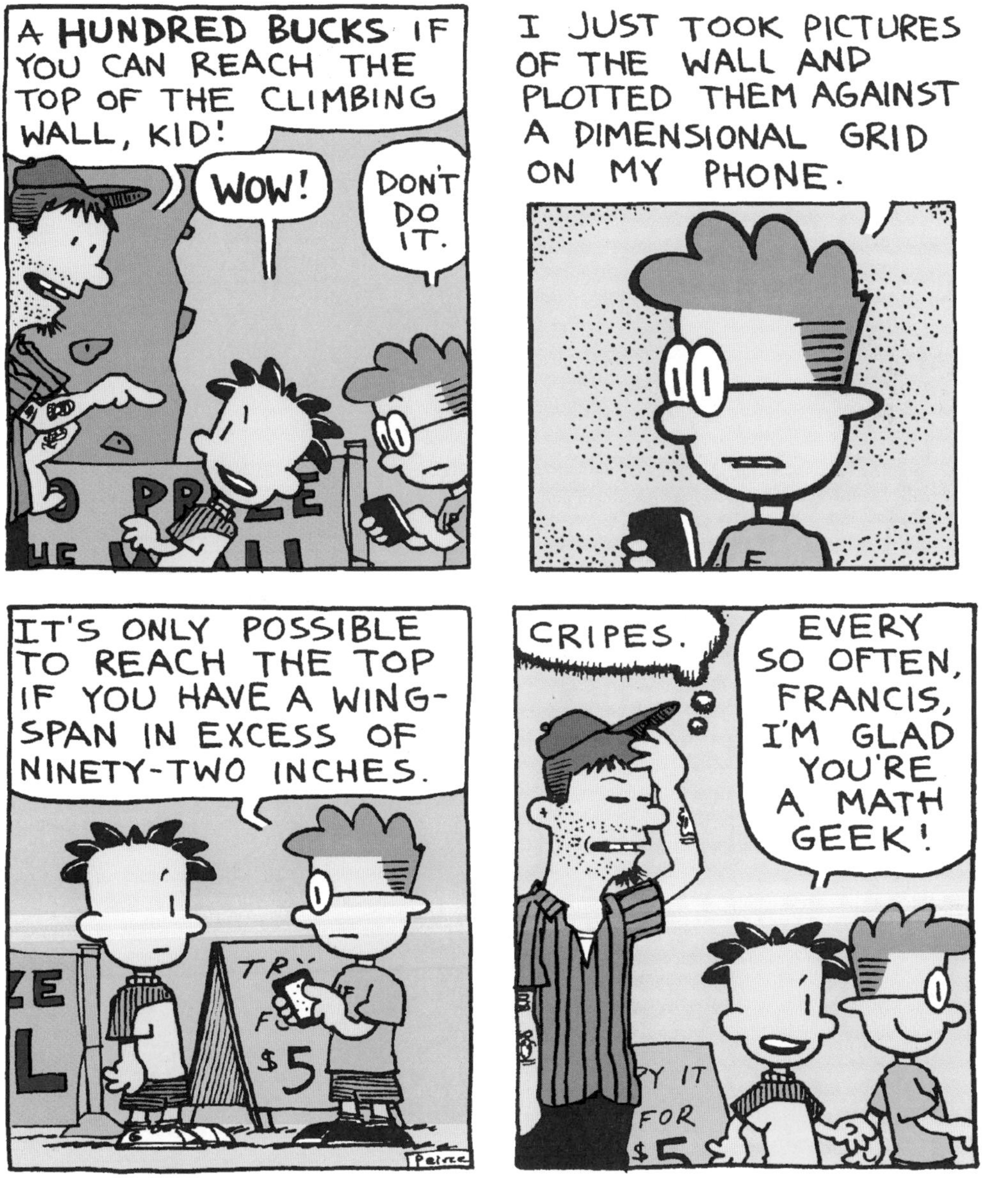
A HUNDRED BUCKS IF YOU CAN REACH THE TOP OF THE CLIMBING WALL, KID!
WOW!
DON'T DO IT.
I JUST TOOK PICTURES OF THE WALL AND PLOTTED THEM AGAINST A DIMENSIONAL GRID ON MY PHONE.
IT'S ONLY POSSIBLE TO REACH THE TOP IF YOU HAVE A WING-SPAN IN EXCESS OF NINETY-TWO INCHES.
CRIPES.
EVERY SO OFTEN, FRANCIS, I'M GLAD YOU'RE A MATH GEEK!

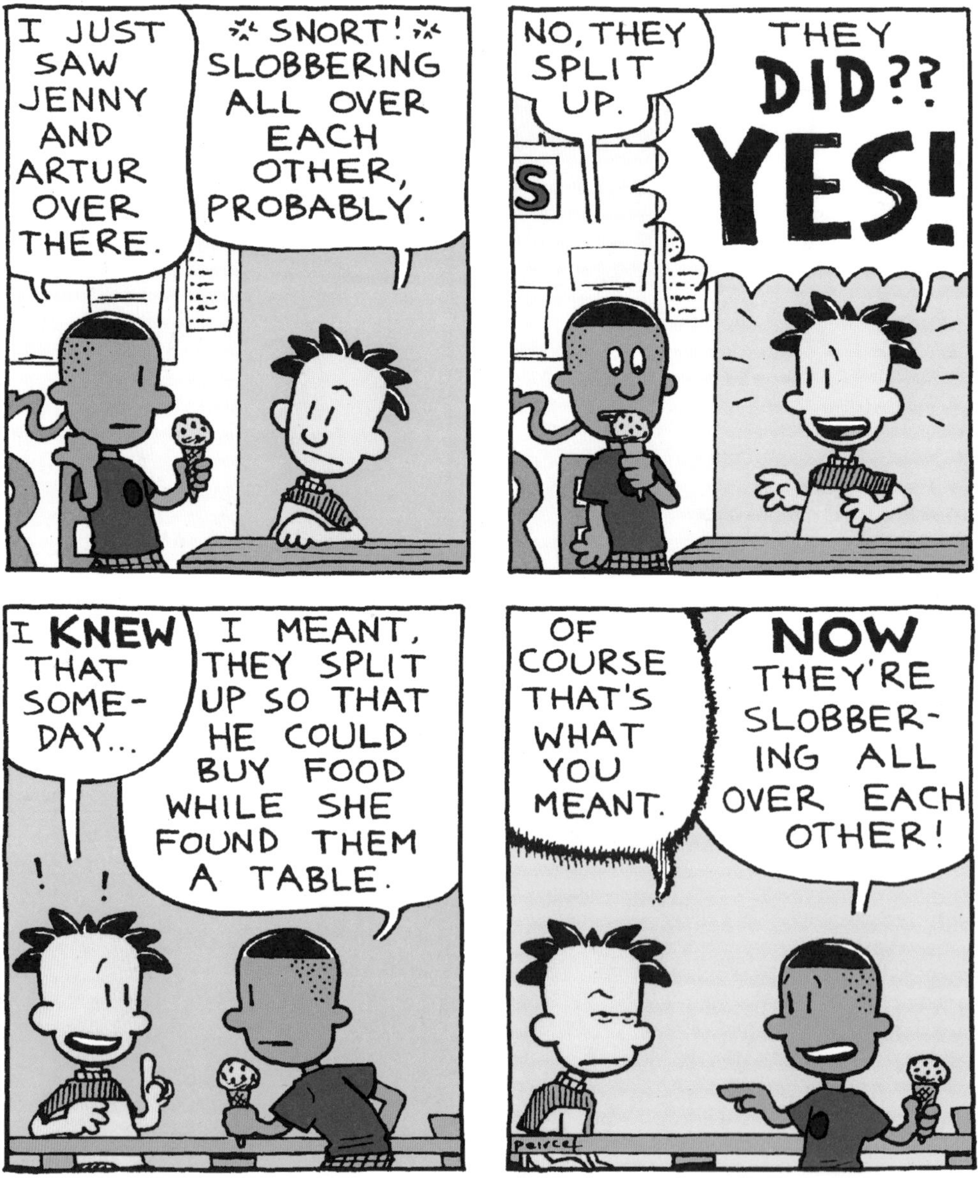
I JUST SAW JENNY AND ARTUR OVER THERE.
SNORT! SLOBBERING ALL OVER EACH OTHER, PROBABLY.
NO, THEY SPLIT UP.
THEY DID?? YES!
I KNEW THAT SOME-DAY...
I MEANT, THEY SPLIT UP SO THAT HE COULD BUY FOOD WHILE SHE FOUND THEM A TABLE.
! !
OF COURSE THAT'S WHAT YOU MEANT.
NOW THEY'RE SLOBBER-ING ALL OVER EACH OTHER!
peirce

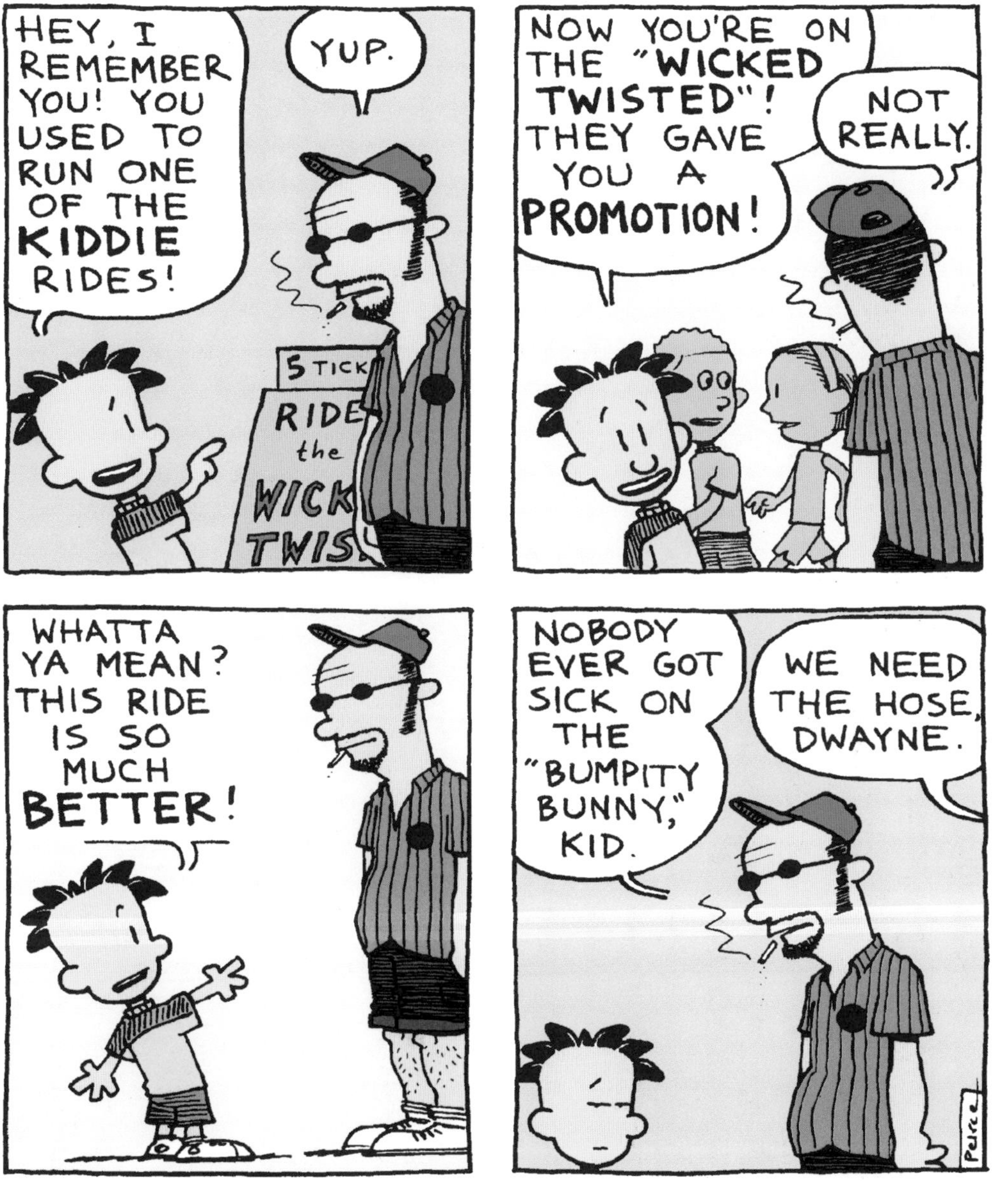
HEY, I REMEMBER YOU! YOU USED TO RUN ONE OF THE **KIDDIE** RIDES!
YUP.
5 TICK
RIDE the WICK TWIS
NOW YOU'RE ON THE "**WICKED TWISTED**"! THEY GAVE YOU A **PROMOTION**!
NOT REALLY.
WHATTA YA MEAN? THIS RIDE IS SO MUCH **BETTER**!
NOBODY EVER GOT SICK ON THE "BUMPITY BUNNY," KID.
WE NEED THE HOSE, DWAYNE.

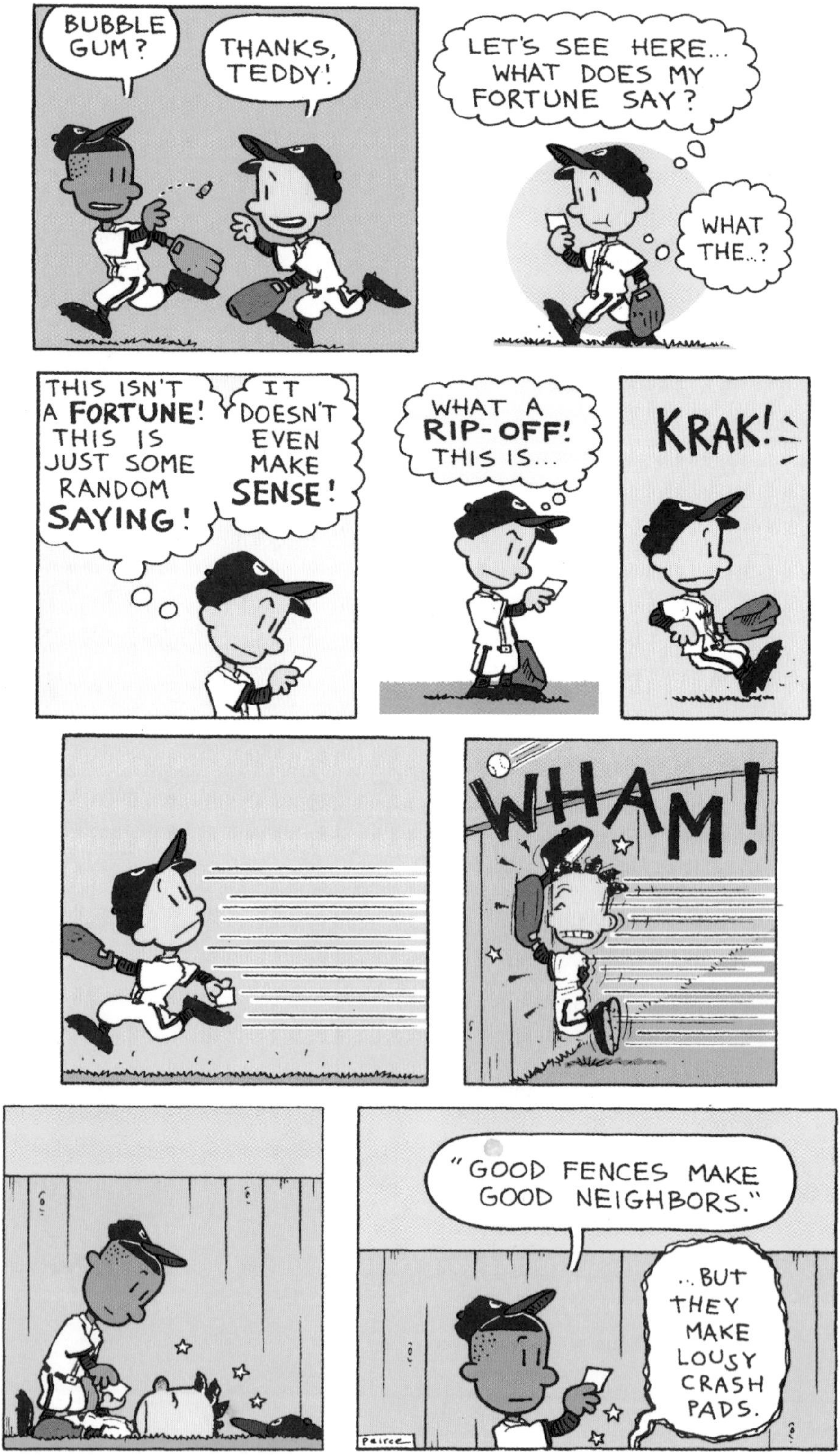
BUBBLE GUM?
THANKS, TEDDY!
LET'S SEE HERE... WHAT DOES MY FORTUNE SAY?
WHAT THE..?
THIS ISN'T A FORTUNE! THIS IS JUST SOME RANDOM SAYING!
IT DOESN'T EVEN MAKE SENSE!
WHAT A RIP-OFF! THIS IS...
KRAK!
WHAM!
"GOOD FENCES MAKE GOOD NEIGHBORS."
...BUT THEY MAKE LOUSY CRASH PADS.
PEIRCE

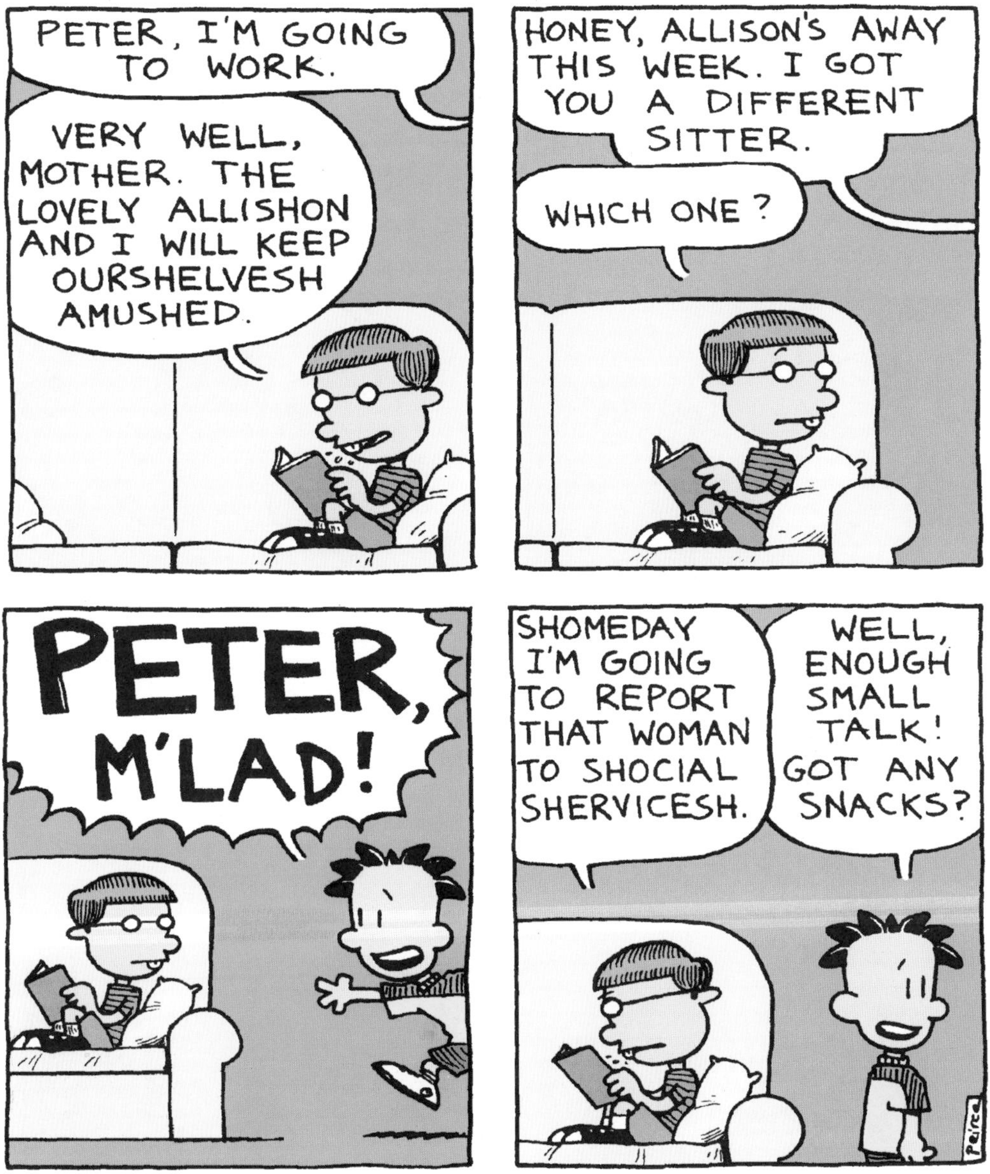
PETER, I'M GOING TO WORK.
VERY WELL, MOTHER. THE LOVELY ALLISHON AND I WILL KEEP OURSHELVESH AMUSHED.
HONEY, ALLISON'S AWAY THIS WEEK. I GOT YOU A DIFFERENT SITTER.
WHICH ONE?
PETER, M'LAD!
SHOMEDAY I'M GOING TO REPORT THAT WOMAN TO SHOCIAL SHERVICESH.
WELL, ENOUGH SMALL TALK! GOT ANY SNACKS?
Peirce

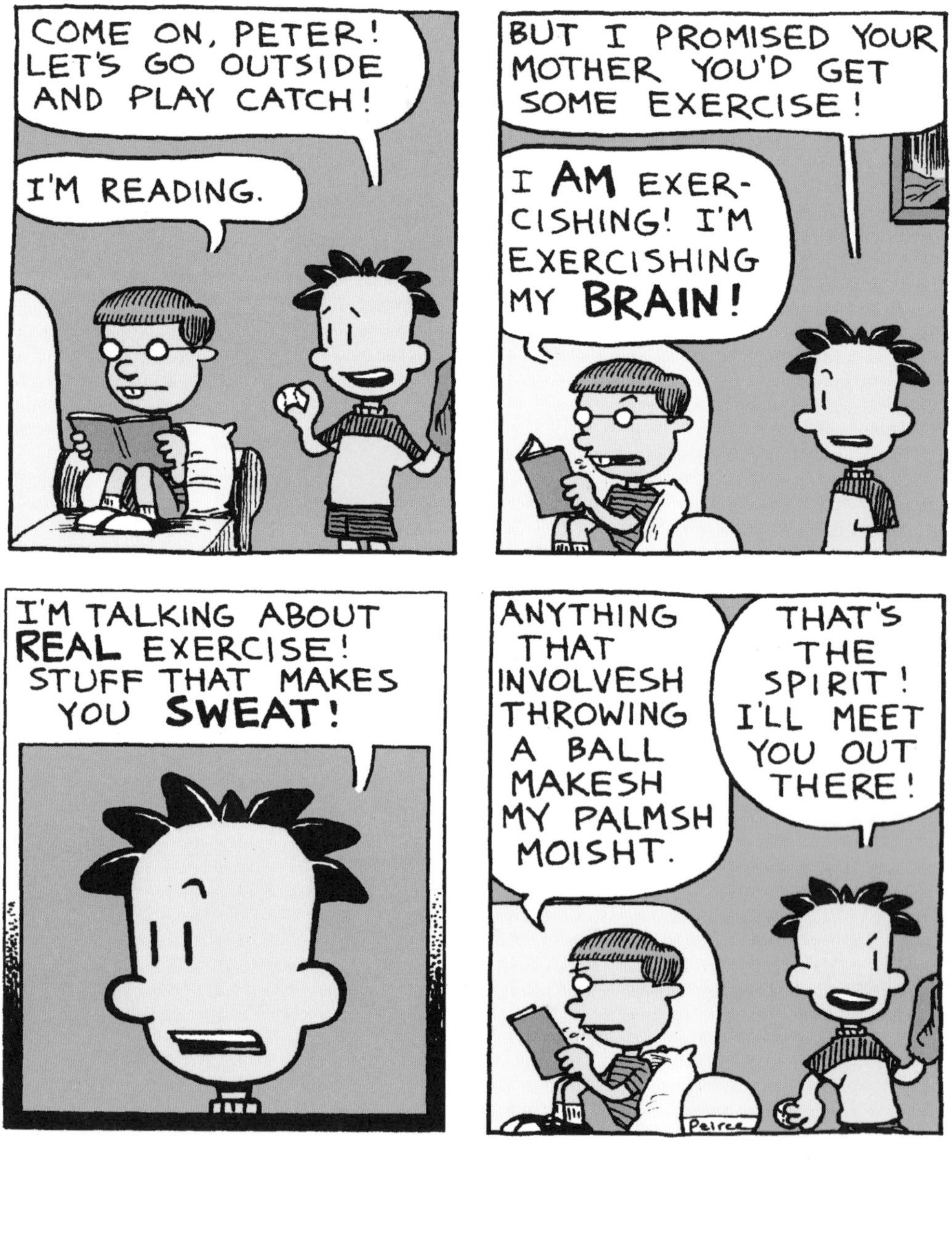
COME ON, PETER! LET'S GO OUTSIDE AND PLAY CATCH!
I'M READING.
BUT I PROMISED YOUR MOTHER YOU'D GET SOME EXERCISE!
I AM EXER-CISHING! I'M EXERCISHING MY BRAIN!
I'M TALKING ABOUT REAL EXERCISE! STUFF THAT MAKES YOU SWEAT!
ANYTHING THAT INVOLVESH THROWING A BALL MAKESH MY PALMSH MOISHT.
THAT'S THE SPIRIT! I'LL MEET YOU OUT THERE!
Peirce

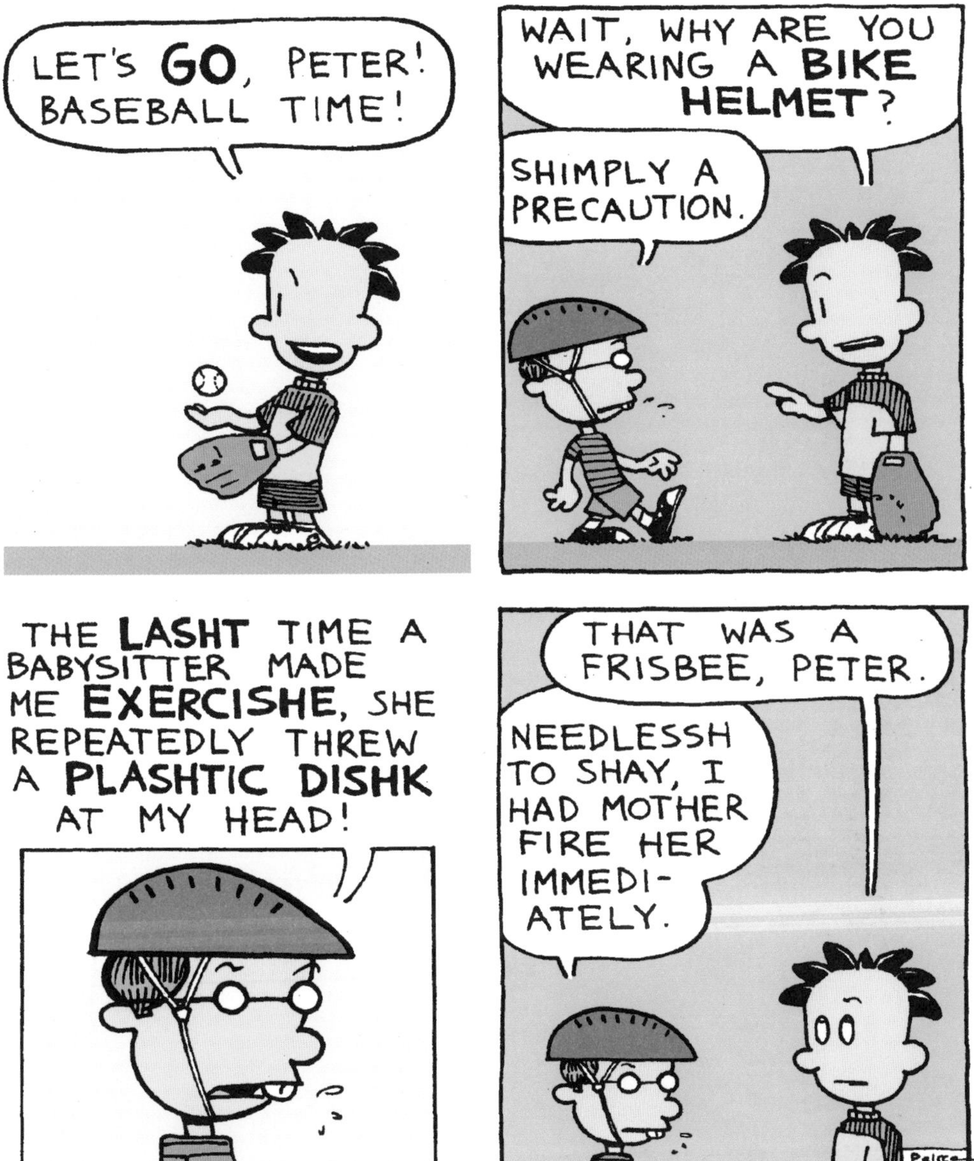
LET'S GO, PETER! BASEBALL TIME!
WAIT, WHY ARE YOU WEARING A BIKE HELMET?
SHIMPLY A PRECAUTION.
THE LASHT TIME A BABYSITTER MADE ME EXERCISHE, SHE REPEATEDLY THREW A PLASHTIC DISHK AT MY HEAD!
THAT WAS A FRISBEE, PETER.
NEEDLESSH TO SHAY, I HAD MOTHER FIRE HER IMMEDI-ATELY.

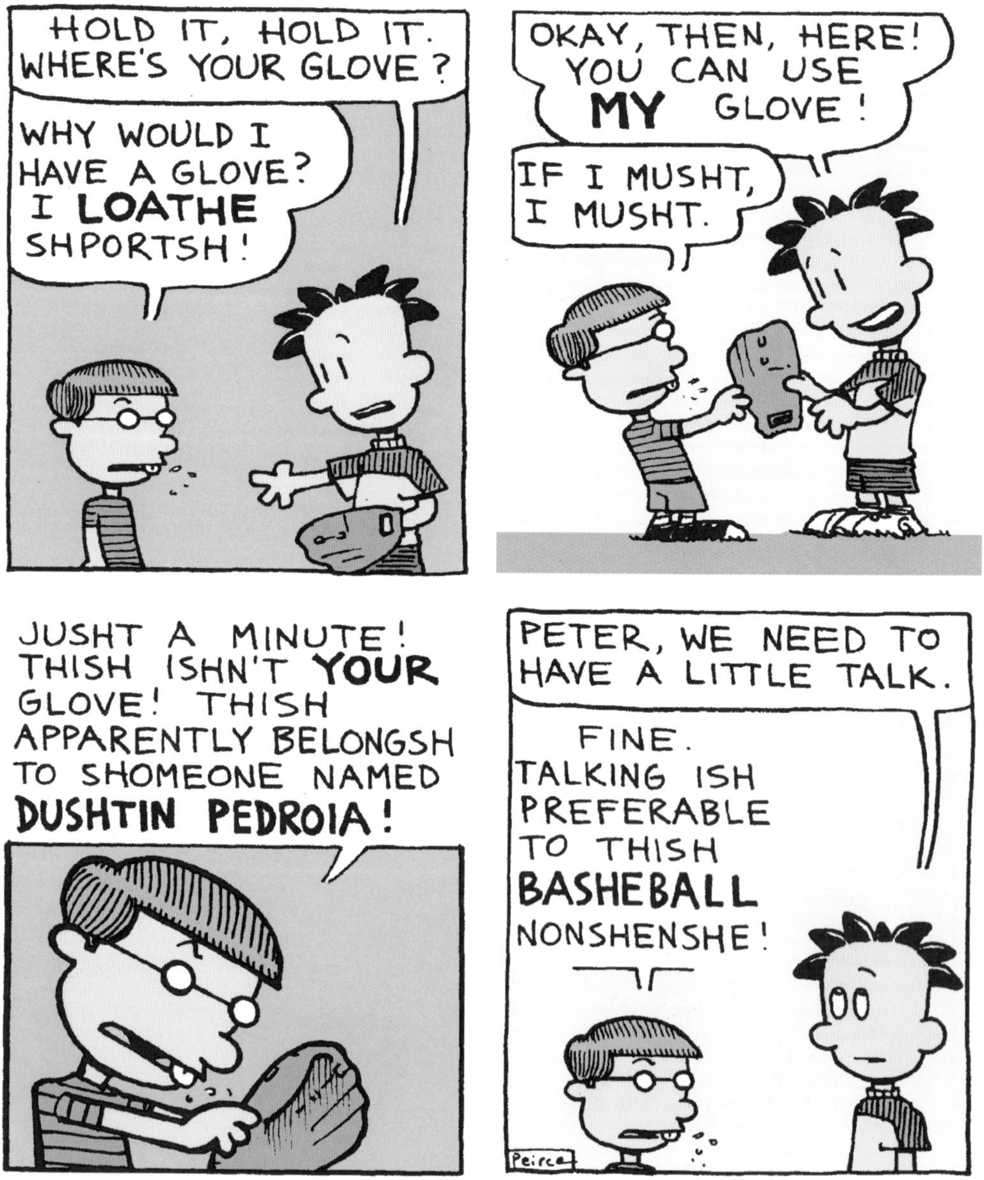
HOLD IT, HOLD IT. WHERE'S YOUR GLOVE?
WHY WOULD I HAVE A GLOVE? I **LOATHE** SHPORTSH!
OKAY, THEN, HERE! YOU CAN USE **MY** GLOVE!
IF I MUSHT, I MUSHT.
JUSHT A MINUTE! THISH ISHN'T **YOUR** GLOVE! THISH APPARENTLY BELONGSH TO SHOMEONE NAMED **DUSHTIN PEDROIA**!
PETER, WE NEED TO HAVE A LITTLE TALK.
FINE. TALKING ISH PREFERABLE TO THISH **BASHEBALL** NONSHENSHE!
Peirce

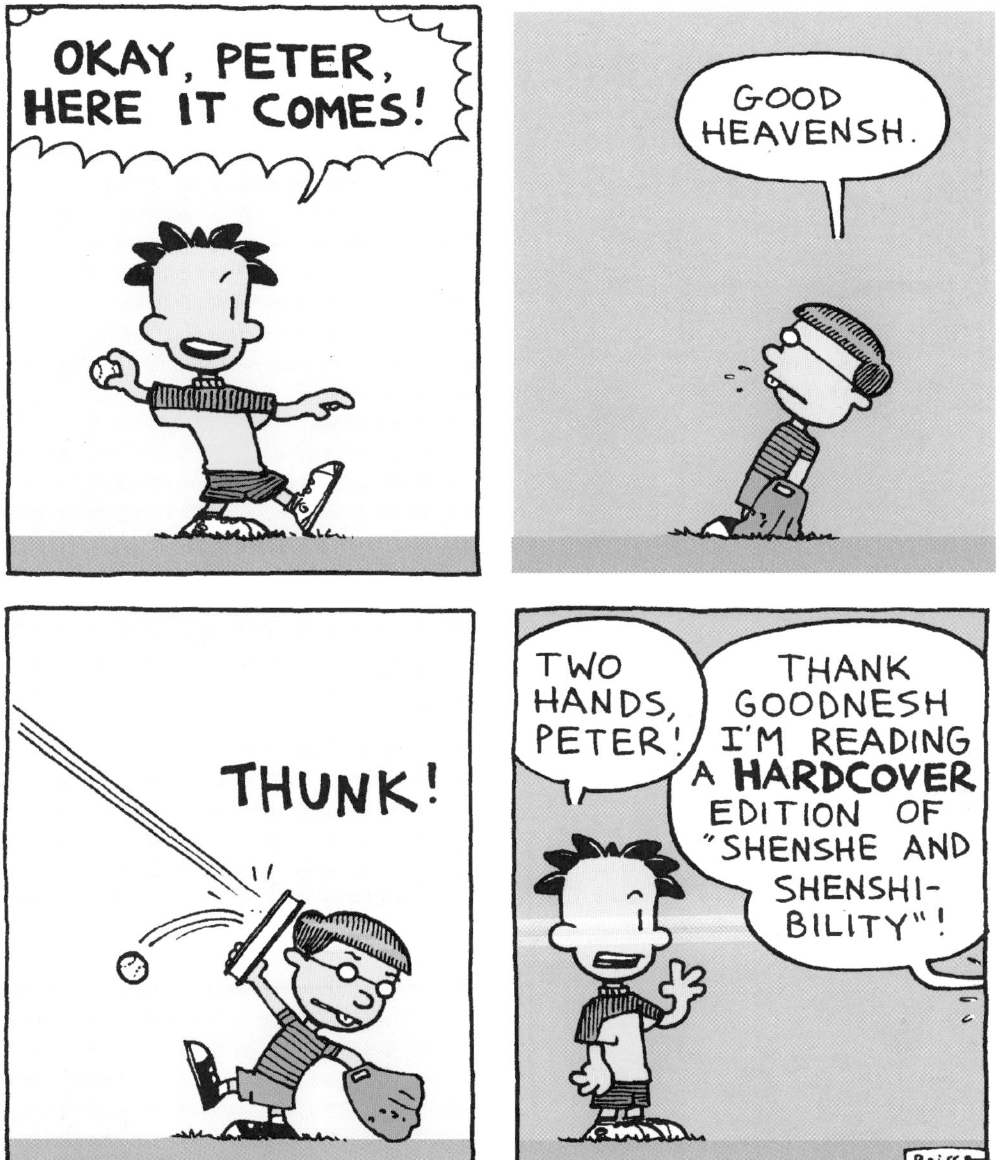
OKAY, PETER, HERE IT COMES!
GOOD HEAVENSH.
THUNK!
TWO HANDS, PETER!
THANK GOODNESH I'M READING A **HARDCOVER** EDITION OF "SHENSHE AND SHENSHI-BILITY"!
Peirce

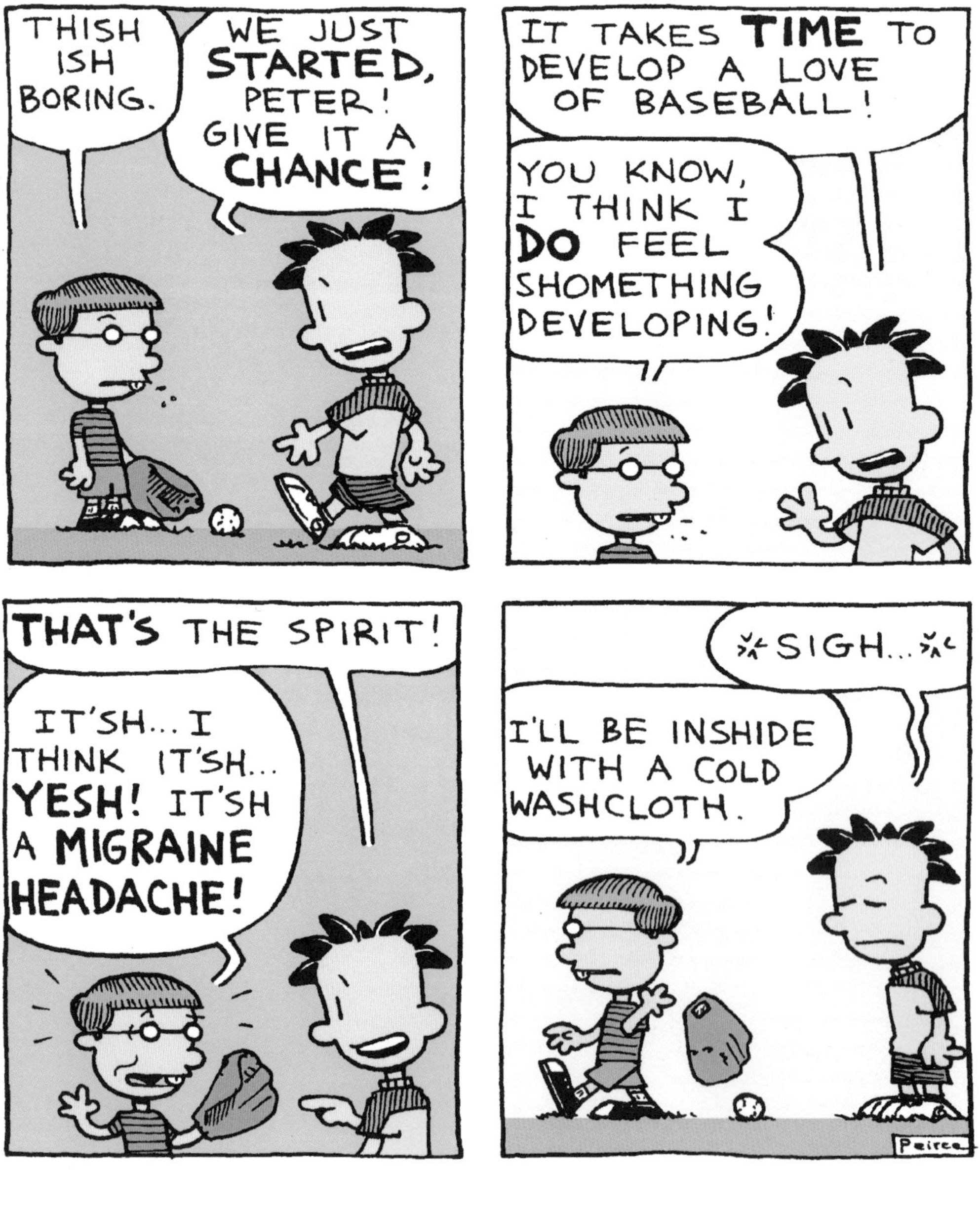
THISH ISH BORING.
WE JUST STARTED, PETER! GIVE IT A CHANCE!
IT TAKES TIME TO DEVELOP A LOVE OF BASEBALL!
YOU KNOW, I THINK I DO FEEL SHOMETHING DEVELOPING!
THAT'S THE SPIRIT!
IT'SH... I THINK IT'SH... YESH! IT'SH A MIGRAINE HEADACHE!
SIGH...
I'LL BE INSHIDE WITH A COLD WASHCLOTH.
Peirce

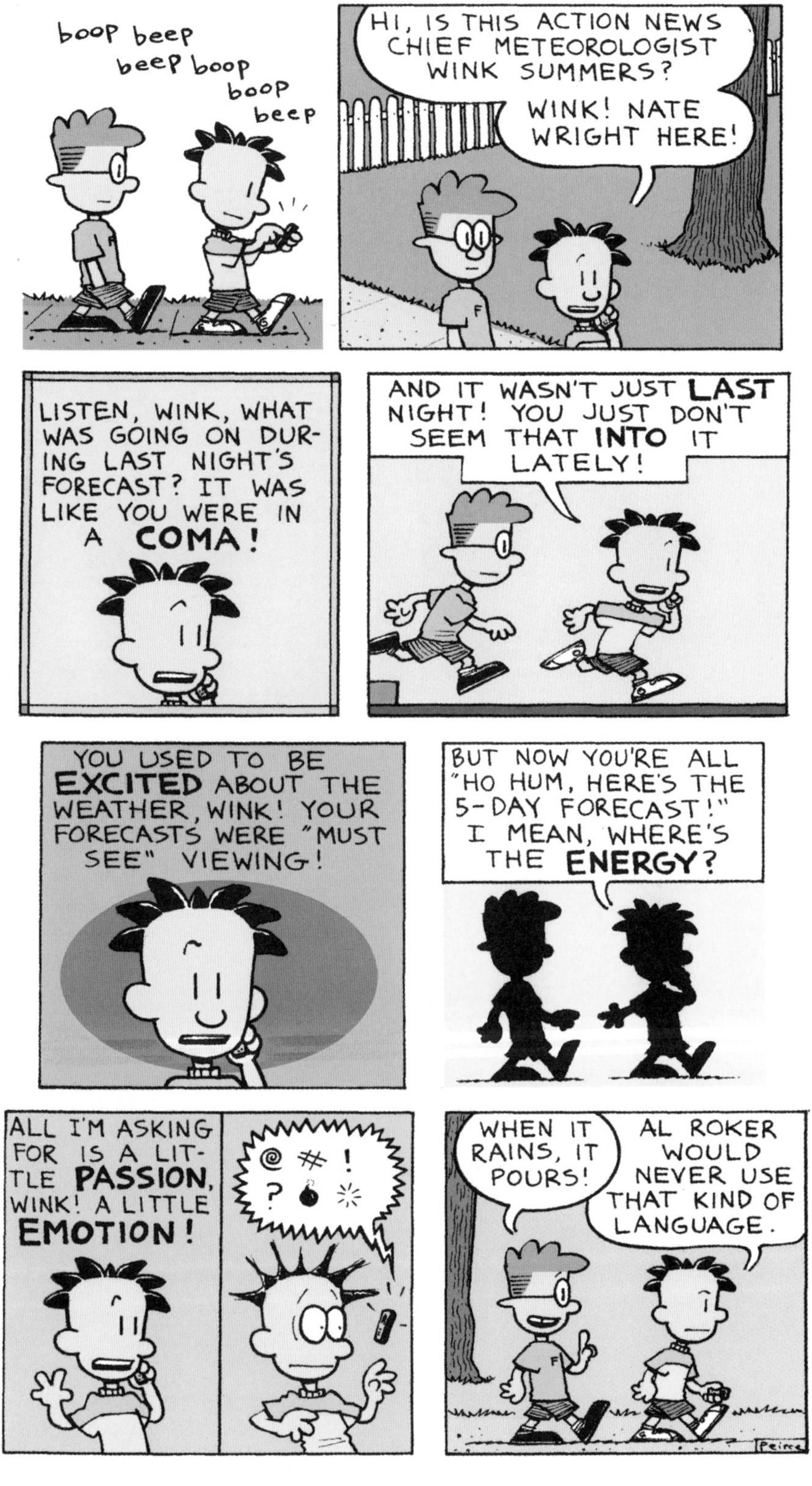
boop beep
beep boop
boop
beep
HI, IS THIS ACTION NEWS CHIEF METEOROLOGIST WINK SUMMERS?
WINK! NATE WRIGHT HERE!
LISTEN, WINK, WHAT WAS GOING ON DURING LAST NIGHT'S FORECAST? IT WAS LIKE YOU WERE IN A **COMA**!
AND IT WASN'T JUST **LAST** NIGHT! YOU JUST DON'T SEEM THAT **INTO** IT LATELY!
YOU USED TO BE **EXCITED** ABOUT THE WEATHER, WINK! YOUR FORECASTS WERE "MUST SEE" VIEWING!
BUT NOW YOU'RE ALL "HO HUM, HERE'S THE 5-DAY FORECAST!" I MEAN, WHERE'S THE **ENERGY**?
ALL I'M ASKING FOR IS A LITTLE **PASSION**, WINK! A LITTLE **EMOTION**!
@ # ! ?
WHEN IT RAINS, IT POURS!
AL ROKER WOULD NEVER USE THAT KIND OF LANGUAGE.
Peirce

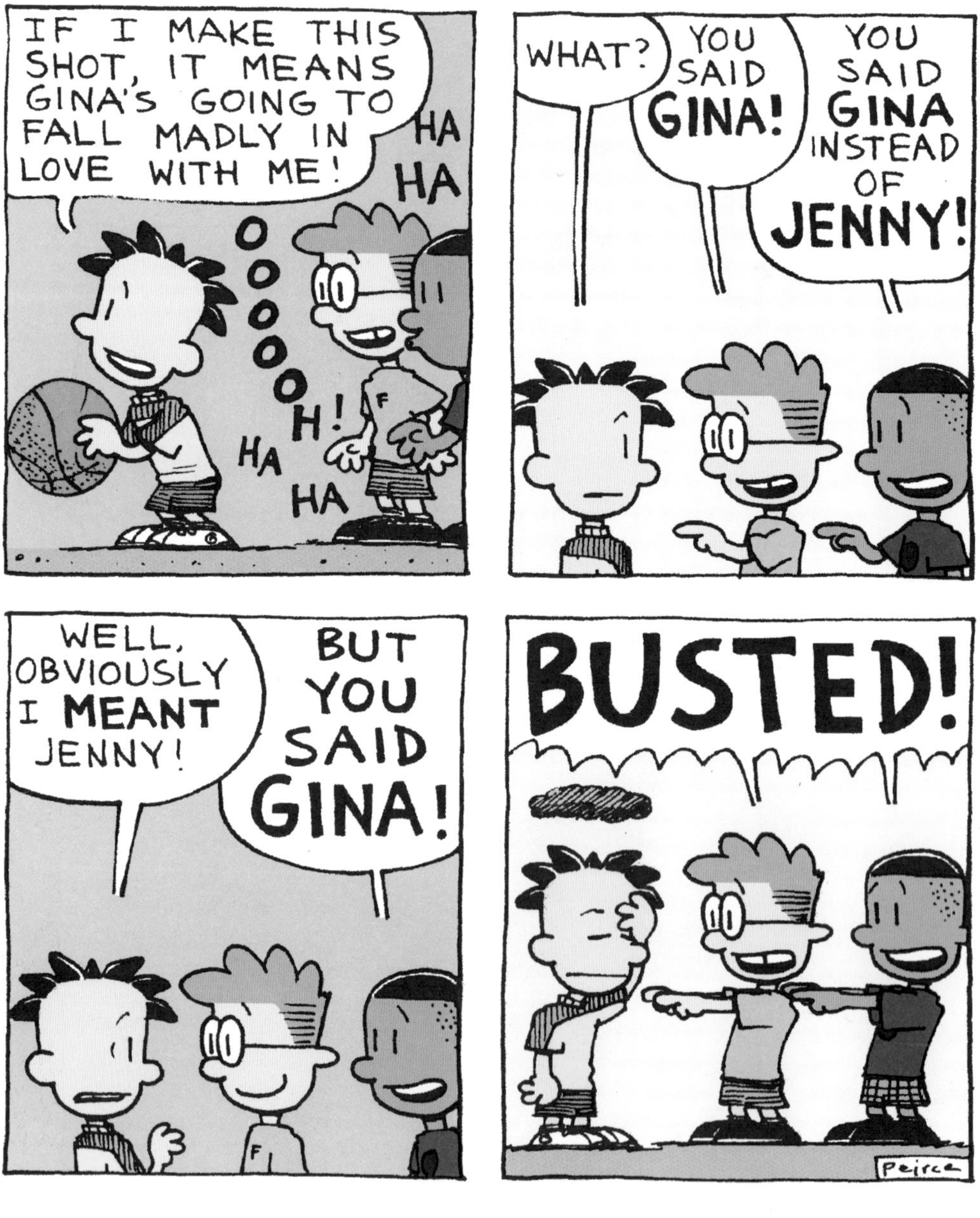
IF I MAKE THIS SHOT, IT MEANS GINA'S GOING TO FALL MADLY IN LOVE WITH ME!
HA HA
OOOOOOH!
HA HA
WHAT?
YOU SAID GINA!
YOU SAID GINA INSTEAD OF JENNY!
WELL, OBVIOUSLY I MEANT JENNY!
BUT YOU SAID GINA!
BUSTED!
Peirce

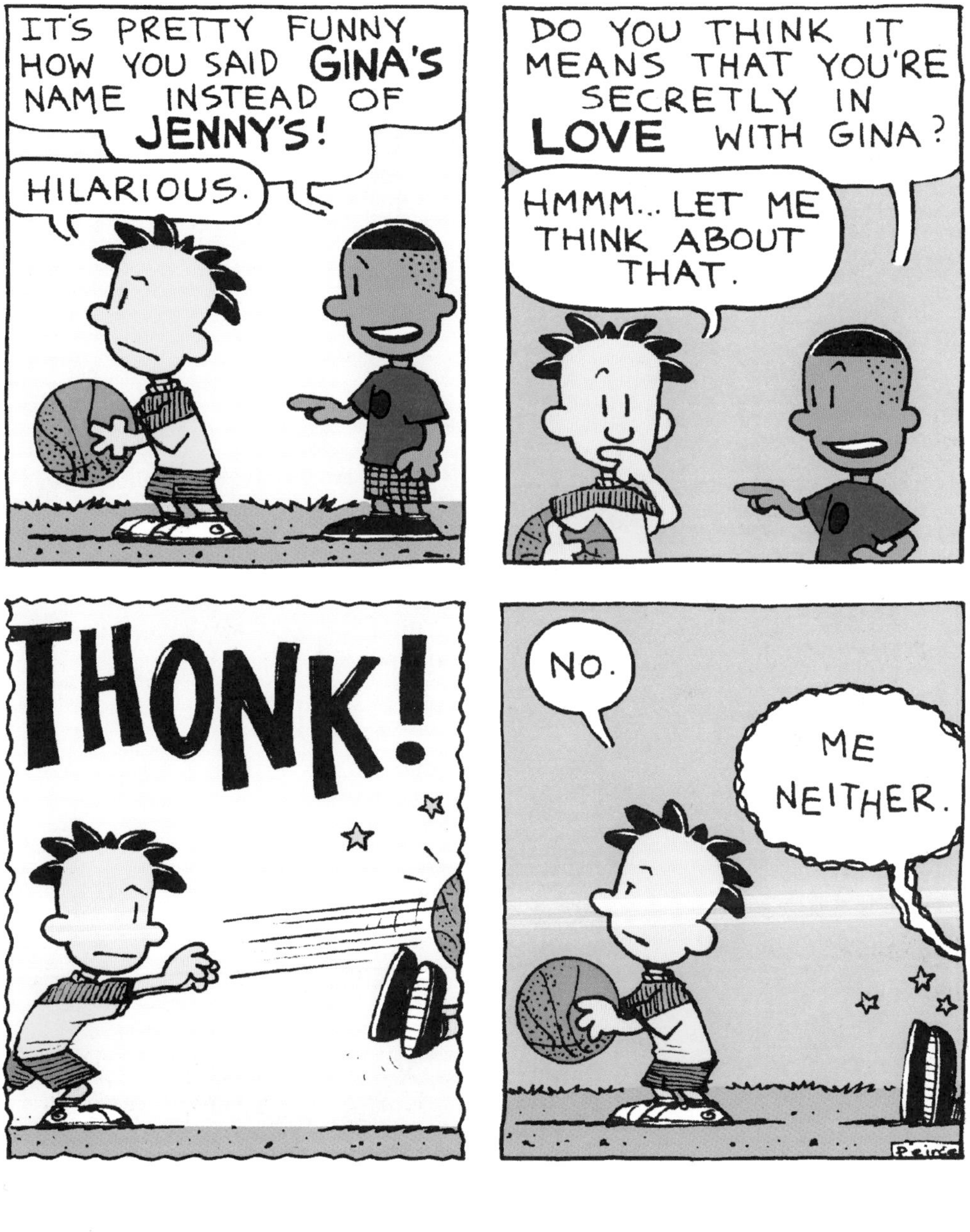
IT'S PRETTY FUNNY HOW YOU SAID GINA'S NAME INSTEAD OF JENNY'S!
HILARIOUS.
DO YOU THINK IT MEANS THAT YOU'RE SECRETLY IN LOVE WITH GINA?
HMMM... LET ME THINK ABOUT THAT.
THONK!
NO.
ME NEITHER.
Peirce

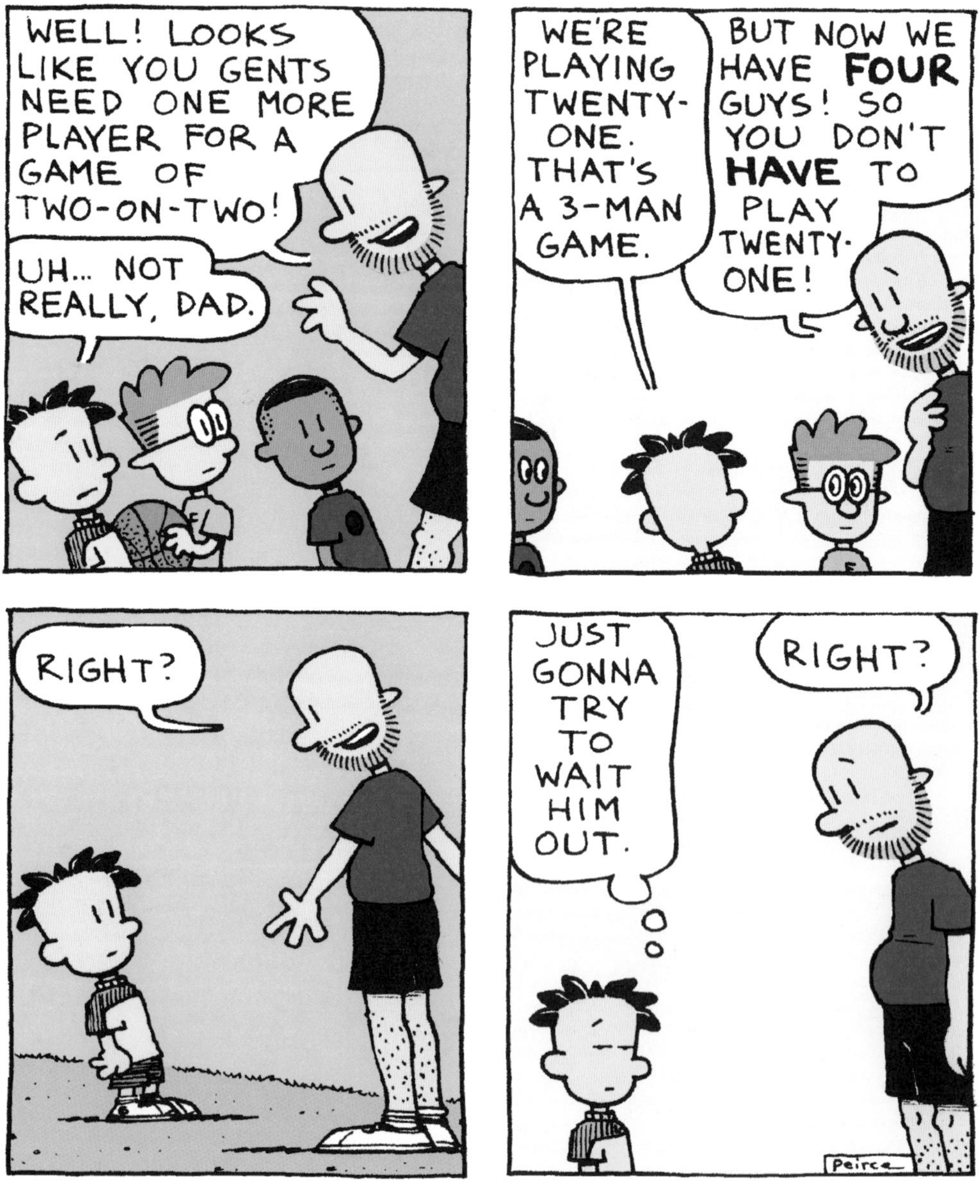
WELL! LOOKS LIKE YOU GENTS NEED ONE MORE PLAYER FOR A GAME OF TWO-ON-TWO!
UH... NOT REALLY, DAD.
WE'RE PLAYING TWENTY-ONE. THAT'S A 3-MAN GAME.
BUT NOW WE HAVE **FOUR** GUYS! SO YOU DON'T **HAVE** TO PLAY TWENTY-ONE!
RIGHT?
JUST GONNA TRY TO WAIT HIM OUT.
RIGHT?
Peirce

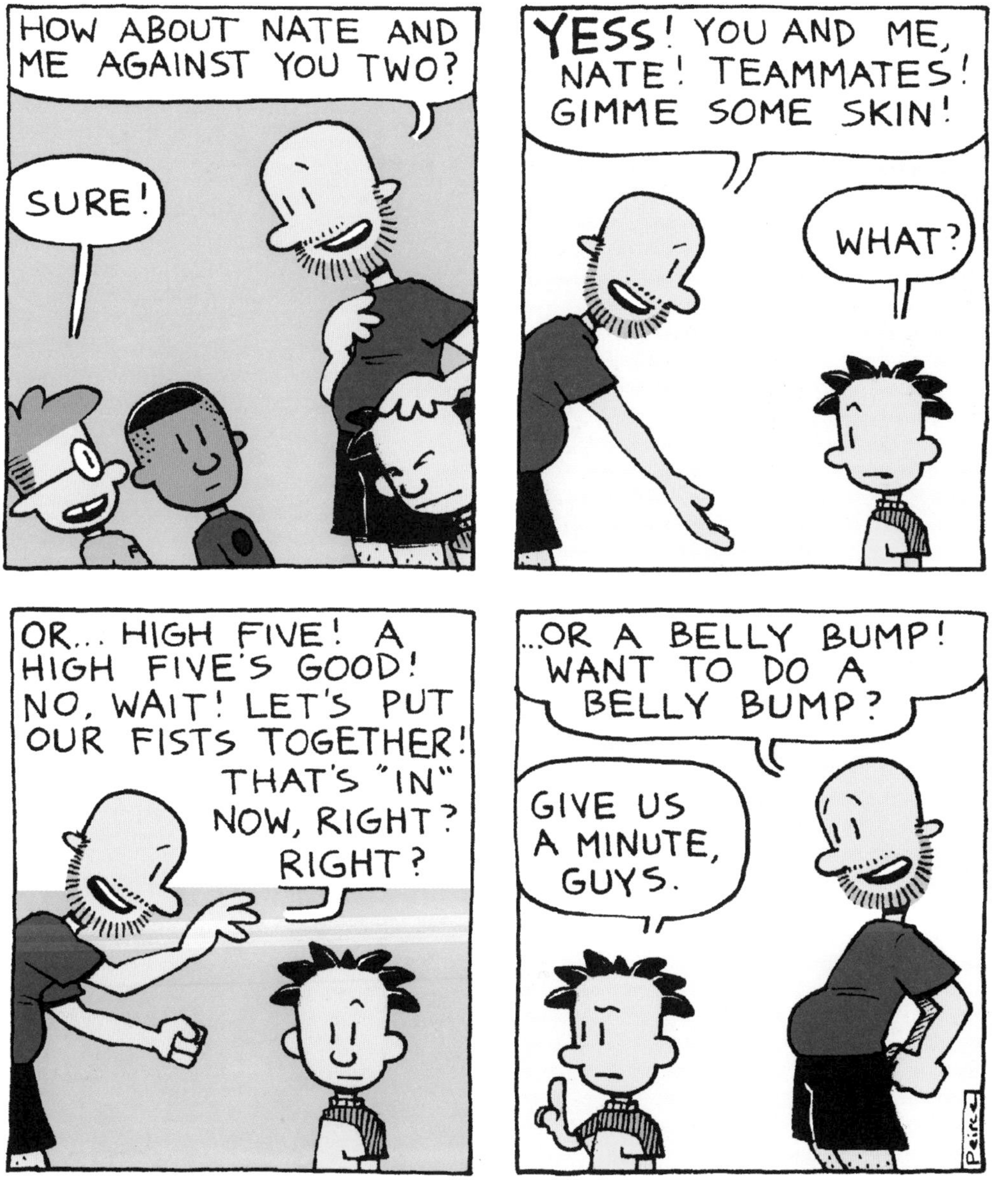
HOW ABOUT NATE AND ME AGAINST YOU TWO?
SURE!
YESS! YOU AND ME, NATE! TEAMMATES! GIMME SOME SKIN!
WHAT?
OR... HIGH FIVE! A HIGH FIVE'S GOOD! NO, WAIT! LET'S PUT OUR FISTS TOGETHER! THAT'S "IN" NOW, RIGHT? RIGHT?
...OR A BELLY BUMP! WANT TO DO A BELLY BUMP?
GIVE US A MINUTE, GUYS.
Peirce

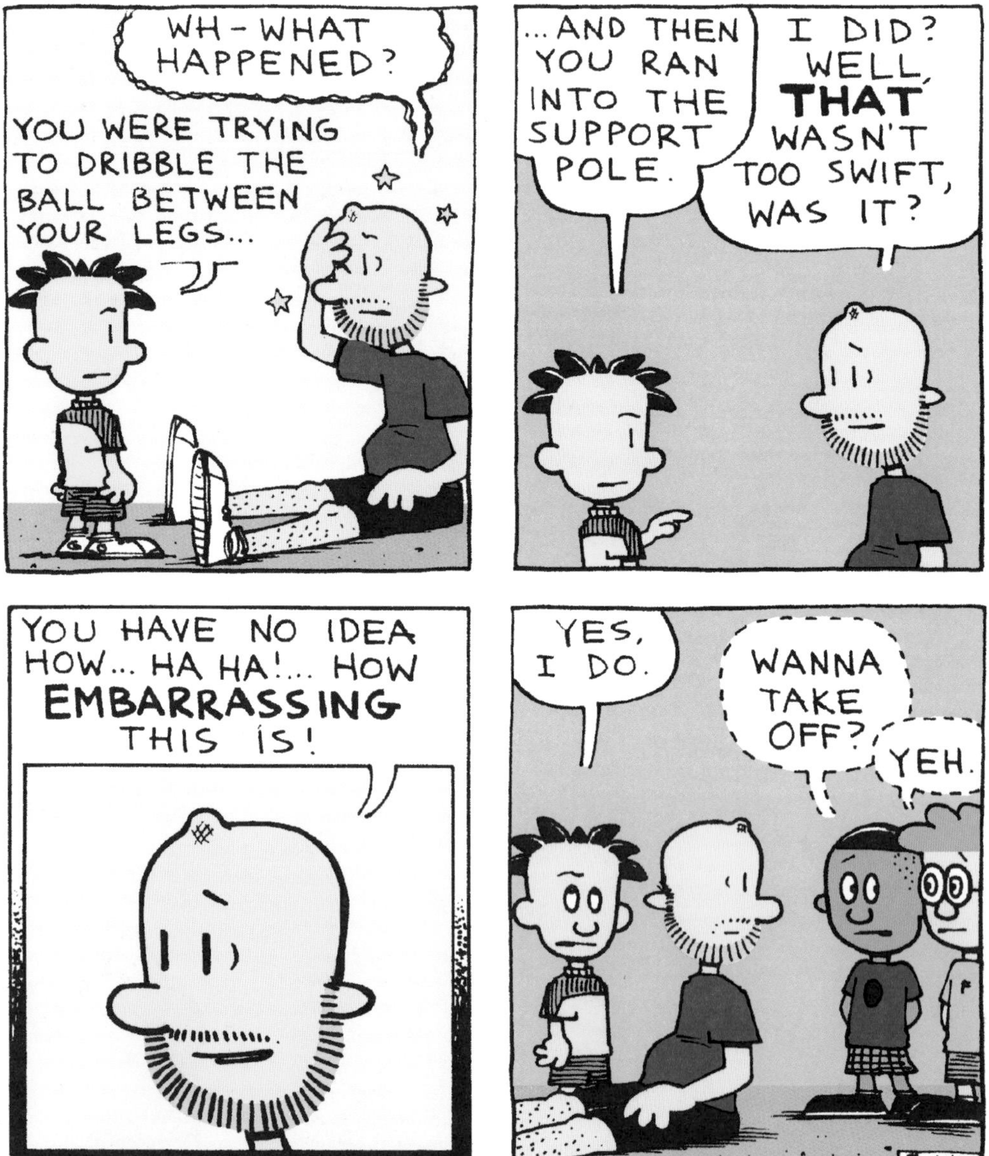
WH-WHAT HAPPENED?
YOU WERE TRYING TO DRIBBLE THE BALL BETWEEN YOUR LEGS...
...AND THEN YOU RAN INTO THE SUPPORT POLE.
I DID? WELL, **THAT** WASN'T TOO SWIFT, WAS IT?
YOU HAVE NO IDEA HOW... HA HA!... HOW **EMBARRASSING** THIS IS!
YES, I DO.
WANNA TAKE OFF?
YEH.
Peirce

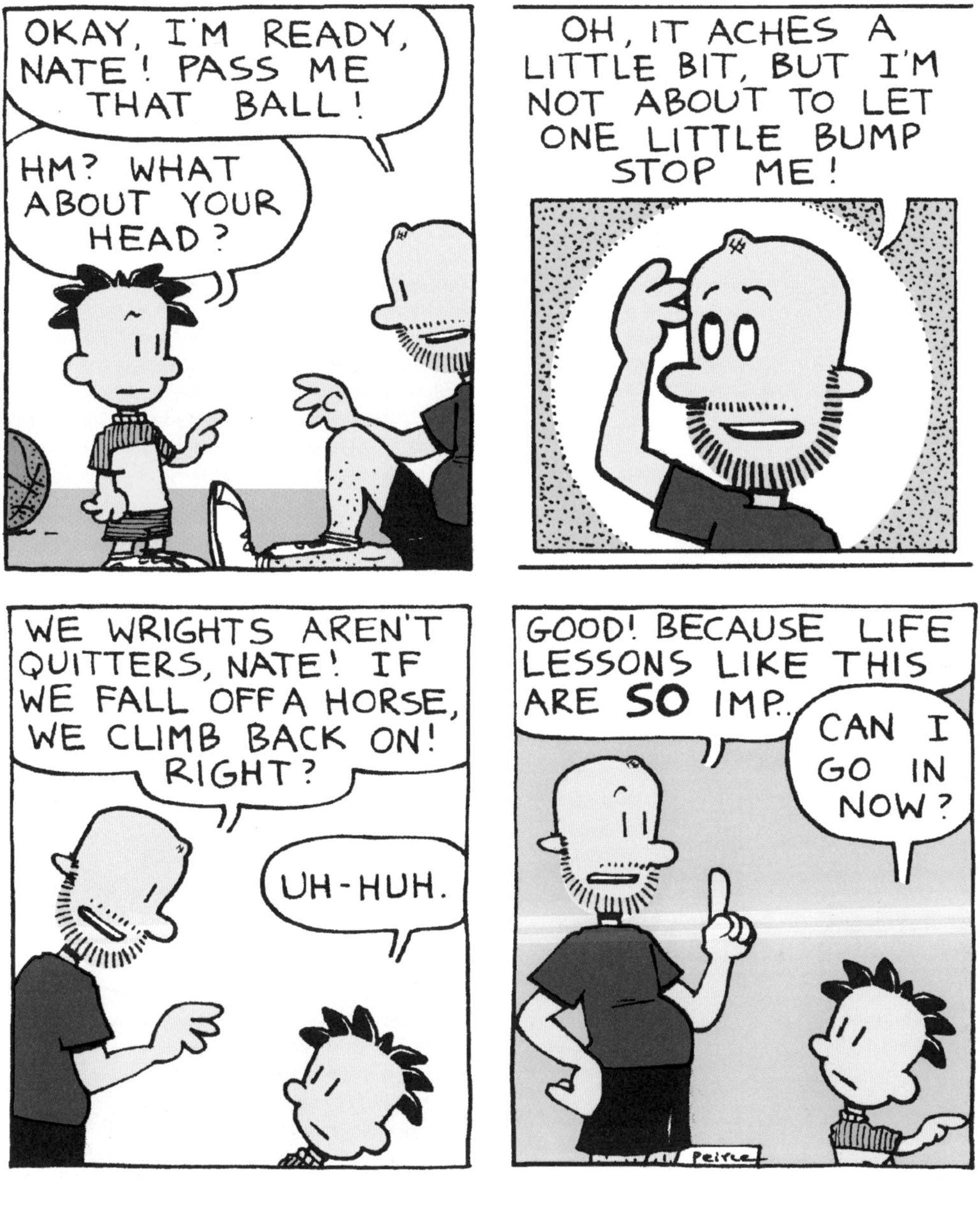
OKAY, I'M READY, NATE! PASS ME THAT BALL!
HM? WHAT ABOUT YOUR HEAD?
OH, IT ACHES A LITTLE BIT, BUT I'M NOT ABOUT TO LET ONE LITTLE BUMP STOP ME!
WE WRIGHTS AREN'T QUITTERS, NATE! IF WE FALL OFF A HORSE, WE CLIMB BACK ON! RIGHT?
UH-HUH.
GOOD! BECAUSE LIFE LESSONS LIKE THIS ARE SO IMP..
CAN I GO IN NOW?
Peirce

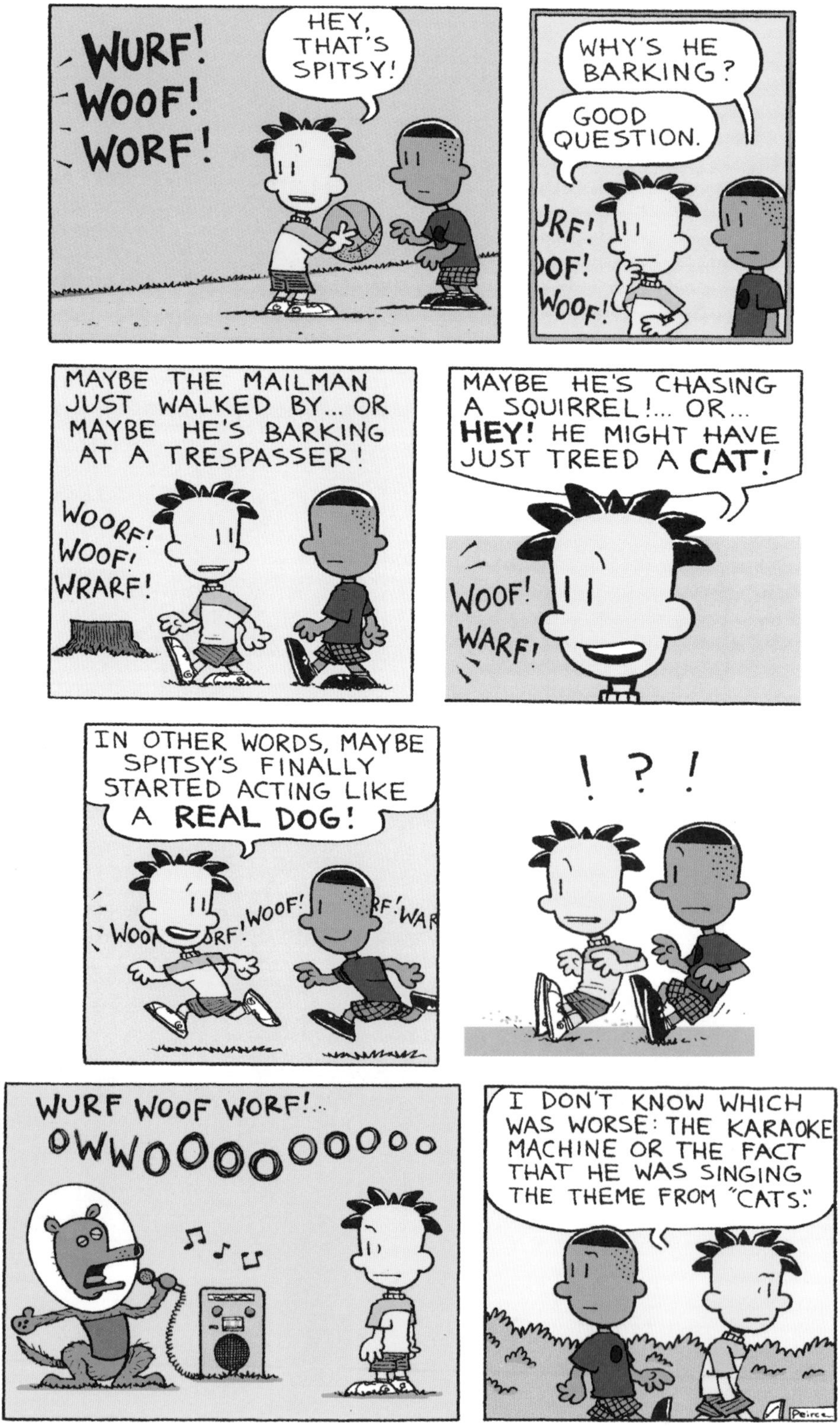
WURF! WOOF! WORF!
HEY, THAT'S SPITSY!
WHY'S HE BARKING?
GOOD QUESTION.
RF! OF! WOOF!
MAYBE THE MAILMAN JUST WALKED BY... OR MAYBE HE'S BARKING AT A TRESPASSER!
WOORF! WOOF! WRARF!
MAYBE HE'S CHASING A SQUIRREL!... OR... **HEY!** HE MIGHT HAVE JUST TREED A **CAT!**
WOOF! WARF!
IN OTHER WORDS, MAYBE SPITSY'S FINALLY STARTED ACTING LIKE A **REAL DOG!**
WOOF!
! ? !
WURF WOOF WORF!...
OWWOOOOOOOOOOo
I DON'T KNOW WHICH WAS WORSE: THE KARAOKE MACHINE OR THE FACT THAT HE WAS SINGING THE THEME FROM "CATS."
Peirce

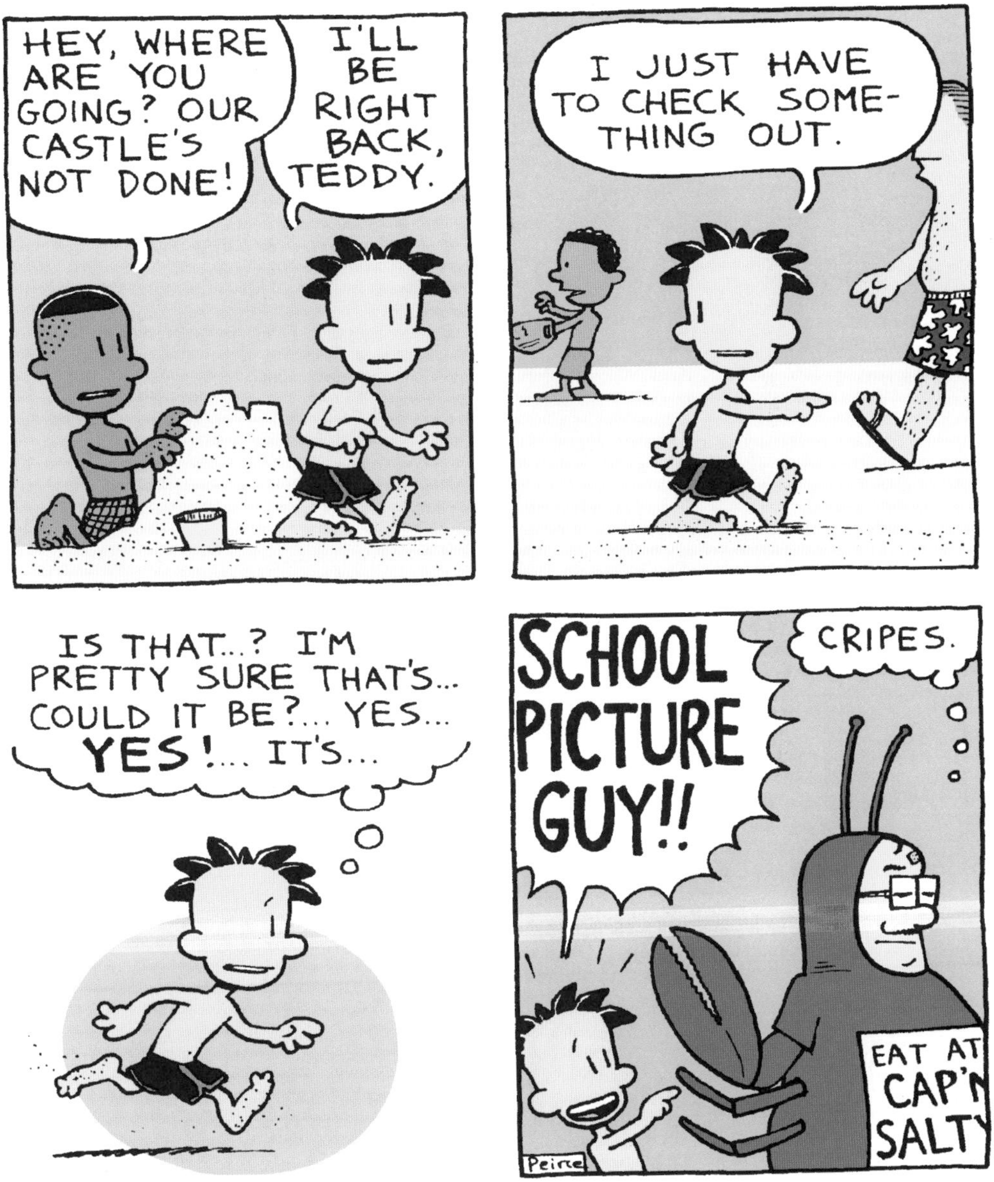
HEY, WHERE ARE YOU GOING? OUR CASTLE'S NOT DONE!
I'LL BE RIGHT BACK, TEDDY.
I JUST HAVE TO CHECK SOME-THING OUT.
IS THAT...? I'M PRETTY SURE THAT'S... COULD IT BE?... YES... YES!... IT'S...
SCHOOL PICTURE GUY!!
CRIPES.
EAT AT CAP'N SALTY
Peirce

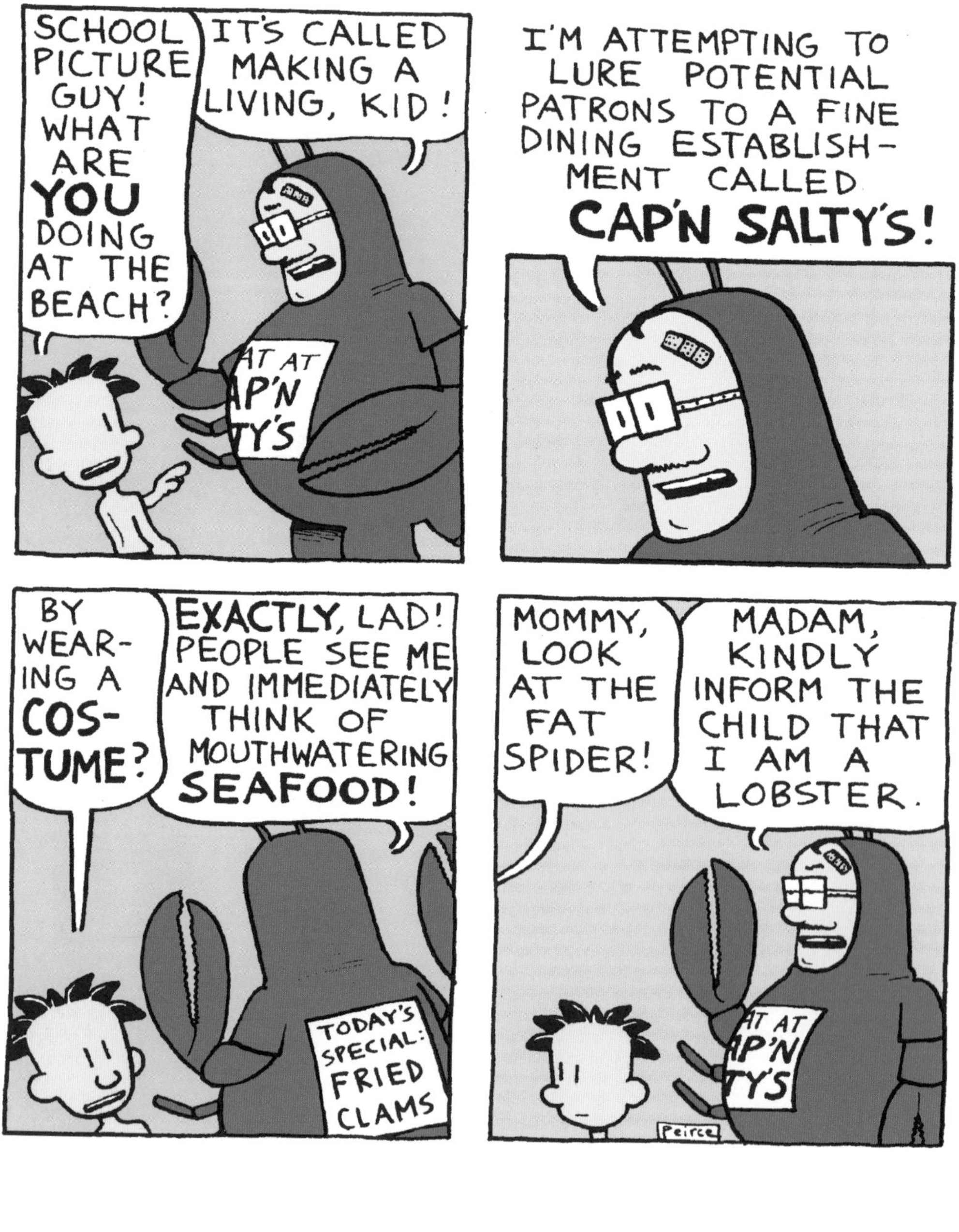
SCHOOL PICTURE GUY! WHAT ARE **YOU** DOING AT THE BEACH?
IT'S CALLED MAKING A LIVING, KID!
AT AT
P'N
TY'S
I'M ATTEMPTING TO LURE POTENTIAL PATRONS TO A FINE DINING ESTABLISHMENT CALLED **CAP'N SALTY'S!**
BY WEARING A **COSTUME?**
EXACTLY, LAD! PEOPLE SEE ME AND IMMEDIATELY THINK OF MOUTHWATERING **SEAFOOD!**
TODAY'S SPECIAL: FRIED CLAMS
MOMMY, LOOK AT THE FAT SPIDER!
MADAM, KINDLY INFORM THE CHILD THAT I AM A LOBSTER.
AT AT
P'N
TY'S
Peirce

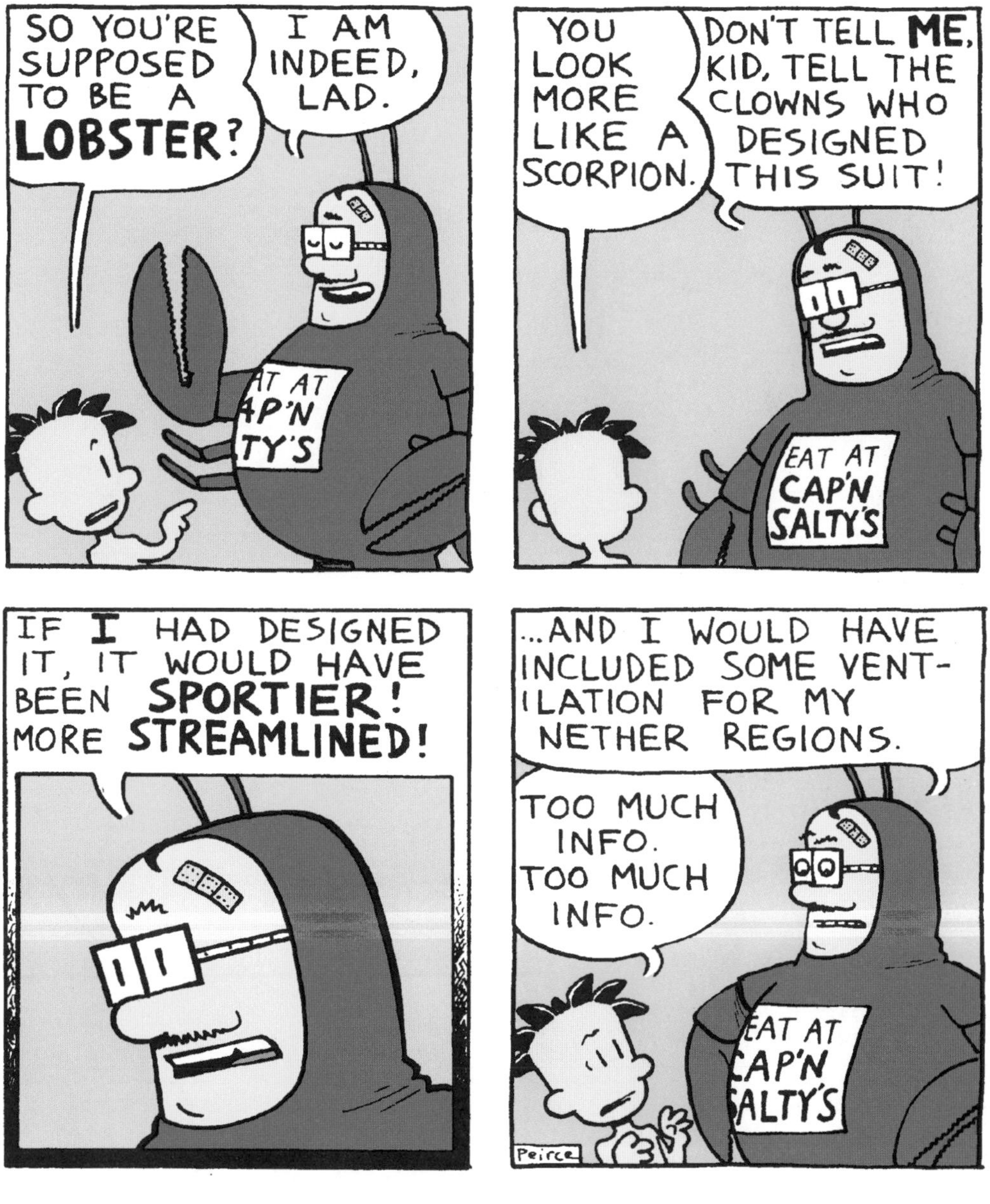
SO YOU'RE SUPPOSED TO BE A LOBSTER?
I AM INDEED, LAD.
EAT AT CAP'N SALTY'S
YOU LOOK MORE LIKE A SCORPION.
DON'T TELL ME, KID, TELL THE CLOWNS WHO DESIGNED THIS SUIT!
EAT AT CAP'N SALTY'S
IF I HAD DESIGNED IT, IT WOULD HAVE BEEN SPORTIER! MORE STREAMLINED!
...AND I WOULD HAVE INCLUDED SOME VENT-ILATION FOR MY NETHER REGIONS.
TOO MUCH INFO. TOO MUCH INFO.
EAT AT CAP'N SALTY'S
Peirce

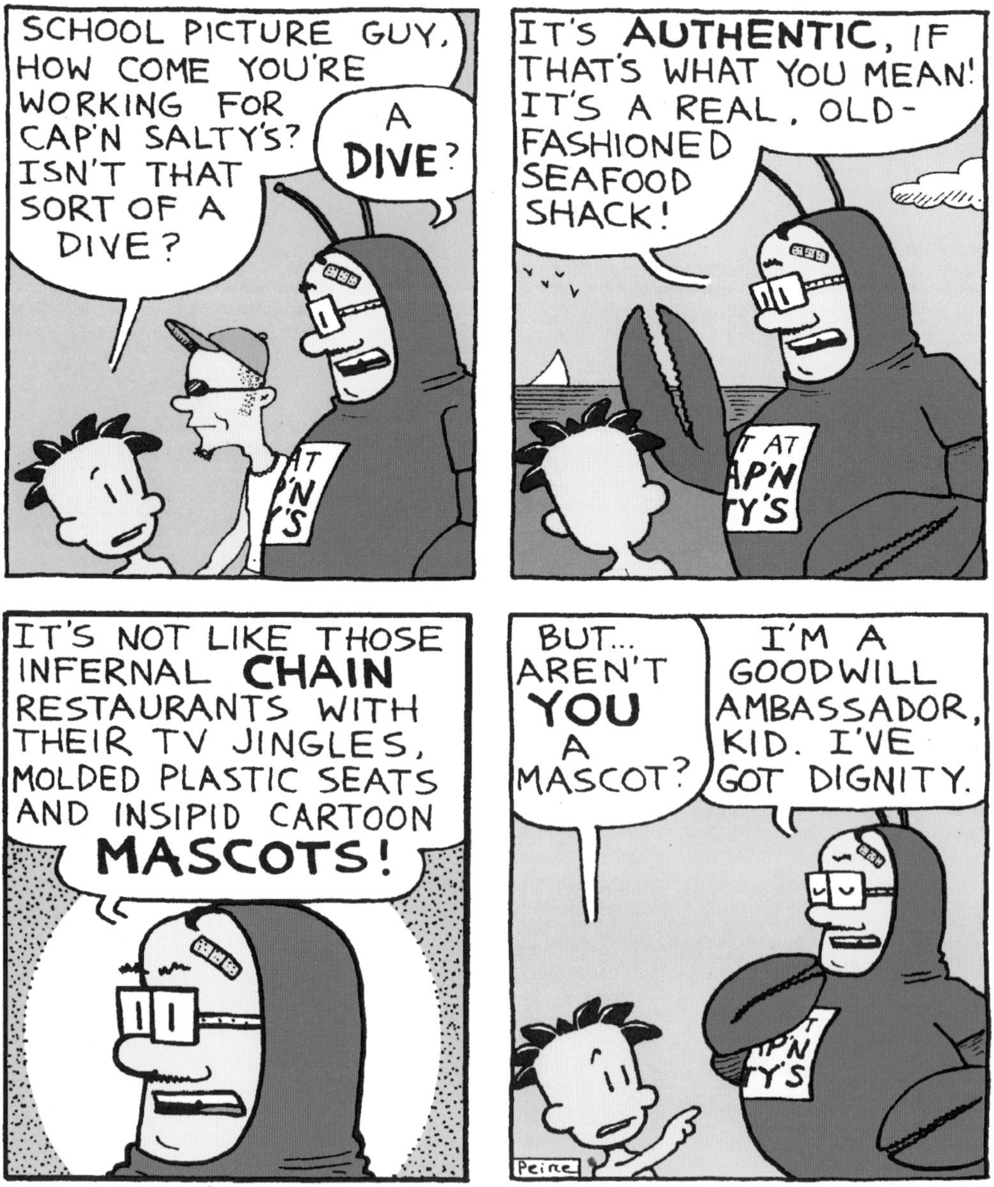
SCHOOL PICTURE GUY, HOW COME YOU'RE WORKING FOR CAP'N SALTY'S? ISN'T THAT SORT OF A DIVE?
A DIVE?
IT'S AUTHENTIC, IF THAT'S WHAT YOU MEAN! IT'S A REAL, OLD-FASHIONED SEAFOOD SHACK!
IT'S NOT LIKE THOSE INFERNAL CHAIN RESTAURANTS WITH THEIR TV JINGLES, MOLDED PLASTIC SEATS AND INSIPID CARTOON MASCOTS!
BUT... AREN'T YOU A MASCOT?
I'M A GOODWILL AMBASSADOR, KID. I'VE GOT DIGNITY.
Peirce

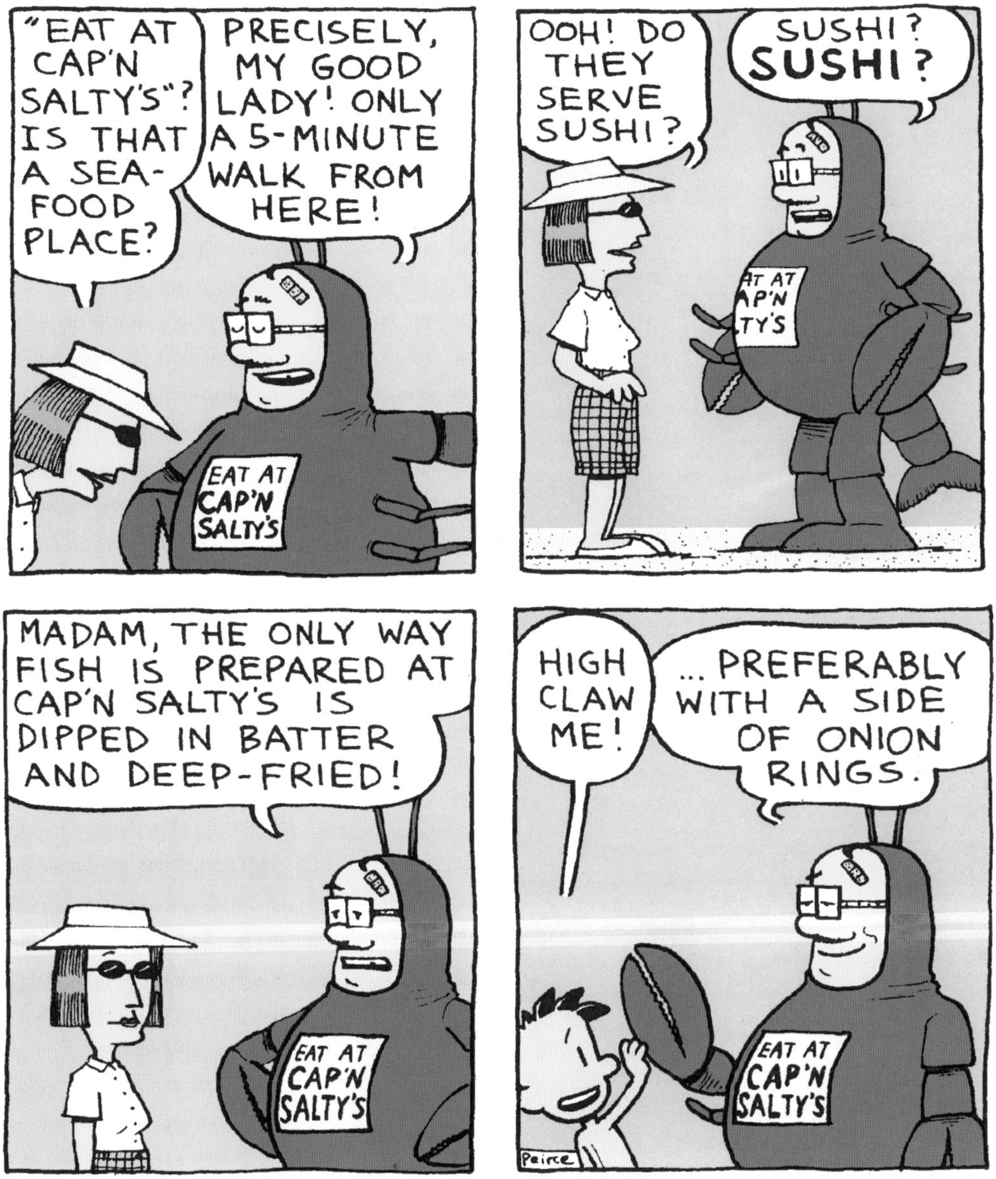
"EAT AT CAP'N SALTY'S"? IS THAT A SEA-FOOD PLACE?
PRECISELY, MY GOOD LADY! ONLY A 5-MINUTE WALK FROM HERE!
EAT AT CAP'N SALTY'S
OOH! DO THEY SERVE SUSHI?
SUSHI? **SUSHI?**
MADAM, THE ONLY WAY FISH IS PREPARED AT CAP'N SALTY'S IS DIPPED IN BATTER AND DEEP-FRIED!
EAT AT CAP'N SALTY'S
HIGH CLAW ME!
...PREFERABLY WITH A SIDE OF ONION RINGS.
EAT AT CAP'N SALTY'S
Peirce

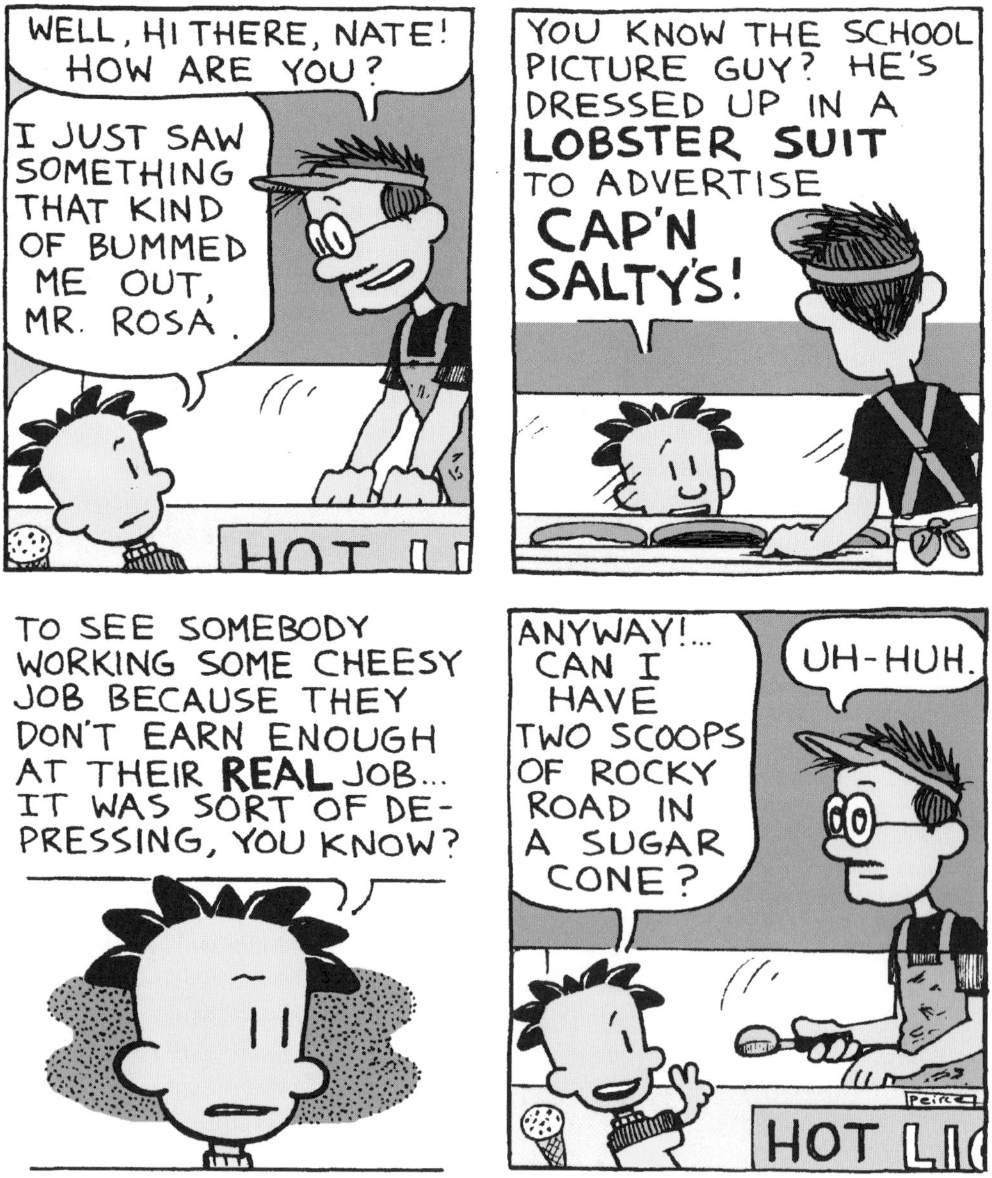
WELL, HI THERE, NATE! HOW ARE YOU?
I JUST SAW SOMETHING THAT KIND OF BUMMED ME OUT, MR. ROSA.
HOT LI
YOU KNOW THE SCHOOL PICTURE GUY? HE'S DRESSED UP IN A LOBSTER SUIT TO ADVERTISE CAP'N SALTY'S!
TO SEE SOMEBODY WORKING SOME CHEESY JOB BECAUSE THEY DON'T EARN ENOUGH AT THEIR REAL JOB... IT WAS SORT OF DE-PRESSING, YOU KNOW?
ANYWAY!... CAN I HAVE TWO SCOOPS OF ROCKY ROAD IN A SUGAR CONE?
UH-HUH.
PEIRCE
HOT LI

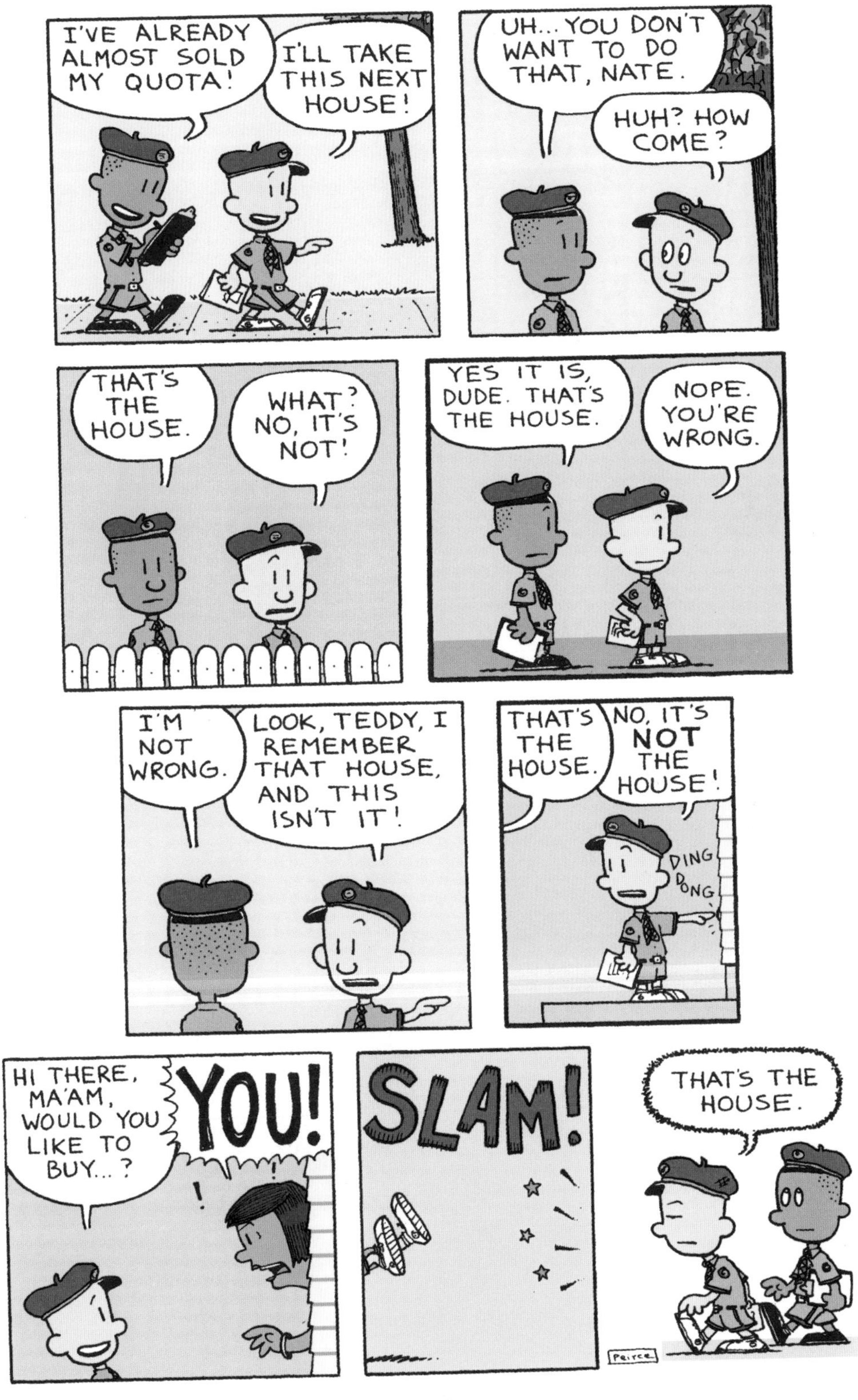
I'VE ALREADY ALMOST SOLD MY QUOTA!
I'LL TAKE THIS NEXT HOUSE!
UH... YOU DON'T WANT TO DO THAT, NATE.
HUH? HOW COME?
THAT'S THE HOUSE.
WHAT? NO, IT'S NOT!
YES IT IS, DUDE. THAT'S THE HOUSE.
NOPE. YOU'RE WRONG.
I'M NOT WRONG.
LOOK, TEDDY, I REMEMBER THAT HOUSE, AND THIS ISN'T IT!
THAT'S THE HOUSE.
NO, IT'S **NOT** THE HOUSE!
DING DONG
HI THERE, MA'AM, WOULD YOU LIKE TO BUY...?
YOU!
!
!
SLAM!
THAT'S THE HOUSE.
PEIRCE

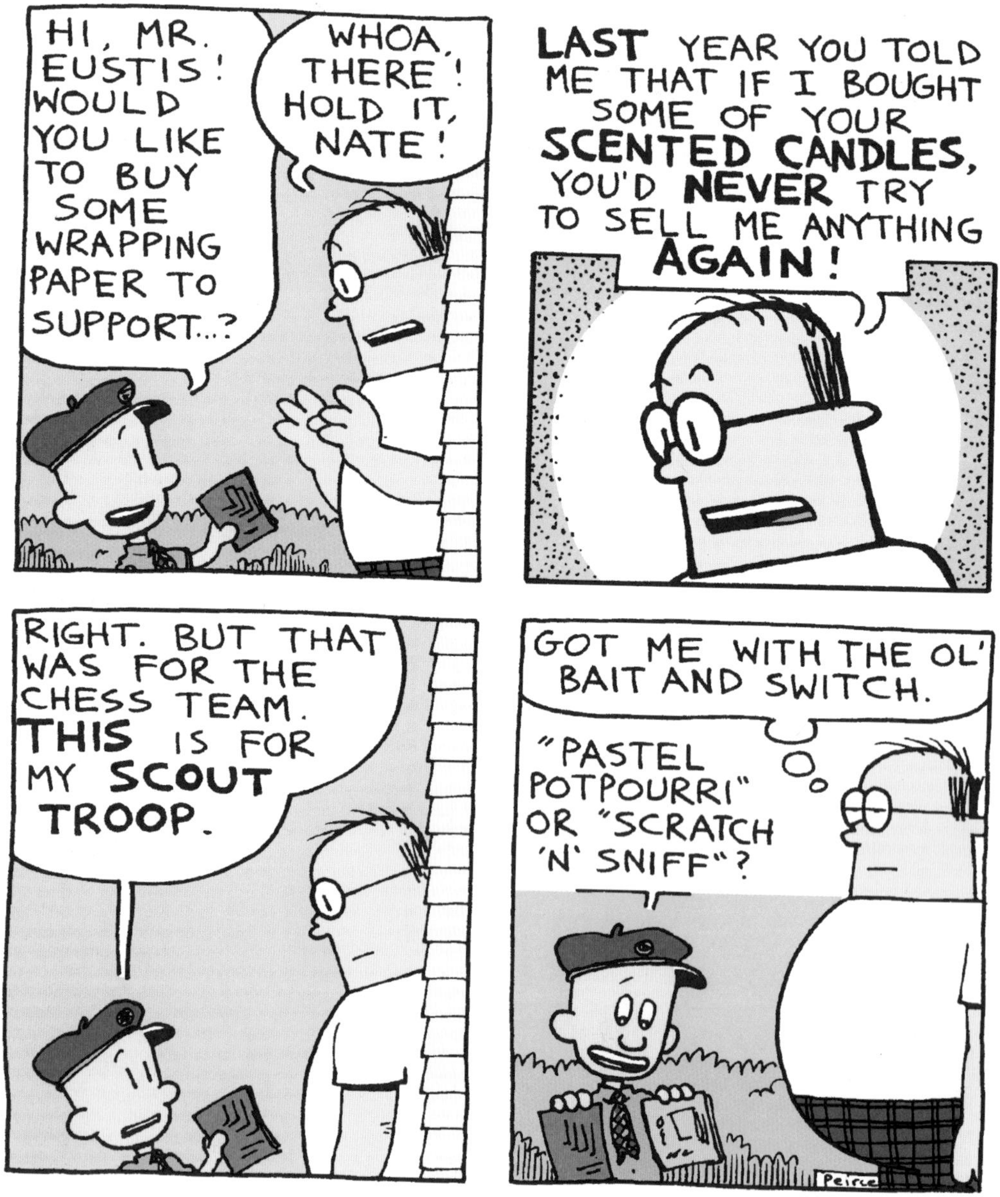
HI, MR. EUSTIS! WOULD YOU LIKE TO BUY SOME WRAPPING PAPER TO SUPPORT...?
WHOA, THERE! HOLD IT, NATE!
LAST YEAR YOU TOLD ME THAT IF I BOUGHT SOME OF YOUR SCENTED CANDLES, YOU'D NEVER TRY TO SELL ME ANYTHING AGAIN!
RIGHT. BUT THAT WAS FOR THE CHESS TEAM. THIS IS FOR MY SCOUT TROOP.
GOT ME WITH THE OL' BAIT AND SWITCH.
"PASTEL POTPOURRI" OR "SCRATCH 'N' SNIFF"?
Peirce

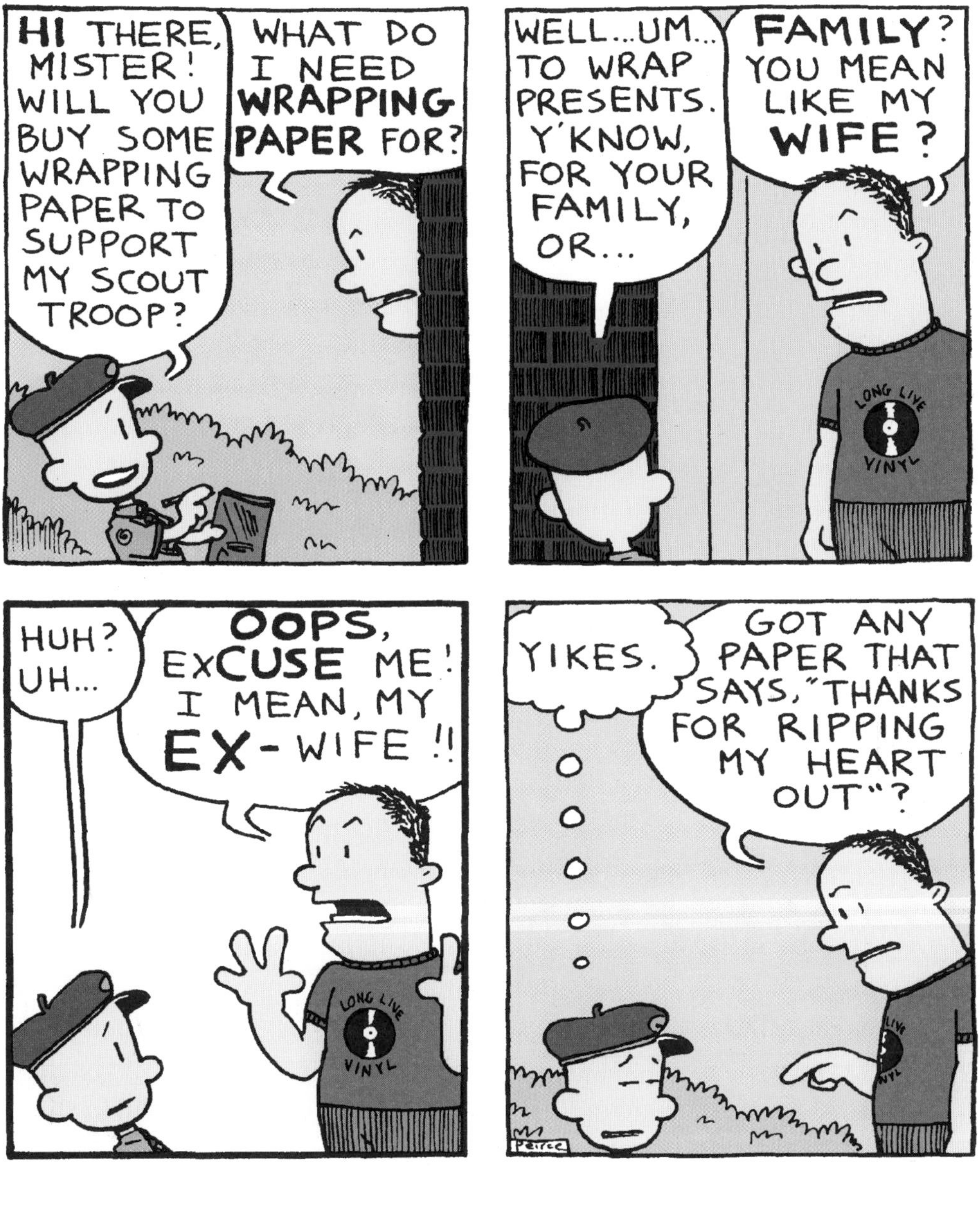
HI THERE, MISTER! WILL YOU BUY SOME WRAPPING PAPER TO SUPPORT MY SCOUT TROOP?
WHAT DO I NEED WRAPPING PAPER FOR?
WELL...UM... TO WRAP PRESENTS. Y'KNOW, FOR YOUR FAMILY, OR...
FAMILY? YOU MEAN LIKE MY WIFE?
LONG LIVE VINYL
HUH? UH...
OOPS, EXCUSE ME! I MEAN, MY EX-WIFE!!
LONG LIVE VINYL
YIKES.
GOT ANY PAPER THAT SAYS, "THANKS FOR RIPPING MY HEART OUT"?
PEIRCE

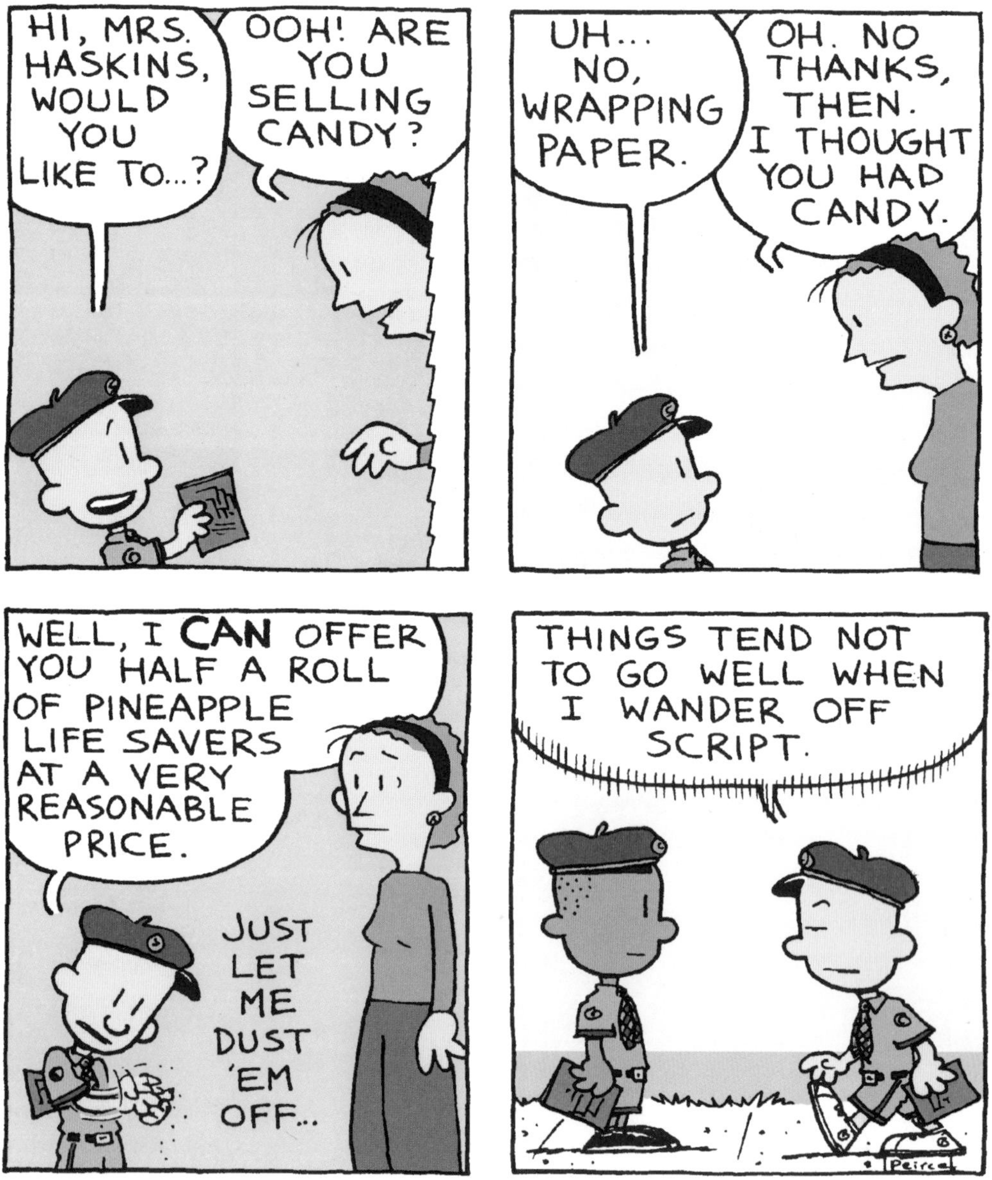
HI, MRS. HASKINS, WOULD YOU LIKE TO...?
OOH! ARE YOU SELLING CANDY?
UH... NO, WRAPPING PAPER.
OH. NO THANKS, THEN. I THOUGHT YOU HAD CANDY.
WELL, I CAN OFFER YOU HALF A ROLL OF PINEAPPLE LIFE SAVERS AT A VERY REASONABLE PRICE.
JUST LET ME DUST 'EM OFF...
THINGS TEND NOT TO GO WELL WHEN I WANDER OFF SCRIPT.
Peirce

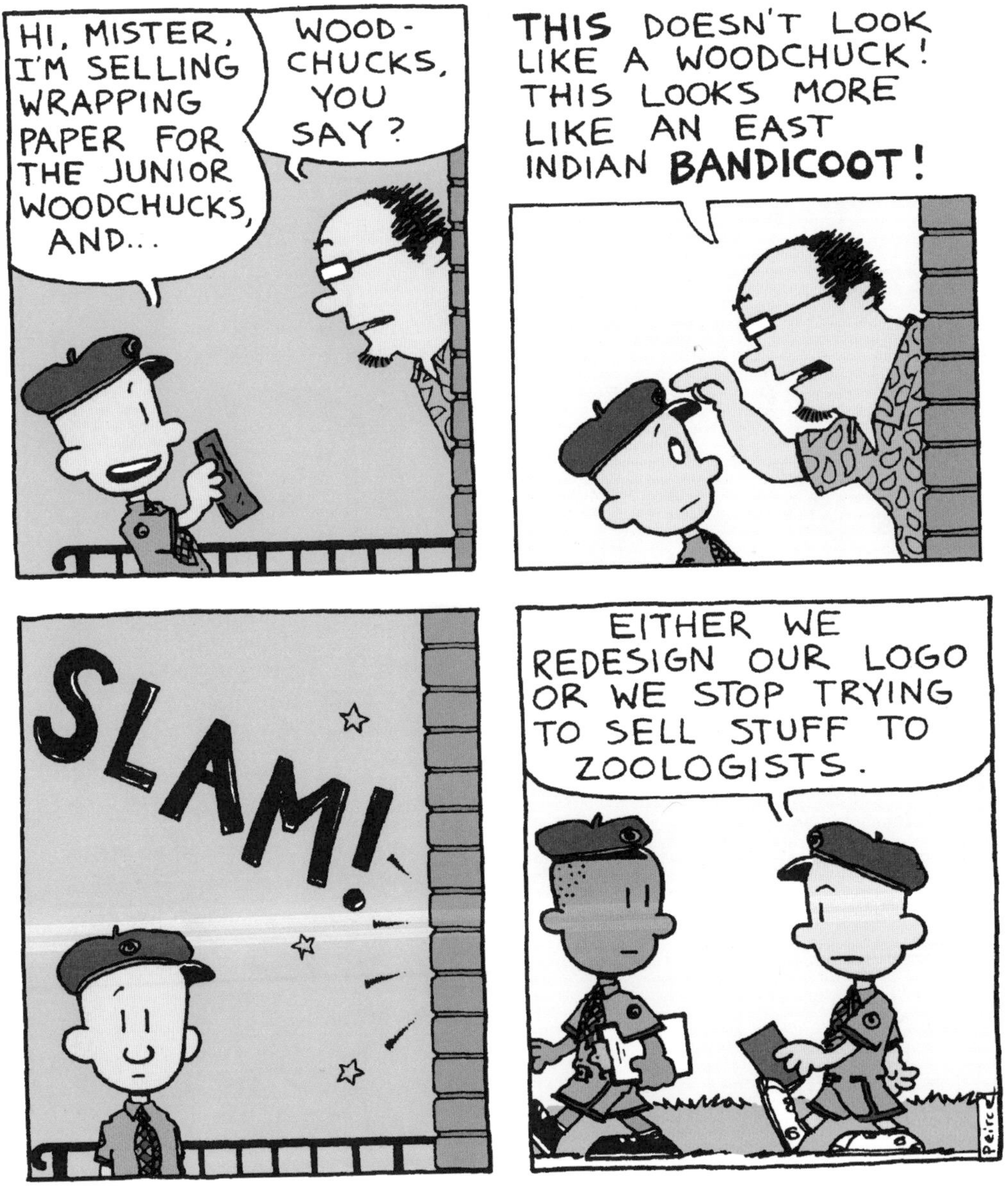

HI, MISTER, I'M SELLING WRAPPING PAPER FOR THE JUNIOR WOODCHUCKS, AND...
WOOD-CHUCKS, YOU SAY?
THIS DOESN'T LOOK LIKE A WOODCHUCK! THIS LOOKS MORE LIKE AN EAST INDIAN BANDICOOT!
SLAM!
EITHER WE REDESIGN OUR LOGO OR WE STOP TRYING TO SELL STUFF TO ZOOLOGISTS.
Peirce

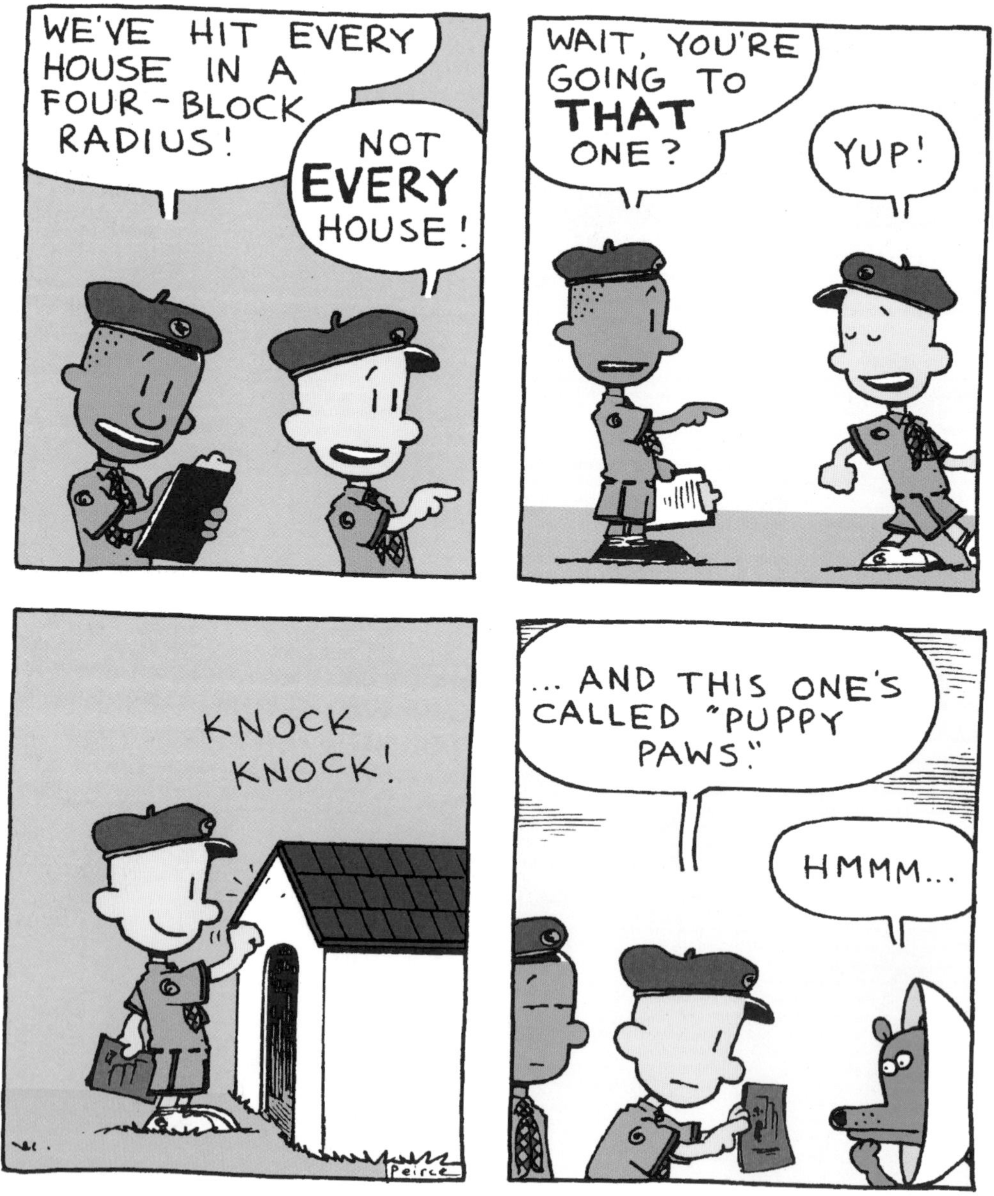
WE'VE HIT EVERY HOUSE IN A FOUR-BLOCK RADIUS!
NOT EVERY HOUSE!
WAIT, YOU'RE GOING TO THAT ONE?
YUP!
KNOCK KNOCK!
Peirce
... AND THIS ONE'S CALLED "PUPPY PAWS."
HMMM...

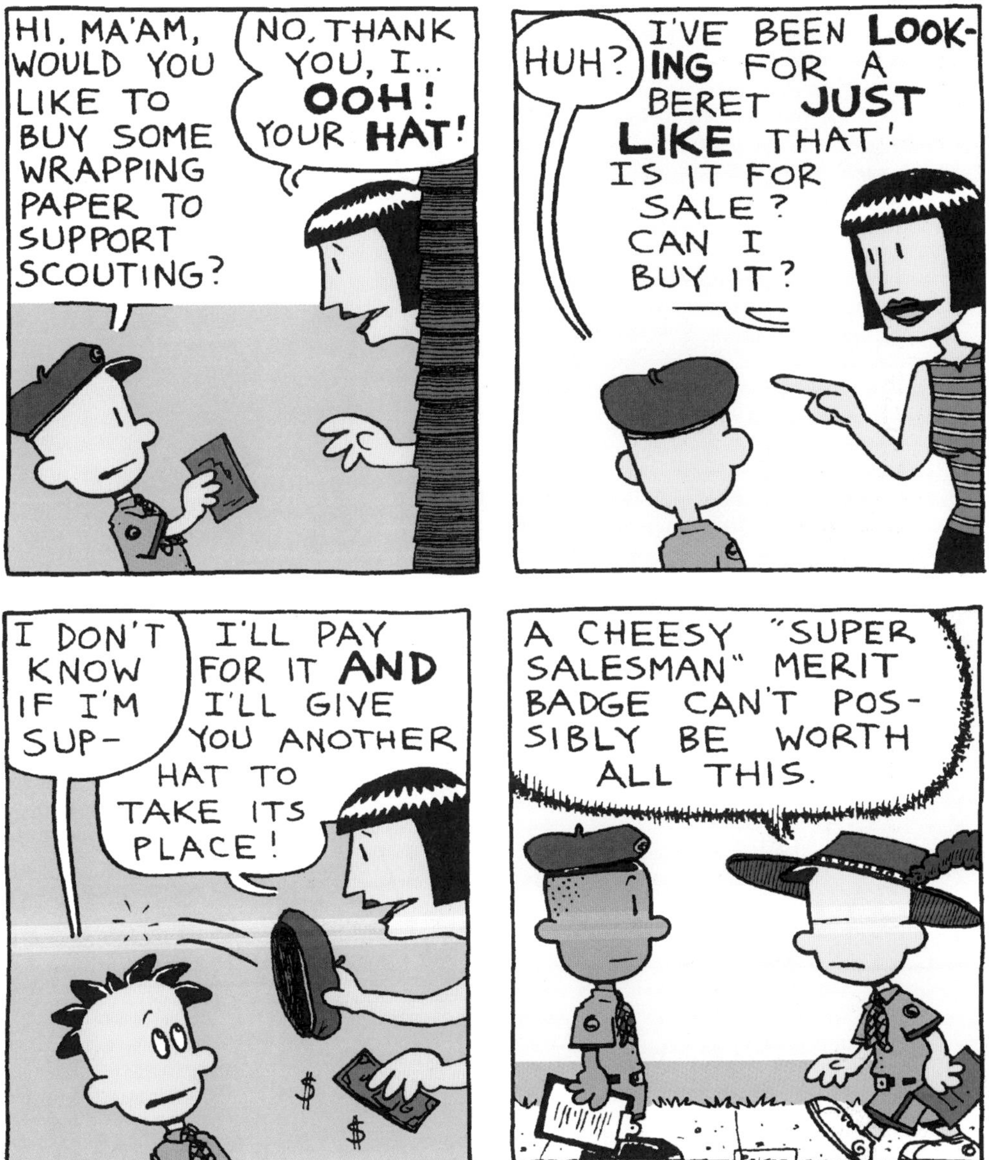

HI, MA'AM, WOULD YOU LIKE TO BUY SOME WRAPPING PAPER TO SUPPORT SCOUTING?
NO, THANK YOU, I... **OOH!** YOUR **HAT!**
HUH?
I'VE BEEN **LOOKING** FOR A BERET **JUST LIKE** THAT! IS IT FOR SALE? CAN I BUY IT?
I DON'T KNOW IF I'M SUP-
I'LL PAY FOR IT **AND** I'LL GIVE YOU ANOTHER HAT TO TAKE ITS PLACE!
$
$
A CHEESY "SUPER SALESMAN" MERIT BADGE CAN'T POSSIBLY BE WORTH ALL THIS.
Peirce

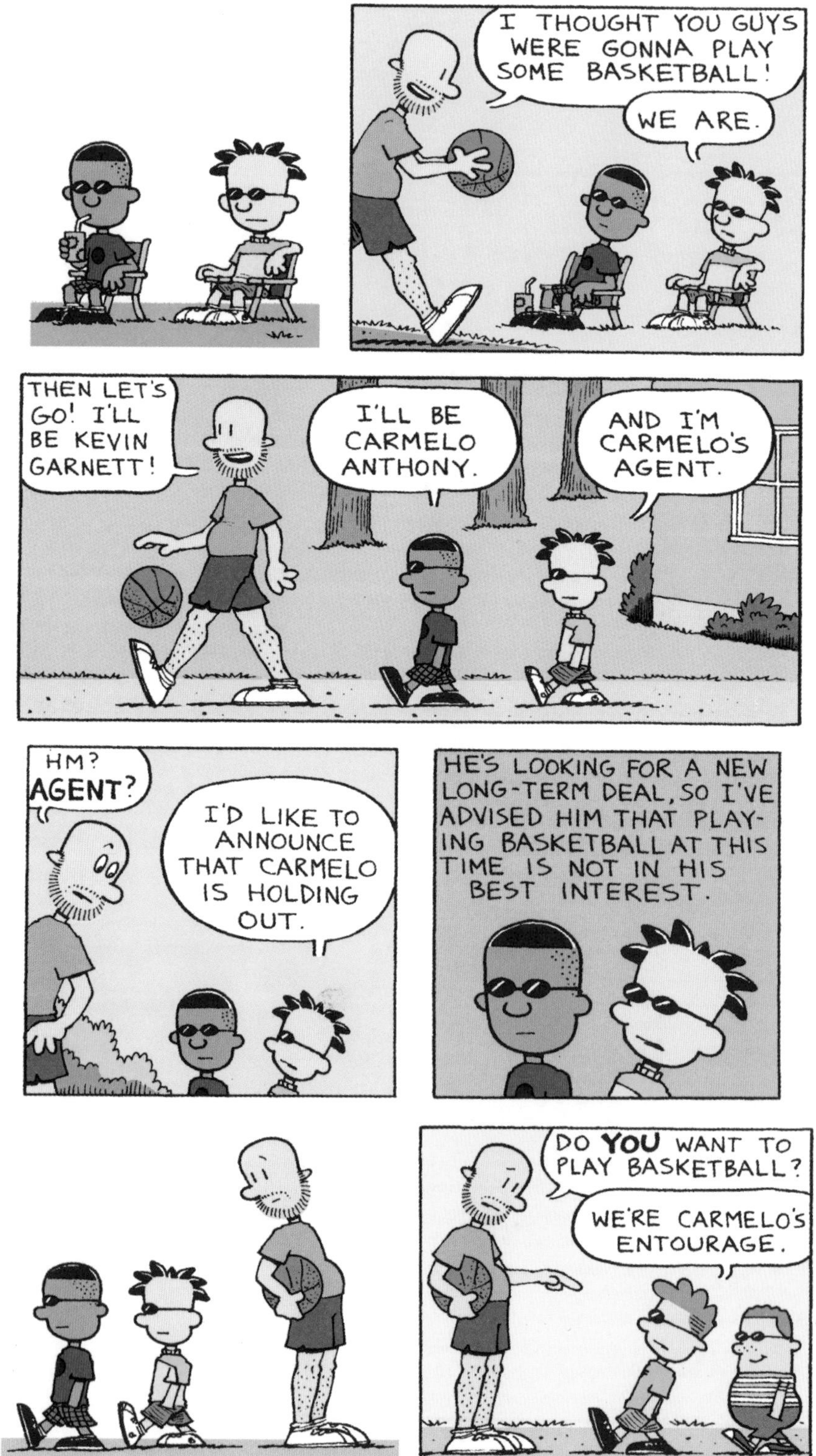
I THOUGHT YOU GUYS WERE GONNA PLAY SOME BASKETBALL!
WE ARE.
THEN LET'S GO! I'LL BE KEVIN GARNETT!
I'LL BE CARMELO ANTHONY.
AND I'M CARMELO'S AGENT.
HM? AGENT?
I'D LIKE TO ANNOUNCE THAT CARMELO IS HOLDING OUT.
HE'S LOOKING FOR A NEW LONG-TERM DEAL, SO I'VE ADVISED HIM THAT PLAYING BASKETBALL AT THIS TIME IS NOT IN HIS BEST INTEREST.
DO YOU WANT TO PLAY BASKETBALL?
WE'RE CARMELO'S ENTOURAGE.
Peirce

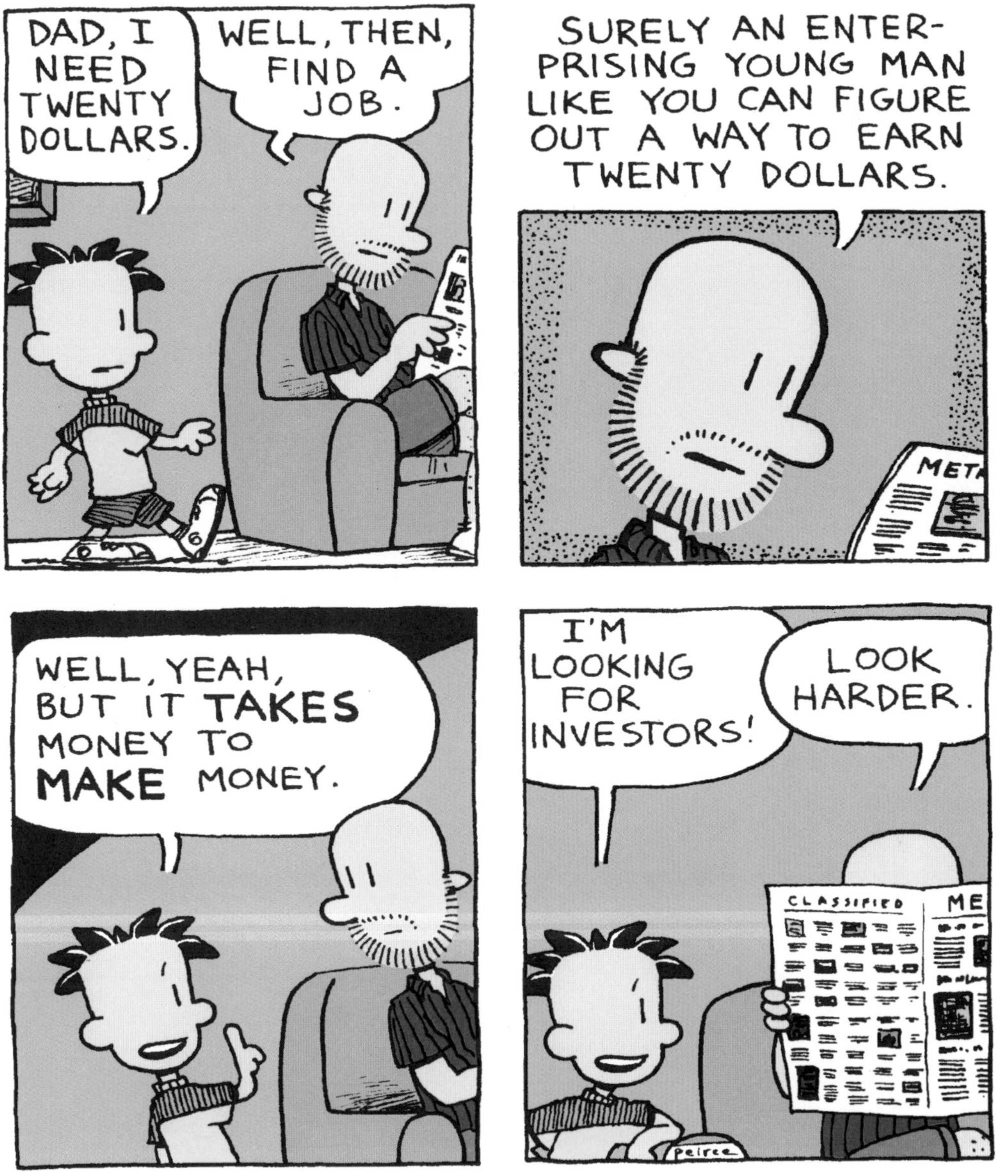
DAD, I NEED TWENTY DOLLARS.
WELL, THEN, FIND A JOB.
SURELY AN ENTERPRISING YOUNG MAN LIKE YOU CAN FIGURE OUT A WAY TO EARN TWENTY DOLLARS.
METR
WELL, YEAH, BUT IT **TAKES** MONEY TO **MAKE** MONEY.
I'M LOOKING FOR INVESTORS!
LOOK HARDER.
CLASSIFIED
ME
peirce

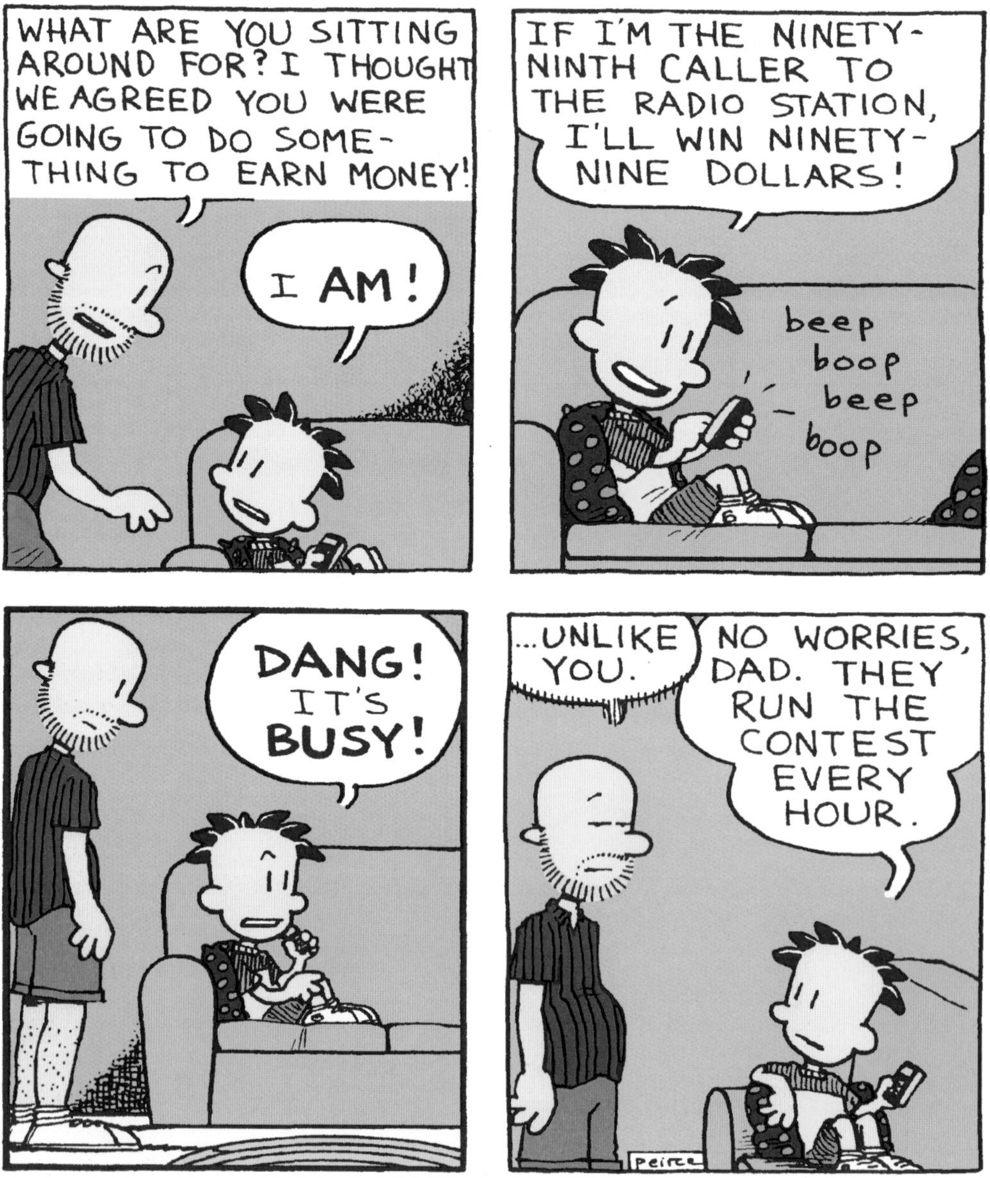
WHAT ARE YOU SITTING AROUND FOR? I THOUGHT WE AGREED YOU WERE GOING TO DO SOME-THING TO EARN MONEY!
I AM!
IF I'M THE NINETY-NINTH CALLER TO THE RADIO STATION, I'LL WIN NINETY-NINE DOLLARS!
beep boop beep boop
DANG! IT'S BUSY!
NO WORRIES, DAD. THEY RUN THE CONTEST EVERY HOUR.
...UNLIKE YOU.
peirce

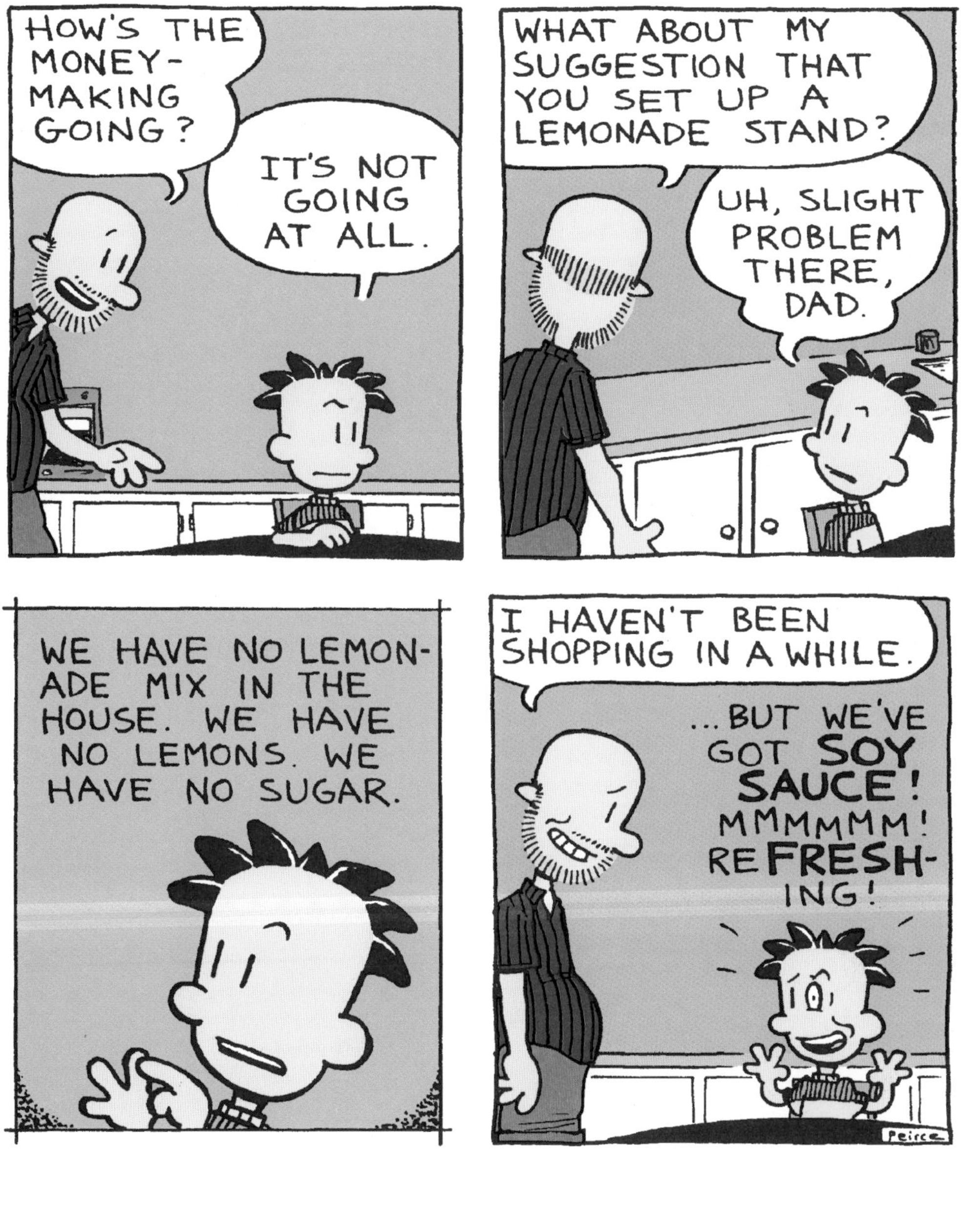

HOW'S THE MONEY-MAKING GOING?
IT'S NOT GOING AT ALL.
WHAT ABOUT MY SUGGESTION THAT YOU SET UP A LEMONADE STAND?
UH, SLIGHT PROBLEM THERE, DAD.
WE HAVE NO LEMONADE MIX IN THE HOUSE. WE HAVE NO LEMONS. WE HAVE NO SUGAR.
I HAVEN'T BEEN SHOPPING IN A WHILE.
...BUT WE'VE GOT SOY SAUCE! MMMMMM! REFRESHING!
Peirce

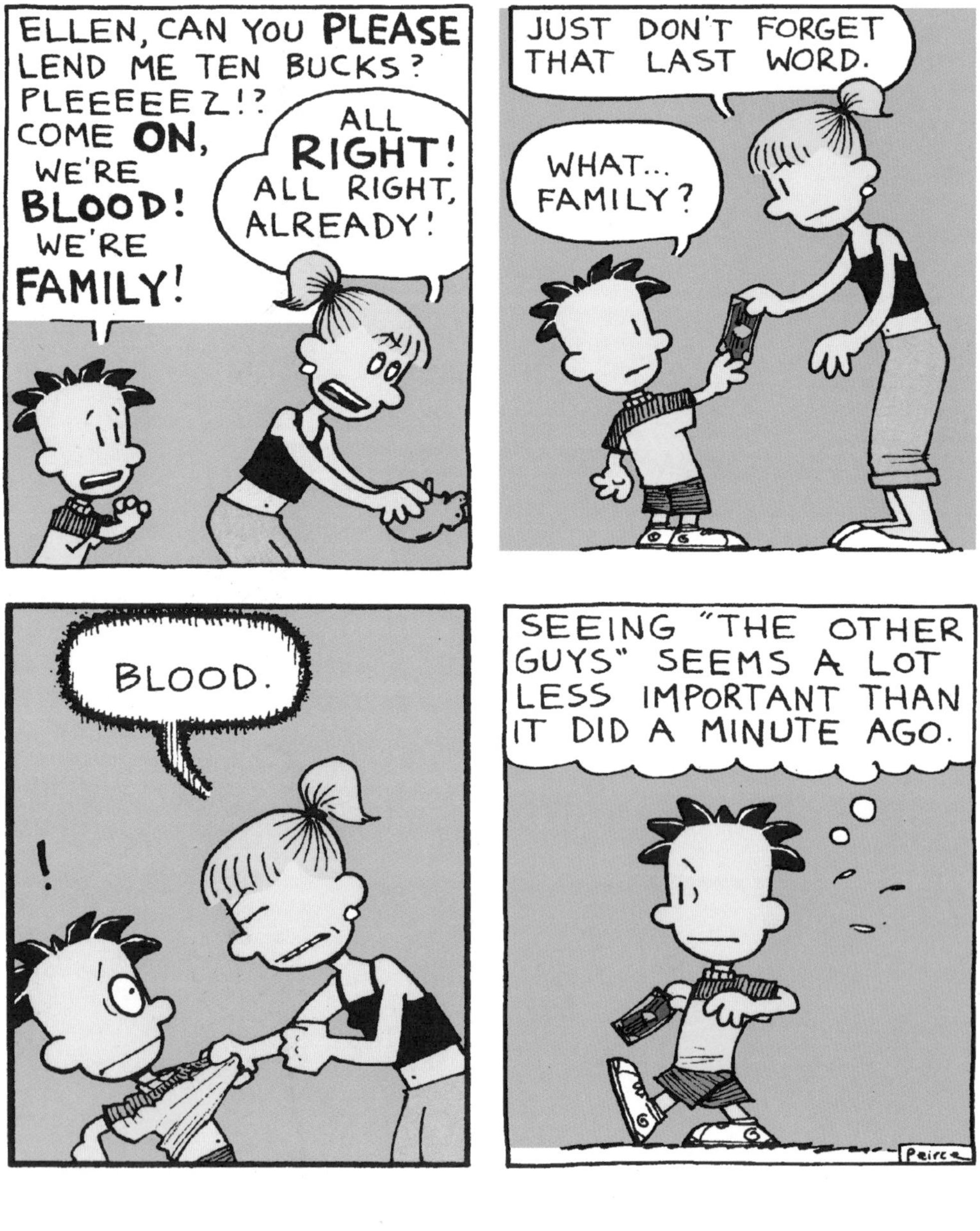
ELLEN, CAN YOU PLEASE LEND ME TEN BUCKS? PLEEEEEZ!? COME ON, WE'RE BLOOD! WE'RE FAMILY!
ALL RIGHT! ALL RIGHT, ALREADY!
JUST DON'T FORGET THAT LAST WORD.
WHAT... FAMILY?
BLOOD.
!
SEEING "THE OTHER GUYS" SEEMS A LOT LESS IMPORTANT THAN IT DID A MINUTE AGO.
Peirce

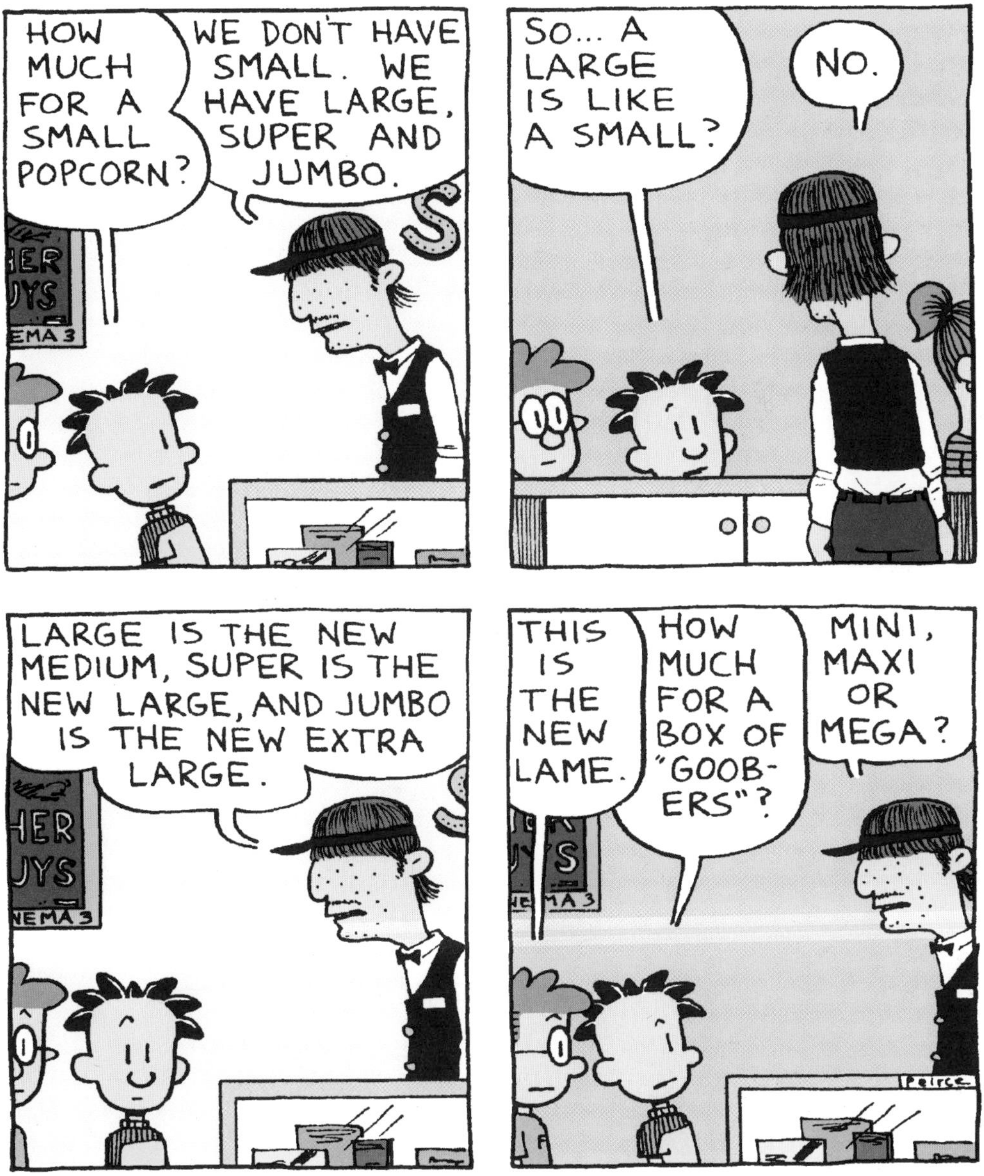
HOW MUCH FOR A SMALL POPCORN?
WE DON'T HAVE SMALL. WE HAVE LARGE, SUPER AND JUMBO.
SO... A LARGE IS LIKE A SMALL?
NO.
LARGE IS THE NEW MEDIUM, SUPER IS THE NEW LARGE, AND JUMBO IS THE NEW EXTRA LARGE.
THIS IS THE NEW LAME.
HOW MUCH FOR A BOX OF "GOOBERS"?
MINI, MAXI OR MEGA?
Peirce

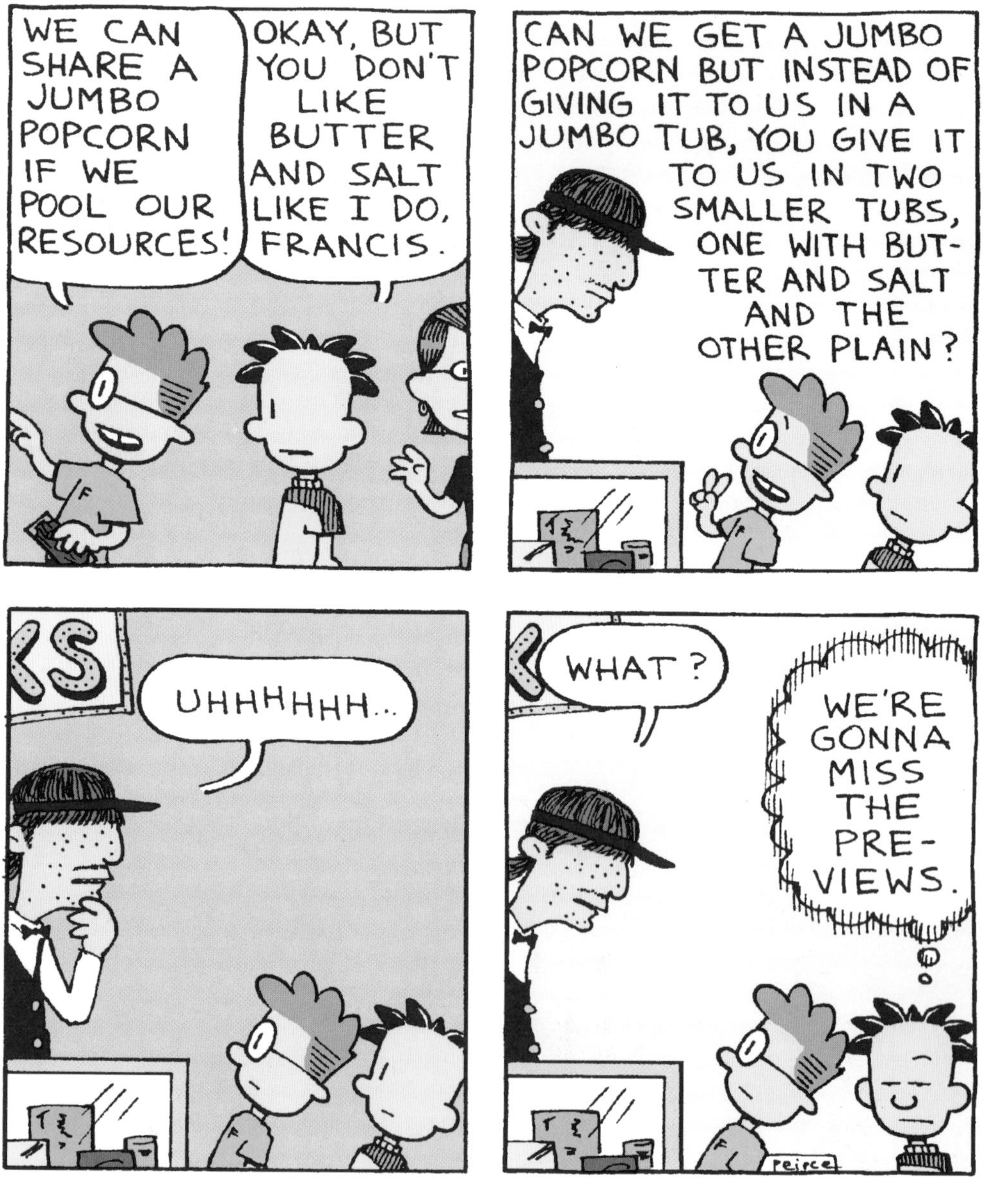
WE CAN SHARE A JUMBO POPCORN IF WE POOL OUR RESOURCES!
OKAY, BUT YOU DON'T LIKE BUTTER AND SALT LIKE I DO, FRANCIS.
CAN WE GET A JUMBO POPCORN BUT INSTEAD OF GIVING IT TO US IN A JUMBO TUB, YOU GIVE IT TO US IN TWO SMALLER TUBS, ONE WITH BUTTER AND SALT AND THE OTHER PLAIN?
UHHHHHH...
WHAT?
WE'RE GONNA MISS THE PREVIEWS.
peirce

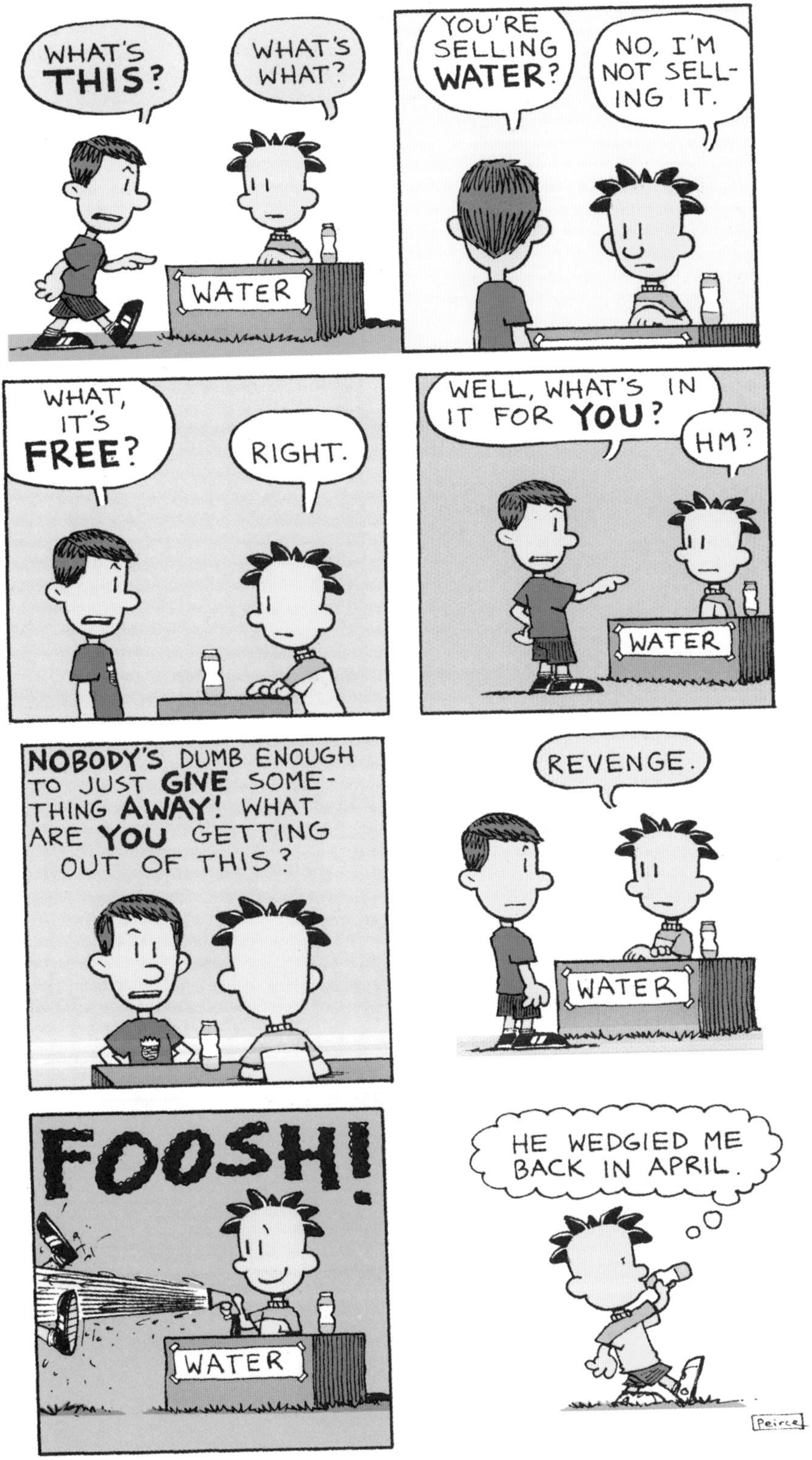
WHAT'S THIS?
WHAT'S WHAT?
YOU'RE SELLING WATER?
NO, I'M NOT SELL- ING IT.
WHAT, IT'S FREE?
RIGHT.
WELL, WHAT'S IN IT FOR YOU?
HM?
NOBODY'S DUMB ENOUGH TO JUST GIVE SOME- THING AWAY! WHAT ARE YOU GETTING OUT OF THIS?
REVENGE.
FOOSH!
HE WEDGIED ME BACK IN APRIL.
WATER
Peirce

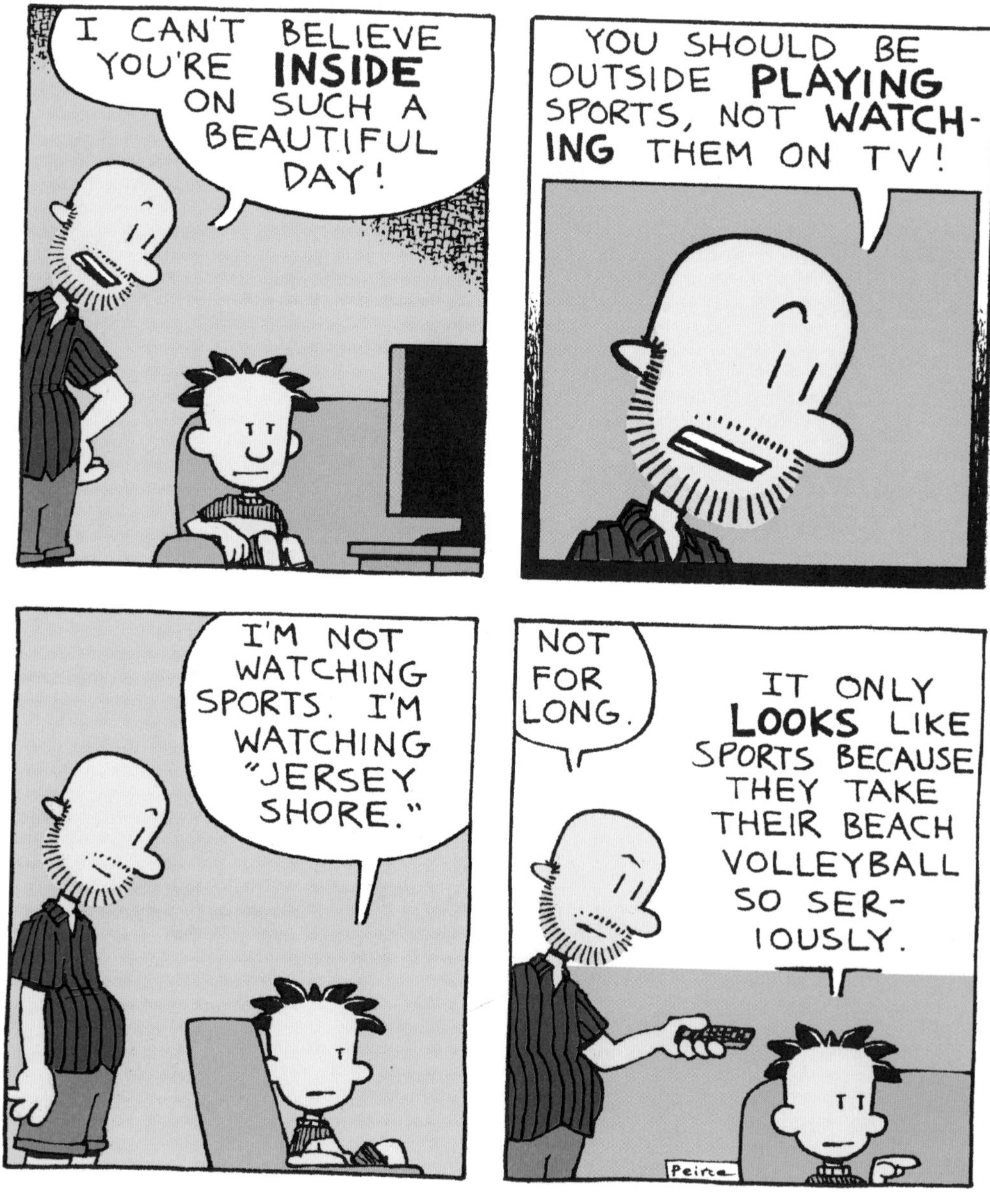
I CAN'T BELIEVE YOU'RE **INSIDE** ON SUCH A BEAUTIFUL DAY!
YOU SHOULD BE OUTSIDE **PLAYING** SPORTS, NOT **WATCHING** THEM ON TV!
I'M NOT WATCHING SPORTS. I'M WATCHING "JERSEY SHORE."
IT ONLY **LOOKS** LIKE SPORTS BECAUSE THEY TAKE THEIR BEACH VOLLEYBALL SO SERIOUSLY.
NOT FOR LONG.
Peirce

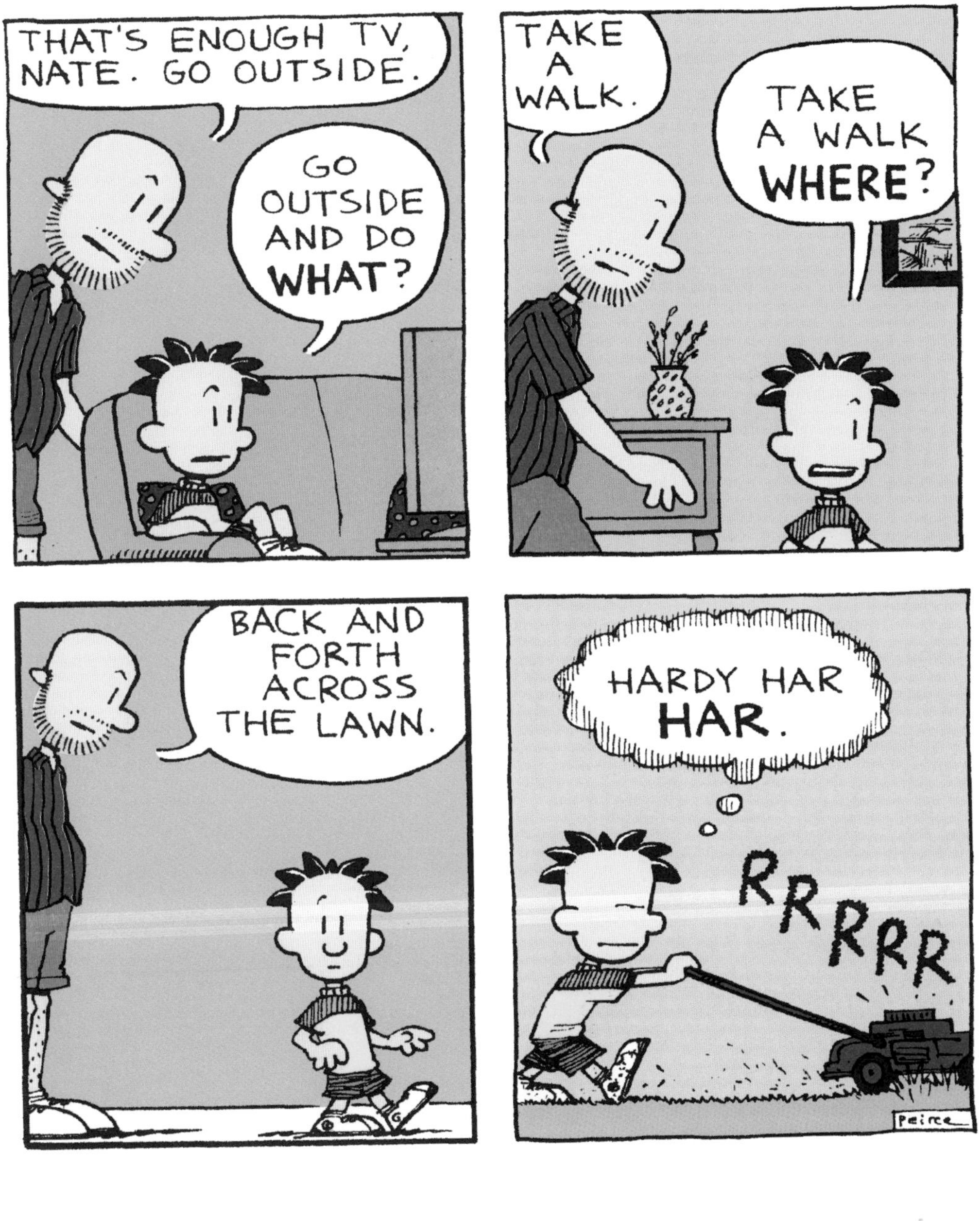
THAT'S ENOUGH TV, NATE. GO OUTSIDE.
GO OUTSIDE AND DO **WHAT**?
TAKE A WALK.
TAKE A WALK **WHERE**?
BACK AND FORTH ACROSS THE LAWN.
HARDY HAR **HAR**.
RRRRRR
Peirce

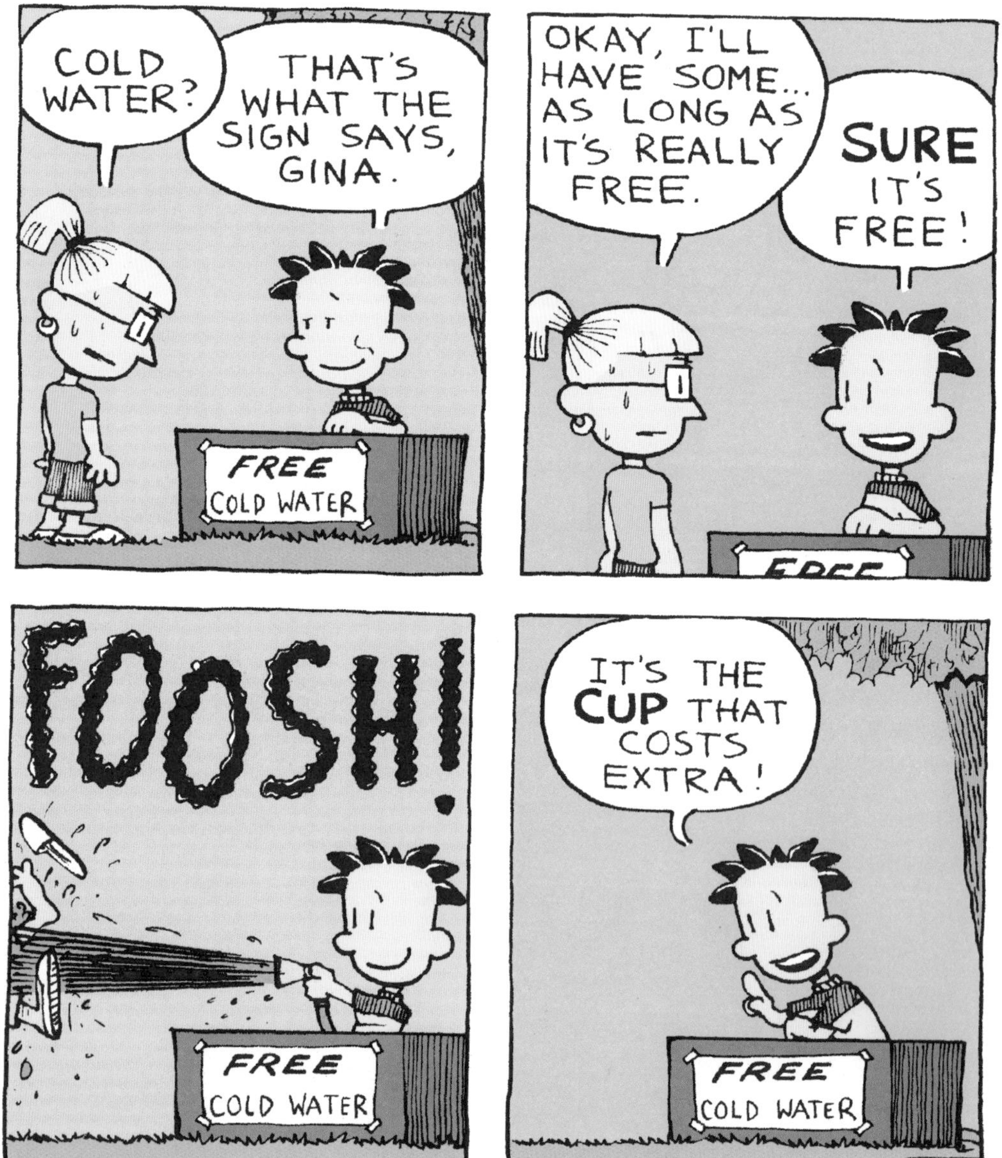
COLD WATER?
THAT'S WHAT THE SIGN SAYS, GINA.
FREE COLD WATER
OKAY, I'LL HAVE SOME... AS LONG AS IT'S REALLY FREE.
SURE IT'S FREE!
FOOSH!
FREE COLD WATER
IT'S THE CUP THAT COSTS EXTRA!
FREE COLD WATER
Peirce

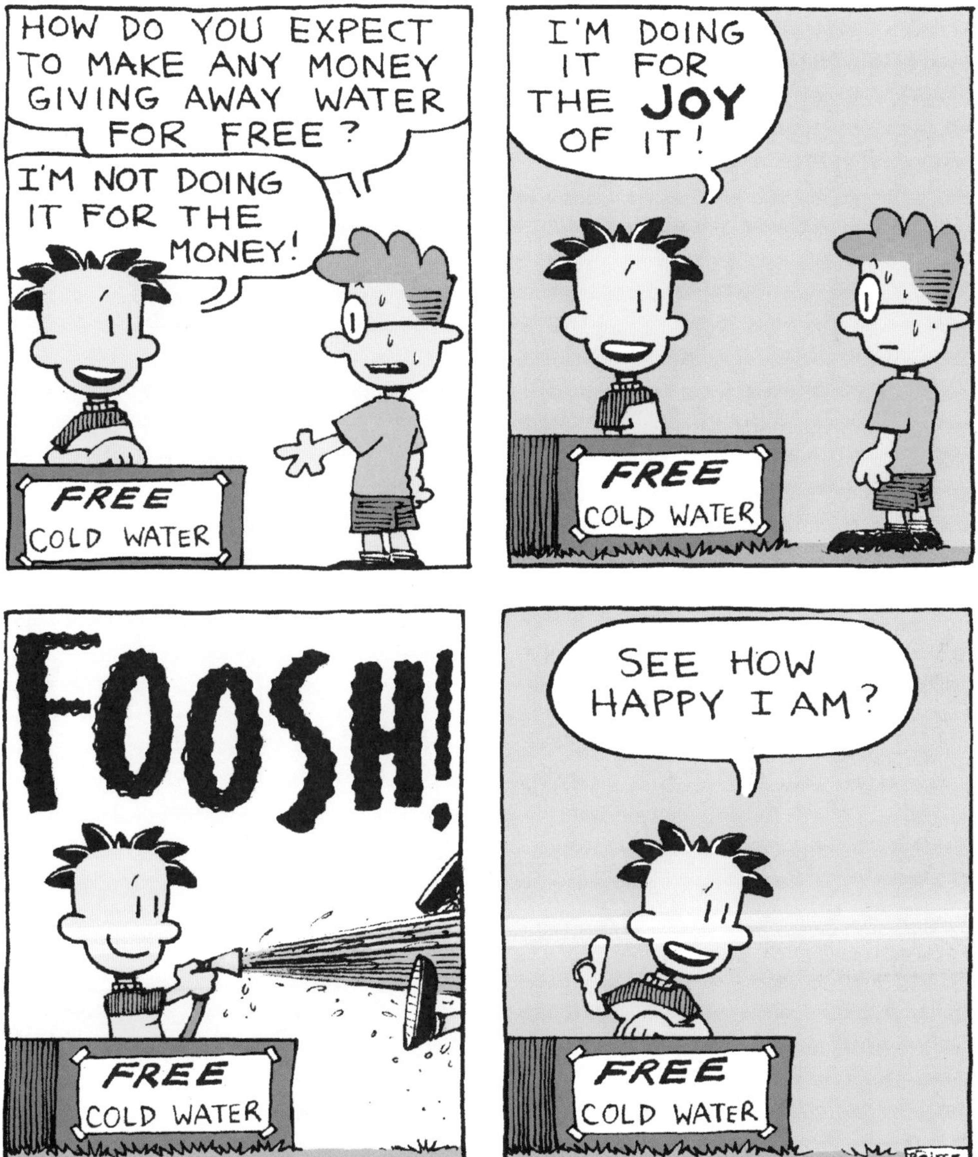
HOW DO YOU EXPECT TO MAKE ANY MONEY GIVING AWAY WATER FOR FREE?
I'M NOT DOING IT FOR THE MONEY!
FREE COLD WATER
I'M DOING IT FOR THE JOY OF IT!
FREE COLD WATER
FOOSH!
FREE COLD WATER
SEE HOW HAPPY I AM?
FREE COLD WATER
Peirce

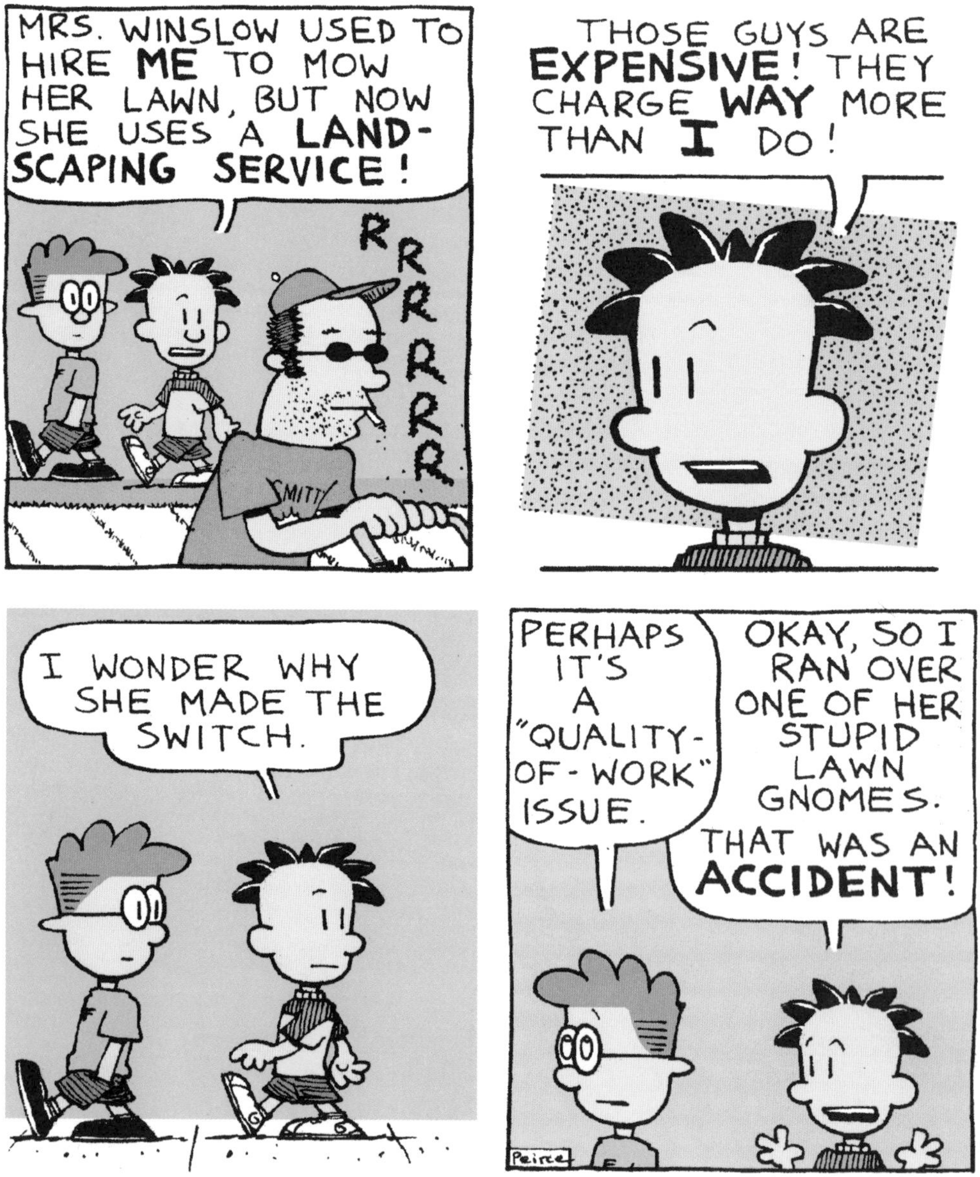
MRS. WINSLOW USED TO HIRE **ME** TO MOW HER LAWN, BUT NOW SHE USES A **LAND-SCAPING SERVICE**!
RRRRRRR
SMITTY
THOSE GUYS ARE **EXPENSIVE**! THEY CHARGE **WAY** MORE THAN **I** DO!
I WONDER WHY SHE MADE THE SWITCH.
PERHAPS IT'S A "QUALITY-OF-WORK" ISSUE.
OKAY, SO I RAN OVER ONE OF HER STUPID LAWN GNOMES. THAT WAS AN **ACCIDENT**!
Peirce

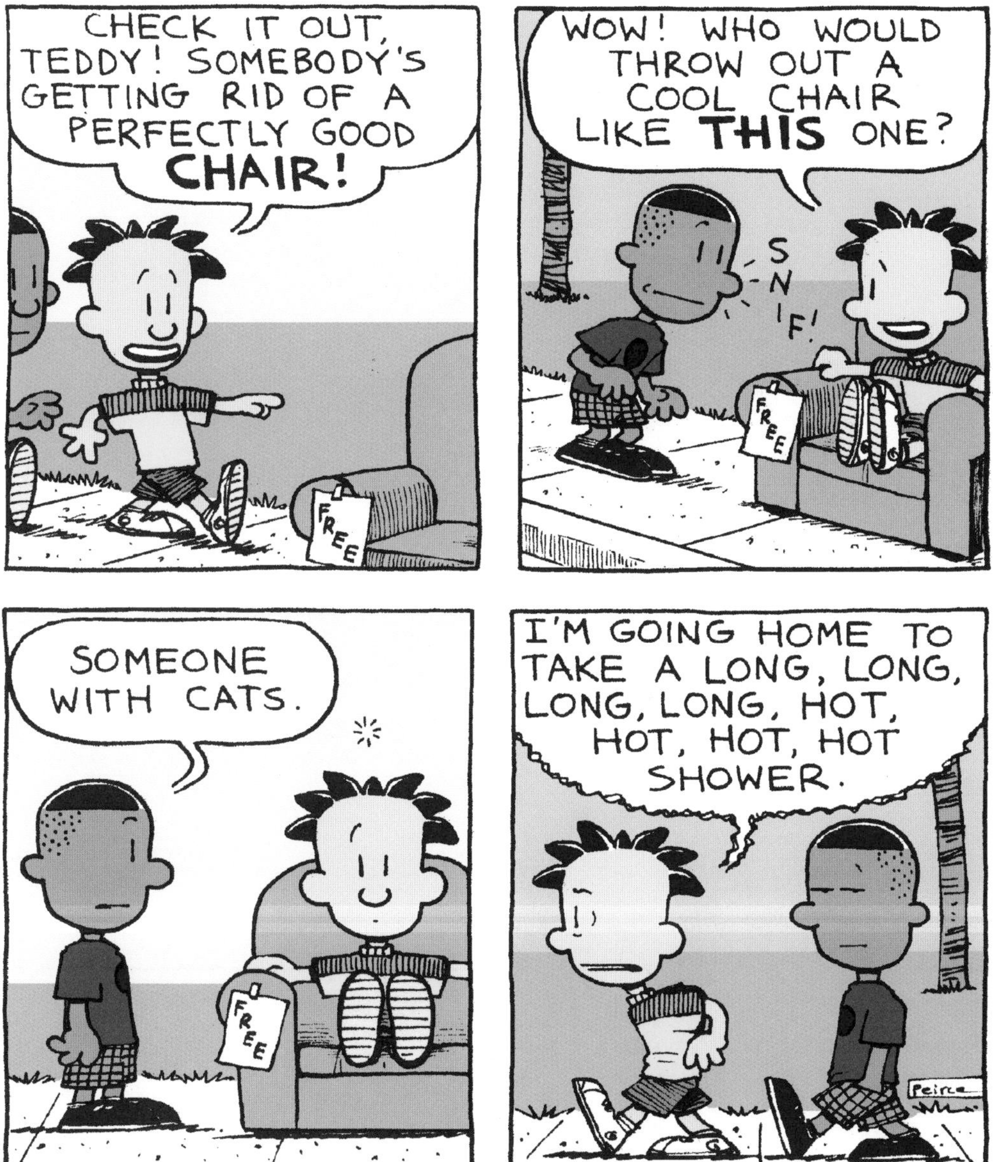
CHECK IT OUT, TEDDY! SOMEBODY'S GETTING RID OF A PERFECTLY GOOD CHAIR!
FREE
WOW! WHO WOULD THROW OUT A COOL CHAIR LIKE THIS ONE?
SNIF!
FREE
SOMEONE WITH CATS.
FREE
I'M GOING HOME TO TAKE A LONG, LONG, LONG, LONG, HOT, HOT, HOT, HOT SHOWER.
Peirce

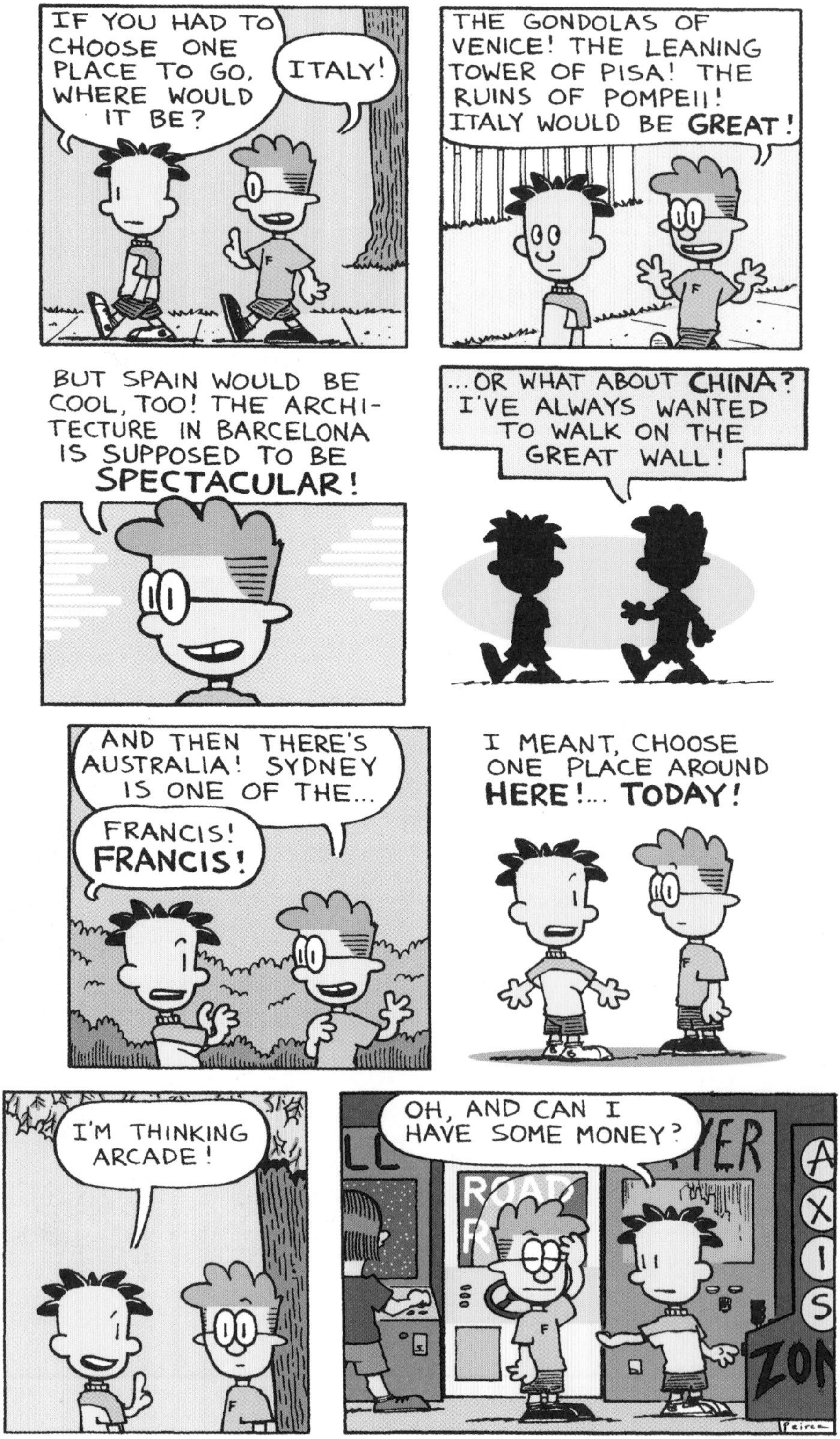
IF YOU HAD TO CHOOSE ONE PLACE TO GO, WHERE WOULD IT BE?
ITALY!
THE GONDOLAS OF VENICE! THE LEANING TOWER OF PISA! THE RUINS OF POMPEII! ITALY WOULD BE **GREAT**!
BUT SPAIN WOULD BE COOL, TOO! THE ARCHITECTURE IN BARCELONA IS SUPPOSED TO BE **SPECTACULAR**!
...OR WHAT ABOUT **CHINA**? I'VE ALWAYS WANTED TO WALK ON THE GREAT WALL!
AND THEN THERE'S AUSTRALIA! SYDNEY IS ONE OF THE...
FRANCIS! **FRANCIS!**
I MEANT, CHOOSE ONE PLACE AROUND **HERE!... TODAY!**
I'M THINKING ARCADE!
OH, AND CAN I HAVE SOME MONEY?

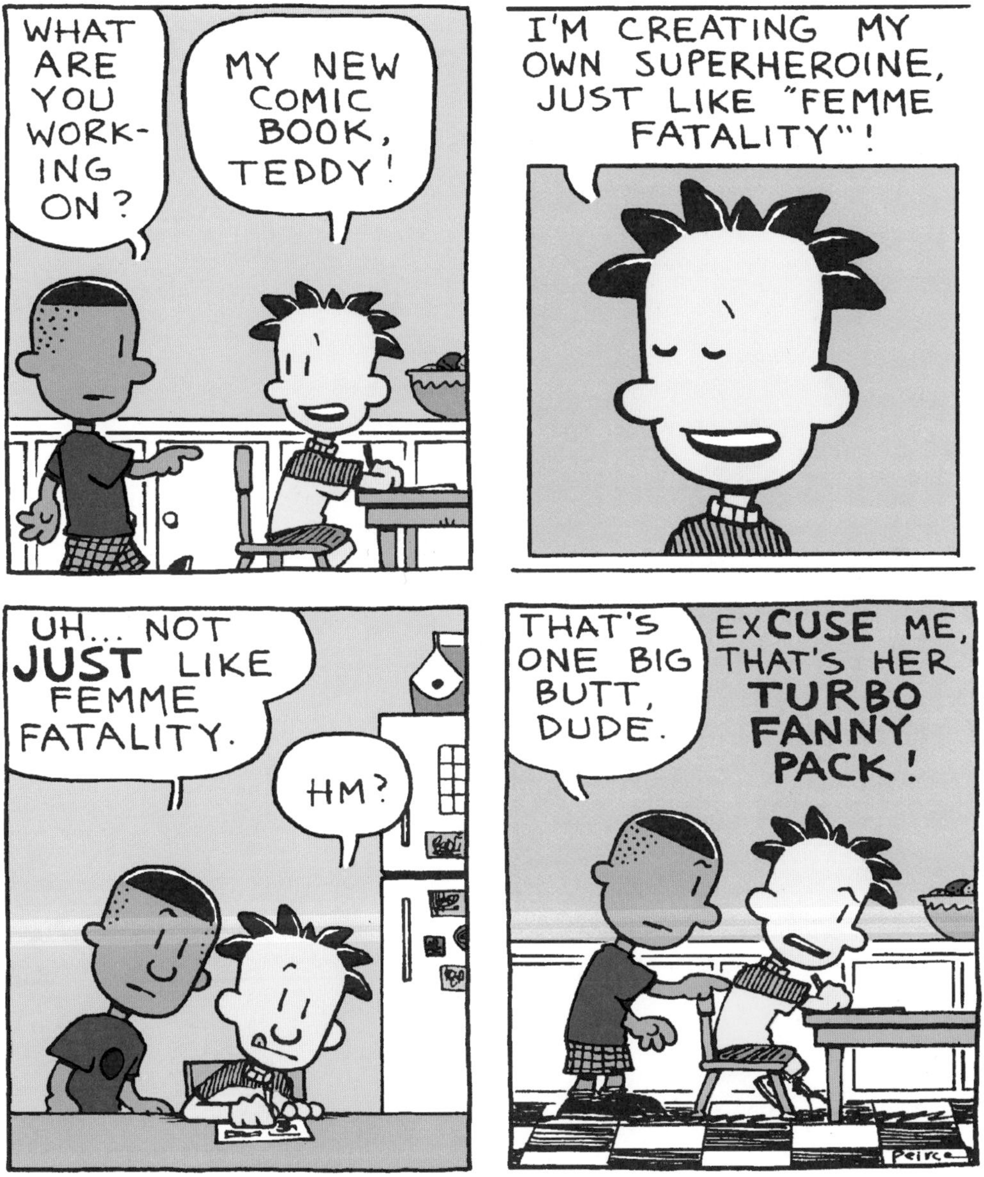
WHAT ARE YOU WORKING ON?
MY NEW COMIC BOOK, TEDDY!
I'M CREATING MY OWN SUPERHEROINE, JUST LIKE "FEMME FATALITY"!
UH... NOT **JUST** LIKE FEMME FATALITY.
HM?
THAT'S ONE BIG BUTT, DUDE.
EX**CUSE** ME, THAT'S HER **TURBO FANNY PACK!**
Peirce

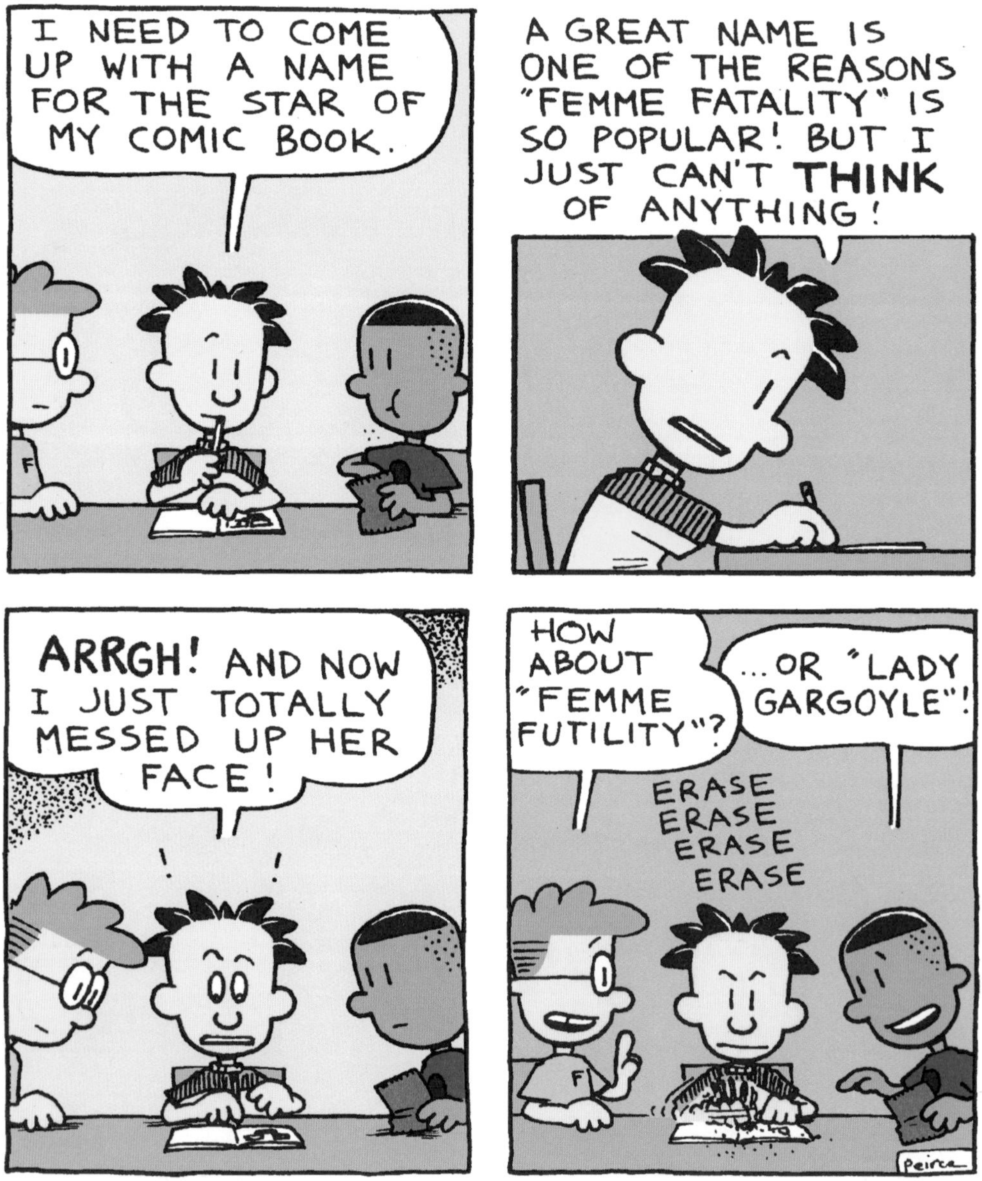
I NEED TO COME UP WITH A NAME FOR THE STAR OF MY COMIC BOOK.
A GREAT NAME IS ONE OF THE REASONS "FEMME FATALITY" IS SO POPULAR! BUT I JUST CAN'T THINK OF ANYTHING!
ARRGH! AND NOW I JUST TOTALLY MESSED UP HER FACE!
! !
HOW ABOUT "FEMME FUTILITY"?
...OR "LADY GARGOYLE"!
ERASE ERASE ERASE ERASE
peirce

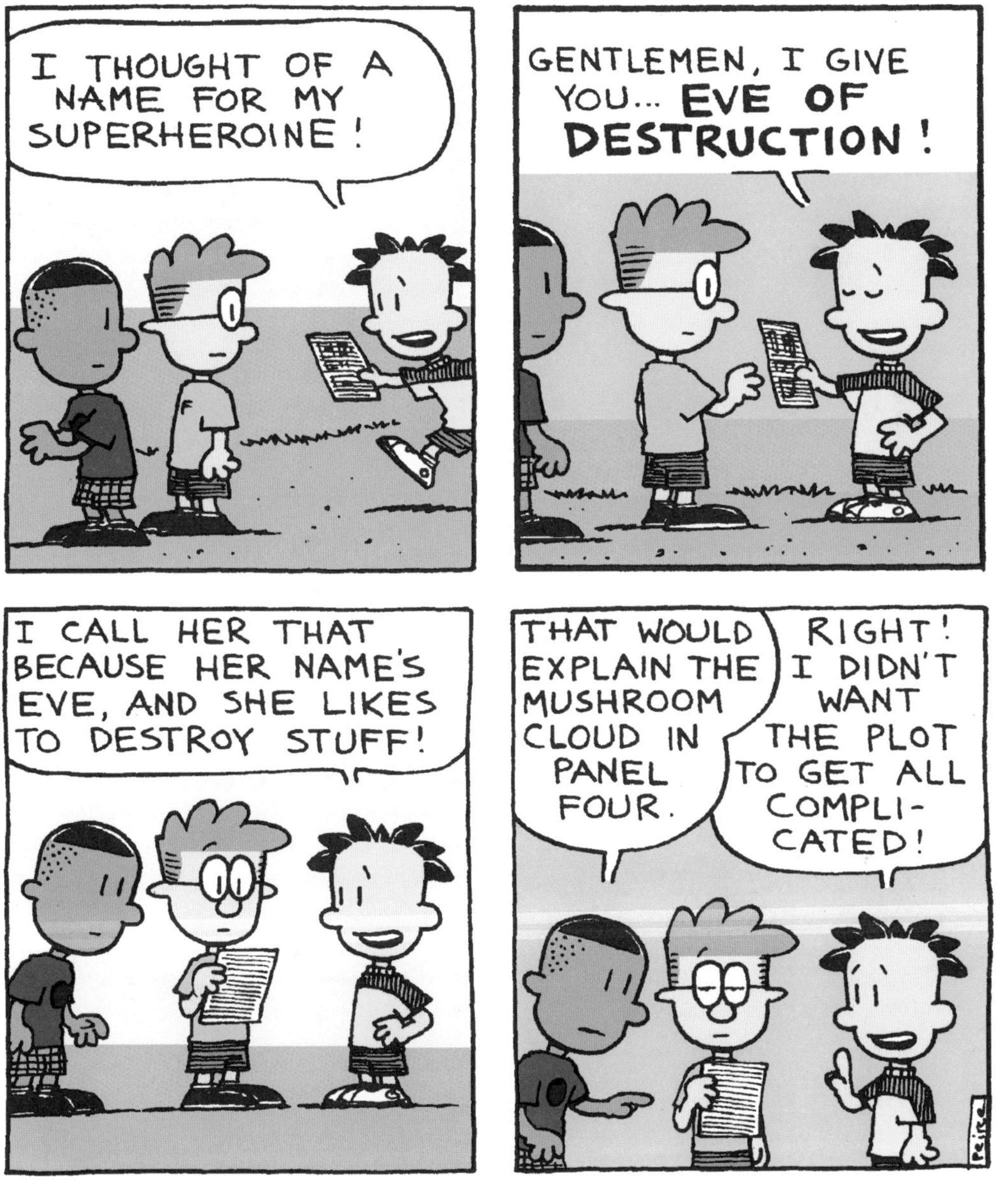
I THOUGHT OF A NAME FOR MY SUPERHEROINE!
GENTLEMEN, I GIVE YOU... EVE OF DESTRUCTION!
I CALL HER THAT BECAUSE HER NAME'S EVE, AND SHE LIKES TO DESTROY STUFF!
THAT WOULD EXPLAIN THE MUSHROOM CLOUD IN PANEL FOUR.
RIGHT! I DIDN'T WANT THE PLOT TO GET ALL COMPLI-CATED!
PEIRCE

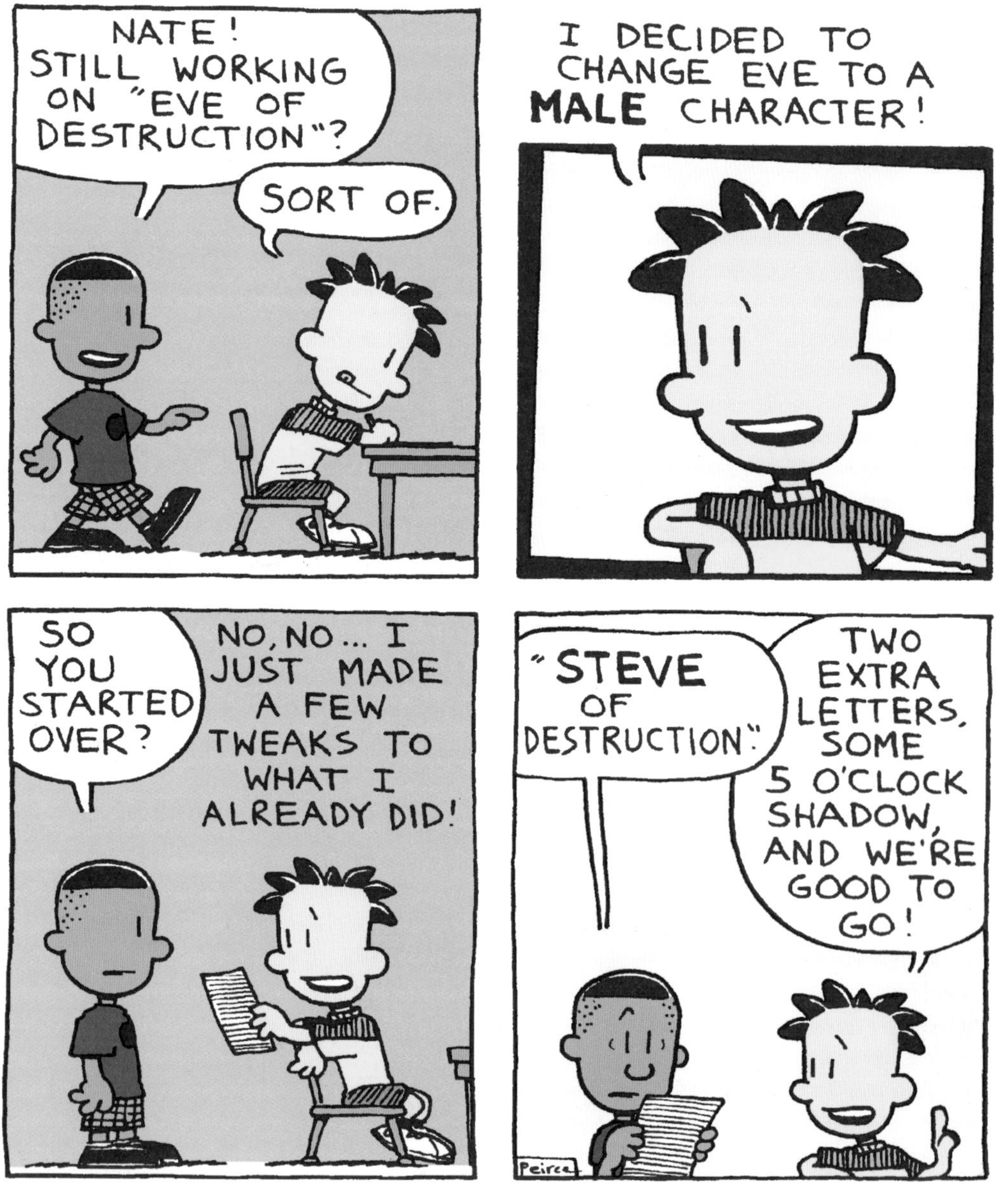
NATE! STILL WORKING ON "EVE OF DESTRUCTION"?
SORT OF.
I DECIDED TO CHANGE EVE TO A **MALE** CHARACTER!
SO YOU STARTED OVER?
NO, NO... I JUST MADE A FEW TWEAKS TO WHAT I ALREADY DID!
"**STEVE** OF DESTRUCTION."
TWO EXTRA LETTERS, SOME 5 O'CLOCK SHADOW, AND WE'RE GOOD TO GO!
Peirce

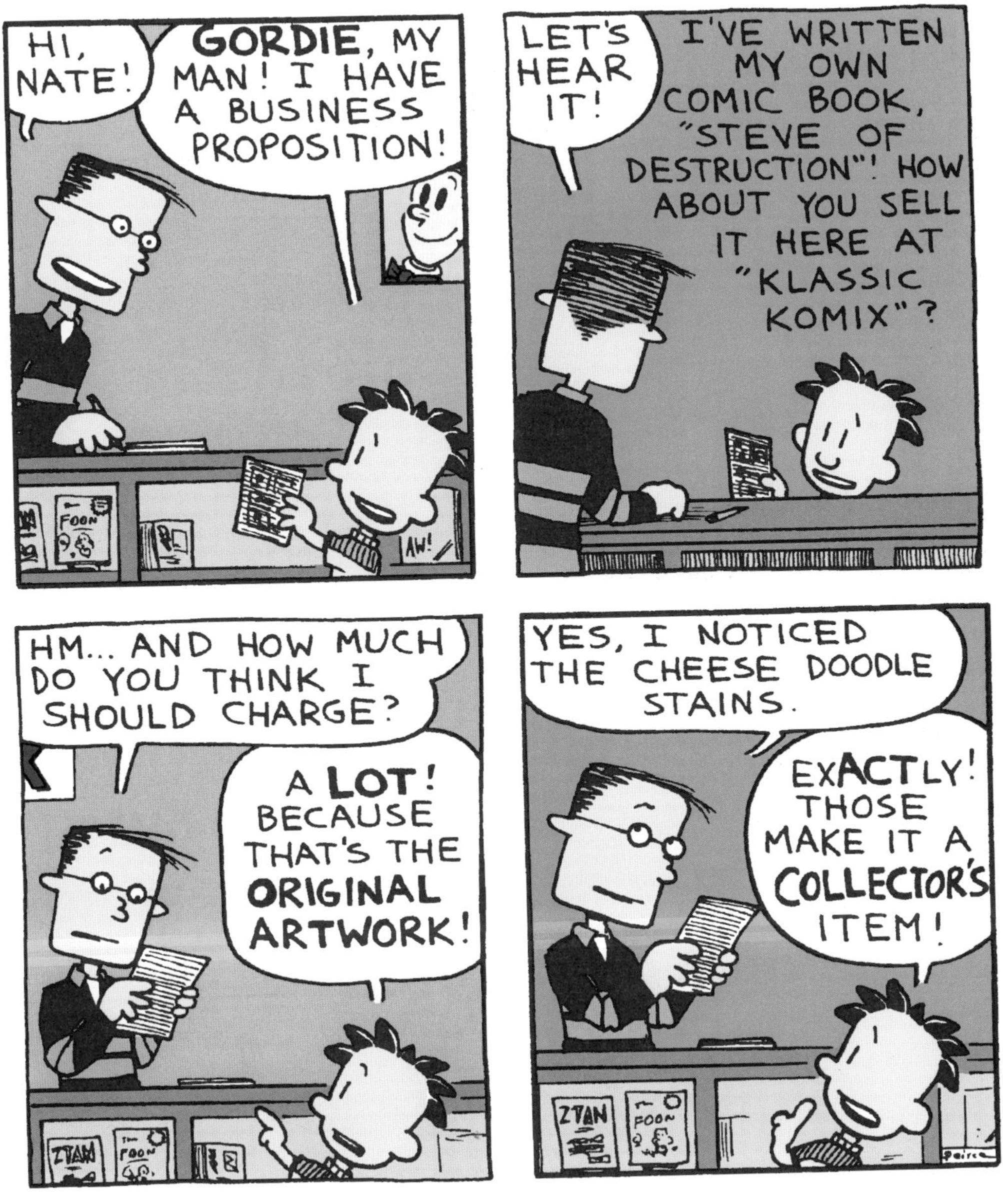
HI, NATE!
GORDIE, MY MAN! I HAVE A BUSINESS PROPOSITION!
LET'S HEAR IT!
I'VE WRITTEN MY OWN COMIC BOOK, "STEVE OF DESTRUCTION"! HOW ABOUT YOU SELL IT HERE AT "KLASSIC KOMIX"?
HM... AND HOW MUCH DO YOU THINK I SHOULD CHARGE?
A LOT! BECAUSE THAT'S THE ORIGINAL ARTWORK!
YES, I NOTICED THE CHEESE DOODLE STAINS.
EXACTLY! THOSE MAKE IT A COLLECTOR'S ITEM!

AH! I SEE YOU'RE A FAN OF ADVENTURE COMIC BOOKS, MISTER!

UH... YEAH.

WELL, THEN, YOU MIGHT ENJOY **THIS** BRAND-NEW CREATION! IT'S CALLED "STEVE OF DESTRUCTION"!

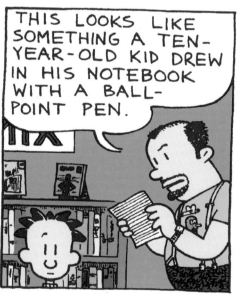

THIS LOOKS LIKE SOMETHING A TEN-YEAR-OLD KID DREW IN HIS NOTEBOOK WITH A BALL-POINT PEN.

YOUR FIRST REVIEW!

FOR THE **RECORD**, PAL, I'M **ELEVEN**!

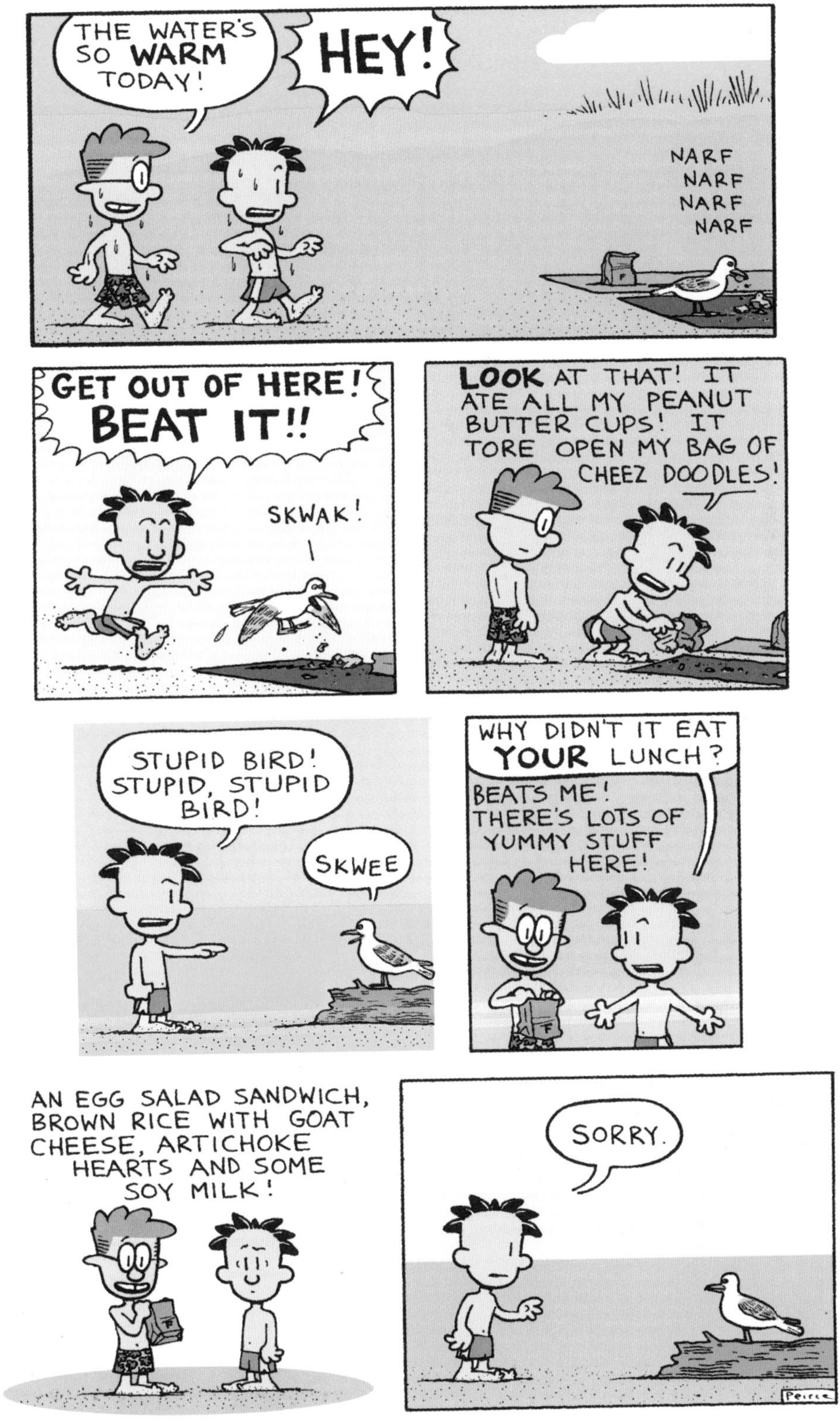
THE WATER'S SO WARM TODAY!
HEY!
NARF NARF NARF NARF
GET OUT OF HERE! BEAT IT!!
SKWAK!
LOOK AT THAT! IT ATE ALL MY PEANUT BUTTER CUPS! IT TORE OPEN MY BAG OF CHEEZ DOODLES!
STUPID BIRD! STUPID, STUPID BIRD!
SKWEE
WHY DIDN'T IT EAT YOUR LUNCH?
BEATS ME! THERE'S LOTS OF YUMMY STUFF HERE!
AN EGG SALAD SANDWICH, BROWN RICE WITH GOAT CHEESE, ARTICHOKE HEARTS AND SOME SOY MILK!
SORRY.
Peirce

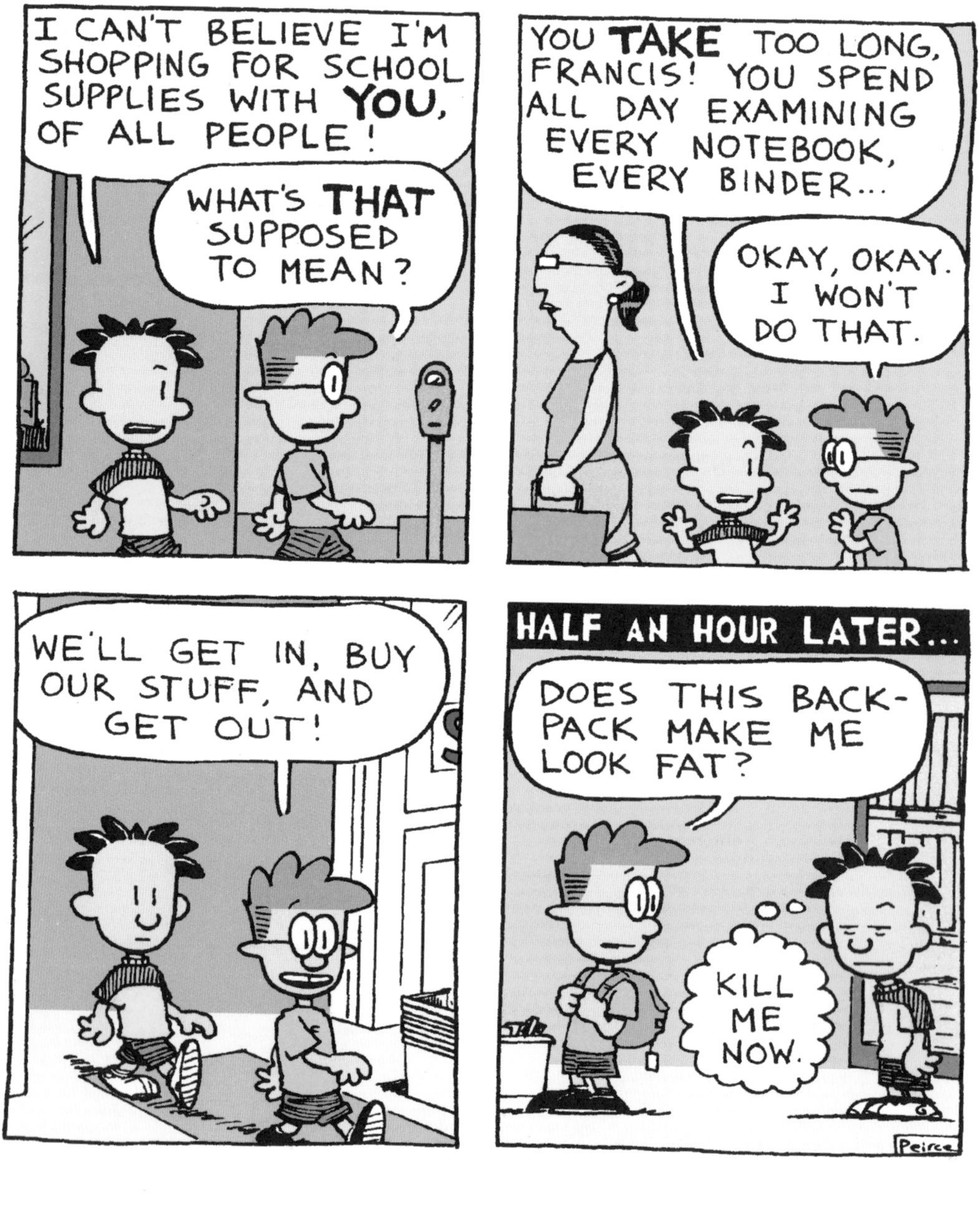
I CAN'T BELIEVE I'M SHOPPING FOR SCHOOL SUPPLIES WITH YOU, OF ALL PEOPLE!
WHAT'S THAT SUPPOSED TO MEAN?
YOU TAKE TOO LONG, FRANCIS! YOU SPEND ALL DAY EXAMINING EVERY NOTEBOOK, EVERY BINDER...
OKAY, OKAY. I WON'T DO THAT.
WE'LL GET IN, BUY OUR STUFF, AND GET OUT!
HALF AN HOUR LATER...
DOES THIS BACK-PACK MAKE ME LOOK FAT?
KILL ME NOW.
Peirce

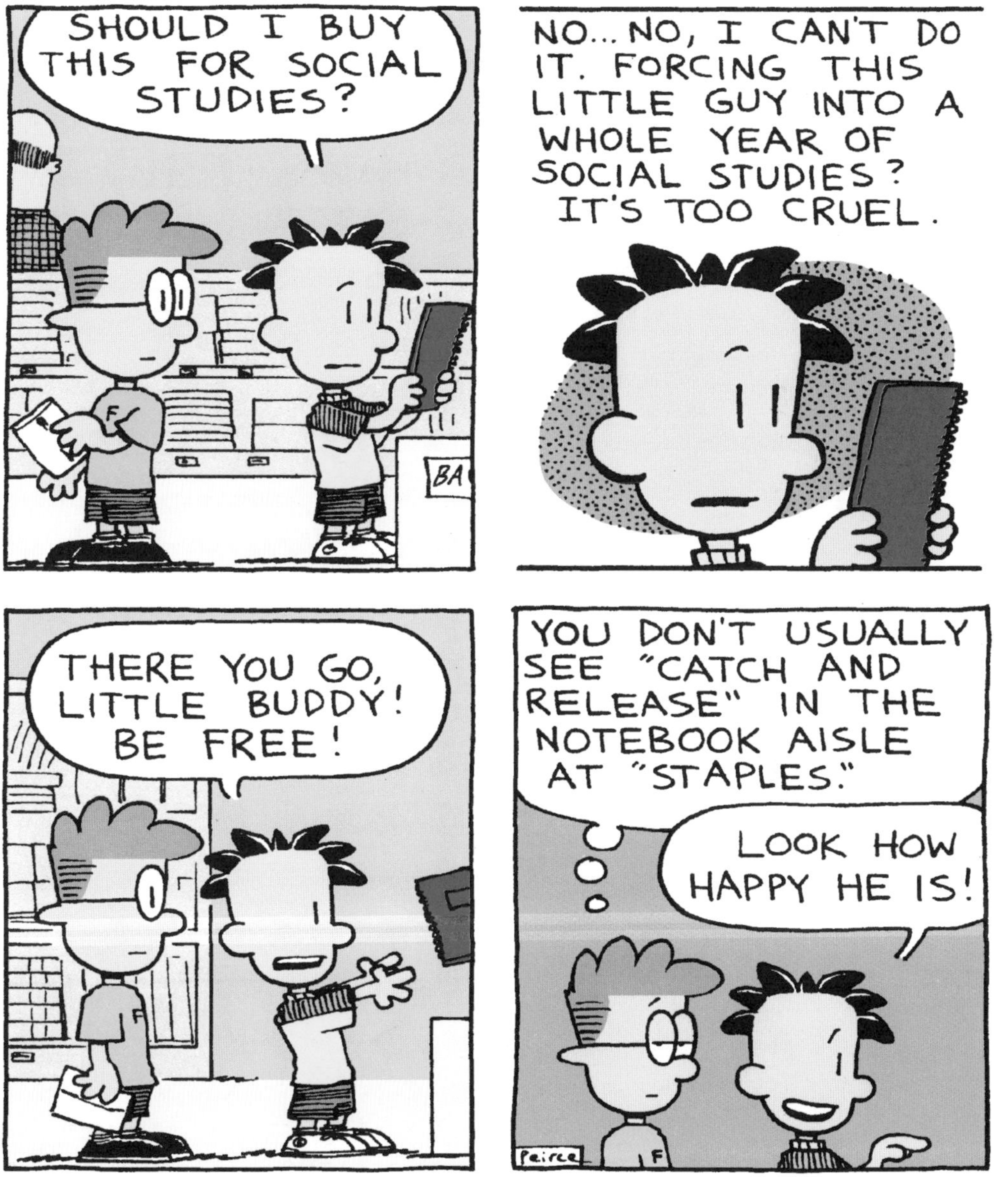
SHOULD I BUY THIS FOR SOCIAL STUDIES?
BA
NO... NO, I CAN'T DO IT. FORCING THIS LITTLE GUY INTO A WHOLE YEAR OF SOCIAL STUDIES? IT'S TOO CRUEL.
THERE YOU GO, LITTLE BUDDY! BE FREE!
YOU DON'T USUALLY SEE "CATCH AND RELEASE" IN THE NOTEBOOK AISLE AT "STAPLES."
LOOK HOW HAPPY HE IS!
Peirce

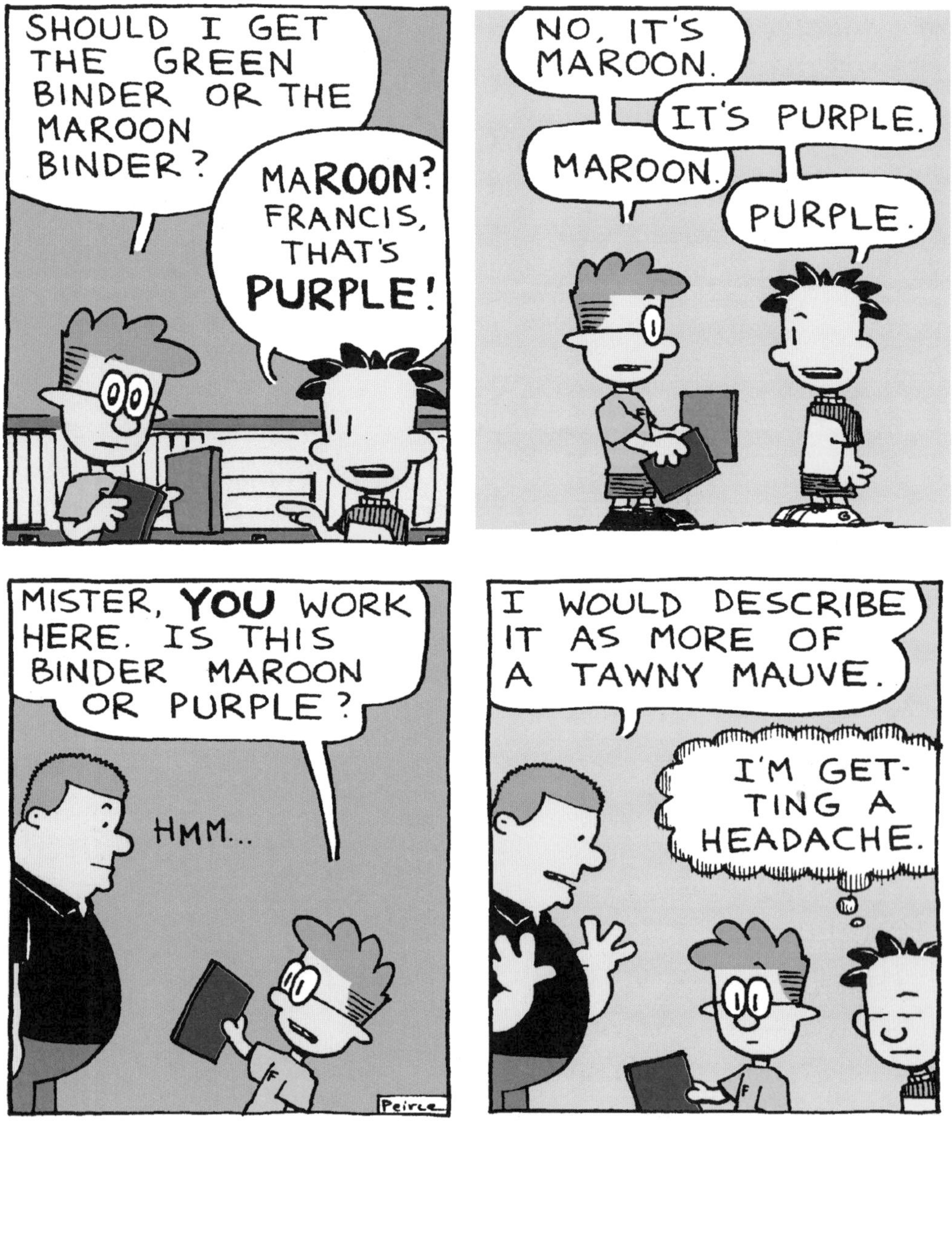
SHOULD I GET THE GREEN BINDER OR THE MAROON BINDER?
MAROON? FRANCIS, THAT'S PURPLE!
NO, IT'S MAROON.
IT'S PURPLE.
MAROON.
PURPLE.
MISTER, YOU WORK HERE. IS THIS BINDER MAROON OR PURPLE?
HMM...
Peirce
I WOULD DESCRIBE IT AS MORE OF A TAWNY MAUVE.
I'M GETTING A HEADACHE.

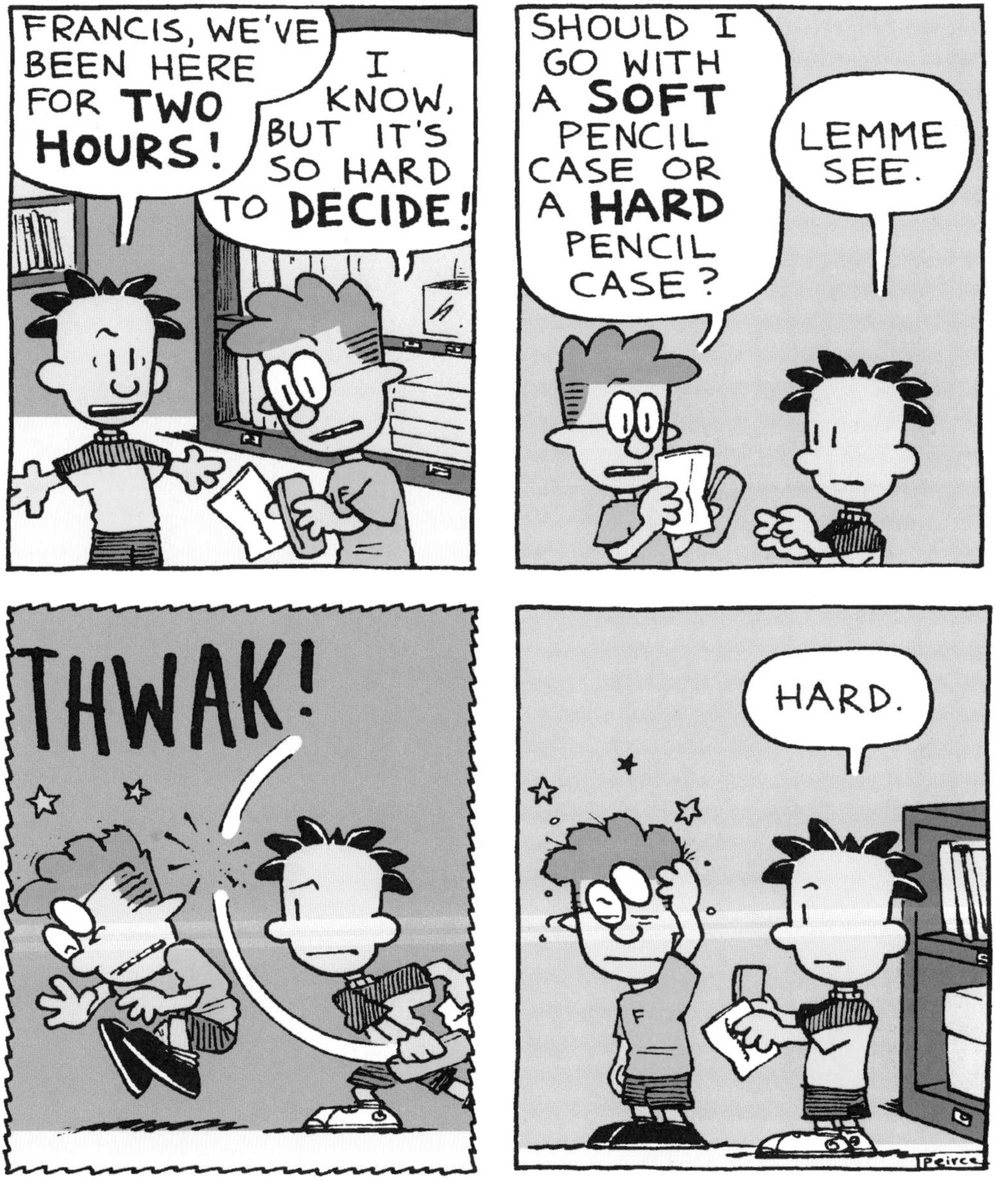
FRANCIS, WE'VE BEEN HERE FOR TWO HOURS!
I KNOW, BUT IT'S SO HARD TO DECIDE!
SHOULD I GO WITH A SOFT PENCIL CASE OR A HARD PENCIL CASE?
LEMME SEE.
THWAK!
HARD.
Peirce

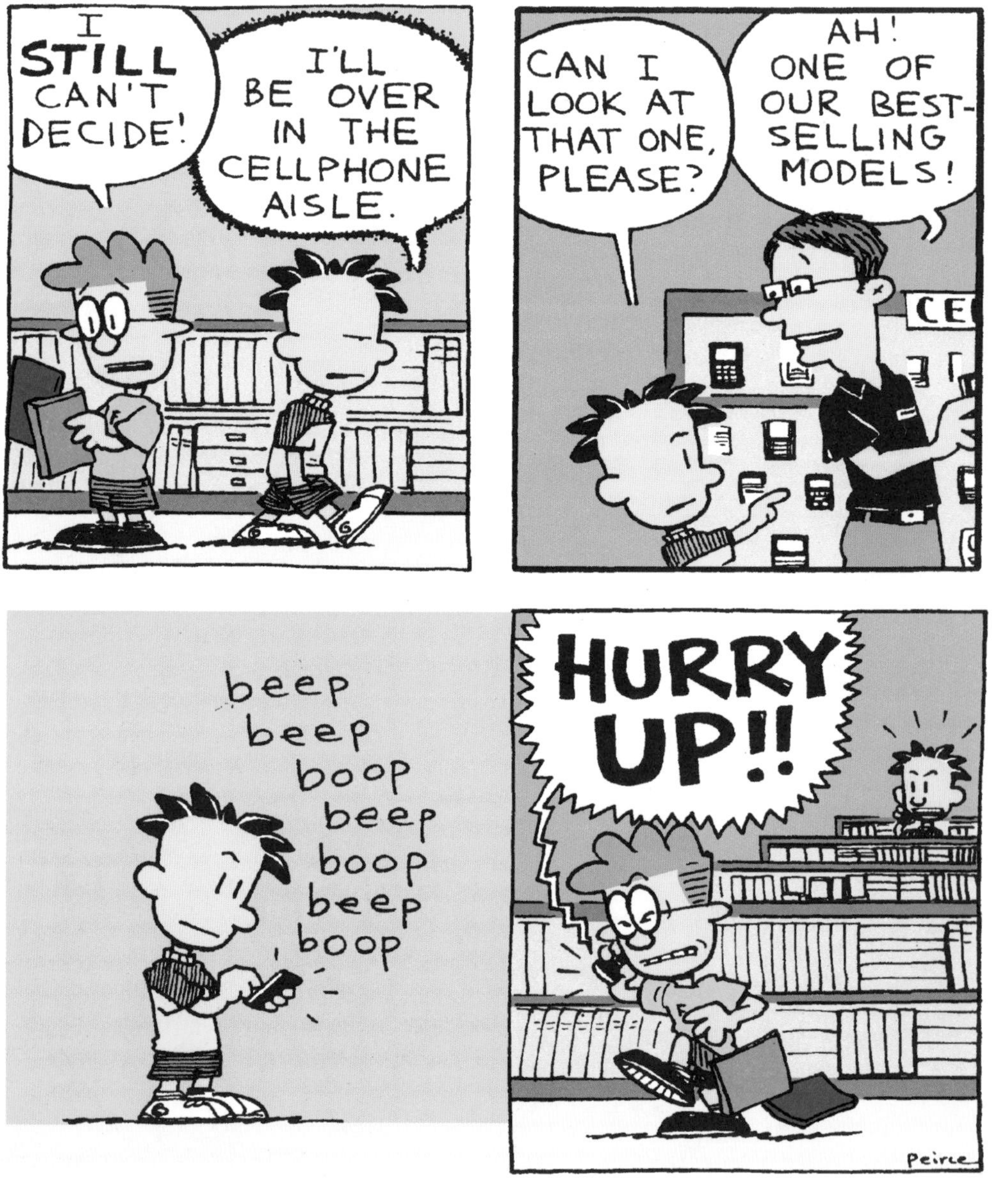
I STILL CAN'T DECIDE!
I'LL BE OVER IN THE CELLPHONE AISLE.
CAN I LOOK AT THAT ONE, PLEASE?
AH! ONE OF OUR BEST-SELLING MODELS!
CE
beep beep boop beep boop beep boop
HURRY UP!!
Peirce

I'M REALLY HAPPY WITH THE BINDER I BOUGHT!

YOU ALREADY TOLD ME THAT, FRANCIS.

DID I **ALSO** TELL YOU HOW MUCH I LOVE THE SOUND OF THE VELCRO POCKETS OPENING AND CLOSING?

RRIP!...SHUCK!
RRIP!...SHUCK!
RRIP!...SHUCK!
RRIP!...SHUCK!

RRIP!... SHUCK... RRIP!...
SHUCK... RRIP!
RRIP!... SHUCK... P
SHUCK... TK
RRIP!... P
SHUCK!... RRIP... SHUCK
RRIP... CK!... RRI
SHU
RRI
SHU
RR
SHU
RRI

I HATE THIS TIME OF YEAR.

Peirce

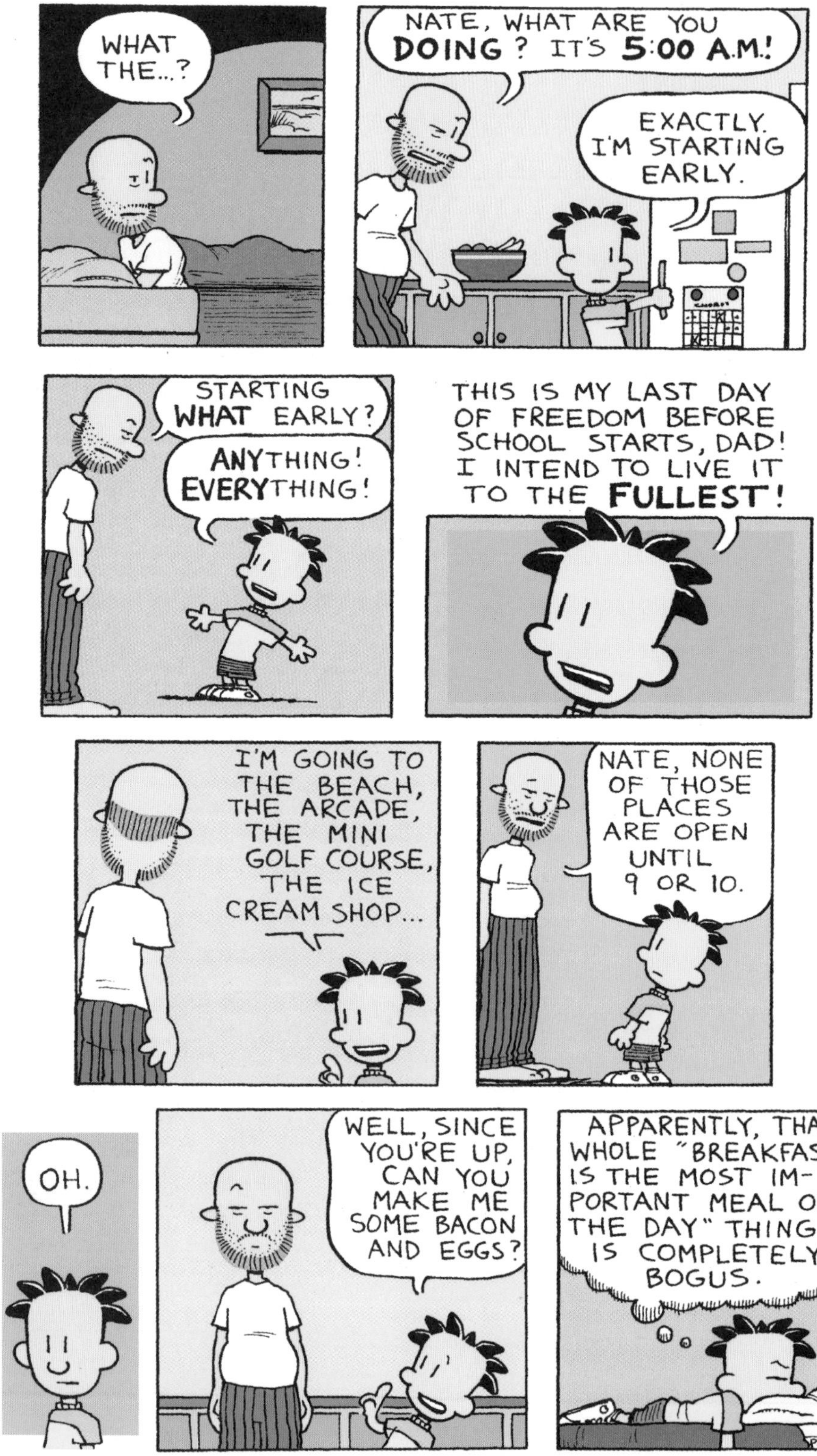
WHAT THE...?
NATE, WHAT ARE YOU DOING? IT'S 5:00 A.M.!
EXACTLY. I'M STARTING EARLY.
STARTING WHAT EARLY?
ANYTHING! EVERYTHING!
THIS IS MY LAST DAY OF FREEDOM BEFORE SCHOOL STARTS, DAD! I INTEND TO LIVE IT TO THE FULLEST!
I'M GOING TO THE BEACH, THE ARCADE, THE MINI GOLF COURSE, THE ICE CREAM SHOP...
NATE, NONE OF THOSE PLACES ARE OPEN UNTIL 9 OR 10.
OH.
WELL, SINCE YOU'RE UP, CAN YOU MAKE ME SOME BACON AND EGGS?
APPARENTLY, THAT WHOLE "BREAKFAST IS THE MOST IMPORTANT MEAL OF THE DAY" THING IS COMPLETELY BOGUS.
Peirce

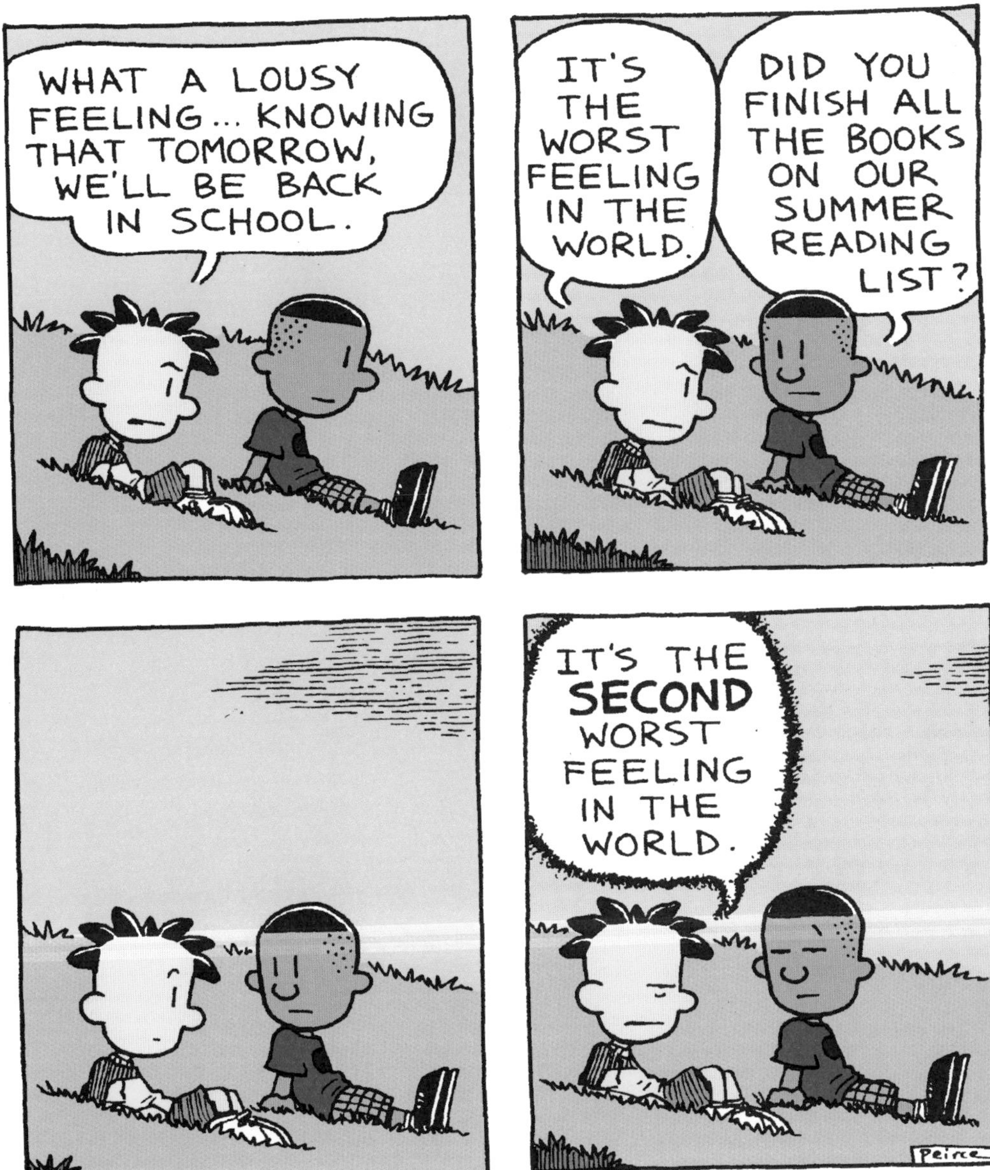
WHAT A LOUSY FEELING... KNOWING THAT TOMORROW, WE'LL BE BACK IN SCHOOL.
IT'S THE WORST FEELING IN THE WORLD.
DID YOU FINISH ALL THE BOOKS ON OUR SUMMER READING LIST?
IT'S THE **SECOND** WORST FEELING IN THE WORLD.
Peirce

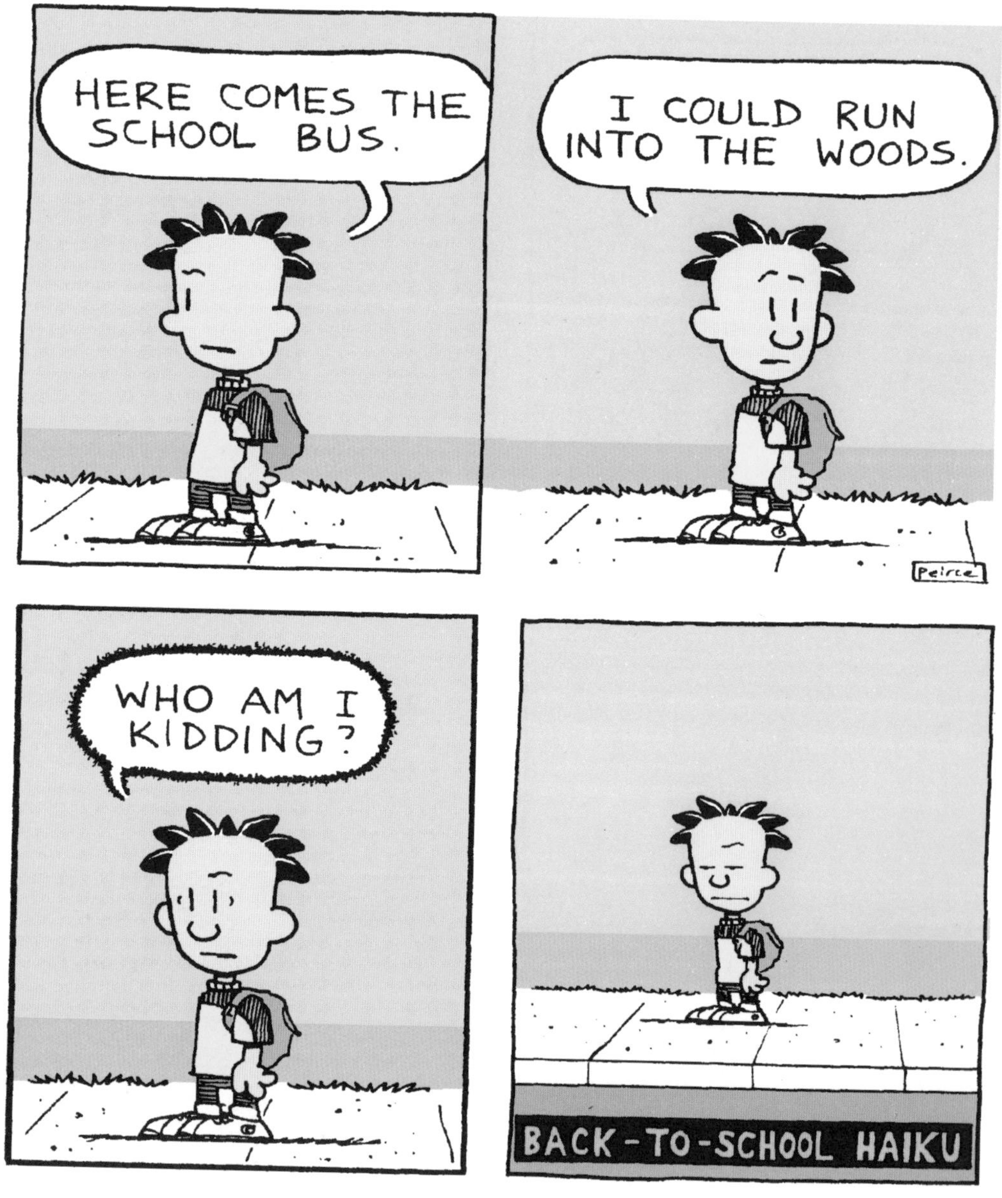
HERE COMES THE SCHOOL BUS.
I COULD RUN INTO THE WOODS.
Peirce
WHO AM I KIDDING?
BACK-TO-SCHOOL HAIKU

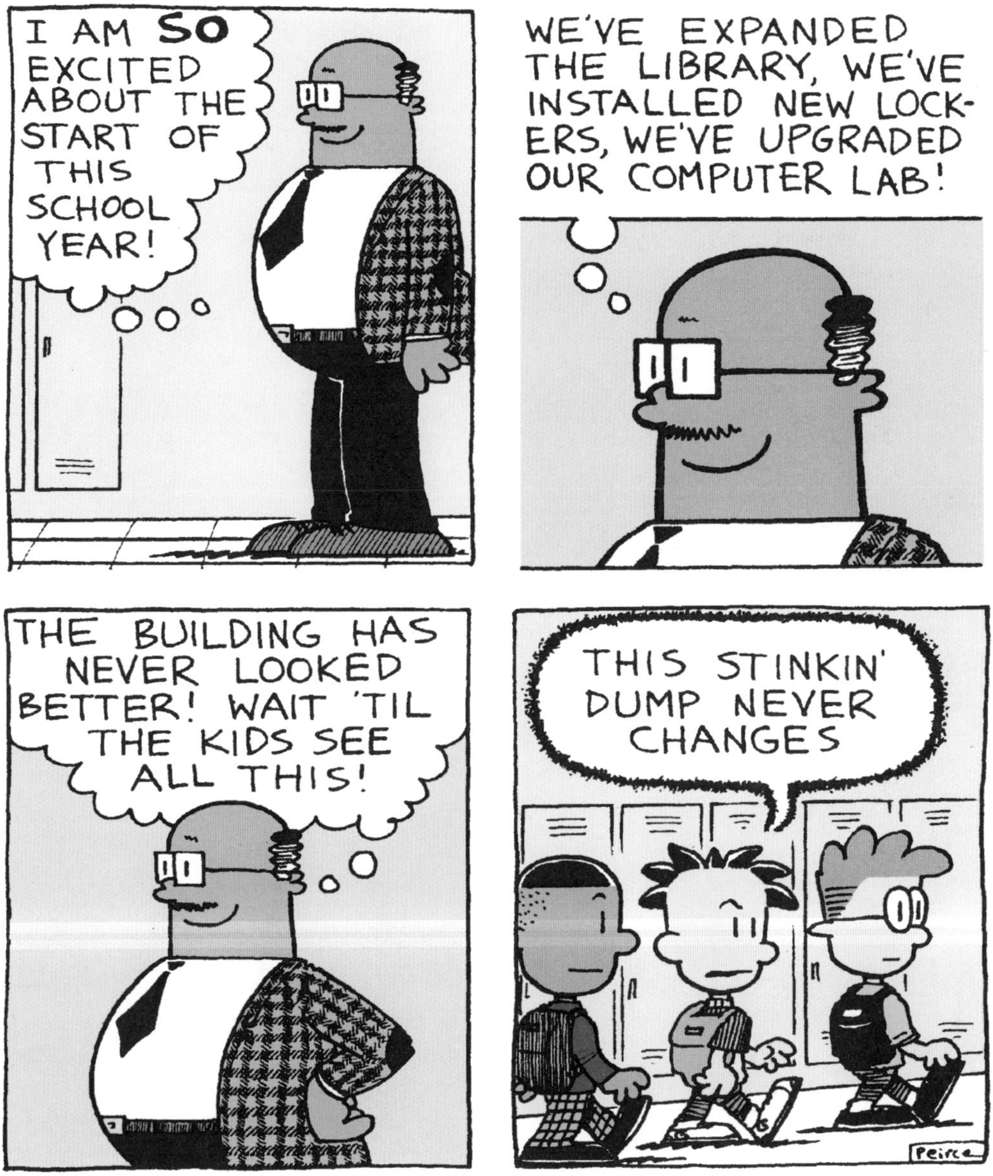
I AM **SO** EXCITED ABOUT THE START OF THIS SCHOOL YEAR!
WE'VE EXPANDED THE LIBRARY, WE'VE INSTALLED NEW LOCKERS, WE'VE UPGRADED OUR COMPUTER LAB!
THE BUILDING HAS NEVER LOOKED BETTER! WAIT 'TIL THE KIDS SEE ALL THIS!
THIS STINKIN' DUMP NEVER CHANGES
Peirce

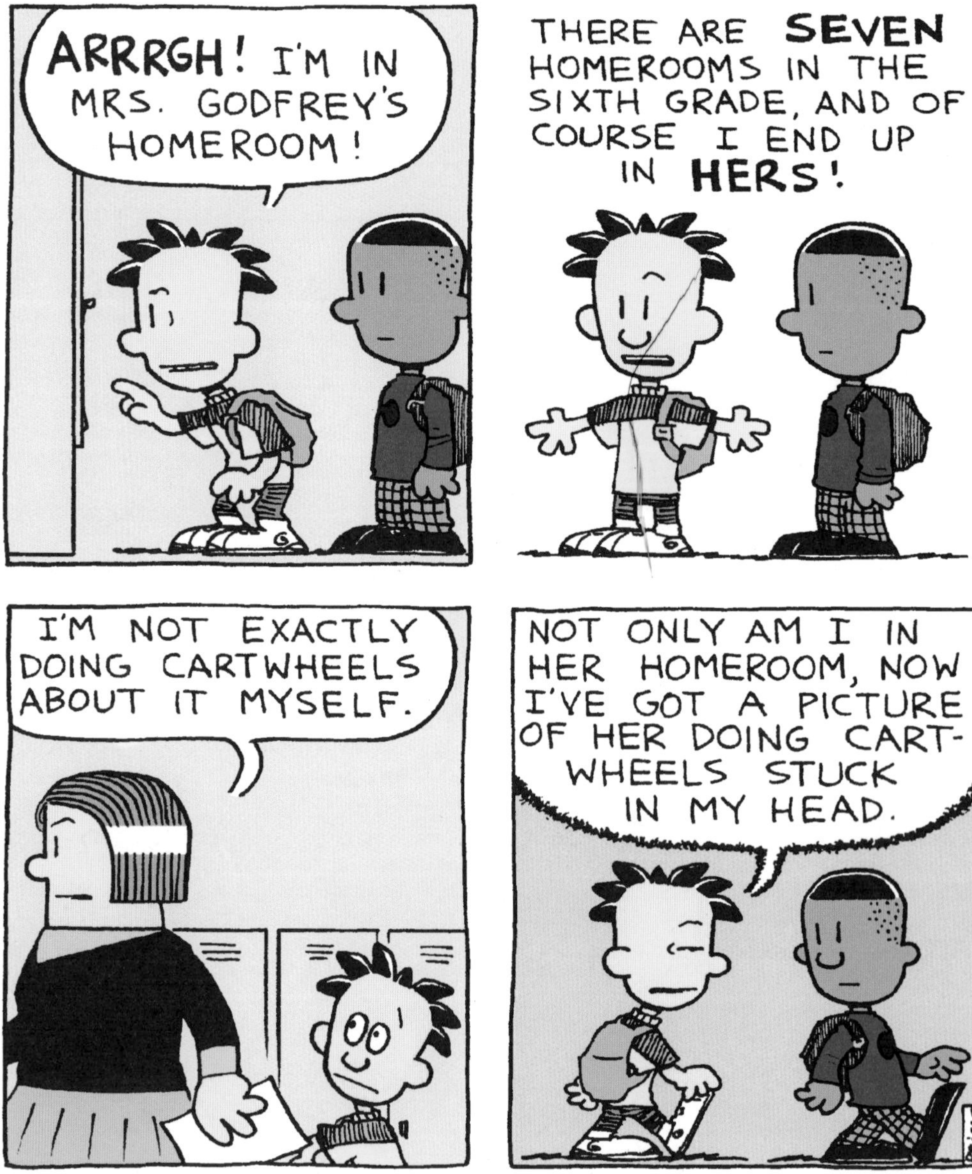
ARRRGH! I'M IN MRS. GODFREY'S HOMEROOM!
THERE ARE SEVEN HOMEROOMS IN THE SIXTH GRADE, AND OF COURSE I END UP IN HERS!
I'M NOT EXACTLY DOING CARTWHEELS ABOUT IT MYSELF.
NOT ONLY AM I IN HER HOMEROOM, NOW I'VE GOT A PICTURE OF HER DOING CART-WHEELS STUCK IN MY HEAD.

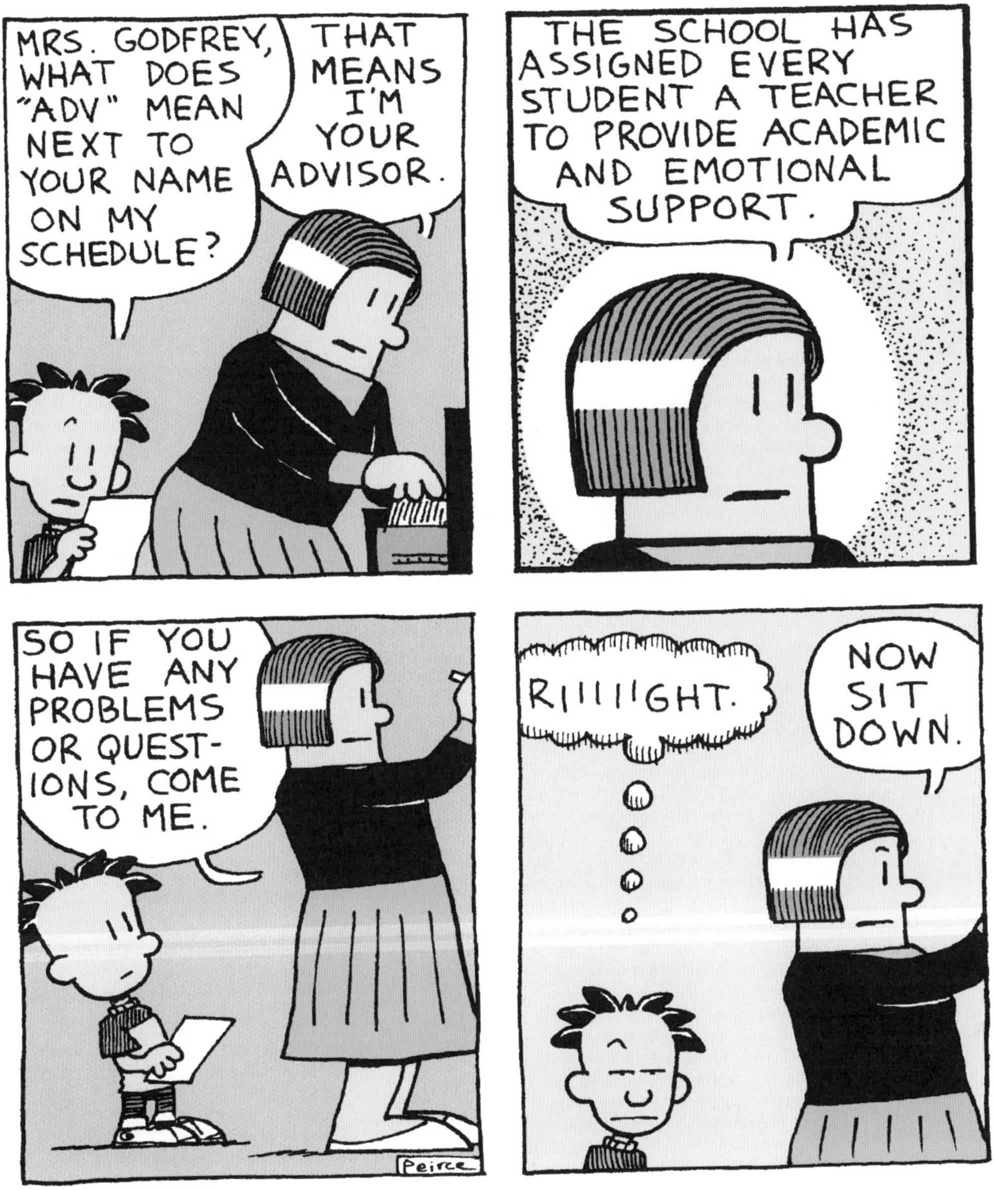
MRS. GODFREY, WHAT DOES "ADV" MEAN NEXT TO YOUR NAME ON MY SCHEDULE?
THAT MEANS I'M YOUR ADVISOR.
THE SCHOOL HAS ASSIGNED EVERY STUDENT A TEACHER TO PROVIDE ACADEMIC AND EMOTIONAL SUPPORT.
SO IF YOU HAVE ANY PROBLEMS OR QUEST- IONS, COME TO ME.
Peirce
RIIIIIGHT.
NOW SIT DOWN.

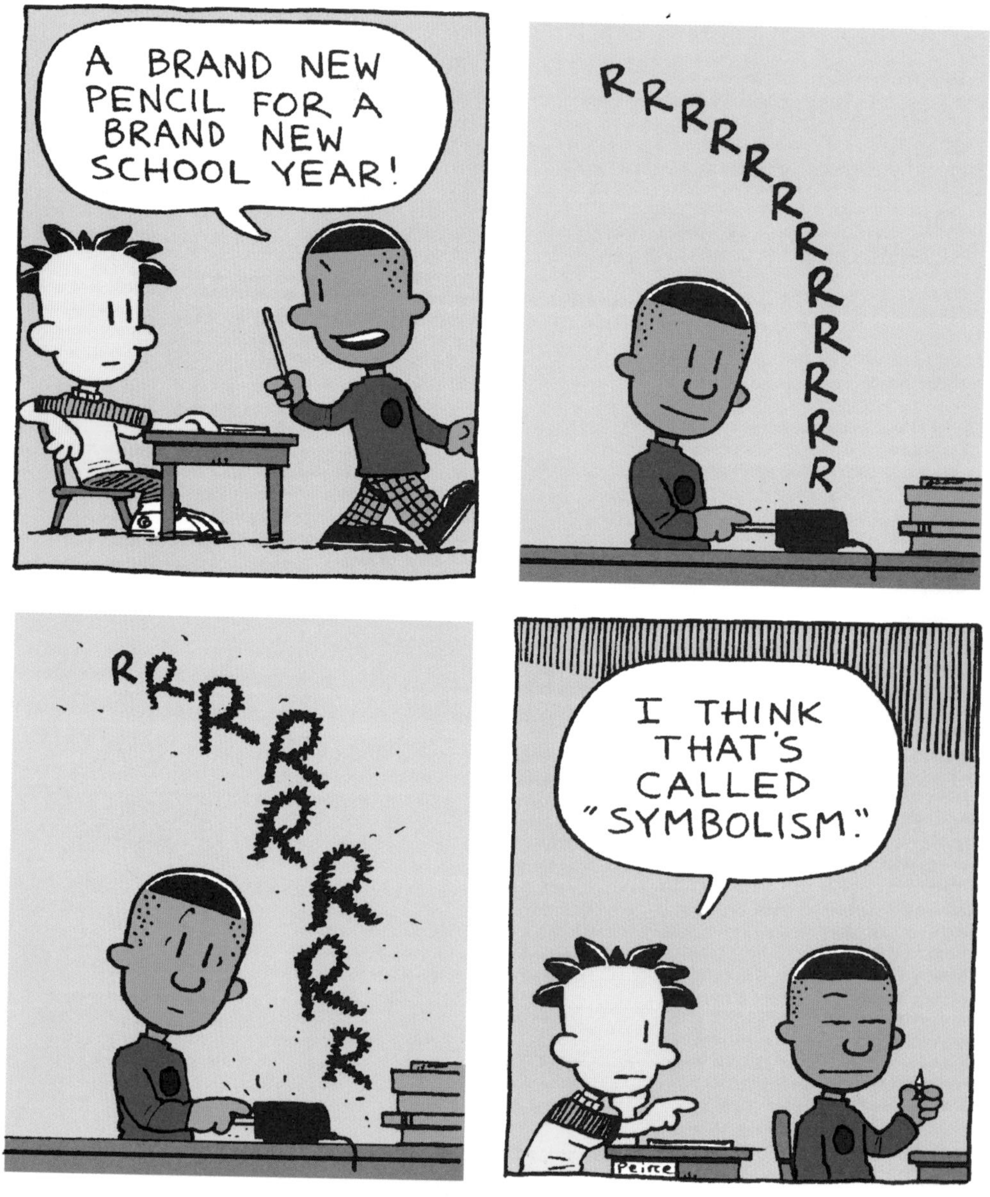
A BRAND NEW PENCIL FOR A BRAND NEW SCHOOL YEAR!
RRRRRRRRRRRR
RRRRRRRR
I THINK THAT'S CALLED "SYMBOLISM."
Peirce

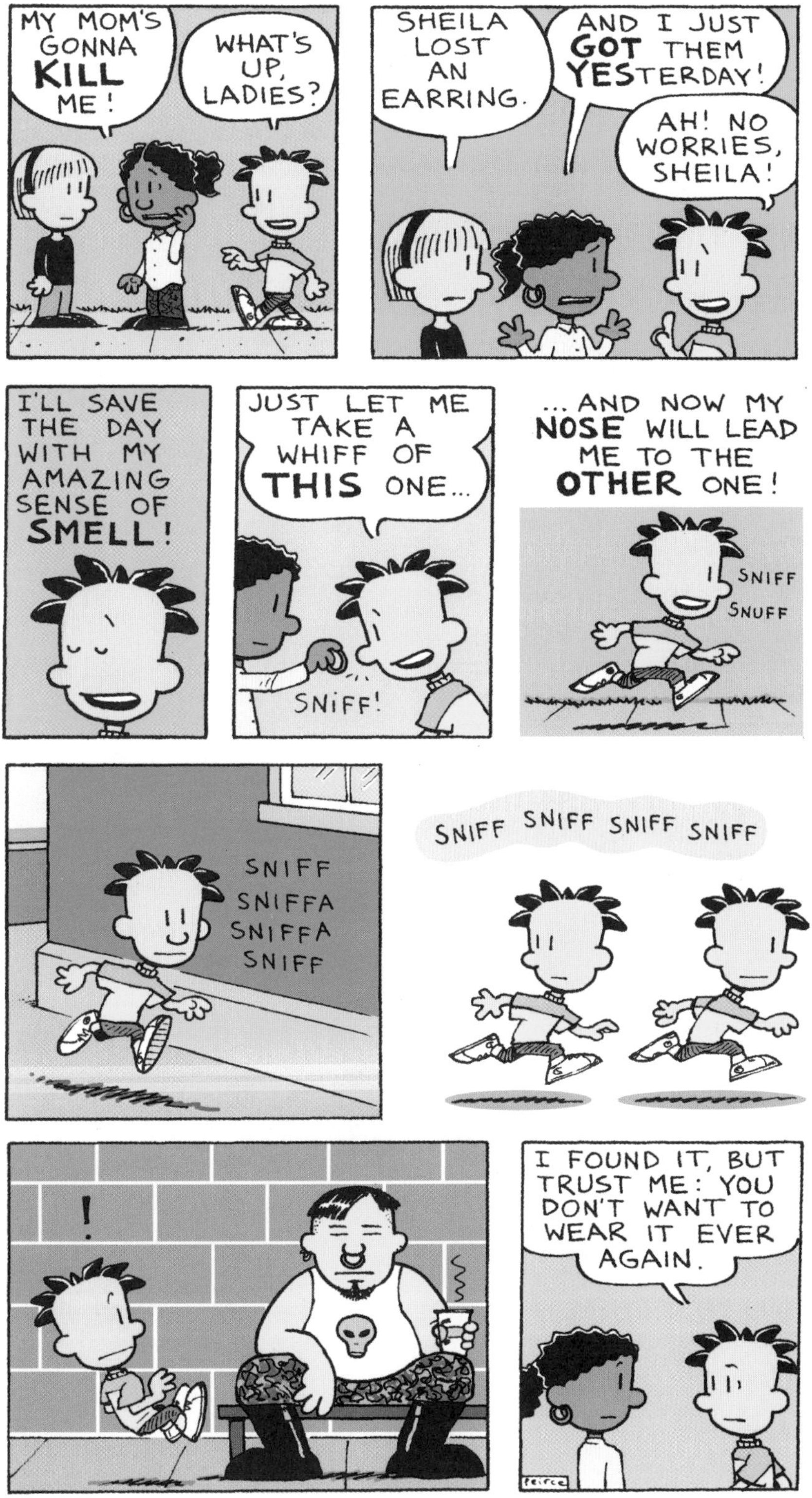
MY MOM'S GONNA KILL ME!
WHAT'S UP, LADIES?
SHEILA LOST AN EARRING.
AND I JUST GOT THEM YESTERDAY!
AH! NO WORRIES, SHEILA!
I'LL SAVE THE DAY WITH MY AMAZING SENSE OF SMELL!
JUST LET ME TAKE A WHIFF OF THIS ONE...
SNIFF!
...AND NOW MY NOSE WILL LEAD ME TO THE OTHER ONE!
SNIFF
SNUFF
SNIFF
SNIFFA
SNIFFA
SNIFF
SNIFF SNIFF SNIFF SNIFF
!
I FOUND IT, BUT TRUST ME: YOU DON'T WANT TO WEAR IT EVER AGAIN.
PEIRCE

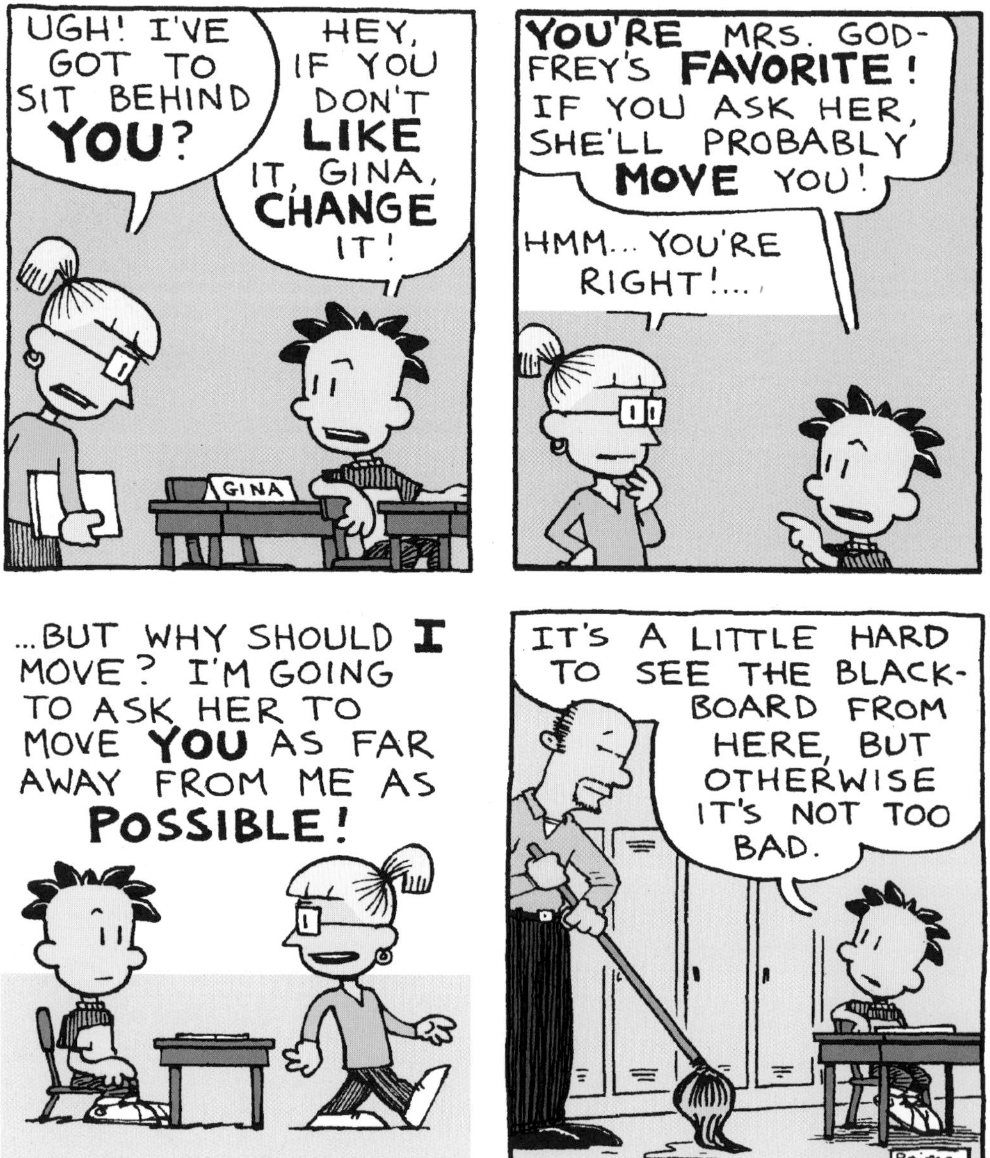
UGH! I'VE GOT TO SIT BEHIND YOU?
HEY, IF YOU DON'T LIKE IT, GINA, CHANGE IT!
GINA
YOU'RE MRS. GODFREY'S FAVORITE! IF YOU ASK HER, SHE'LL PROBABLY MOVE YOU!
HMM... YOU'RE RIGHT!...
...BUT WHY SHOULD I MOVE? I'M GOING TO ASK HER TO MOVE YOU AS FAR AWAY FROM ME AS POSSIBLE!
IT'S A LITTLE HARD TO SEE THE BLACKBOARD FROM HERE, BUT OTHERWISE IT'S NOT TOO BAD.
Peirce

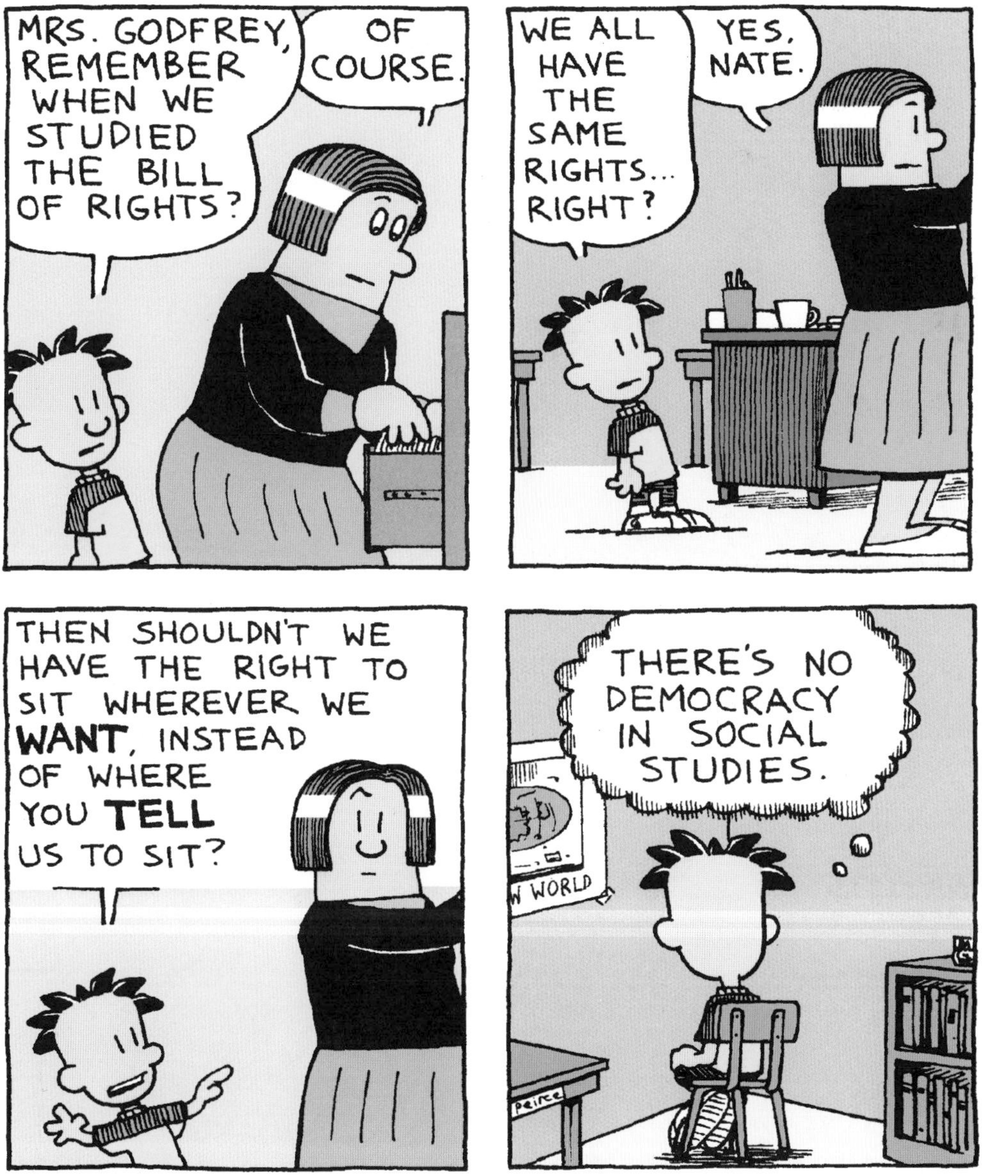
MRS. GODFREY, REMEMBER WHEN WE STUDIED THE BILL OF RIGHTS?
OF COURSE.
WE ALL HAVE THE SAME RIGHTS... RIGHT?
YES, NATE.
THEN SHOULDN'T WE HAVE THE RIGHT TO SIT WHEREVER WE **WANT**, INSTEAD OF WHERE YOU **TELL** US TO SIT?
THERE'S NO DEMOCRACY IN SOCIAL STUDIES.
W WORLD
peirce

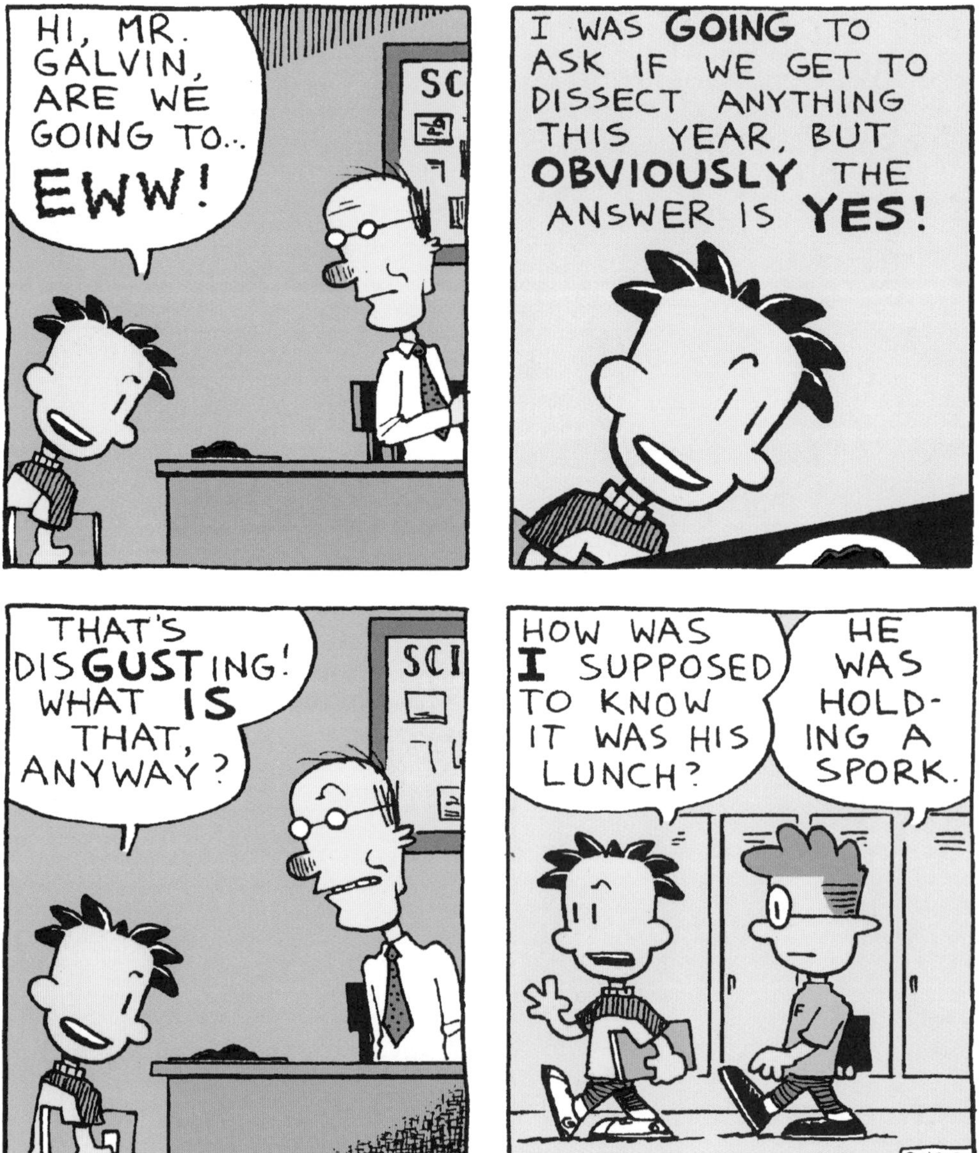
HI, MR. GALVIN, ARE WE GOING TO... EWW!
I WAS GOING TO ASK IF WE GET TO DISSECT ANYTHING THIS YEAR, BUT OBVIOUSLY THE ANSWER IS YES!
THAT'S DISGUSTING! WHAT IS THAT, ANYWAY?
HOW WAS I SUPPOSED TO KNOW IT WAS HIS LUNCH?
HE WAS HOLDING A SPORK.
Peirce

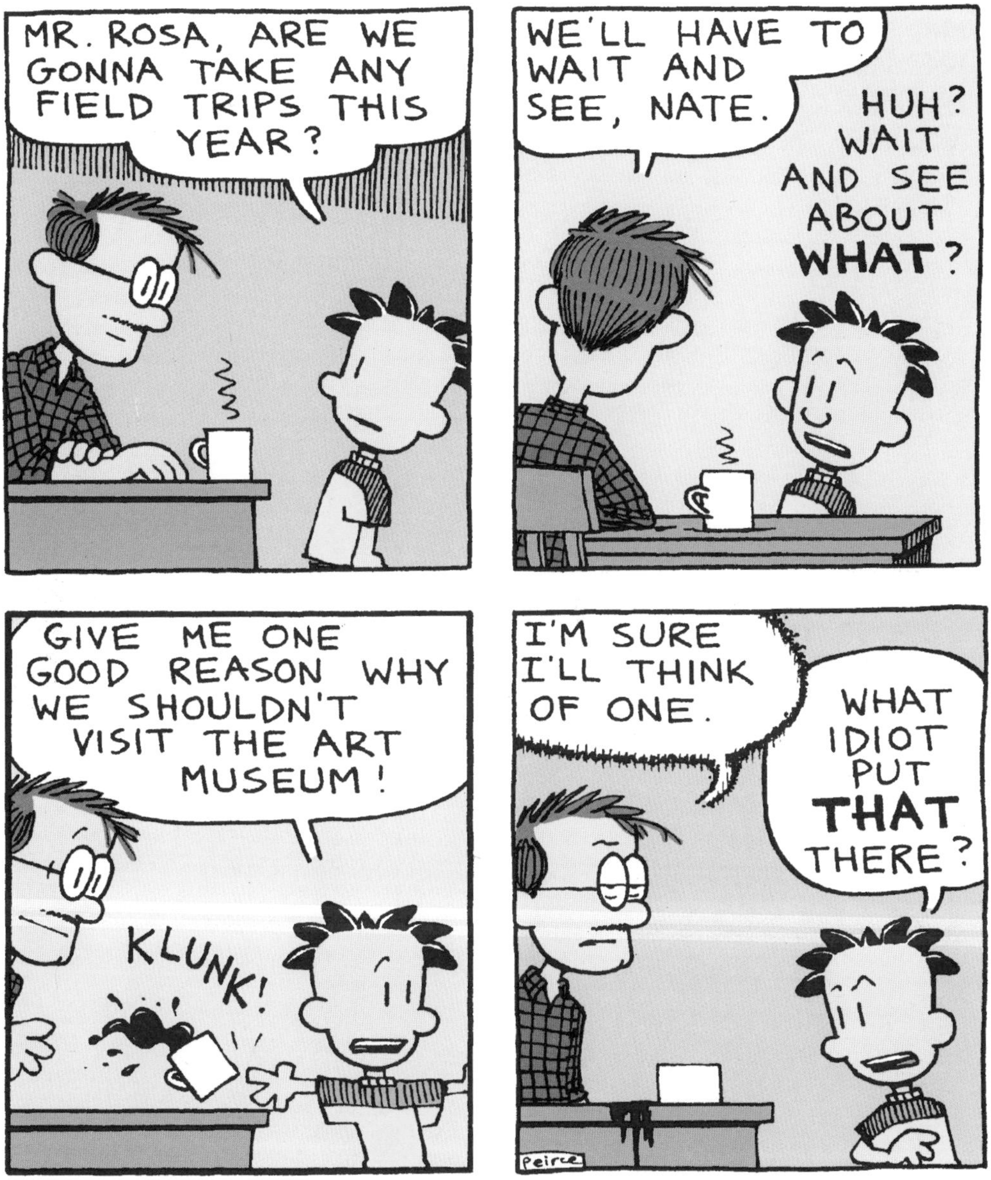
MR. ROSA, ARE WE GONNA TAKE ANY FIELD TRIPS THIS YEAR?
WE'LL HAVE TO WAIT AND SEE, NATE.
HUH? WAIT AND SEE ABOUT WHAT?
GIVE ME ONE GOOD REASON WHY WE SHOULDN'T VISIT THE ART MUSEUM!
KLUNK!
I'M SURE I'LL THINK OF ONE.
WHAT IDIOT PUT THAT THERE?
Peirce

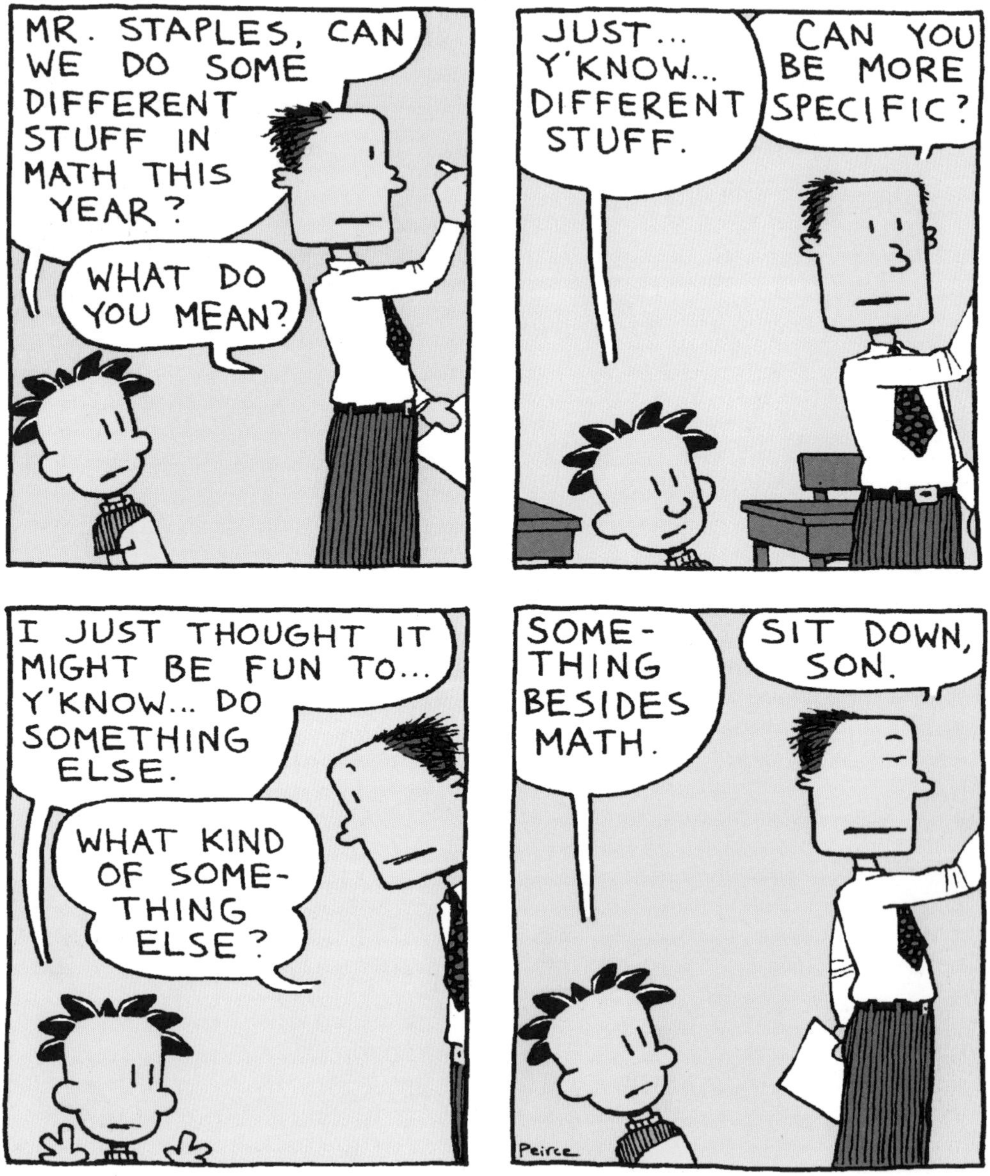
MR. STAPLES, CAN WE DO SOME DIFFERENT STUFF IN MATH THIS YEAR?
WHAT DO YOU MEAN?
JUST... Y'KNOW... DIFFERENT STUFF.
CAN YOU BE MORE SPECIFIC?
I JUST THOUGHT IT MIGHT BE FUN TO... Y'KNOW... DO SOMETHING ELSE.
WHAT KIND OF SOME-THING ELSE?
SOME-THING BESIDES MATH.
SIT DOWN, SON.
Peirce

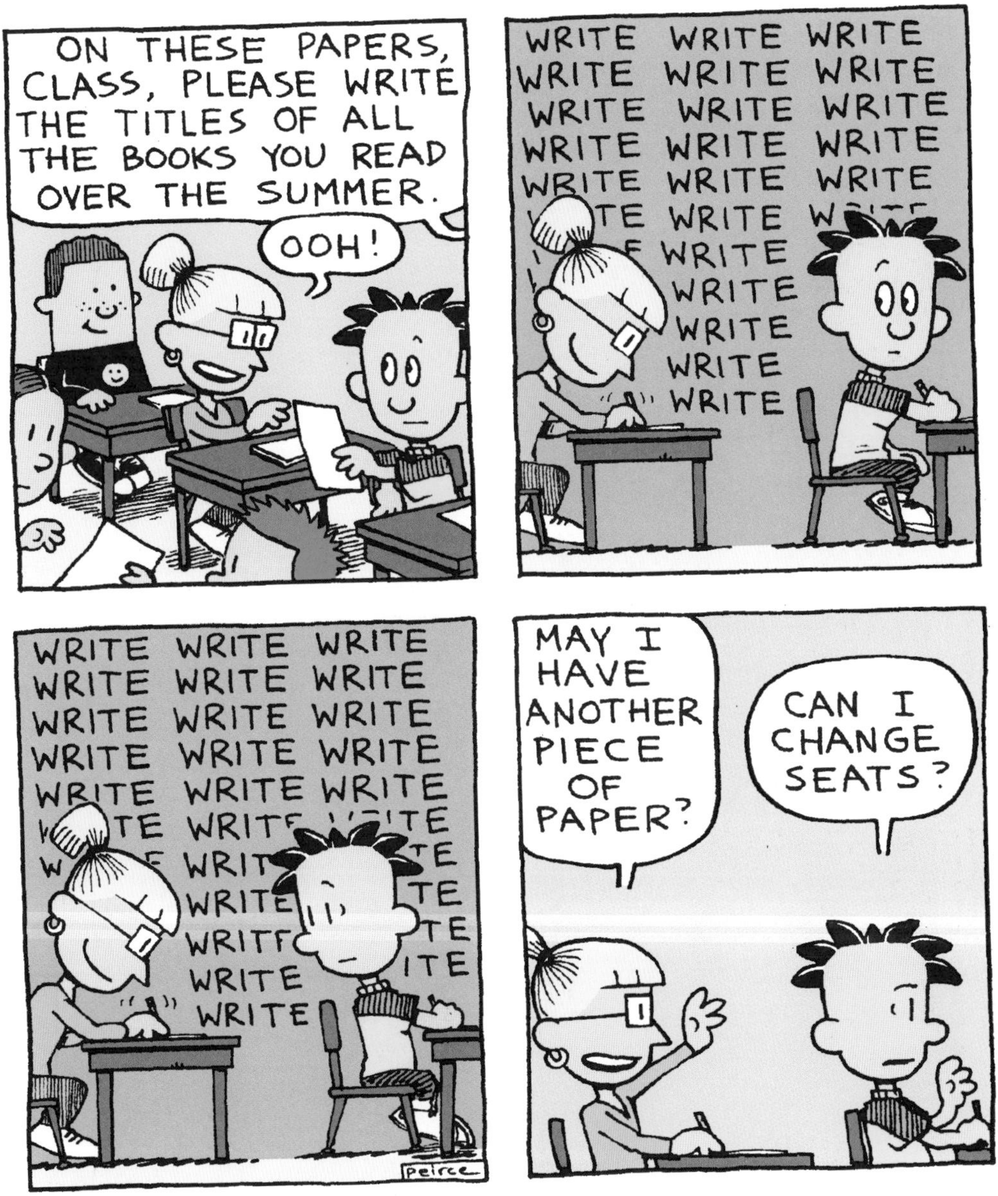
ON THESE PAPERS, CLASS, PLEASE WRITE THE TITLES OF ALL THE BOOKS YOU READ OVER THE SUMMER.
OOH!
WRITE WRITE WRITE
WRITE WRITE WRITE
WRITE WRITE WRITE
WRITE WRITE WRITE
WRITE WRITE WRITE
WRITE
WRITE
WRITE
WRITE
WRITE
WRITE
WRITE WRITE WRITE
WRITE WRITE WRITE
WRITE WRITE WRITE
WRITE WRITE WRITE
WRITE WRITE WRITE
WRITE
WRITE
peirce
MAY I HAVE ANOTHER PIECE OF PAPER?
CAN I CHANGE SEATS?

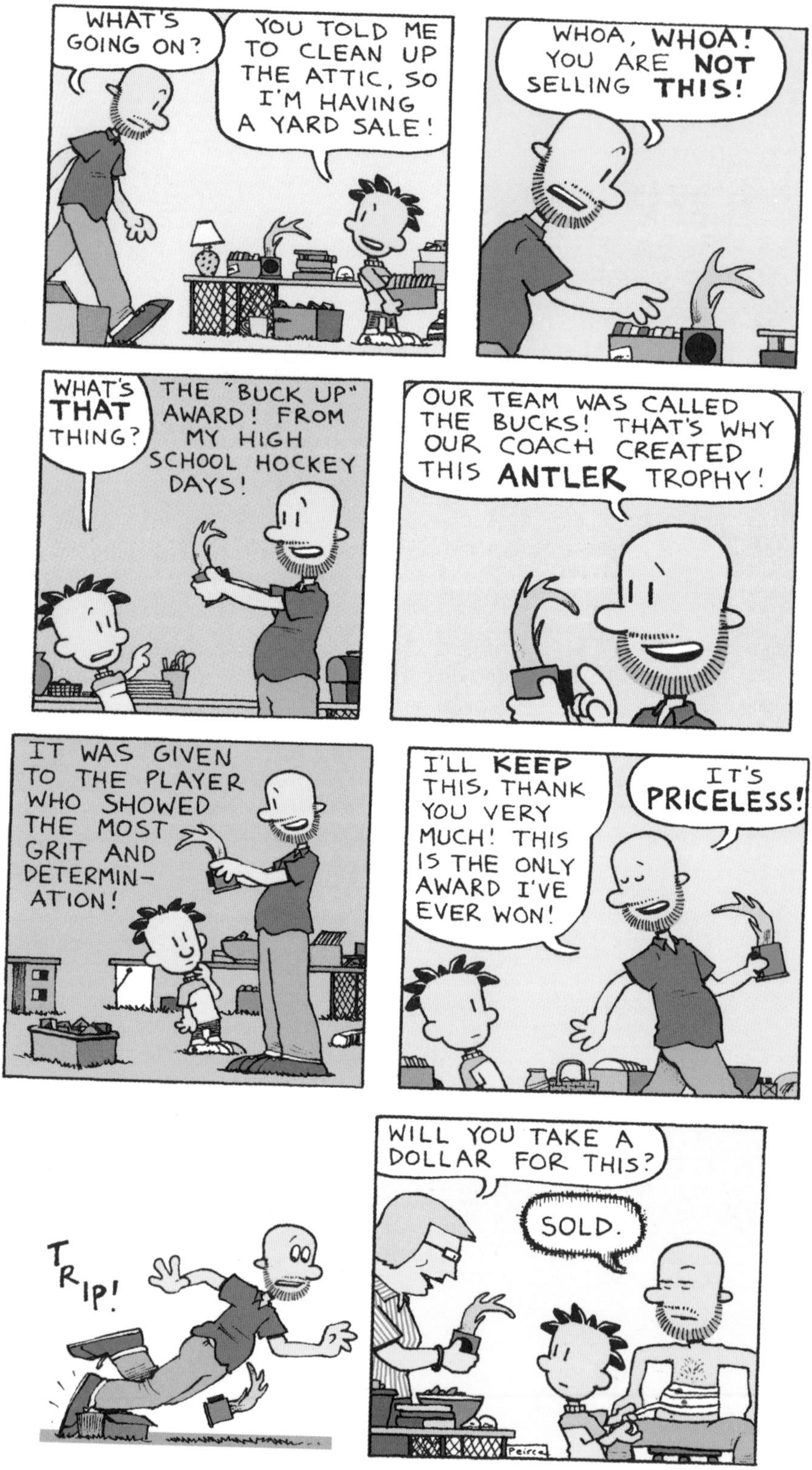
WHAT'S GOING ON?
YOU TOLD ME TO CLEAN UP THE ATTIC, SO I'M HAVING A YARD SALE!
WHOA, WHOA! YOU ARE NOT SELLING THIS!
WHAT'S THAT THING?
THE "BUCK UP" AWARD! FROM MY HIGH SCHOOL HOCKEY DAYS!
OUR TEAM WAS CALLED THE BUCKS! THAT'S WHY OUR COACH CREATED THIS ANTLER TROPHY!
IT WAS GIVEN TO THE PLAYER WHO SHOWED THE MOST GRIT AND DETERMIN-ATION!
I'LL KEEP THIS, THANK YOU VERY MUCH! THIS IS THE ONLY AWARD I'VE EVER WON!
IT'S PRICELESS!
TRIP!
WILL YOU TAKE A DOLLAR FOR THIS?
SOLD.
Peirce

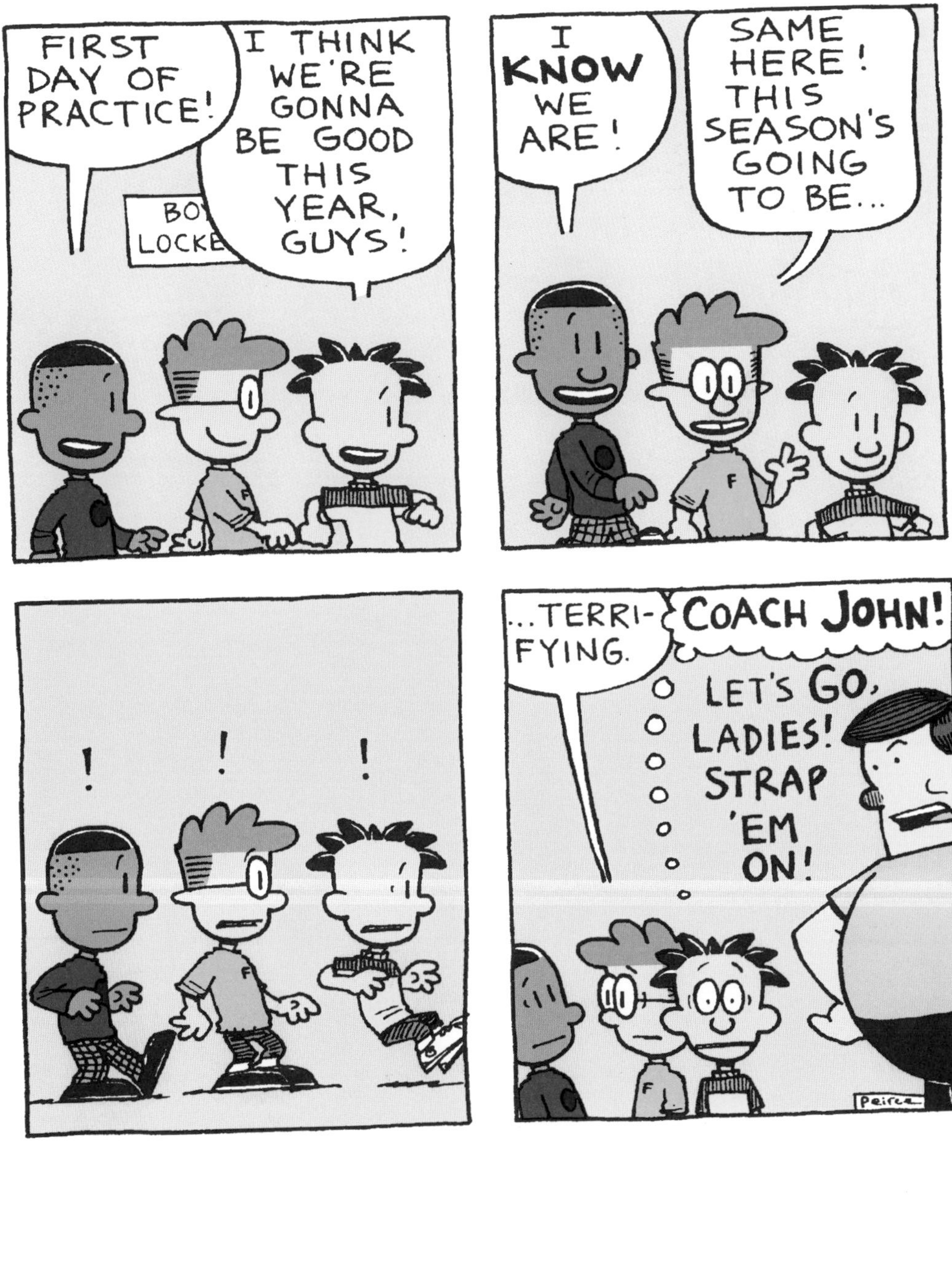
FIRST DAY OF PRACTICE!
I THINK WE'RE GONNA BE GOOD THIS YEAR, GUYS!
BOY LOCKE
I KNOW WE ARE!
SAME HERE! THIS SEASON'S GOING TO BE...
! ! !
...TERRIFYING.
COACH JOHN!
LET'S GO, LADIES! STRAP 'EM ON!
Peirce

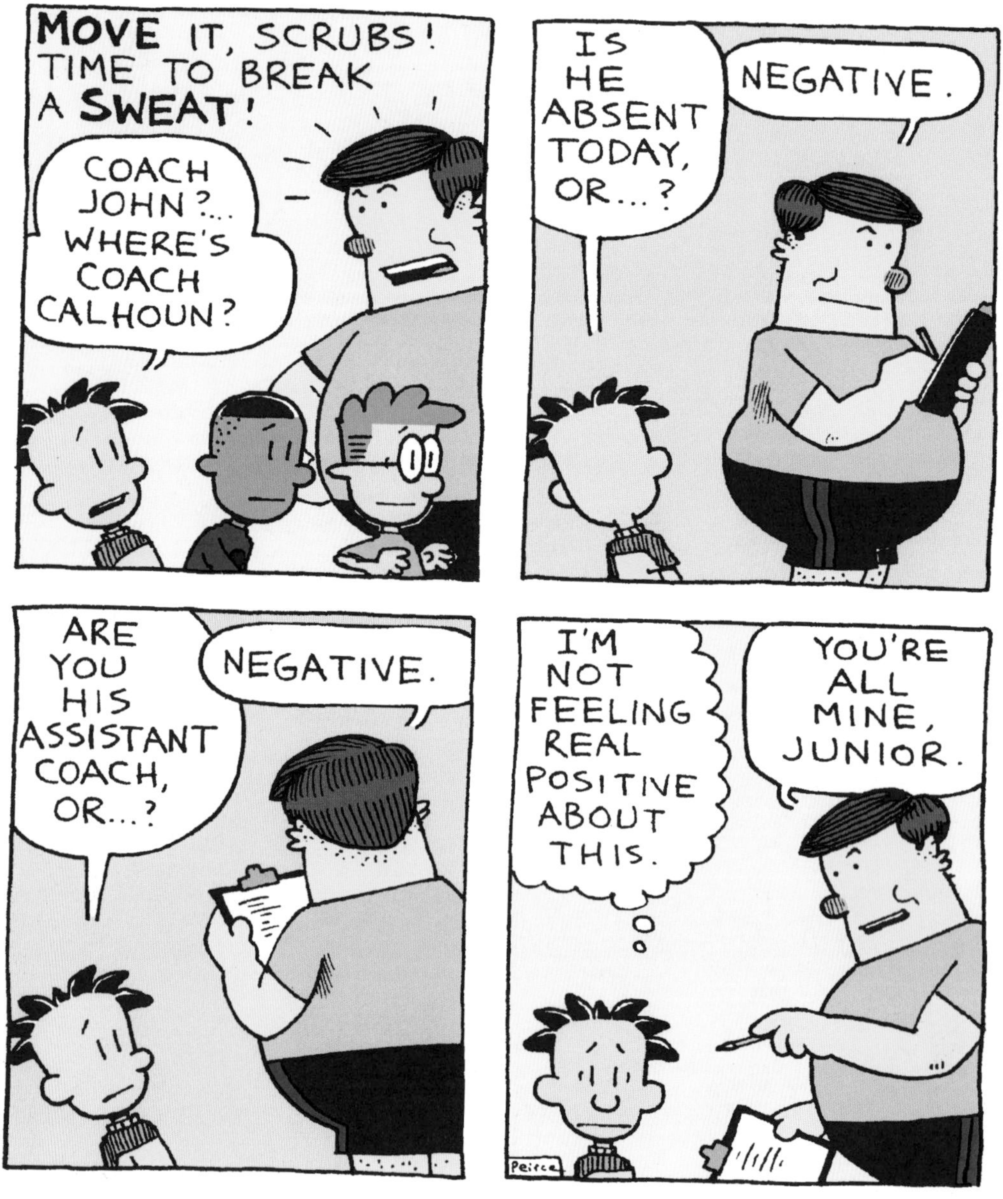
MOVE IT, SCRUBS! TIME TO BREAK A SWEAT!
COACH JOHN?... WHERE'S COACH CALHOUN?
IS HE ABSENT TODAY, OR...?
NEGATIVE.
ARE YOU HIS ASSISTANT COACH, OR...?
NEGATIVE.
I'M NOT FEELING REAL POSITIVE ABOUT THIS.
YOU'RE ALL MINE, JUNIOR.
Peirce

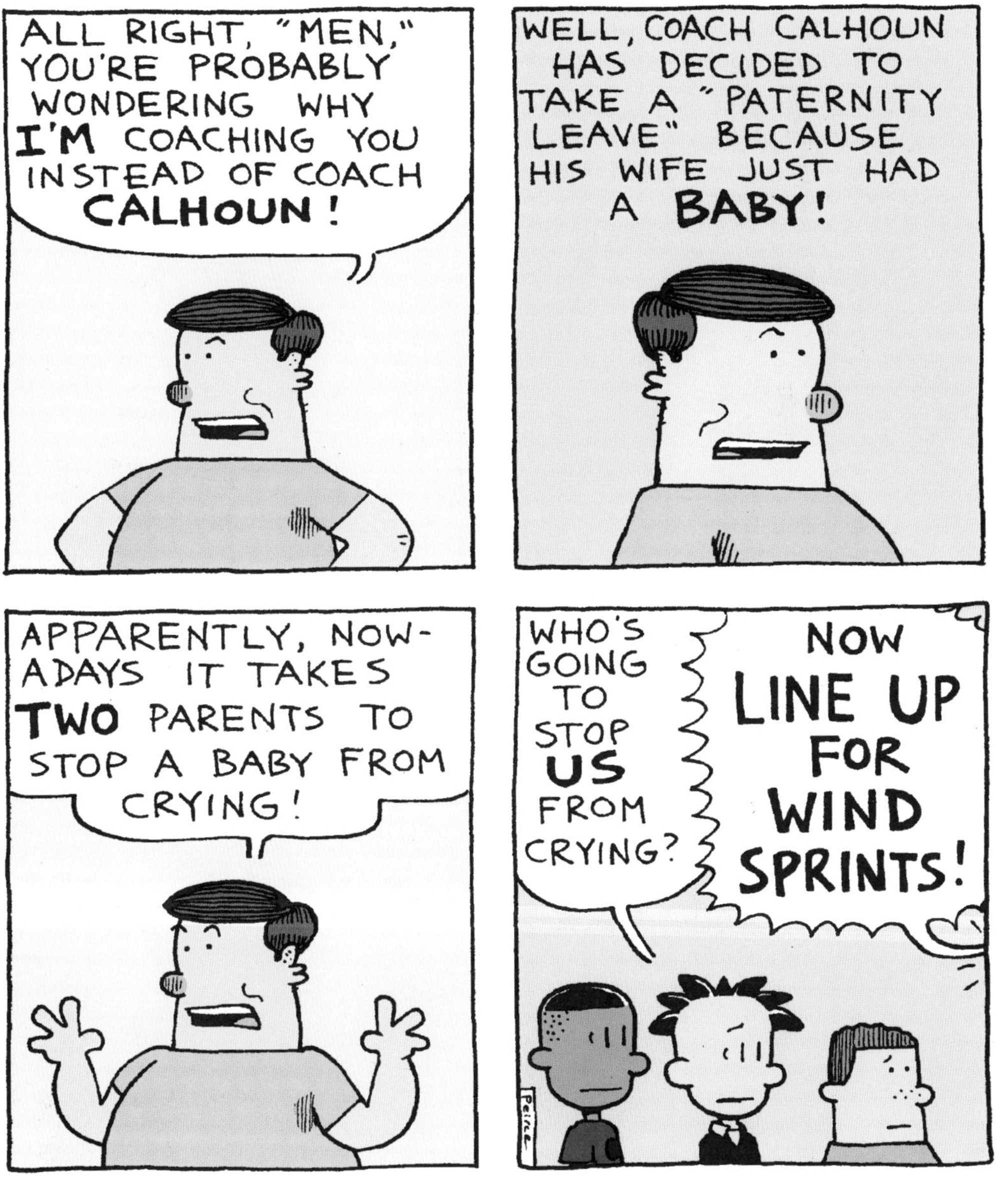
ALL RIGHT, "MEN," YOU'RE PROBABLY WONDERING WHY I'M COACHING YOU INSTEAD OF COACH CALHOUN!
WELL, COACH CALHOUN HAS DECIDED TO TAKE A "PATERNITY LEAVE" BECAUSE HIS WIFE JUST HAD A BABY!
APPARENTLY, NOW-ADAYS IT TAKES TWO PARENTS TO STOP A BABY FROM CRYING!
WHO'S GOING TO STOP US FROM CRYING?
NOW LINE UP FOR WIND SPRINTS!
Peirce

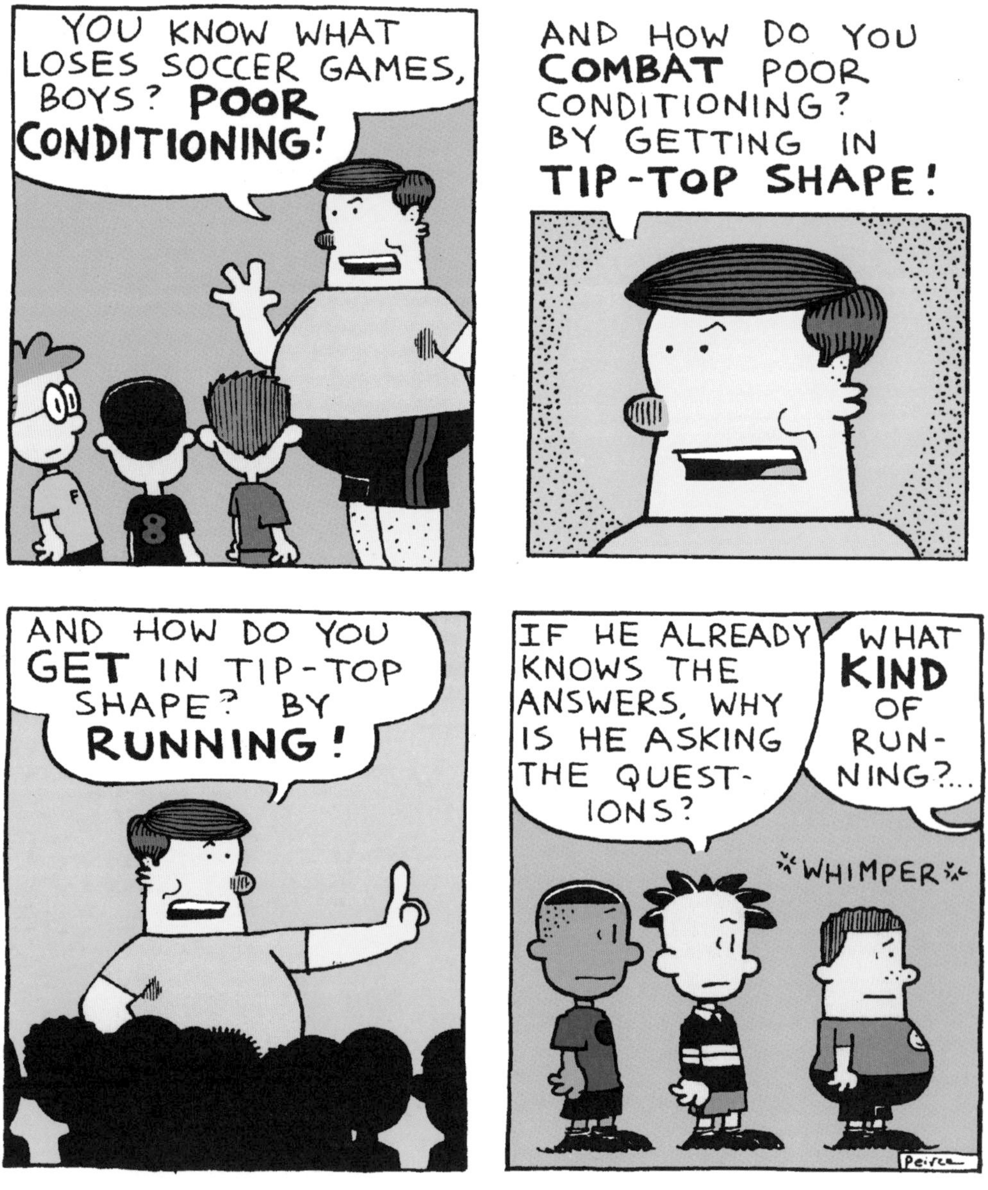
YOU KNOW WHAT LOSES SOCCER GAMES, BOYS? POOR CONDITIONING!
AND HOW DO YOU COMBAT POOR CONDITIONING? BY GETTING IN TIP-TOP SHAPE!
AND HOW DO YOU GET IN TIP-TOP SHAPE? BY RUNNING!
IF HE ALREADY KNOWS THE ANSWERS, WHY IS HE ASKING THE QUESTIONS?
WHAT KIND OF RUNNING?...
WHIMPER
Peirce

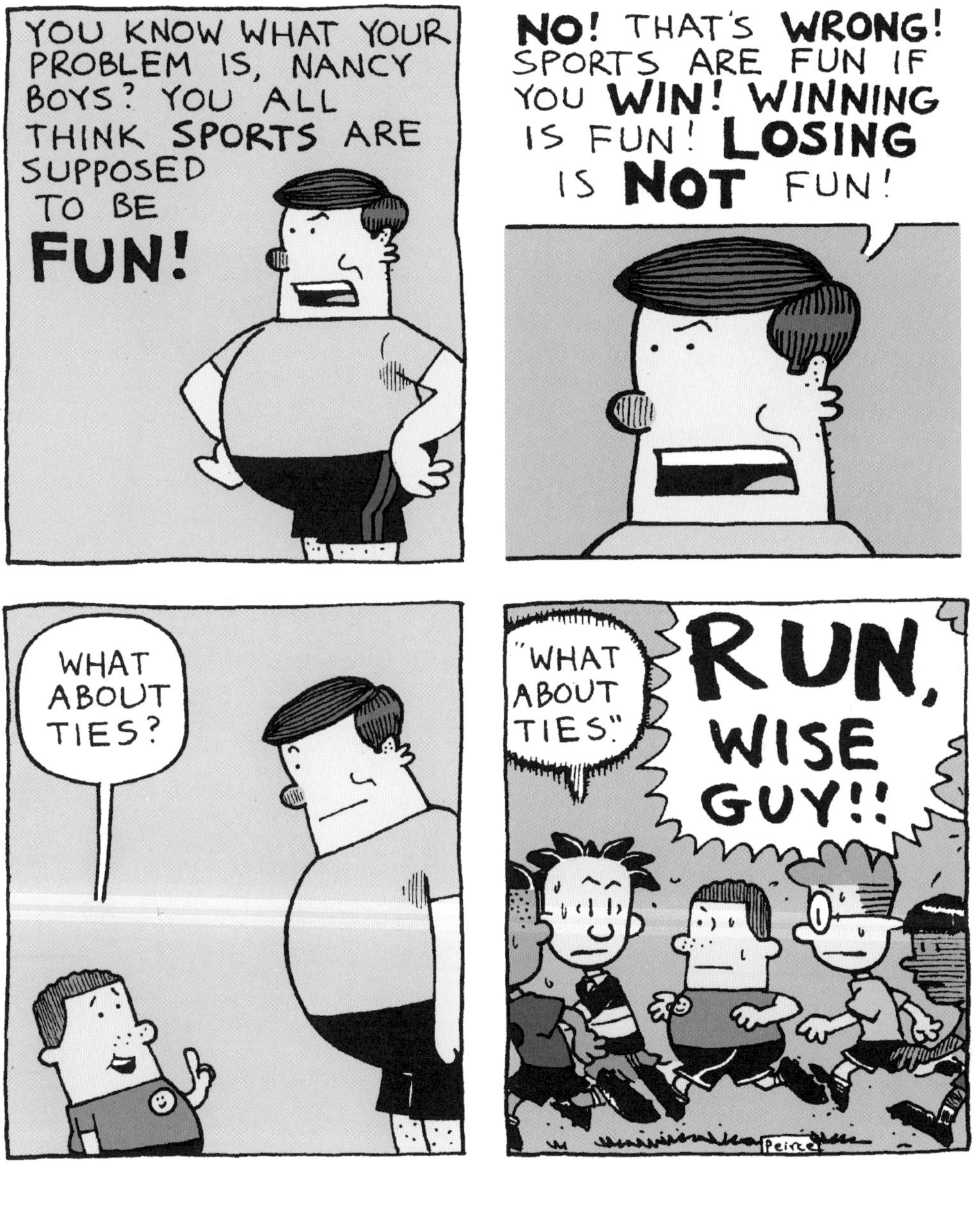
YOU KNOW WHAT YOUR PROBLEM IS, NANCY BOYS? YOU ALL THINK SPORTS ARE SUPPOSED TO BE FUN!
NO! THAT'S WRONG! SPORTS ARE FUN IF YOU WIN! WINNING IS FUN! LOSING IS NOT FUN!
WHAT ABOUT TIES?
"WHAT ABOUT TIES"
RUN, WISE GUY!!
Peirce

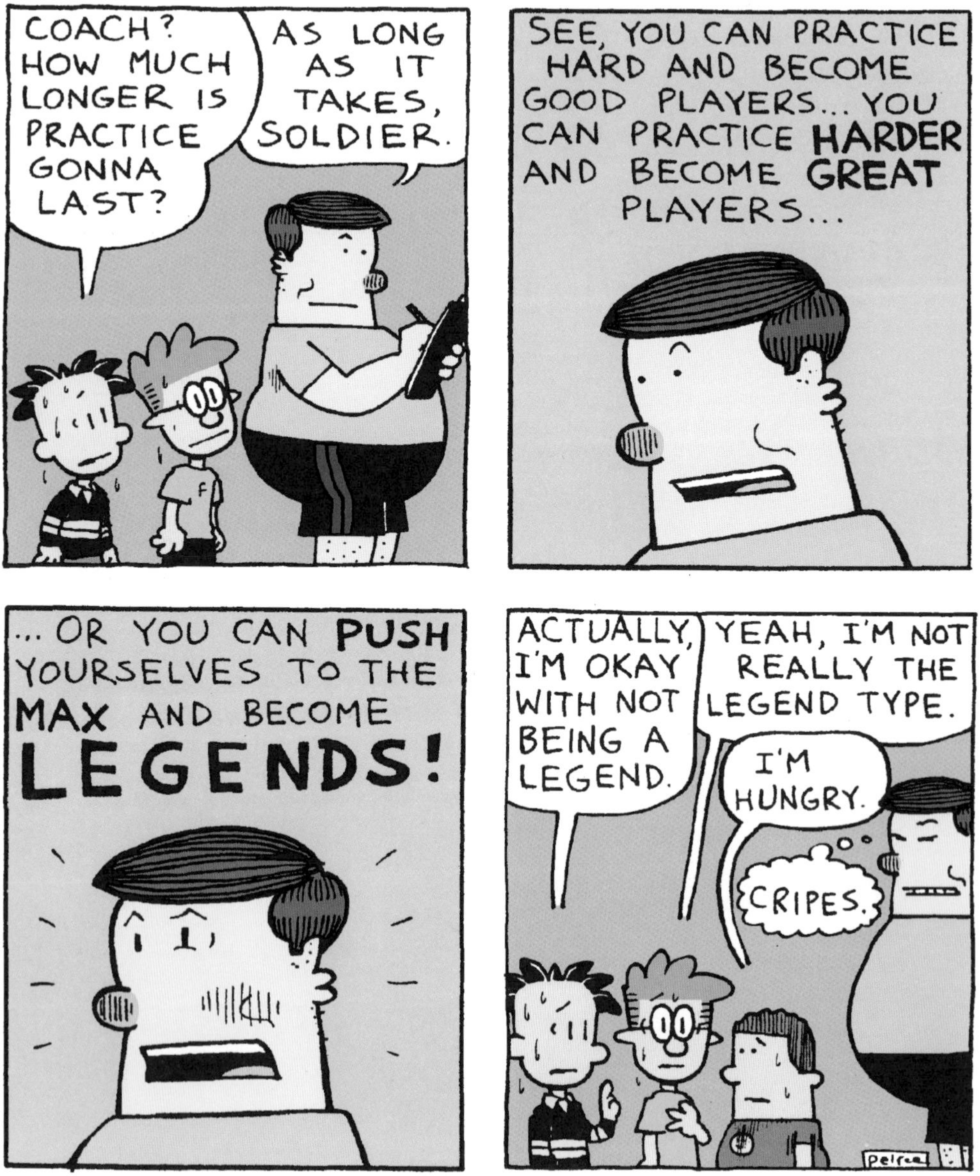
COACH? HOW MUCH LONGER IS PRACTICE GONNA LAST?
AS LONG AS IT TAKES, SOLDIER.
SEE, YOU CAN PRACTICE HARD AND BECOME GOOD PLAYERS... YOU CAN PRACTICE **HARDER** AND BECOME **GREAT** PLAYERS...
... OR YOU CAN **PUSH** YOURSELVES TO THE **MAX** AND BECOME **LEGENDS!**
ACTUALLY, I'M OKAY WITH NOT BEING A LEGEND.
YEAH, I'M NOT REALLY THE LEGEND TYPE.
I'M HUNGRY.
CRIPES.
peirce

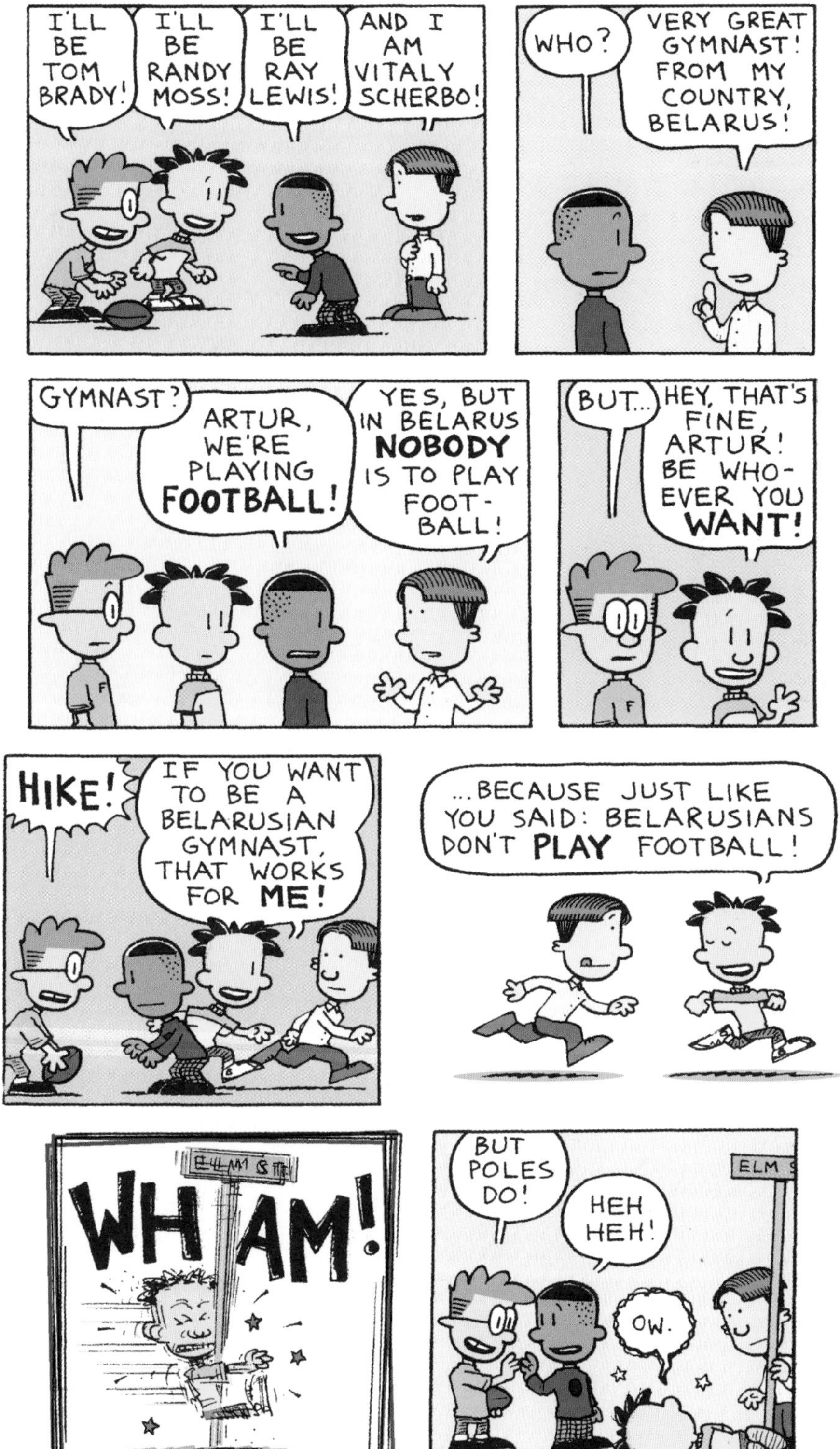
I'LL BE TOM BRADY!
I'LL BE RANDY MOSS!
I'LL BE RAY LEWIS!
AND I AM VITALY SCHERBO!
WHO?
VERY GREAT GYMNAST! FROM MY COUNTRY, BELARUS!
GYMNAST?
ARTUR, WE'RE PLAYING FOOTBALL!
YES, BUT IN BELARUS NOBODY IS TO PLAY FOOT-BALL!
BUT...
HEY, THAT'S FINE, ARTUR! BE WHO-EVER YOU WANT!
HIKE!
IF YOU WANT TO BE A BELARUSIAN GYMNAST, THAT WORKS FOR ME!
...BECAUSE JUST LIKE YOU SAID: BELARUSIANS DON'T PLAY FOOTBALL!
ELM ST
WHAM!
BUT POLES DO!
HEH HEH!
OW.
ELM S
Peirce

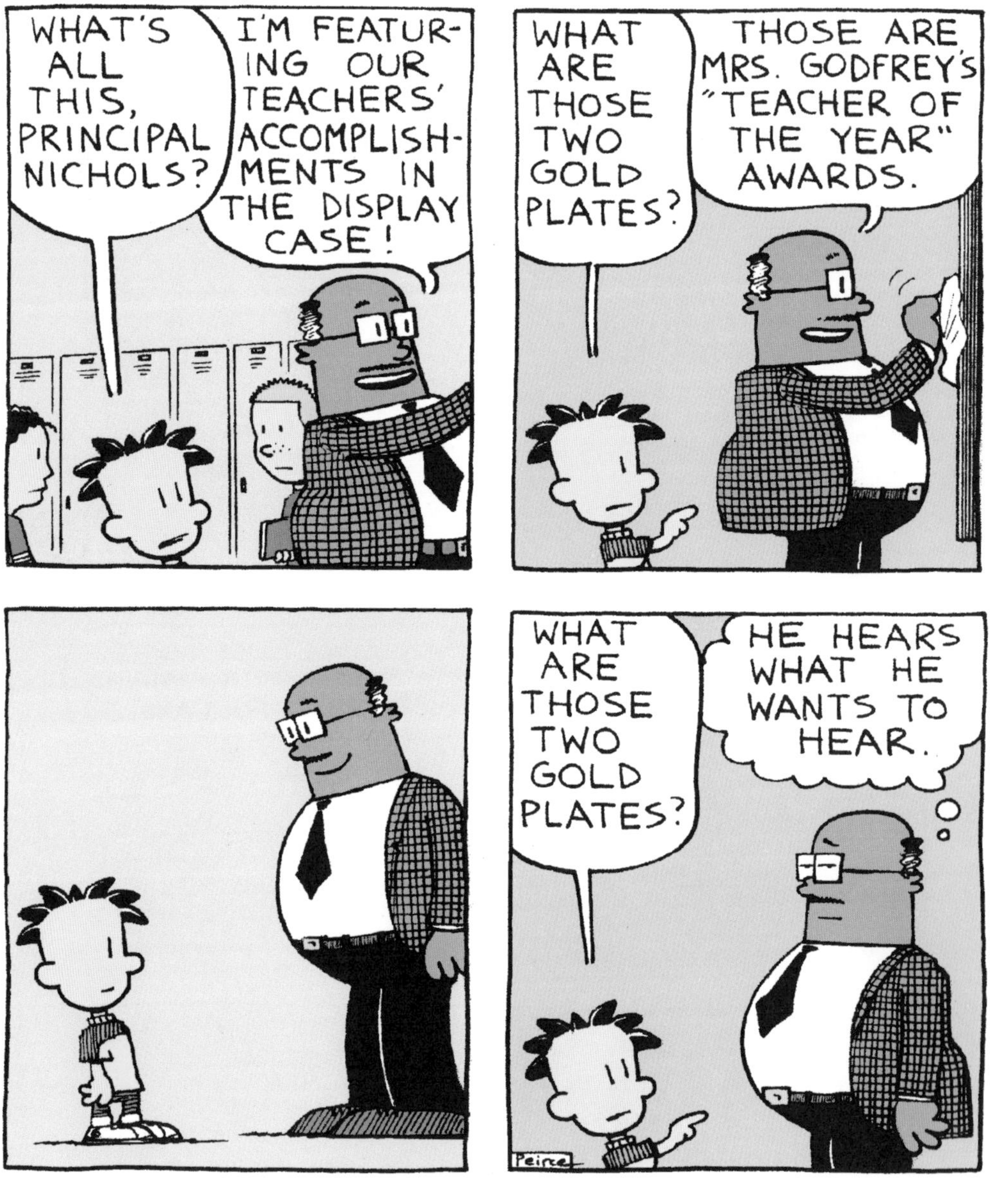
WHAT'S ALL THIS, PRINCIPAL NICHOLS?
I'M FEATURING OUR TEACHERS' ACCOMPLISHMENTS IN THE DISPLAY CASE!
WHAT ARE THOSE TWO GOLD PLATES?
THOSE ARE MRS. GODFREY'S "TEACHER OF THE YEAR" AWARDS.
WHAT ARE THOSE TWO GOLD PLATES?
HE HEARS WHAT HE WANTS TO HEAR.
Peirce

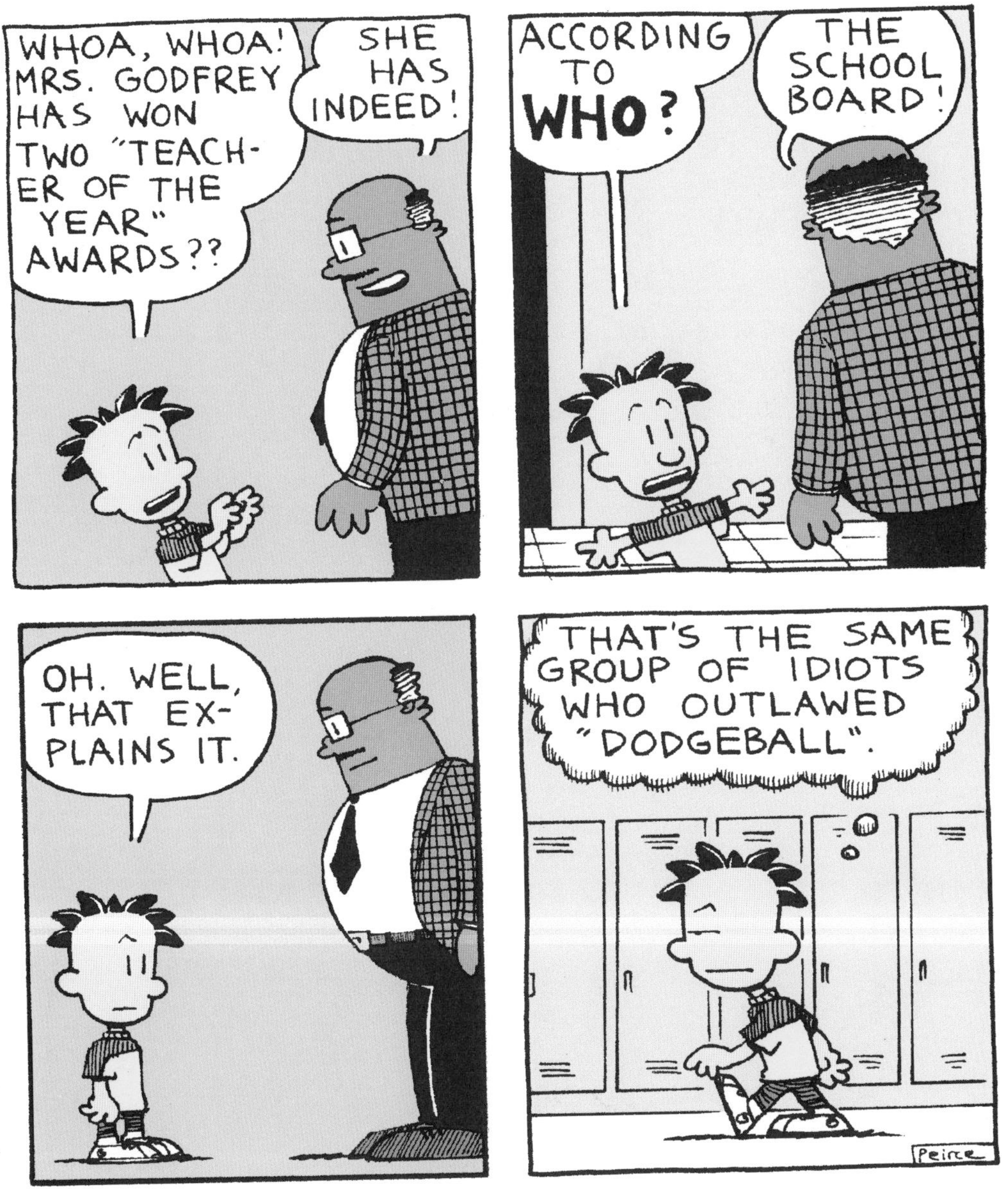
WHOA, WHOA! MRS. GODFREY HAS WON TWO "TEACHER OF THE YEAR" AWARDS??
SHE HAS INDEED!
ACCORDING TO **WHO**?
THE SCHOOL BOARD!
OH. WELL, THAT EXPLAINS IT.
THAT'S THE SAME GROUP OF IDIOTS WHO OUTLAWED "DODGEBALL".
Peirce

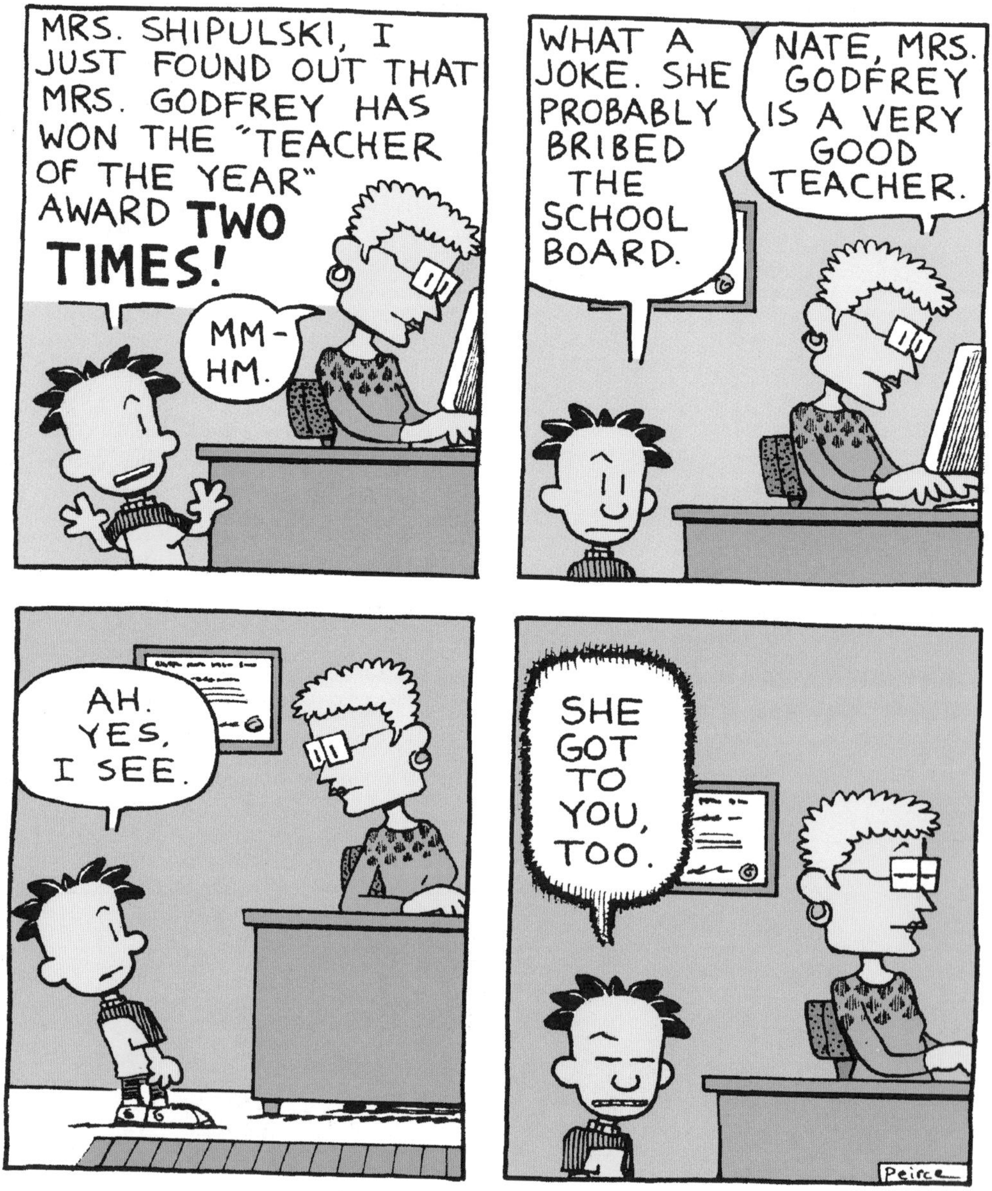
MRS. SHIPULSKI, I JUST FOUND OUT THAT MRS. GODFREY HAS WON THE "TEACHER OF THE YEAR" AWARD **TWO TIMES!**
MM-HM.
WHAT A JOKE. SHE PROBABLY BRIBED THE SCHOOL BOARD.
NATE, MRS. GODFREY IS A VERY GOOD TEACHER.
AH. YES, I SEE.
SHE GOT TO YOU, TOO.
Peirce

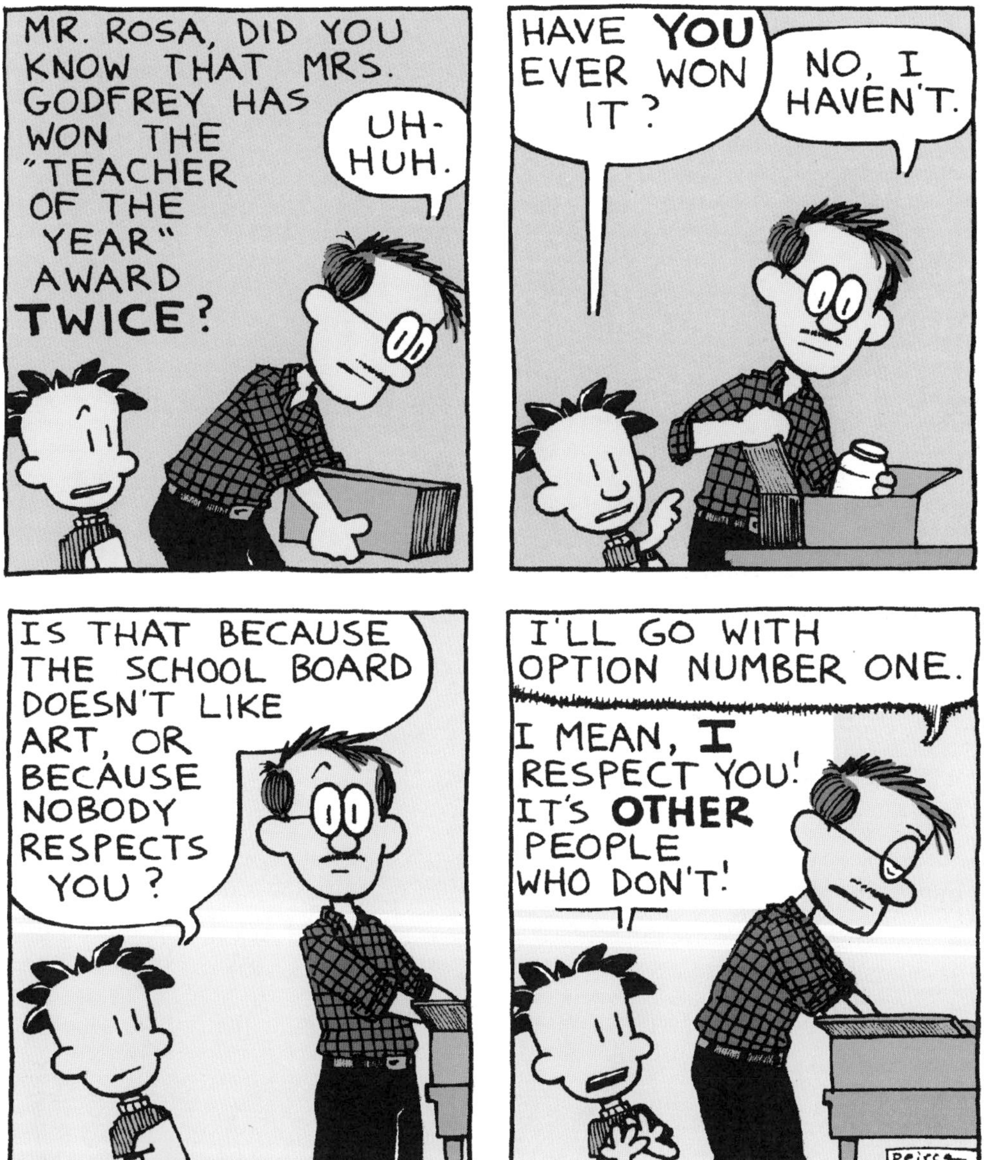
MR. ROSA, DID YOU KNOW THAT MRS. GODFREY HAS WON THE "TEACHER OF THE YEAR" AWARD **TWICE**?
UH-HUH.
HAVE **YOU** EVER WON IT?
NO, I HAVEN'T.
IS THAT BECAUSE THE SCHOOL BOARD DOESN'T LIKE ART, OR BECAUSE NOBODY RESPECTS YOU?
I'LL GO WITH OPTION NUMBER ONE.
I MEAN, **I** RESPECT YOU! IT'S **OTHER** PEOPLE WHO DON'T!
peirce

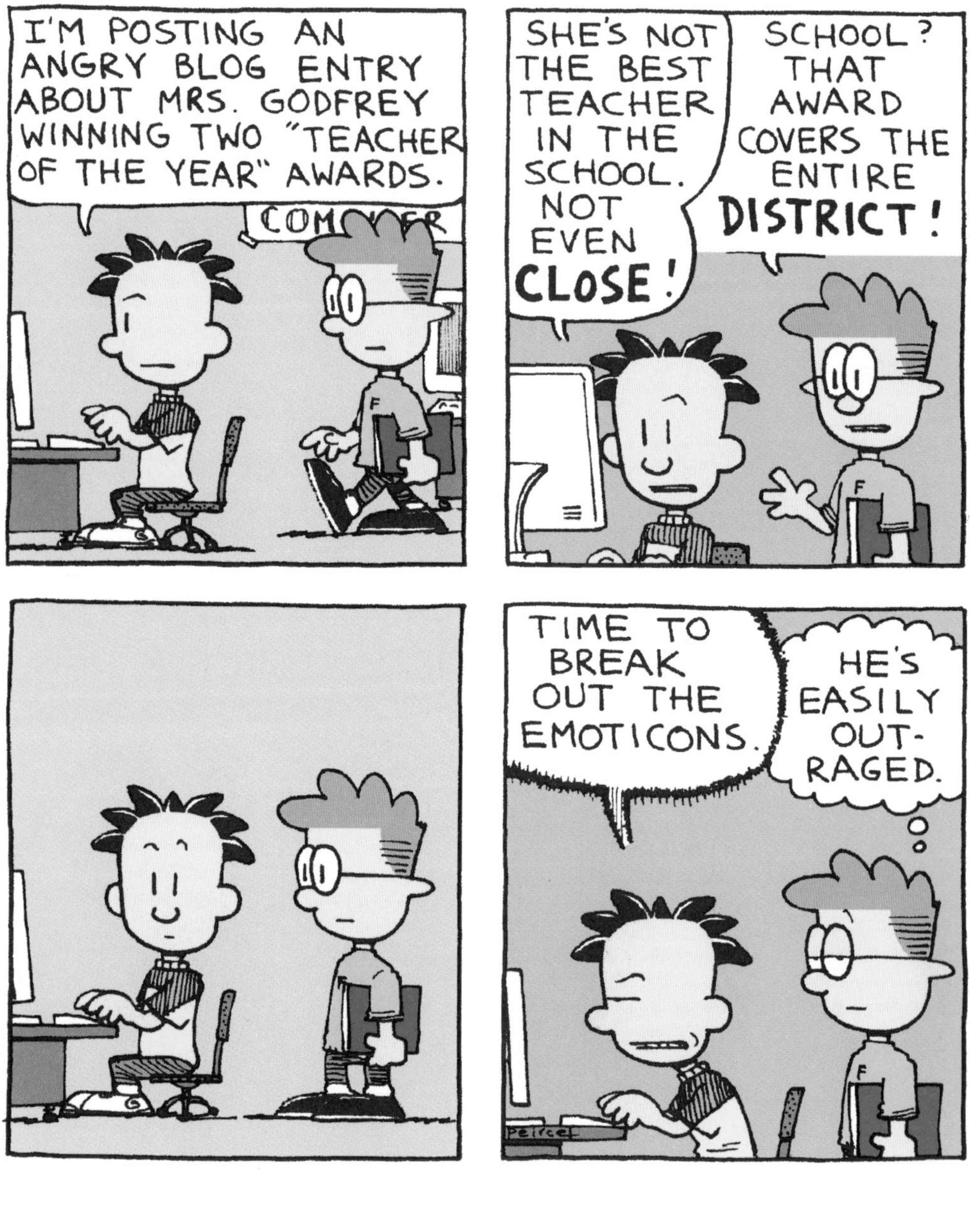
I'M POSTING AN ANGRY BLOG ENTRY ABOUT MRS. GODFREY WINNING TWO "TEACHER OF THE YEAR" AWARDS.
SHE'S NOT THE BEST TEACHER IN THE SCHOOL. NOT EVEN **CLOSE**!
SCHOOL? THAT AWARD COVERS THE ENTIRE **DISTRICT**!
TIME TO BREAK OUT THE EMOTICONS.
HE'S EASILY OUT-RAGED.
peirce

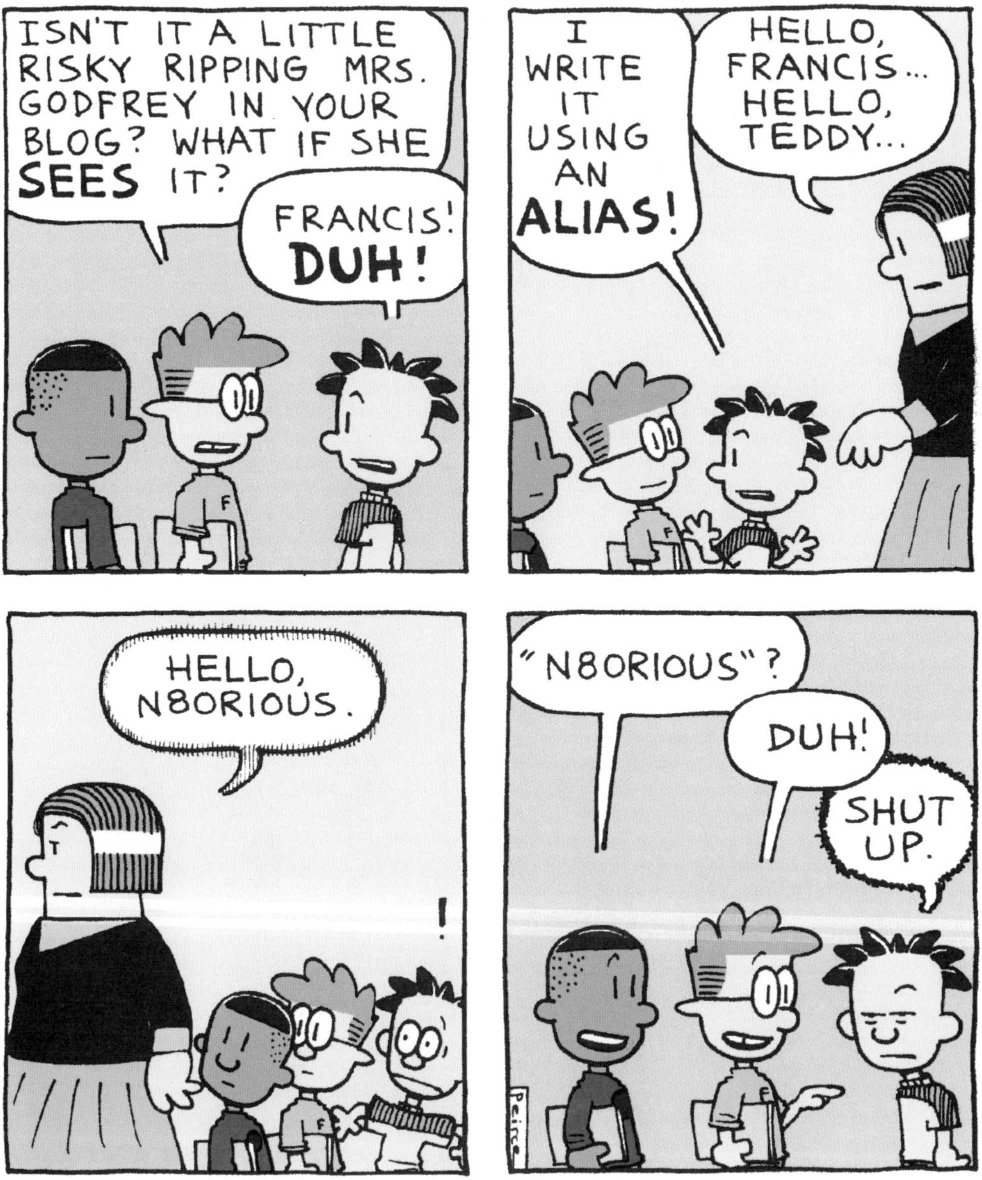
ISN'T IT A LITTLE RISKY RIPPING MRS. GODFREY IN YOUR BLOG? WHAT IF SHE **SEES** IT?
FRANCIS! **DUH**!
I WRITE IT USING AN **ALIAS**!
HELLO, FRANCIS... HELLO, TEDDY...
HELLO, N8ORIOUS.
!
"N8ORIOUS"?
DUH!
SHUT UP.
Peirce

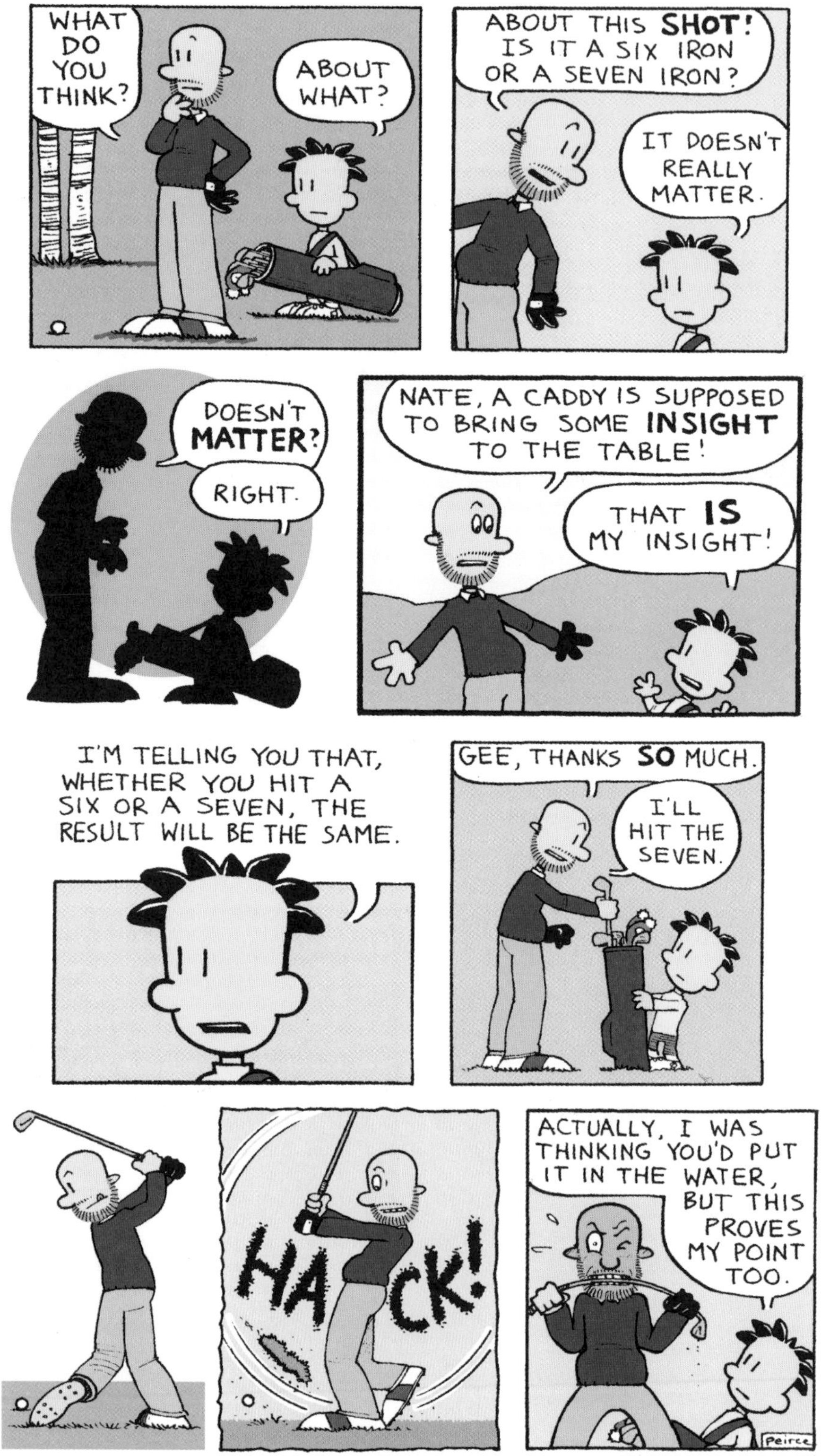
WHAT DO YOU THINK?
ABOUT WHAT?
ABOUT THIS **SHOT!** IS IT A SIX IRON OR A SEVEN IRON?
IT DOESN'T REALLY MATTER.
DOESN'T **MATTER?**
RIGHT.
NATE, A CADDY IS SUPPOSED TO BRING SOME **INSIGHT** TO THE TABLE!
THAT **IS** MY INSIGHT!
I'M TELLING YOU THAT, WHETHER YOU HIT A SIX OR A SEVEN, THE RESULT WILL BE THE SAME.
GEE, THANKS **SO** MUCH.
I'LL HIT THE SEVEN.
HACK!
ACTUALLY, I WAS THINKING YOU'D PUT IT IN THE WATER, BUT THIS PROVES MY POINT TOO.
Peirce

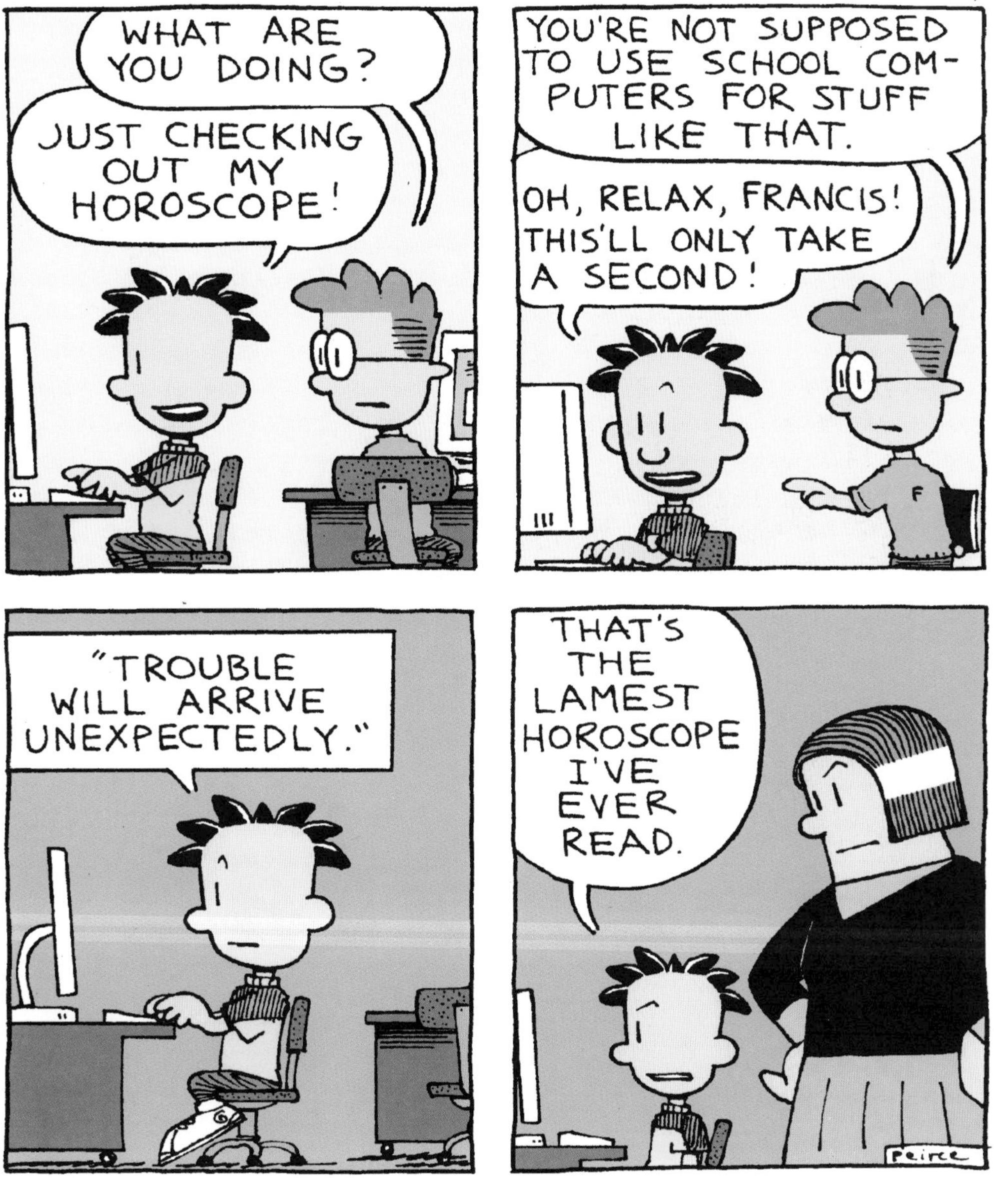
WHAT ARE YOU DOING?
JUST CHECKING OUT MY HOROSCOPE!
YOU'RE NOT SUPPOSED TO USE SCHOOL COM-PUTERS FOR STUFF LIKE THAT.
OH, RELAX, FRANCIS! THIS'LL ONLY TAKE A SECOND!
"TROUBLE WILL ARRIVE UNEXPECTEDLY."
THAT'S THE LAMEST HOROSCOPE I'VE EVER READ.
Peirce

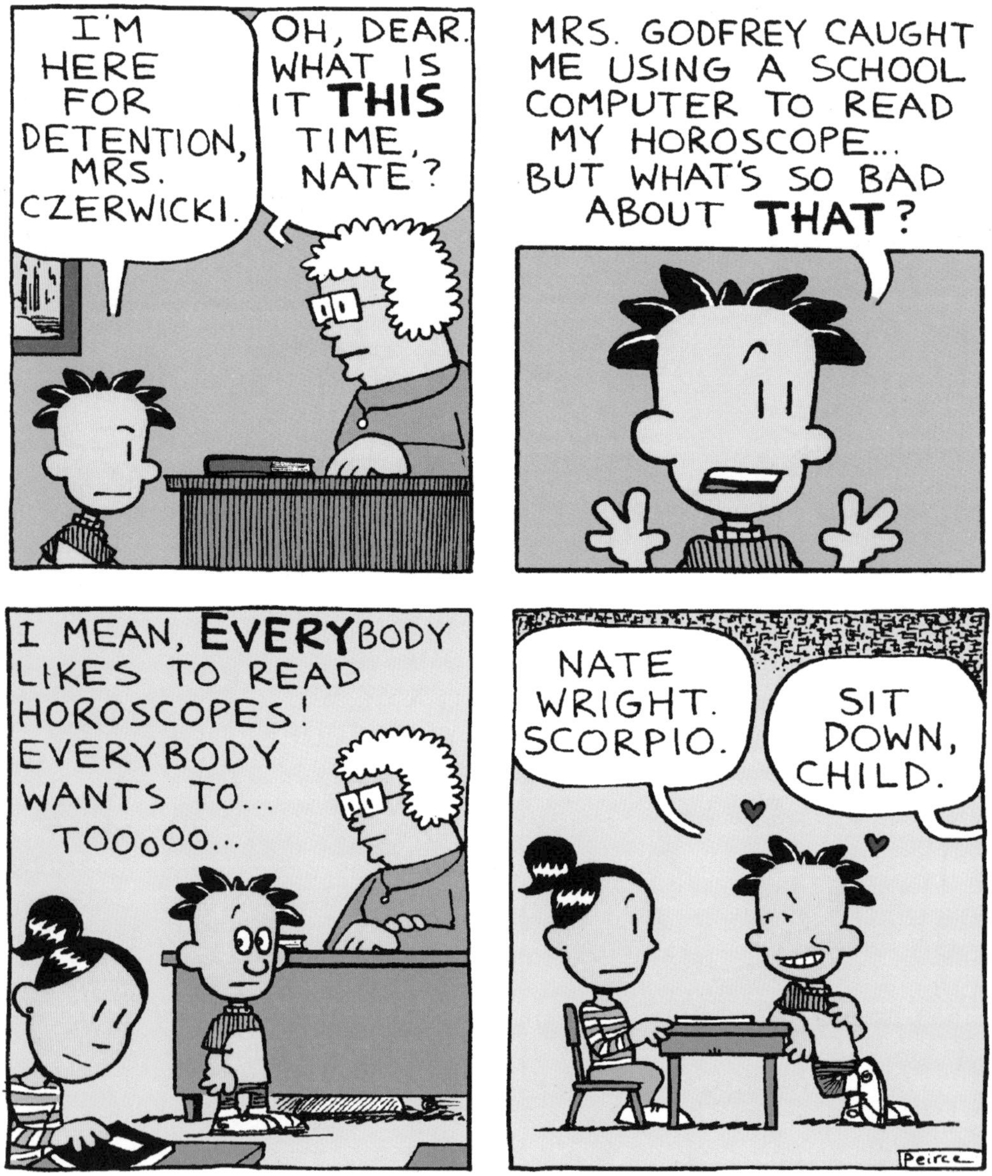
I'M HERE FOR DETENTION, MRS. CZERWICKI.
OH, DEAR. WHAT IS IT **THIS** TIME, NATE?
MRS. GODFREY CAUGHT ME USING A SCHOOL COMPUTER TO READ MY HOROSCOPE... BUT WHAT'S SO BAD ABOUT **THAT**?
I MEAN, **EVERY**BODY LIKES TO READ HOROSCOPES! EVERYBODY WANTS TO... TOOoOO...
NATE WRIGHT. SCORPIO.
SIT DOWN, CHILD.
Peirce

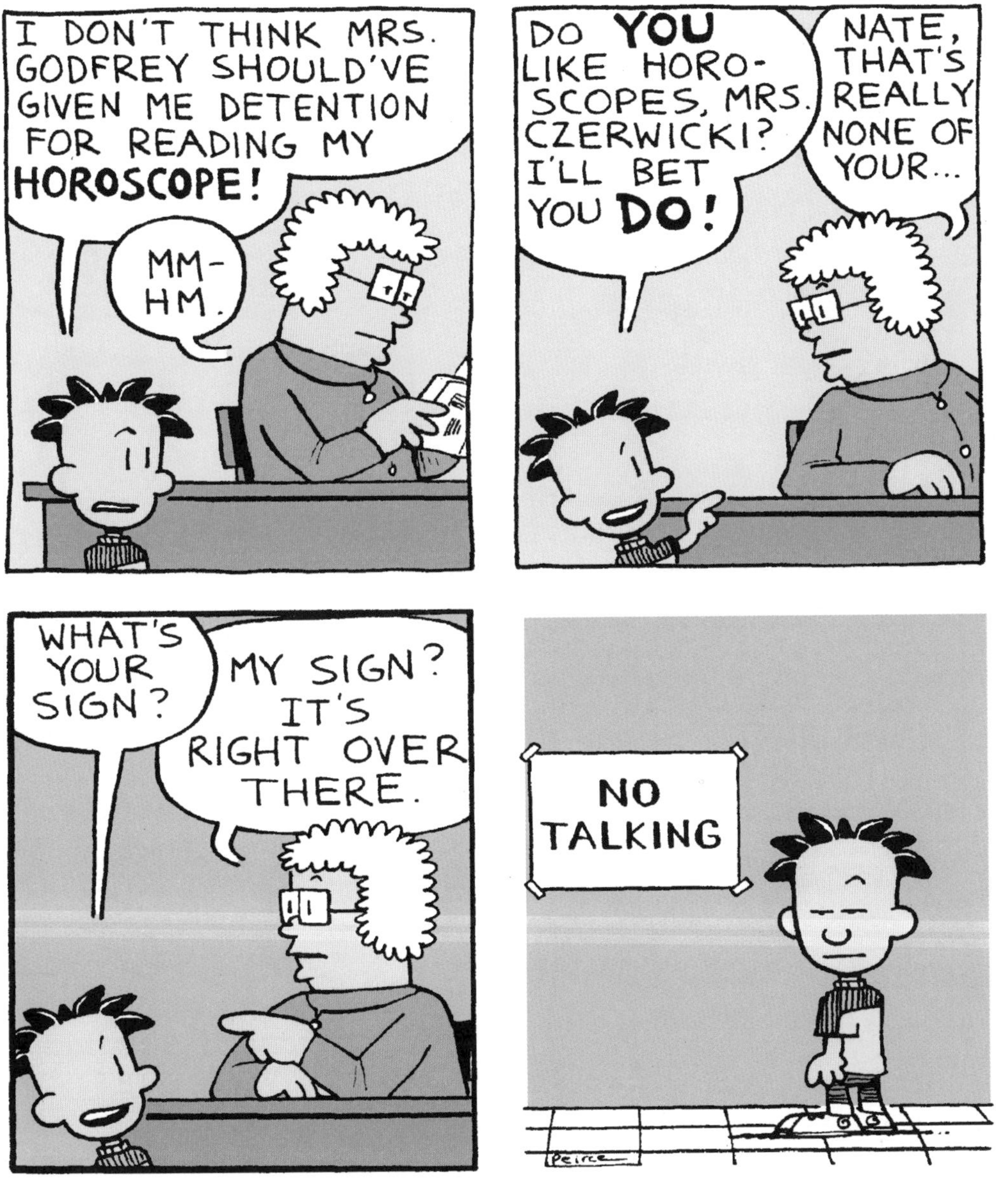
I DON'T THINK MRS. GODFREY SHOULD'VE GIVEN ME DETENTION FOR READING MY **HOROSCOPE**!
MM-HM.
DO **YOU** LIKE HOROSCOPES, MRS. CZERWICKI? I'LL BET YOU **DO**!
NATE, THAT'S REALLY NONE OF YOUR...
WHAT'S YOUR SIGN?
MY SIGN? IT'S RIGHT OVER THERE.
NO TALKING
Peirce

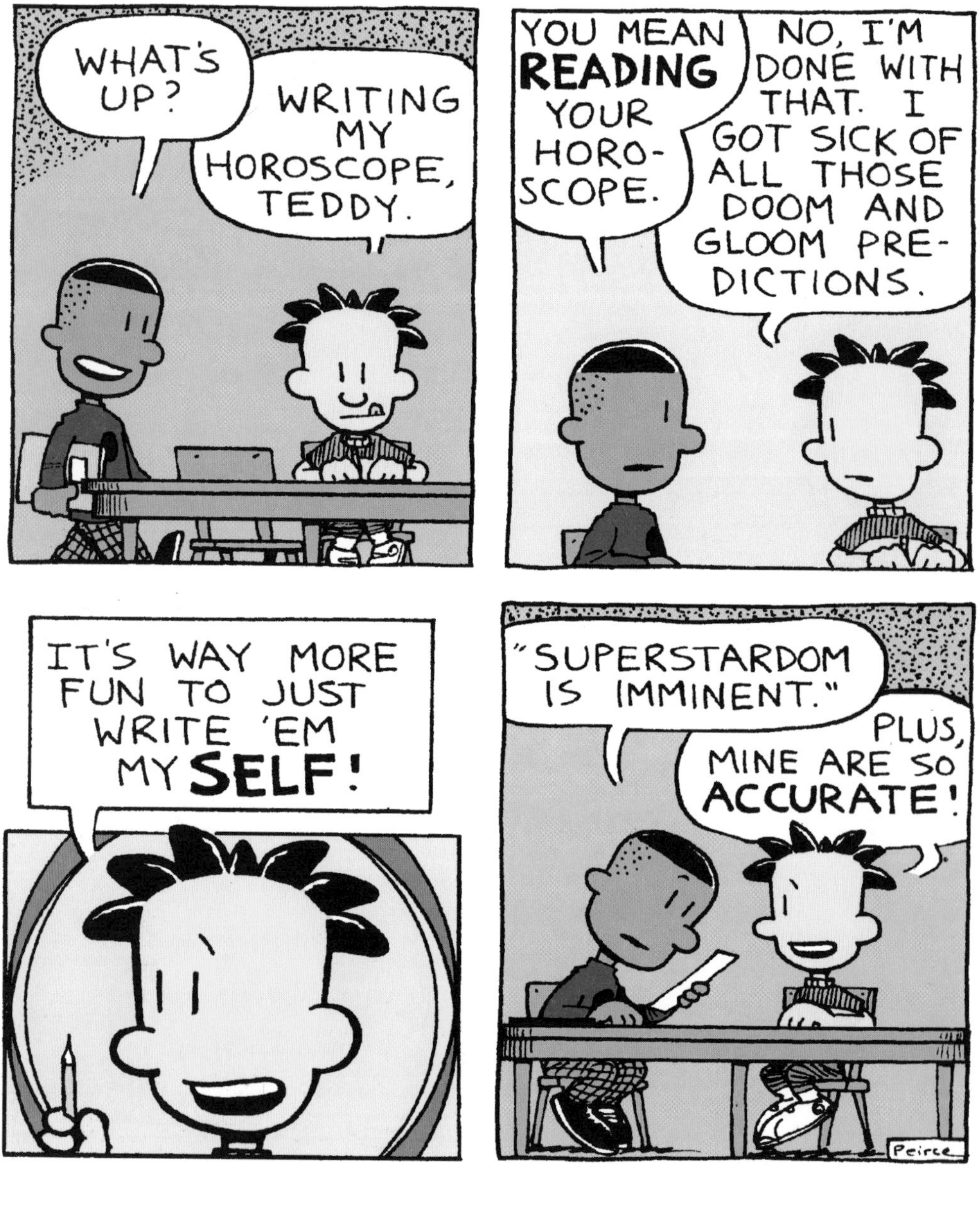
WHAT'S UP?
WRITING MY HOROSCOPE, TEDDY.
YOU MEAN **READING** YOUR HOROSCOPE.
NO, I'M DONE WITH THAT. I GOT SICK OF ALL THOSE DOOM AND GLOOM PREDICTIONS.
IT'S WAY MORE FUN TO JUST WRITE 'EM MY**SELF**!
"SUPERSTARDOM IS IMMINENT."
PLUS, MINE ARE SO **ACCURATE**!
Peirce

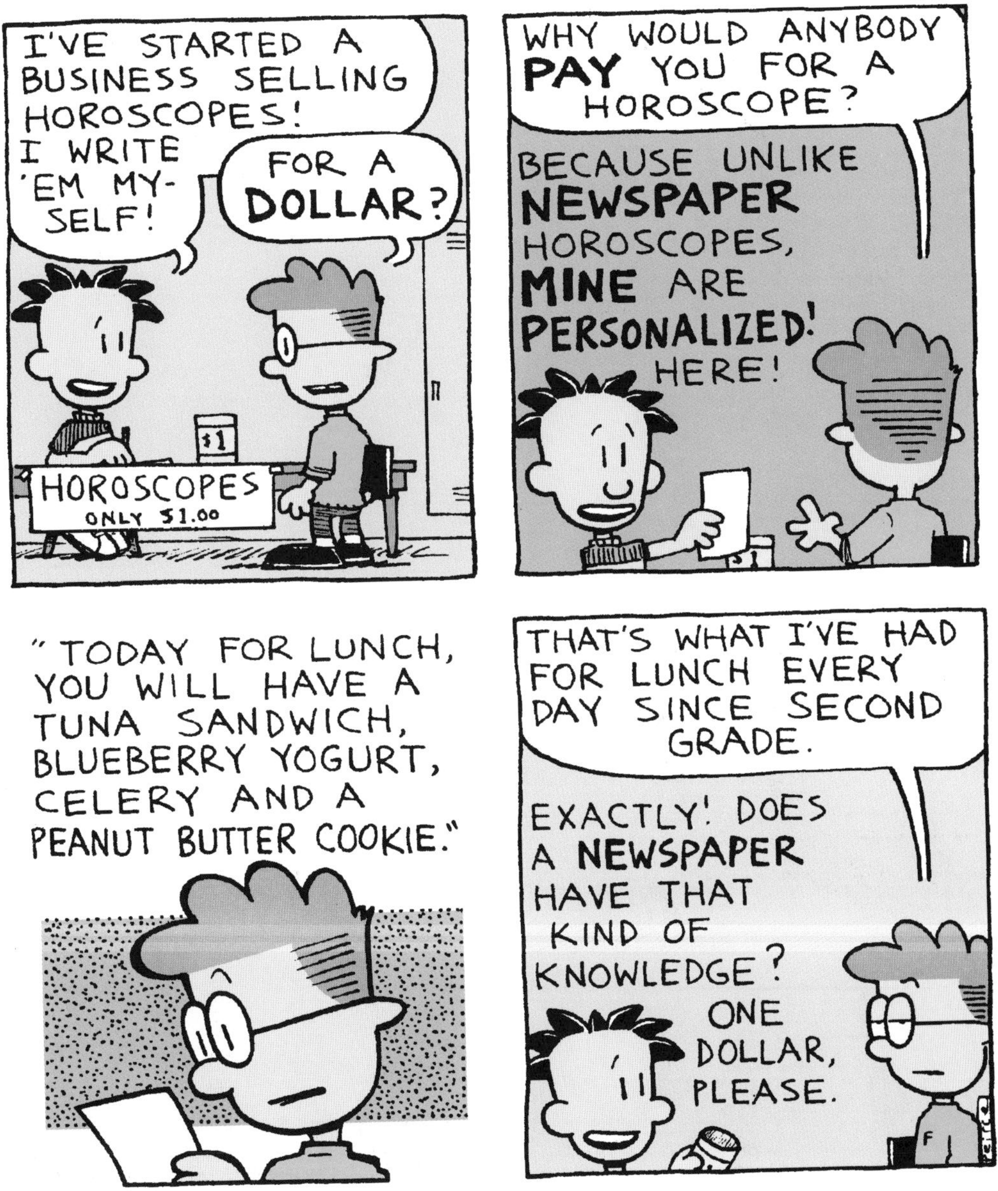
I'VE STARTED A BUSINESS SELLING HOROSCOPES! I WRITE 'EM MYSELF!
FOR A DOLLAR?
HOROSCOPES ONLY $1.00
$1
WHY WOULD ANYBODY PAY YOU FOR A HOROSCOPE?
BECAUSE UNLIKE NEWSPAPER HOROSCOPES, MINE ARE PERSONALIZED! HERE!
"TODAY FOR LUNCH, YOU WILL HAVE A TUNA SANDWICH, BLUEBERRY YOGURT, CELERY AND A PEANUT BUTTER COOKIE."
THAT'S WHAT I'VE HAD FOR LUNCH EVERY DAY SINCE SECOND GRADE.
EXACTLY! DOES A NEWSPAPER HAVE THAT KIND OF KNOWLEDGE?
ONE DOLLAR, PLEASE.

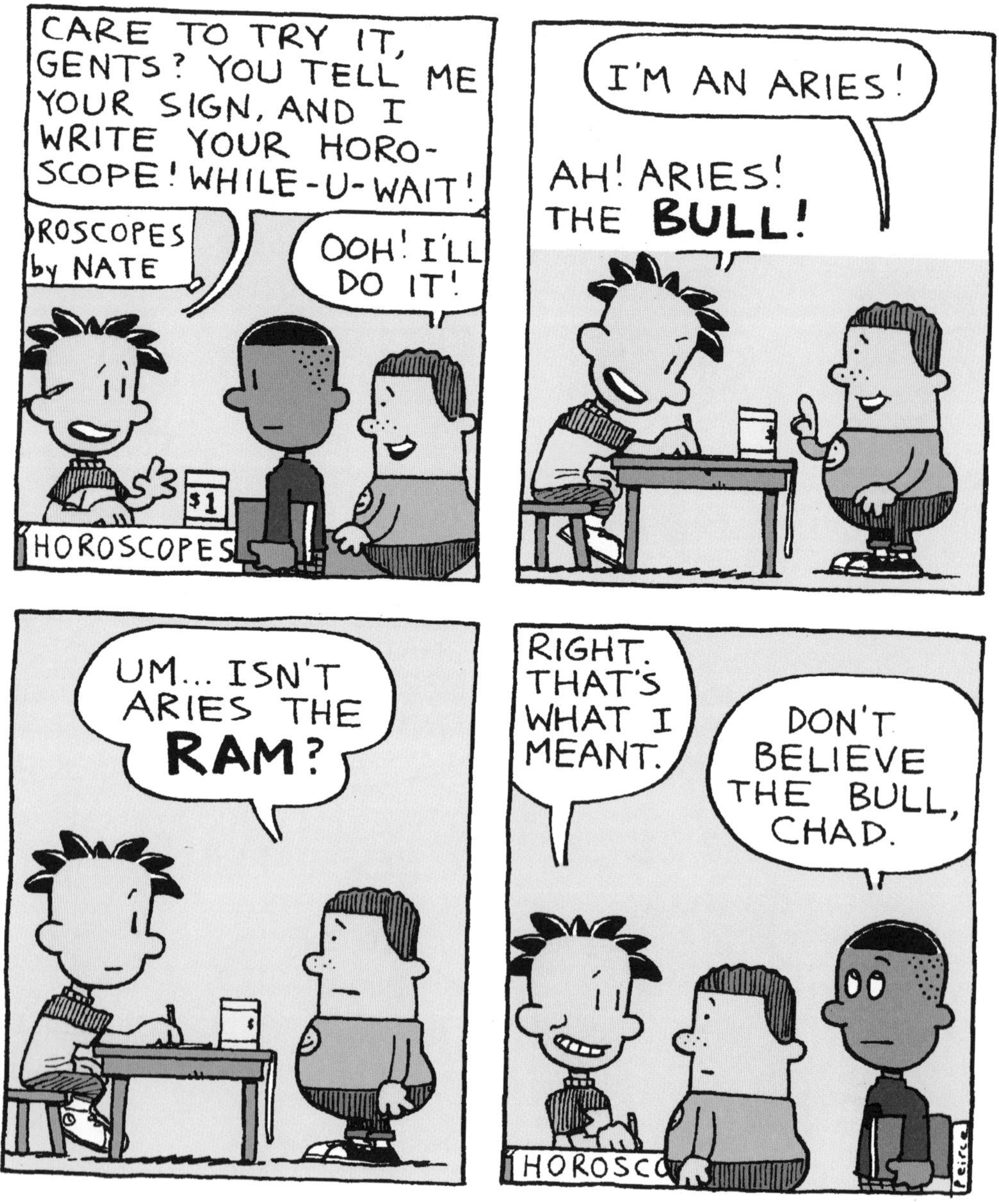
CARE TO TRY IT, GENTS? YOU TELL ME YOUR SIGN, AND I WRITE YOUR HOROSCOPE! WHILE-U-WAIT!
ROSCOPES by NATE
OOH! I'LL DO IT!
$1
HOROSCOPES
I'M AN ARIES!
AH! ARIES! THE **BULL**!
UM... ISN'T ARIES THE **RAM**?
RIGHT. THAT'S WHAT I MEANT.
DON'T BELIEVE THE BULL, CHAD.
HOROSC
Peirce

Big Nate is distributed internationally by Universal Uclick.

Andrews McMeel Publishing, LLC
an Andrews McMeel Universal company
1130 Walnut Street, Kansas City, Missouri 64106

www.andrewsmcmeel.com

14 15 16 17 18 SDB 10 9 8 7 6 5 4 3 2 1

ISBN: 978-1-4494-3634-6

Library of Congress Control Number: 2014931550

Made by:
Shenzhen Donnelley Printing Company Ltd.
Address and location of manufacturer:
No. 47, Wuhe Nan Road, Bantian Ind. Zone,
Shenzhen China, 518129
1st Printing—7/28/14

These strips appeared in newspapers from
March 8, 2010, through October 9, 2010.

Big Nate can be viewed on the Internet at
www.gocomics.com/big_nate

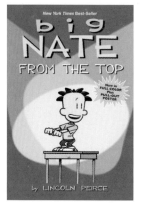